MILLION
THE UNRAVELLER

ALSO BY C.R. BERRY

MILLION EYES: EXTRA TIME

MILLION EYES

MILLION EYES II
THE UNRAVELLER

C.R. BERRY

Elsewhen Press

Million Eyes II: The Unraveller
First published in Great Britain by Elsewhen Press, 2021
An imprint of Alnpete Limited

Elsewhen Press, PO Box 757, Dartford, Kent DA2 7TQ
www.elsewhen.press
British Library Cataloguing in Publication Data.
A catalogue record for this book is available from the British Library.
ISBN 978-1-911409-68-7 Print edition
ISBN 978-1-911409-78-6 eBook edition

Designed and formatted by Elsewhen Press

This book is a work of fiction. All names, characters, places, religious
institutions, evil mega-corporations, and events are either a product of
the author's fertile imagination or are used fictitiously. Any
resemblance to actual events, organisations, institutions, places or
people (living, dead or temporally displaced) is purely coincidental.

For Dan

PREVIOUSLY IN MILLION EYES

"MR FERRO, THE PEOPLE I WORK FOR...
ARE THE PEOPLE YOU'RE LOOKING FOR."

In 2019, Gregory Ferro learns from an anonymous whistleblower that the world's leading technology company, Million Eyes, are time travellers chasing a book from the future.

Million Eyes operative Robert Skinner secretly listens in on the conversation and recognises the whistleblower's voice: Stuart Rayburn.

Skinner murders Ferro and runs over Ferro's accomplice, Jennifer Larson, leaving her for dead.

"WALLS DO NOT HAVE EARS. BUT BOOKS DO."

In 1483, the book – and some of Million Eyes' time travel pills – have fallen into the possession of the Princes in the Tower.

But the book is not a book at all. It's a transcription device that instantly transcribes all conversations in its vicinity.

The princes use the pills to travel in time from 1483 to 1888. When the transcriber is stolen from them, they swallow more pills, travelling to an unknown time.

"I KNOW EXACTLY WHO YOU ARE.
YOU'RE JACK THE RIPPER."

In 1888, crossing-sweeper Harriet Turner encounters a man in a church with a suitcase of human organs. She realises he is Jack the Ripper.

Jack is actually James Rawling, a Million Eyes operative sent back in time to recover the transcriber, who has inadvertently become Britain's most famous serial killer.

When Harriet overhears Rawling talking on the phone about the 'timeline' and 'the future' before vanishing into thin air, she wonders if he may be a time traveller.

"I HAVE TO GET THIS BOOK TO THE QUEEN."

In 1997, the transcriber makes its way into the hands of Diana, Princess of Wales, while she is in Paris. She plans to leave Paris immediately to deliver it to Queen Elizabeth II.

James Rawling travels to 1997 and arranges Diana's assassination to get the transcriber back.

Diana's Mercedes crashes in the Pont de l'Alma tunnel. Rawling's colleagues retrieve the transcriber from the wreckage and destroy it.

"WE'RE ABOUT TO ASSASSINATE BRITAIN'S LONGEST-SERVING MONARCH."

In 2019, Jennifer Larson wakes up in hospital and listens to a voicemail left by Ferro right before his murder, revealing the truth about Million Eyes. After escaping a second attempt on her life, she runs away to Brighton.

In 2021, Jennifer finds a blank transcriber and eavesdrops on a conversation between two Million Eyes operatives about a plot to assassinate Queen Elizabeth II. The blank book transcribes the conversation.

Million Eyes go after Jennifer, forcing her to travel in time. Stranded in 1100, Jennifer is apprehended by two knights and conveyed to King William II.

"YOU'RE GOING TO CLEAR UP YOUR MESS."

When Jennifer travels to the past, history changes and Million Eyes' rise to power never happens. This is because of the information in the transcriber, which Jennifer has taken with her.

With Million Eyes' London headquarters protected from the changes by a temporal shield, CEO Erica Morgan dispatches operatives to recover the transcriber and restore history.

With the timeline repaired, Million Eyes assassinate Elizabeth II as planned.

"WE NEED TO TALK ABOUT MILLION EYES."

In 2026, Adam Bryant is still reeling from the disappearance of Jennifer, his best friend.

One night, a mysterious woman called Dr Samantha Lester phones him telling him she has evidence that Elizabeth II was murdered. This evidence consists of letters from the 1100s. Letters written by Jennifer.

Hinting that Million Eyes were involved somehow, Dr Lester tells Adam they need to meet.

PROLOGUE

A man has discovered the location of a document capable of bringing the world's most powerful institution to its knees. He intends to steal it.

Only he has to go back in time to do so. He has learned that, between 1348 and 1666, the document was stored in St Adela's Church in Paternoster Road, London. In September 1666, hours before the Great Fire of London laid waste to the church, the document was moved. Somewhere. To this day, only two people on Earth know of its location. The man isn't one of them.

So he goes back to August 1666, when St Adela's Church still stands and the document lies protected in its crypt.

He arrives late at night. The church is cold and empty, bar the odd rat scurrying in the shadows. He passes through a door in the chancel and descends a flight of stone steps that terminates with a locked door. He burns through the lock with a disruptor beam and enters the crypt.

He crosses to the other side, threading through pillars, statues and tombs that flicker feebly in the glow of his lantern. Against the wall is a sarcophagus bearing the effigy of a nameless woman. The man lifts the lid. The sarcophagus is a ruse. It is in fact a concealed entrance to another staircase.

The man descends the stairs to a further locked door. He breaches the door and all three Keepers of the Scrolls surround him, waving their ornate spears. Before they charge, the man kills them with his disruptor.

And there it is. The document he will use to destroy his greatest enemy centuries before it can do what it did to him.

The Roman Catholic Church.

The man walks up to the huge elevated spindle. At the centre of the spindle is a circular glass case displaying four scrolls, one on top of the other, each continuous roll divided into two dozen pages of ancient Aramaic penmanship. The inscription on the spindle's polished marble plinth reads, in English capital letters:

THE GOSPEL ACCORDING TO JESUS.

The man swings his hammer against the case, shattering the glass and the silence. He carefully removes the scrolls, rolls them up and slips them inside an aluminium canister.

Then he turns and leaves.

1

66 Million Years Ago

Where – *when* – had those damned red pills brought them this time?

The elder of the Princes in the Tower, Edward V of England, got to his feet, gulped the air and took in various pungent but pleasant smells – earth, flowers, fresh pine. His leather satchel still hung from his shoulder, the pot of red pills rolling about inside. It took a moment for his dizziness to abate and his surroundings to sharpen. His brother, Richard, Duke of York, was already on his feet and rubbing his head.

The ground was dusted with sand and pebbles and patches of vegetation. Lots of ferns, mosses and horsetails. Edward's eye was drawn by some big, unusual-looking bushes with cone-shaped leaves and bulbous, scaly blooms. They were horrific and beautiful at the same time, like nothing Edward had seen before. There were a few tall trees that looked like pines, hence the smell, and others that were like cycads – trees he had only seen in drawings, because they grew in the tropics. But then the air was so warm and humid it *felt* tropical. The blisteringly hot sun was making Edward – who like his brother was in a thick black tunic and hose – break out in a sweat.

This certainly didn't feel like England anymore.

The uncrowned boy king lifted his gaze. He and Richard were standing on a slight elevation in the middle of a vast, uneven plain, scattered with trees and shrubs but not a single building. And although half of the plain was dry and being burned yellow by the sun, the other half, where the land sloped gently downwards, was a waterlogged maze of marshes, lakes and meandering rivers.

Which may have been something to do with the vast blue expanse of sea stretching out beyond it, gentle waves whipping whorls of froth at miles of glistening mudflats. It also explained the other smell Edward had been having trouble pinpointing: salty sea air.

Suddenly they were by the coast – but how?

Edward noticed that Richard was looking fixedly at something in the other direction, his eyes wide, mouth hanging open. All the blood had drained from his small face. "Brother – look!"

Edward turned and followed Richard's stare. Initially he couldn't see what his brother was looking at with such fright. Then he saw them. Far off in the distance, close to a line of deformed-looking trees with wild, erratic branches, was a herd of dark blue-grey beasts. They had small heads, long necks, huge barrel-shaped guts, long whip-like tails and elephantine legs.

"Are they… dragons?" cried Richard.

Edward's stomach knotted. He shook his head, "They don't look much like dragons to me."

Richard snapped his gaze to Edward. "And you have seen one to know, have you?"

"I have seen plenty in bestiaries. In all the pictures and descriptions, dragons have wings like –"

"Like… *those?*" Richard was staring at something above Edward's head. Edward wheeled round to look.

An immense flock of *somethings* was coming straight for them. If they were birds, they were bigger – *stranger* – than any Edward had ever seen. Red-brown skin with the wings of a bat, the beak of a pelican and, protruding from the backs of their heads, the sharp horn of a unicorn.

Edward's whole body started to tremble as the

creatures soared towards them. They were many in number. If they wanted to attack, the princes didn't stand a chance.

Suddenly, a shrill screech burst from the gullet of one of the creatures and made both boys dive forwards onto the ground on their fronts.

"Brother!" cried Richard.

"Quiet. Don't move."

Edward held his breath and stared at the ground, hoping to God that the flock would fly over and be gone. His heartbeat thundered in his ears, harder and harder, till he could feel it pulsing through every extremity.

"Have they seen us?" whispered Richard.

"Ssshh."

The whoosh of wings made Edward look over his shoulder, eyes tilted upwards. The creatures were passing over them, flying in the direction of the herd in the distance.

A bead of sweat dribbled into Edward's eye, making him squint. He waited for all the creatures to pass. The ones at the head of the flock were now far ahead, the sound of their wings dying away.

Edward swallowed. "I don't think they saw us. If they did, they were not interested." His taut body began to loosen and he and Richard climbed to their feet.

"Where have you taken us?" said Richard, panic in his voice.

The piece of parchment Edward had picked up before they arrived here flashed into his mind. The one dated *Thursday, August 30, 1888.* The one that revealed exactly what had happened to them after they swallowed those first two red pills in the Tower of London in 1483: that they'd come forwards in time. Four centuries into the future. It was the reason London looked so different.

"I told you to take me home to Mother," said Richard bitterly.

"I will, brother." The words just came out. It was his job, as elder brother, to look after Richard, to comfort him when he was scared or upset. But he shouldn't have been making promises he couldn't keep.

"When?" said Richard.

When. Not as simple a question as it once was.

Richard didn't give Edward a chance to answer. "We have to get back to London. The pills clearly aren't working. Now they have brought us someplace else entirely. I do not think we are even in England anymore."

Was Richard right? If they had moved in time before but remained in the same place, then it stood to reason that they had simply moved in time again. Which meant this was still London. Still England. Perhaps instead of forwards, they had travelled back. Far back. Could this have been shortly after the Flood? It would make sense, given the watery landscape. And it would mean the flock and the herd were among the animals that had been taken aboard Noah's Ark. The ones God saved.

Edward looked at the herd of monsters. Did He really save *those?*

Sighing heavily, Edward placed his hand on his brother's shoulder. "Richard, I have to tell you something that may alarm you."

"What?"

"I think we *are* in London."

Richard frowned and shook his head. "What? Brother, we are by the sea."

"Yes, I know. We have entered a different time, a time when the sea is much higher and closer and the city is not built."

"What in the world are you talking about?"

Edward thought it best to take this in stages. "You remember when we were in the Tower and each ate one of the red pills, and we ended up in some strange, dizzying place surrounded by ghosts before emerging back into our room? But when we did, our room had changed – as had the entirety of the Tower itself?"

"Yes. And there was that… that mysterious flag. And strange boats on the river. And people in strange clothes speaking in a foreign tongue – like the man who stole the Book That Listens."

Edward swallowed. A pang of guilt rippled through him. Besides its astonishing powers, the Book That Listens was an omen, detailing a threat that the monarchy would one day face. It had been guarded and protected for centuries by his predecessors and Edward had lost it in a matter of minutes to a foreign man who'd assaulted his brother. What kind of king was he? He didn't deserve his crown, he realised. That's why God had denied it him.

Edward pushed back the guilt. Now wasn't the time to dwell on his kingly failures. "That's right," he said. "And London looked totally different, didn't it. And then I saw a piece of parchment lying on the ground that told me why."

Richard's eyes flared. "What? You never said anything about that."

"I tried, but you were desperate to go. You wanted to eat another pill and get out of there."

Richard sighed but didn't argue, meaning he probably remembered how insistent he had been. He snapped, "Tell me now then."

"There was a date written on the parchment. Thursday, August 30th, 1888."

His brother's eyes narrowed. "1888? But that's –"

"Yes. More than four hundred years in our future. I believe the red pills caused us to travel from 1483 to 1888, which was why London looked so different. We were seeing four centuries of change."

"That's preposterous, Edward!" Richard looked angry, but it was probably more frustration and confusion.

He wasn't wrong, though. It *was* preposterous. Edward said softly, "I agree with you. Nevertheless, it is the best explanation we have."

"I should never have listened to you. We should never have eaten those pills."

"We might be dead right now if we hadn't."

"Uncle Richard would *not* have murdered us!" His

brother was clearly still in denial about the political reality of the England they had left. He'd been reluctant to accept that their uncle, Richard, Duke of Gloucester and Lord Protector of the Realm, who'd left both of them to languish in the Tower behind a locked door, might have done so to seize England's throne for himself.

But there was no point arguing over what might have happened if they'd stayed and not eaten the pills. They were here now. It was time to work out what they were going to do next.

"Let's forget Uncle Richard for a moment," said Edward. "We need to think. Decide on a course of action."

"So you think we have moved in time."

"Yes. I do."

"Both times? You think we travelled forwards in time four hundred years and... what about now? *When* do you think we are now?"

Richard always seemed to think his elder brother had all the answers. Edward couldn't honestly blame him, because he often made out that he did. Being their father's heir had made Edward very self-assured, sometimes imperious. Richard wavered between being irritated by it and depending on it.

On this occasion Edward had to admit, "I do not know. We have come to a time when the city of London does not exist. I would say that it is most likely that we are in the distant past, before the city was built. I have been wondering if this is shortly after God sent the Flood. It would explain the water, the sea. But equally it could be that we are in the distant future. And perhaps..." Edward swallowed, not wanting to imagine the alternative. "... Perhaps London has been destroyed."

Richard visibly shivered. It wasn't the cold. His face shone with sweat, the sun searing both their scalps.

"So how do we get back to 1483?"

Edward thought about this for a moment. He remembered the first time they travelled in time. He remembered being in the realm of ghosts, after swallowing the pills, feeling like he was floating. Their bedchamber was suddenly filled with strangely dressed people – transparent people – walking through, literally through, one another. He could see through the walls, through the furniture, through the floor to the room below. He could see beyond the Tower to the river. Everything and everyone were eerily ethereal and blurred together in front of his eyes. And Edward remembered that when he concentrated on one thing amid the haze, it sharpened into focus, all the other ghosts falling away. There was a painting. A painting that looked like it was of him and his brother. It was transparent at first, like everything else. But as Edward stared at it, it became clear, and everything else started to fade. A moment later, they were back in their bedchamber and all the ghosts had gone, but it was four hundred years later.

Things happened in much the same way when they ate the second pill only minutes ago, standing on the streets of London in 1888. Edward remembered returning to the realm of ghosts, the streets filled with shiny horse-less carriages, people in eccentric clothes and giant structures all around. All transparent of course. Ghosts, like before.

Only Edward couldn't remember fixing on anything that time. He couldn't remember seeing anything shift into focus while the rest fell away.

So how did they get here?

He told his brother his theory on how they ended up in 1888, that his focusing on one thing in particular seemed to pull them out of whatever it was they were actually in and into a specific period in time. But he admitted he couldn't remember what he had focused on before they arrived here.

"That's because it wasn't you," said Richard after a moment's thought.

"What?" said Edward.

"It was me. I looked at something. I focused on it. It became clear, like you said. Everything else – all the

9

ghosts – started fading away. We were holding hands at the time. A moment later, we were here."

It was presumptuous of Edward to think that he was the only one with the ability to plot their journey, as though time itself was only going to respond to him. Richard had brought them here.

"So what did you see?" said Edward. "What was it you focused on?"

It was like two tiny flames went out in Richard's eyes. His face paled and his throat bulged with a swallow. An aura of fear had come over him like a deep shadow.

"What's wrong?" said Edward.

"I saw… a monster," replied Richard, looking down at his feet. "It was coming towards me. Charging at me like a bull. I was terrified. Did you not see it?"

"I saw creatures. I saw a lot of things. None could see me, though. What did the monster look like?"

Richard sighed, raised his head and looked at Edward. He opened his mouth to answer, then the direction of his gaze shifted slightly and his whole face dropped.

"That," he whispered, rigid.

Edward spun round, following his gaze.

Lord have mercy.

Not far from where they stood, standing partly shaded beneath a cycad and trampling a large patch of hornworts, was a creature three times as tall as them, with dark green, brown-flecked skin that was scaly like a snake. Dangling from its bulbous middle were two small arms with three-fingered hands ending in sickle-shaped claws. Its two legs and feet were similar, only much larger and longer, and along its back was a row of tall, bony spines linked by skin. It waved a long tail that was as thick as a tree at the base and tapered to a point, and looked like it could propel a carriage into the air with a single whack. Its long head bore two horns and a tapered jaw, the hot sun gleaming off multiple, tightly packed rows of ravenous-looking teeth.

Edward's heart was pounding as they watched the

creature lean forwards, its two eyes – like yellow billiard balls – staring straight at them.

Neither boy moved. Richard whispered, "What do we do?"

Edward swallowed hard. He plunged his hand into his satchel and pulled out the pot of red pills.

"We have to –" started Edward.

"Edward!" his brother screamed.

The creature stooped low and launched into a run.

"Run!"

The boys spun on the spot and hurtled down the incline that led to the rivers and marshes. Their legs had never moved faster.

The beast's enormous footfalls hammered the earth behind them. Edward glanced back. With each stride the creature covered startling amounts of ground.

It nearly has us.

Edward had the pot of pills in his hand. If he could slip a pill into Richard's hand and another into his own mouth as they ran, they could escape.

He looked at his brother, running maybe a foot or two behind him, and shouted, "Richard, I'm going to pass you a pill. Swallow it as soon as you have it!"

Richard nodded but then the creature's colossal shadow engulfed him.

No.

The creature lunged fast and caught him. Richard's entire upper body disappeared inside its huge crocodilian jaws.

"Richard!" Edward's blood-curdling scream shivered across the plain. He stopped dead and watched helplessly as his brother was hoisted violently into the air.

Richard frantically thrashed his limbs as the monster swung him back and forth like a chew toy. Then the beast lifted its head and squeezed its jaws, crushing Richard's body between its teeth. The crack of his brother's bones skewered painfully into Edward like a sword to the heart.

Richard's limbs flopped. Edward watched, frozen, as

the monster shuffled his body fully inside its deadly cage of teeth and swallowed him whole. Richard slid down easily, the creature's pale green throat bulging only slightly.

Edward was cold, numb. The only thing he could feel was hot vomit churning in his stomach. He stood inert, broken. Running was useless.

As soon as the monster had finished, its vicious yellow eyes were on Edward.

He was still holding the pot of pills. He could still escape.

He went to unscrew the lid.

No time.

Everything went dark. Edward felt multiple agonising stabs all over his body, but the pain only lasted a moment. A tingling sensation coursed instantly through his limbs and extremities. He was floating.

In a moment the darkness began to lift. A beautiful light glimmered. Someone was emerging. Coming towards him from the light, calling his name. Reaching for him.

He could see her smiling face now, and a great welling of warmth filled him up.

Mother...

2

October 26th 2026

Adam Bryant felt his breath grow short at the mention of Million Eyes. Sitting rigid on the sofa next to his girlfriend, Izzy, he gripped the phone tighter.

Why was this *Dr Lester* screwing with him like this? His old best friend, Jennifer, had travelled back in time and his employers were involved somehow? The words 'what the fuck' were teetering on his tongue.

He should've hung up, but the tug of curiosity won out. He had to see where Dr Lester was going with this.

"What about Million Eyes?" he asked.

"They're the ones who assassinated the Queen," Lester replied.

The fact that Lester was a Liz Truther – people who believed that Queen Elizabeth II had been assassinated five years ago – drained her of credibility. All the assassination claims had been judged baseless. Liz Truthers were nothing more than your garden-variety, tin-foil-hat-wearing conspiracy theorists. Aka, fruitcakes.

"You're kidding, right?" Adam sniffed and wiped a couple of stray tears with his finger. All this Jennifer talk had triggered a bunch of emotions to surface unexpectedly. He glanced at Izzy, who sipped her beer, face shadowed with worry. She'd only seen him cry once, and that was when his mum died two years ago. It took a lot for him to cry.

"No, I'm not," said Lester. "And not only that, Million

Eyes were the ones trying to kill Jennifer. They're the reason she travelled in time."

What? He'd been trying to hold them back – the memories – but the dam broke and they poured through in a drowning deluge.

Jennifer at the hospital, raving about people trying to kill her, saying that they'd murdered Gregory Ferro, that conspiracy theorist she'd been meeting up with. The phone call he had with her a few hours later, when she was in a state, saying she'd run from the hospital, that a nurse was trying to kill her, and asking Adam to come pick her up.

At the time, Adam thought Jennifer might be suffering from some form of psychosis, so he got in his car and went to find her. He couldn't. He searched Queen Victoria Park where she said she was, and the roads around it. She was nowhere. He headed for the hospital, but the road was closed, police everywhere. Somebody told him there'd been a 'terrorist incident'.

He remembered the guilt and panic that had ripped through him in that moment. The awful realisation that perhaps Jennifer hadn't lost it at all, and *was* being chased by someone wanting her dead. And he hadn't believed her.

And then she disappeared. Adam was overcome with worry that she might be dead, until – *thank God* – he got a letter from her. She told him she'd run away but didn't say where or who was after her, just that she was safe and that she'd be back.

Only she didn't come back. And Adam didn't hear from her again.

"Adam, you're scaring me," said Izzy. He'd never told her about Jennifer – what was the point? But he was going to have to explain this somehow.

"Mr Bryant, did you hear what I said?" said Lester. Adam realised he'd been silent for several moments, trying to hold back the queasy rush of emotions that were threatening to spill out.

"Why are you doing this?" he murmured, swallowing the bile that had collected at the back of his throat.

"Doing what?"

"There have always been conspiracy theories about Million Eyes, just like there are about all successful companies. All you've done is imaginatively tie those theories to Jennifer's disappearance – not caring who you hurt in the process." He felt his brow tighten and jaw clench. He rarely got angry but this woman had just pushed all the right buttons.

Lester gave a sigh. "I know this is difficult, Mr Bryant, but it's true. It's all in Jennifer's letters. Million Eyes invented time travel. It's how she went back in time. She had a bottle of red pills that she took from a Million Eyes operative's house. It was through swallowing one of those pills that she ended up in the year 1100."

"Pills? Oh, come on. A flying DeLorean's more realistic than that."

"Jennifer said you'd take some convincing. She said you didn't believe her about Gregory Ferro either."

Adam didn't believe anything unless there was proof – but Jennifer was the same. Scepticism and not falling for bullshit were among the few things they had in common. *Used to.*

"Gregory Ferro was a nutjob," said Adam. "Jennifer knew that."

"Did she? She was starting to believe him. She told you she was starting to. At the pub. The night she got run over."

Adam shivered. How could she know all this?

She was tricking him; these people had ways of knowing things, of finding out stuff. "I'm hanging up now," he said.

"Mr Bryant, please. I know you still work for Million Eyes. I know you've been promoted to headquarters. We need to work together. Find out what they're up to."

Yes, he had been. He'd just had his first day working as a senior developer in the productivity apps office, and he wasn't about to get sucked into anything that might jeopardise that. It was his most exciting role yet. "Sorry."

"But –"

He hung up and threw down his phone. Leaning forwards, he grabbed his beer off the coffee table and took a hefty swig.

"What the hell was that about?" said Izzy, frustration and a touch of anger in her voice, which was often how her worrying would manifest.

"Some conspiracy theorist trying to tell me Million Eyes are bad news."

"But you don't believe him?"

"Her. And no, I don't. Million Eyes are a great company. She's one of those people who has to see the worst in everything, can't understand how a company can be successful without having a whole bunch of skeletons in the closet." *Weird time-travelling skeletons.*

A moment later, "Who's Jennifer?"

He knew that was coming. He downed some more beer. "An old friend. Long gone now."

"You never mentioned her."

"That's because she disappeared years ago." Adam felt an ache in his chest. "And I think she's probably dead."

Izzy's eyes sprang wide. "Dead? Shit! Why do you think that?"

"I really don't wanna talk about it, okay?"

His words came out a bit sharper than he intended, but it honestly wasn't something he wanted to go over again. Jennifer's disappearance was a scar that wouldn't heal. But it was one he was pretty good at covering up. It was time to reapply the band-aid.

Izzy put a comforting hand on Adam's thigh. "Okay. But you *can* talk to me about it. If you want to. Just saying."

"Yeah, thanks. Can we just go back to *Eastenders*?" They'd been watching the recently cancelled soap opera's final episode and right now he wanted nothing more than to get back to all the shit acting, overblown plots and dialogue, and cartoon villainy.

Izzy flashed an uneasy grin. "Geez, it must be bad if you're saying that."

Yeah, it was. He'd take *Eastenders* over thinking about Jennifer any day.

But the dismal soap wasn't enough of a distraction and Adam couldn't help his mind swinging back to the things Lester had said. Jennifer travelling in time. Million Eyes inventing time travel and assassinating the Queen. Jennifer writing letters in the 1100s that proved everything. He remembered Gregory Ferro's whackadoo theories about time travellers buggering about with history, and he remembered trying to persuade Jennifer that the 'evidence' Ferro had found *must've* been hoaxes and lies because time travel was scientifically impossible. And now, here was someone else, presumably not connected to Ferro in any way, spewing forth the same kind of bollocks.

Getting into bed that night, having drunk more beers than he'd planned and feeling woozy, Adam let the question creep into his mind: could any of it *not* be bollocks? *Any* of it?

Turning over and closing his eyes, he laughed inwardly and pushed the question back. *No, you dickhead. Of course not.*

3

March 29th 2027

Dr Samantha Lester, a senior palaeontologist and archaeologist for LIPA – the London Institute of Palaeontology and Archaeology – was returning home to the commuter town of Gravesend in Kent on the same quiet road she always took, the one that wound through little villages instead of the busy A2. The journey was usually uneventful, but today, driving through one of the villages, Lester spotted a little girl up ahead, skipping happily along the pavement in the same direction. She was alone.

Lester's heart leapt into her throat. The long, shining ginger hair was unmistakable. And the denim dungarees.

Georgia?

Her eyes stayed on the girl as she drove past. She needed to see her face, confirm it wasn't Georgia. Just another little ginger girl with similar dungarees.

Oh my God. She saw a flash of the girl's face. Her daughter's distinctive cheeky grin made her tremble all over.

Lester was forced to turn her eyes back on the road, but she had to see her again. She had to go back.

There was a mini roundabout up ahead. She made a fast turn all the way around and went back up the road, her breath quickening.

Georgia was gone. It was a solid row of terraced houses she'd been skipping past, no alleyways for her to run up.

Lester checked the pavement on the other side, just in case she'd missed her crossing the road. A man with three small dogs was walking one way, a partly hunched-over old lady the other. No Georgia.

A driver blasted his horn behind her. She'd inadvertently slowed to fifteen miles per hour while she scoured the street for her daughter. She pressed the accelerator and continued up the road, turning around at the next roundabout so she could resume her journey home.

She knew she must've imagined it, but that didn't stop her from scanning both sides as she came back along the same stretch of road for a third time, this time being careful not to dip below thirty. She didn't see Georgia again. She switched on the radio to try and distract herself. It didn't work.

I'm losing it.

It was four months, four days since Georgia died. She was only six. At age one she was diagnosed with necrocythemia, a rare and unstoppable blood disease, for which the only treatment was regular blood transfusions and organ transplants. From that moment on, every few months, sometimes weeks, a new organ would fail. Before long all of Georgia's organs had belonged to other people, and Lester had donated so much blood to her daughter she was surprised she had any left herself.

Then, after five years of constant trauma, doctors administered a revolutionary new drug and, defying all the odds, Georgia's condition started to improve. Lester was a scientist and an atheist, but admittedly she had started to wonder if a higher power had given Georgia another chance.

Until it happened. Georgia was playing with her teddies in the lounge one evening, Lester on the sofa on her laptop reading the results of geophysical survey on a site in Hampshire, and her husband, Brody, in the kitchen cooking lasagne. Georgia put her teddies to bed, then said she was going to have a little sleep with them and got under the blanket, snuggling up with her favourite, Mary Alice. Lester assumed she was pretending to sleep since she'd never voluntarily put herself to bed. But a minute or so went by and she still hadn't moved. Lester checked on her, found her unconscious and unrousable with a rapidly weakening pulse. An ambulance came but Georgia was already gone. The new drug had slowed things down, but it hadn't fixed anything, and Georgia's tired little body had had enough.

It was such a cruel twist. Just when things seemed like they were getting better, Lester's entire world came crashing down around her with no warning, no chance to say goodbye, to hold Georgia's warm little body in her arms and tell her one last time that she loved her. How do you go on when your six-year-old daughter lies down and dies right in front of you?

"You go on knowing that she's at peace," her counsellor would say.

She's not at peace, she's dead, Lester felt like replying. *Death isn't peaceful. Death is death.*

To be honest, Lester's own heart basically stopped the moment her daughter's did. Yes, she got on with things, threw herself into her work, but she just felt cold, empty, like nothing really mattered anymore. Alive but not living. And they say time's a healer. Rubbish. Time was making things worse. She'd stopped going to her counsellor because it just wasn't helping. Last week her GP had increased her dose of antidepressants. And now she was seeing visions of Georgia. She felt like she was two steps away from a breakdown.

She got home and the smell of burnt chicken hit her the moment she stepped through the front door. "Brody, you alright?" she said as she hung up her coat.

"Yeah," Brody replied quietly. "I burnt dinner again. Sorry. I'll order us a takeaway now you're back."

Lester could hear faint laughing coming from the lounge, followed by a very familiar squeal. As she went up the hallway, several excitable voices became more distinct. One was her own.

She came into the lounge. The room was dark. It had been a dull, cloudy day all day and now the sun was going down. Brody hadn't switched any lamps on, so the only light in the room was coming from the TV, which Brody stared blankly at while slumped corpse-like on their three-seater. And although he wasn't crying at that moment, there was wetness on his cheeks, glowing in the TV's light.

She looked at the screen. Brody, in a pair of swim shorts, was running around the garden with a water pistol, chasing Georgia, in her T-Rex swimming costume, screaming and giggling and occasionally getting Daddy back with her own pistol, while Lester, behind the camera, snorted and sniggered.

Lester smiled briefly, felt a tear squirm free and run to the corner of her mouth. She licked it away, sniffed and said, "Sean, lamps on." Their MEye virtual assistant, which had the voice of Sean Bean, switched on the floor lamp by the two-seater and the lamp on the table by Brody. Warm, mellow light filled the room. Then she said, "Sean, June 2026 water fight, off," and the home movie clip faded into the menu screen.

Brody looked at her, frowning. "What are you doing?"

"You can't keep doing this," she replied softly. "Every time I come home, you're watching these. It's not good for you."

"I'll decide what's good for me. Sean, June 2026 water fight, resume."

"No. Stop it, Brody. Sean, TV, off."

The screen faded to black. Lester went to sit next to Brody on the sofa.

"What do you want?" he said, eyes wide.

"I don't know – to talk?"

Brody shook his head and huffed. "You haven't wanted to talk to me in months. What's changed?"

"What do you mean?"

"I mean we've barely spoken since it happened. I've

tried, you close up every time. It's like you can't even mention her name."

Why was he doing this? "It's just hard, okay."

Brody's voice went up in pitch and volume. "Oh, it's hard, is it? Shit. If only I knew what you were going through."

"Brody, don't."

"I'm sorry but it's like you've forgotten about her –"

Lester interjected quickly and with resentment, "Of course I haven't," but her words were buried under his.

"– and you've switched your fucking feelings off or something. And it's like I'm going through this on my own."

Lester raised her voice to match his. "Trust me, you're not."

"Then why aren't we comforting each other? Helping each other through it? You know, we haven't touched each other since before Georgia died."

She felt a spark of fury. "Are you serious? This is about sex? Our daughter's dead and you're worried about getting laid?"

"Oh fuck off, Sam." Brody shot to his feet and stormed out of the room.

Lester followed him into the kitchen. Brody opened the Eat Now app on his MEpad, charging on the worksurface, and started perusing takeaway menus.

"What then?" she said.

He looked up. "Intimacy, Sam. I'm talking about intimacy. We both need it, now more than ever. Don't we?"

She breathed a heavy sigh, shook her head. "I don't know what we need." She did, though. Help. Some kind of. Neither of them were coping. This conversation was proving it.

Her phone started buzzing in her pocket. She took it out and stepped into the hallway. It was Becca Tiedemann, one of the excavators at the dig in Tower Hamlets, for which she was project officer. Several weeks ago, construction workers digging the foundations for a new shopping centre had come upon some fossil fragments. LIPA was called in and Lester and her team were now lifting the remains of a previously unknown species of dinosaur out of its primeval bed. It was the sort of thing Lester would be bursting with excitement over, if she still got excited about anything.

"Hi Becca," said Lester.

"Hey. You have to come see this." She sounded elated, breathless.

"See what?" Lester could hear voices and hammering in the background and shot a glance at her watch. "Are you still on site?"

"Yeah. We're all still here. No one wanted to go home."

"Why? What have you found?"

"Probably better that you see it for yourself. Can you come?"

Lester's gaze drifted towards the kitchen. She knew Brody was in there stewing. It was a bad time to head out.

But she needed a distraction right now. "Yeah. I'll be there. Are you going to give me a hint?"

"Sure. We've found something... impossible."

Lester's curiosity surged. "Okay. I'll be there soon."

Hanging up and stepping into the kitchen, "I have to go."

Refusing to look up from the MEpad, Brody replied dourly, "Yeah, I heard. Dinner for one, then."

"We'll pick this up later, okay?"

"Mm-hmm."

She sighed and got ready to leave. She wasn't sure what else to say.

Forty minutes later, Lester arrived at the dig site in Tower Hamlets. The dusk had thickened into night but the floodlights they'd erected around the site were so bright it would've been easy to mistake it for the middle of the day. Lester parked in the road and walked to the edge of the deep open pit where she could see her two-dozen-strong excavation team working away purposefully. There was no evidence that anyone was packing up and going home any time soon.

She climbed down one of several ladders placed around the perimeter and walked over to the dinosaur skeleton. Her team having removed most of the overburden, the contour of the creature was visible, the bones partly poking through their rock encasements like a body touching the surface of a lake. It was lying on its right side, its skull long and narrow, its tail stretched out. At somewhere between eighty and ninety percent complete, it was remarkably preserved, early visual inspection suggesting that it might be a close relation of the Spinosaurus.

Lester surveyed the scene. Some of the excavators were bringing the still-buried leg bones to the surface with chisels and rock hammers. Others were using knives, awls and brushes to dislodge and scrape rock and loose sediment from between the long bones that protruded from the spinal column, and a few had started trenching around the sufficiently unearthed parts of the skeleton, removing earth from beneath and around the bones and their surrounding matrix so that they sat on pedestals; at that point they would be wrapped in protective plaster jackets in order to be removed and transported safely.

However, most of the team, including Becca, were currently huddled around the area just below the creature's ribcage, where its stomach would've been.

Becca looked up when she heard Lester's footsteps crunching over the bedrock. "Hey, Sam. This is going to blow your mind."

Lester stepped closer. When she saw it, the blood in her veins froze. "My God."

"Yeah," said Becca. "I know."

The team were gently picking at the rock encasing a small framework of bones. Enough had been brushed away for them to discern what it was. The frontal bone and cavernous eye sockets were unmistakable. A skull. A *human* skull.

"I see what you mean by 'impossible'," said Lester. "Does anyone else know about this?"

"Only you," said Becca.

"Good. Let's keep it that way, for now. The moment this gets out, we'll have reporters coming out of our ears."

4

November 17th 28

Dr Jesus M. Hirschfield opened his eyes and found himself staggering, disoriented, into a sloping town square. Everything was shifting in and out of focus but moments of clarity revealed small double- and single-storey clay-brick houses with flat roofs, orchards and enclosures for livestock, and a much bigger stone building with a clerestory roof that towered over everything. Hammers banged and saws scraped and farm animals bleated and brayed, and yet it was peaceful – blissfully so – compared to where Jesus just was. No screaming. No weapons fire. No ships in the sky.

What happened? Where am I? How did I get here?

The air stank of shit and freshly cut timber. Jesus trudged along a dirt road, passing men in simple cotton robes and women with colourful shawls over their shoulders and heads. They stared at him warily and went silent until he had passed.

Why are you all dressed like that?

He passed a small structure built into the hillside, with a stone arch leading inside it, saw a throng of people gathered around and inside the arch on a paved area partly enclosed by a wall, holding jugs and buckets. He felt faint, the people with the jugs starting to spin and blur into each other. He blinked but couldn't shake the spinning. It was because he was starving, probably. His belly ached and groaned. He had to eat something.

An intense wave of dizziness made him nearly collide with a small, two-wheeled cart pulled by a donkey. He stopped and doubled over, clutching his knees. He gulped a lungful of air.

"Are you all right?"

His dizziness easing, Jesus straightened. The man standing in front of him wore a dark blue turban and white robe, fastened with a jewelled belt. Jesus found himself staring unwittingly at his bushy brown beard. Jesus had never seen anyone with a beard.

Jesus's throat felt dry and sore but he was able to reply, weakly, "W-where am I?"

"Nazareth," the man replied.

Though his head still felt like it had been in a laundry pod, the fog over Jesus's eyes had lifted. Inhaling deeply, he drank in his surroundings. To his left he saw a woman spinning thread with a spindle; across the square, a donkey was pulling a millstone to grind wheat; on the hillside a shepherd tended his flock in an olive grove; and coming down the dirt road towards him was a man riding a camel. There were carpenters everywhere, hence the prevailing sounds of hammers and saws. Their benches were just outside their doors in seas of wood shavings, planks of all sizes resting up against their pale walls, and they were using simple lathes to carve bowls, tools, tables – anything. He saw one boring a hole through a plank with some kind of primitive drill – simply a bow with a string attached to a cylindrical shaft. His gaze roamed back to the building with the stone arch and the people coming away from it with jars and buckets now sloshing with water. It was a well.

One thing was painfully clear. The question wasn't *where* he was. The question was *when*.

"What year is it?" said Jesus.

"You *have* come from afar. I could tell. It is the fourteenth year of Tiberius Caesar."

His knowledge of history was scant but that sounded like an ancient Roman emperor to him. What on earth happened? He tried to think but the fog that had lifted from his eyes continued to smother his memory. The last thing he remembered was taking cover in an abandoned building in the year 2222 – then here.

"What's that?" said the man, pointing at Jesus's side. Jesus looked down; his medical kit was still hanging from his shoulder. He hadn't even realised it was there.

"Nothing," he said quickly, wrapping his arm around it protectively. If he really had come back to the time of the Roman Empire, the items inside could completely derail the course of history.

Although – would that be a bad thing? Where – *when* – he'd come from, humanity was perishing around him. Everyone, everywhere, dying. Jesus felt his gut twist, everything that had happened to him flooding back like a huge drowning wave. The horrors that befell his friends, his family. He'd lost everything. But so had everyone else. And those left behind and still fighting were so scarred by what they'd been through, what they'd witnessed, that in spirit they were dead too.

So perhaps derailing the course of history was a great idea.

"Do you need help?" said the man. "Some proper clothes, perhaps?"

Jesus yanked himself from a harrowing past to a bewildering present – although the definitions of 'past' and 'present' weren't so simple anymore. The man's comment made him realise why everybody was staring at him. He was wearing a bright, fitted, silvery blue Twelfth Remnant uniform, a far cry from their rough, rudimentary coverings.

"I need a place to stay," said Jesus.

The man looked him up and down and frowned, clearly still deciding what to make of him. After a moment, he nodded, "With me. You can stay with me. I have a house on the other side of town. I can take you there."

The man had kind eyes and his beard made him appear warm and genuine. If this wasn't all some bizarre dream and Jesus really had come back in time two thousand or so years, he was going to need as much help as he could get.

"Thank you," said Jesus, smiling. "That's very kind."

The man's eyebrows twitched. "I presume you have a name. It would probably be sensible to let me have that first."

"Yes. Sorry. Dr Jesus M. Hirschfield."

The man shook his head. "What kind of name is that?"

"Jesus is fine. And you are?"

"Joseph. Joseph of Arimathea."

"Pleased to meet you." He felt another pang of hunger. "Do you have anything to eat?"

Joseph nodded. "Yes. Come. My wagon is this way."

Jesus followed Joseph up the road, hoping it wasn't far. He felt so weak and unsteady. He wished he could remember how he got here. Perhaps some sustenance would help with that.

People continued staring at him and giving him a wide berth. He couldn't blame them.

Then one of the starers caught his eye: a young-looking woman standing several metres ahead, in an ankle-length, pale blue tunic, sandals and a long white shawl spilling over her shoulders, concealing most of her long brown hair. A deep-looking sadness wilted her lips and glazed her eyes.

Jesus kept his eyes on her, expecting her to back away from him like everyone else as he got closer. She didn't.

A single tear glinted on her cheek as she raised her right arm towards him, revealing the small silver gun in her hand. When she mouthed what looked like 'I'm so sorry,' Jesus knew she was here to kill him.

Two hands slammed into Jesus's side. The ground rushed towards his face, his hands and knees shooting out in front of him to break his fall, palms grazing the gravel, stinging pains darting up his arms and thighs. The corner of his eye caught the green bolt of light surging overhead with a hiss.

He turned over on the ground, saw a man in a long black robe with a deep hood that cast half his face in shadow, clasping a similar-looking gun to the one wielded by the woman. The man looked down at Jesus briefly, then whipped his gaze in the direction of the woman and charged into the knots of townspeople who were running screaming.

Joseph jostled through to help Jesus to his feet. "What just happened?"

"I – I'm not sure." He dusted the sand and stones off his palms and looked up the road to try to see the woman or the hooded man. A bright white light flashed in the distance. Nobody else seemed to notice, but that's because they were frantically taking cover from a woman capable of conjuring bolts of green lightning.

Jesus took a deep breath. His heart was racing. "I think… I think someone just tried to kill me."

Joseph frowned. "Why would someone want to kill you?"

"I don't know."

He did, though. That woman, that man. They were from the future, like he was. If the woman was trying to kill him, then it was because she was trying to stop him from impacting the timeline. If the man was trying to save him, then he was trying to ensure that whatever changes Jesus made, stood.

But Jesus had a chance to change the timeline for the *better*. Warn humanity about the apocalypse it was facing. Give people two thousand years to make sure things turned out differently.

Saving the human race from extinction could only be a good thing.

"Perhaps it is the way you are dressed," Joseph smirked.

Jesus gave an uneasy smile.

"Come. Let's get you away from here."

5

April 1ˢᵗ 2027

It didn't take long for the press to get wind of what was happening in Tower Hamlets. Lester suspected that it might even have been her boss, Ethan, LIPA's head of Field Operations, who'd tipped them off. Even though he knew the crowds would make her excavation team's job more difficult, he was always trying to get LIPA more attention in the media. And now LIPA was right at the centre of the story of the century.

Arriving at the dig site late that afternoon to give a press statement at Ethan's request, Lester counted at least eight news vans parked haphazardly in the road and along the pavement, along with police cars and other vehicles. There were people everywhere, some journalists with microphones and camera crews, others just nosy spectators trying to get closer to the site and being held back by a perimeter of police and LIPA-contracted security personnel Ethan had stationed there earlier that day.

With nowhere to park, Lester parked in a no-parking zone. Why not? Everybody else was doing it. She jostled through to the front of the crowd and was stopped by a security man.

"Can't go any further, ma'am."

She arched one eyebrow and flashed her LIPA card. "This is *my* dig."

The guard shot a glance at her card and flushed slightly

with embarrassment. "Sorry, ma'am. Please go through."

He stepped aside and she walked to the edge of the pit, climbed down and walked over to Becca, who was looking at her phone and grinning. "How are we doing?" said Lester.

"Good," said Becca, slipping her phone into her trousers. "Social media's going mad. Everybody's got a theory."

Lester nodded. "Everybody always has."

"In normal circumstances, your press statement would put an end to the speculation. But since we haven't got a fucking clue ourselves, I doubt it. Do you even know what you're going to say?"

"The only thing I can say at this point. Lots of 'don't know yets'."

Lester looked down at the two small skeletons gradually emerging from their cocoon of rock. Many of the bones were still buried but her excavators had trimmed the rock that encased them, revealing clear body shapes. There could be no doubt that both skeletons were human and, judging by their size, children.

"Just be prepared. Those reporters are going to be on you like feeding sharks. I certainly don't envy –"

Becca fell silent when one of the diggers dislodged some rock close to one of the children's hands. Loose brown sediment fell into the trench around the body and both Becca and Lester noticed a cluster of tiny red stones go with it.

"Hey – what are those?" said Lester, diving forwards and collecting up the stones in her palm. She held them out and both she and Becca stared at them, frowning.

No. They weren't stones. They were too uniform – all capsule-shaped. They looked manmade.

"They look like..." *Oh my God.* Lester swallowed hard, remembering Jennifer Larson's letters. "... pills."

"Pills!" said Becca. "This is getting crazier by the minute."

Lester walked over to the conservator she trusted the

most, Keiko Hamasaki. "Keiko, I need you to bag these, discreetly, and get them to the labs." She handed her the red pills.

Keiko's acne-scarred features narrowed with confusion. "What are they?"

"That's what we need to find out. Take them with the next batch of bones. And don't mention or show them to anyone else."

Keiko nodded, "Understood," and scurried away.

Roger, one of LIPA's communications assistants, walked over to Lester. "Sam, some of the reporters are asking for an ETA on your statement."

Lester nodded. "I'm coming now. Just give me a moment."

She got out her phone to re-read her press statement. A message flashed up from Brody, simply saying I love you with a beating heart emoji.

She swiped the message away without replying. As she re-read her statement, her gaze drifted back to the exhumation, a hundred questions crowding her head.

One dominated them all: was all this Million Eyes' doing?

6

November 17th 28

Jesus followed Joseph to his wagon, which was parked in a narrow side street just off Nazareth's main square and being looked after by a servant, or probably more aptly a slave: a boy in his early teens who was in desperate need of a bath. The wagon was large and pulled by a pair of oxen. In the back were dozens of large sheets of tin tied together with rope, along with baskets of fruits and vegetables, dried meats and bread. Joseph handed Jesus some bread, a pomegranate and a bag-like drinks receptacle made from animal skin.

Jesus sat next to Joseph on a wooden seat at the front of his wagon and ate the bread and fruit hungrily. It felt so good to eat. He drank from the skin, hoping for water, getting wine. Wine that was not good. The slave boy rode in the back with the tin and baskets of food. He hadn't spoken a word. Maybe he wasn't allowed. Maybe he couldn't.

On the ten-minute journey up the hillside to Joseph's house, Jesus thought about the woman who'd just tried to shoot him. Sure, he was used to attempts on his life. They were par for the course back in war-torn 2222. Back? Forward in war-torn 2222. *Whatever.*

But this one was different. This one was personal. Somebody wanted him dead because of his impact on the course of history. An impact he was yet to have.

Jesus's mind was back on Joseph, who was saying

nothing as the wagon rumbled over the rough and heavily rutted road. He just let Jesus eat. But Jesus knew an onslaught of questions was coming. The first, most important question for him now was how on earth he was going to answer the rest.

Perhaps by being honest. What exactly did he have to lose? Nothing, frankly. Nothing at all.

Joseph's house was single-storey and made from yellow clay bricks, with an open courtyard at the front, furnished with a large clay stove and a water cistern. While his slave remained in the courtyard to feed and water his oxen, Joseph led Jesus into a small room, evidently a kitchen. Against one wall was a bench laid with spoons and other utensils, next to a store of food in the corner – baskets of bread and fruit and a goat carcass Joseph was obviously planning to cook. Above the bench were some recessed shelves holding earthenware bowls, cups and a pitcher, and in the centre of the room was a large wooden table with two stools. Glancing up, Jesus saw that the ceiling was just reeds layered with mud and supported by timber beams – very basic and rural. Through a doorway he could see into a second room where there was a lumpy-looking mattress and a pile of blankets. It seemed there were only two rooms: one for eating, one for sleeping.

Jesus was surprised. He expected the house to be bigger, more lavish. He'd already seen houses that were much bigger than this in his short time in the town. And Joseph didn't look like a poor man.

"Do you live here alone?" said Jesus.

"Only when I'm in Nazareth," said Joseph. He brought down the earthenware pitcher and poured each of them a cup of wine. "I travel a lot. In some of those places I have houses. My wife and children live in Arimathea."

That explained it. He had several houses. They didn't *all* need to be lavish.

Joseph invited Jesus to sit on one of the stools at the table and sat down opposite him. There was a short silence and Jesus realised his interrogation was about to start. He was ready.

Joseph's first question was not the one he expected. "So, are you a madman?"

"I'm sorry?"

"A madman. You are certainly dressed like one."

"If you think I am, why have you invited me into your home?"

Joseph sipped his wine. "I enjoy interesting people, and sometimes the most interesting are the maddest."

Jesus smiled, then laughed inwardly. What Jesus was about to tell him was surely going to make him sound like a madman.

"I'm not mad," said Jesus. "But you will think I am before this conversation is over."

Joseph nodded, "Probably," laughing.

Jesus looked at his wine. It was likely the same as what he was drinking from that wineskin. It was brown and had bits floating in it. He sipped it to be polite. Yep, still gross. But he couldn't expect the wine-making process to be as refined in Ancient Roman times as it was in the 23rd century.

"I'm from the future," said Jesus.

Joseph frowned. "The future?"

"I've come back in time from the year 2222. I don't know how or why. I don't remember what happened. One minute I was there, the next I was here. And I don't know where the 'fourteenth year of Tiberius Caesar' fits into the calendar we use in the future, but I think 2222 is about two thousand years from now, give or take a couple of centuries."

Joseph leaned forwards, arched one bushy eyebrow. "You mean you have seen the future? You have had visions of the days to come? You make claims of prophethood?"

"No. I'm not a prophet. I haven't just seen the future. I have *come from* the future. Thousands of tomorrows from now. Today is a very distant yesterday for me."

"What? Nonsense. That isn't possible. You can't... none of us can travel to yesterday. It is past. Lived. Gone. It can't be lived again. Only God has such powers."

Jesus nodded, "I know it doesn't seem possible. But one day it will be."

Joseph started twiddling his beard. "Let's say I believe you. I would be most curious to know what you profess the world to be like, two thousand years from now."

Jesus sighed, "Ending."

Joseph's eyes widened. "Ending?"

"Yes. In two thousand years' time, humankind faces extinction. We are fighting a losing war. We call it the Last War."

"A war against whom?"

Jesus told Joseph all about the Last War, trying to be as honest as he could without confusing him. Joseph listened, nodding often, although Jesus couldn't tell whether he believed him or was just humouring him.

Afterwards, Joseph stood up. He walked up and down the room for a minute or so, saying nothing. He gazed out of the window that was simply a hole in the wall.

Jesus sat there silently, rubbing his hands together, anxious to know what Joseph thought of it all.

Finally Joseph looked at him and said, "If you have come from two thousand years in the future, tell me something. How are we able to speak?"

"What do you mean?"

"You and I are speaking exactly the same language. That would seem to suggest that the language people speak in these lands has not changed in two thousand years. That is folly."

This man didn't miss a thing. He tried to explain, "You're right. We're not actually, *physically*, speaking the same language. But there is a tiny machine in my head that makes it seem like we are."

"So you are a magus."

"No. There's no magic involved. This machine in my head, it's the work of ordinary people. Two thousand years from now, humankind will have a much wider range of skills. We can build all kinds of complex machines that would seem like magic to you, to anyone here, but are not."

Joseph sighed thoughtfully. "Do you have any proof of this? Of any of this?"

Jesus's medical kit was by his feet on the packed-dirt floor. He reached to grab it, placed it on the table. "Do you have a knife?"

Joseph stood and walked over to his food preparation bench. He lifted a knife made of what looked like flint from the pile of utensils and handed it to Jesus.

"And a blanket?"

Joseph went to fetch a blanket from the other room. Jesus folded it several times and placed it in his lap. Then he pulled back the sleeve of his Twelfth Remnant uniform and drove the point of the knife into his forearm, feeling a sharp scratch.

"What are you doing?" said Joseph, voice slightly raised.

"Showing you something."

The deep wound he'd just made bled heavily into the blanket. He opened his medical kit with his other hand and took out a tubular contraption. He pointed the wider end at the wound and pressed his thumb against the narrower end.

Joseph noticeably recoiled as the device began emitting a pale blue light, which Jesus projected over the wound.

"Look," said Jesus, raising his arm.

Joseph leaned in closer, his eyes wide with awe as he watched the edges of the wound draw together under the light.

His skin resealed, the sting fading, Jesus turned off the device and placed it on the table, and wiped the excess blood with the blanket. He held up his healed arm to Joseph.

"You *are* a magus! God's divinity flows through you!"

"No. I'm not a magus, and I'm not divine. I have no

41

powers of my own." He gestured to the device. "This is one of the machines I was just talking about. It's called a regenerator. In the future I am a physician. A healer. This is something healers use. There are thousands of them in hospitals all around the world. But there's nothing special or magical about them. They're just very clever."

Joseph picked up the regenerator, holding it gently and carefully in both hands like it was a bomb.

Jesus pointed at the other items in his medical kit. "The rest of these things are not magic either." He picked up the tiny round device resembling a miniature hockey puck. "This, for example, is a diagnode. It attaches to a person's skin and tells me if they're unwell – and what might be the cause of it." He then picked up the pistol-like jet injector and one of the drug vials that went inside it. "And this is a pharmacator. It's used to put liquids inside people's bodies to help them get better."

"Stop. Say no more," said Joseph, shaking his head and placing the regenerator back down on the table. He looked at Jesus, his face flushed. "When I invited you here, I expected that your madness might offer me some amusement. I can see now that I was wrong."

"About what? My being mad? Or my being funny?"

"Both. I do not think you are mad, although I could be mad for thinking so. And there is nothing about any of this that I would deem funny."

Joseph sighed deeply and sat back down, entwining his fingers over the table and staring at Jesus's medical instruments. There was confusion and angst all over his face.

"What are you thinking?" said Jesus.

"That God's mysteriousness is greater than I could have imagined, and whether you are man or divine is not for me to decide or even understand. What I do know is this. You *are* a prophet, Jesus. And you are part of God's plan. I believe he has sent you here to save us. Save us from this Last War you speak of."

Part of what Jesus was saying was getting through, but Joseph was still interpreting everything Jesus said through a religious lens, no doubt because it was the mindset of the time. Religion was part and parcel of people's lives here. That building Jesus saw when he arrived, the big stone one with the clerestory roof, was probably a temple.

Joseph had mentioned this particular god several times now. "Which god is that?"

Joseph's eyes flared like it was abominable that Jesus didn't already know. "Adonai, the God of Israel! The one and only!"

Jesus hadn't heard of that one, but that wasn't surprising. Religion didn't exist in 2222. No one believed in gods anymore. People learned about some of the old faiths at school in history, but Jesus hated history and had tried to pay as little attention as possible, to his teacher's irritation.

"Is that one of the Roman gods?" asked Jesus.

Now Joseph looked like Jesus had just stabbed his child. "No. I am not a Roman. I am a Jew. I am a member of the council of rabbis, the Sanhedrin."

Jesus had heard of the Jews. He was a Jew himself, technically – *ethnically*. It wasn't a religion anymore, in his time. And it wasn't really an ethnicity anymore either, just because nobody talked about ethnicity. People were just people.

"Okay," said Jesus. "Well, I don't think it was the God of Israel who sent me here, Joseph."

"Then how did you get here?"

Jesus had no answer for that. "I don't know."

"That is because it was God. There is no other explanation. You have told me that a great evil is coming. The Devil and his army of demons is coming to destroy us all. And God has sent you here to make us ready so that we can beat them."

It wasn't quite how Jesus would have put it, but he had already decided that his coming here was a chance to change everything. To prevent the obliteration of humanity. It was seeming like Jesus and Joseph were aligned on that.

Joseph could help him. This man, who was likely more intelligent and open-minded than most in this time, could be his guide to Ancient Israel.

"What do you suggest I do?" said Jesus.

"You must tell the world about the Last War."

"Will you help me?"

"Is that not obvious?"

Jesus smiled. He figured, if he was stuck here – and it was looking increasingly certain that he was – then the least he could do was try and change the future. Even cruel, stark and primitive Ancient Israel was better than that.

1

April 1ˢᵗ 2027

Adam had been shimmying up the ranks of Million Eyes not because he wanted to, or was particularly ambitious, but because he loved, and was good at, his job. He'd gone from IT technician at the Basingstoke MEstore to programmer, then developer, at the Guildford office, to senior developer at headquarters – the grandiose London skyscraper everybody called the Looming Tower. It had meant moving to London, not something he'd ever been keen on, but since Izzy, an astrophysicist for BRSA, the British Republic Space Agency, already lived and worked there, it made sense.

That morning, Adam had been debugging the new photo editor for MEps, the 'Million Eyes productivity suite', and had barely looked up from his MEc in two hours. Shortly before midday, his friend, Curtis O'Brien, set a coffee down on the desk in front of him.

"Cheers, mate," said Adam.

"No worries." A moment later, "Well, I can't believe I've been back three seconds and you haven't asked me how it went."

Adam turned his head as Curtis set down his own coffee and sat at the MEc next to him. "Oh, shit, yeah. How'd it go?"

"I got it."

"That's great, mate. Congrats."

Adam and Curtis had only been friends since Adam's

promotion to headquarters five months ago, but they'd hit it off over a shared love of zorbing, vintage video games and curry. Now that Curtis had been promoted to principal software engineer for MEow – 'Million Eyes online world', the company's main cloud computing service – and the MEow office was the next floor up, it meant that Adam and Curtis would no longer be working together. Adam had concurred with Curtis's sentiment that that part 'sucked massive hairy donkey bollocks'.

"So how much longer do I have to stare at your sexy bum?" said Adam. Curtis loved it when Adam flirted with him.

Curtis grinned. "Next week they want me to start. Then this awesome arse is outta here."

Straight-faced, Adam said quietly, "I'll miss it."

"I know." Curtis's eyes flitted over his MEc and suddenly sprang wide. "Fuck me."

"Later," said Adam, following Curtis's gaze to floor eleven's lifts. Out of one of them stepped the CEO, Miss Morgan. Instantly it was like someone had turned down the volume on the office, several employees ending their conversations and scuttling back to their seats.

A knot formed at the pit of Adam's stomach that was one part awe, two parts terror. As the brains behind the most powerful technology company in the world, the woman was a celebrity to him, and this was the first time he was seeing her in person. He clearly wasn't the only one. A few of his colleagues had looked up from their MEcs and were gawking at Miss Morgan like she'd just parted the sea.

Adam also knew by reputation that she was a force to be reckoned with, and her fuse was short. Hence the terror.

"Shit," whispered Adam. "What do you think she's doing here? She never comes down here."

"Never ever," said Curtis. "I kinda want to get my phone out and take a photo. That's sad, right?"

"Yeah, that's lame." He paused. "I want to too."

Miss Morgan stopped to talk to Jemma Gates, deputy

manager of MEps. She had a serious look on her face, although from the pictures and video clips Adam had seen, she always had a serious look on her face.

"How old do you think she is?" said Curtis quietly.

"Sixties?" A wild guess. Erica Morgan's age was one of the world's big mysteries, since she'd never revealed it publicly. People had been guessing it for years.

"She looks fucking good for sixties. She looks more like forties."

Adam regarded her. Her face had the odd line but was otherwise vibrant and alluring, augmented with subtle eye makeup and dark purple lipstick. Her jet-black hair spilled over a charcoal skirt suit with a ruffled-collar blouse the same shade as her lipstick and she walked on black suede ankle boots with stiletto heels. The epitome of elegance – and intimidation.

"She can't be in her forties," said Adam. "She's been CEO since 1998. She would've been a teenager."

"Then I guess she just doesn't age. Maybe she's got powers. I could do with some of those."

"Oh, you'll always be gorgeous, darling."

Curtis flashed him a flirty side-eye. "Thanks babe."

"Get a room, you two," whispered their colleague, Ruth, sitting opposite them.

Curtis sniggered. "I don't think he's ready for that."

"Hey, I can take it."

"I bet you can."

Ruth's mouth twisted in disgust. "Gross."

Curtis smirked and raised both eyebrows. "Homophobe."

Finishing her conversation with Gates, Miss Morgan strode purposefully across the room, exuding confidence, and stepped inside the office of MEps manager Peter Elba, who stood up to greet her. Shutting the door behind her, she walked to the internal windows and closed the Venetian blinds.

"Ooo, secretive," said Curtis.

"Yeah," murmured Adam uneasily. His mind swung

back to that unnerving phone call with Dr Samantha
Lester five months ago. No one but Izzy knew about it,
and he'd certainly not told Curtis or anyone else at
Million Eyes. But it had prompted him to dig through the
many conspiracy theories about Million Eyes on Google,
feeling more uncomfortable the more he read. Nothing
had ever been proven, but scores of people suspected
Million Eyes' involvement in things that had nothing to
do with computers. Of course, the general consensus
judged such claims as unfounded and unhinged, and
Adam had always counted himself among them. Yet now
he found himself questioning things that happened at
Million Eyes a lot more than he ever used to.

Every company had secrets. Did Million Eyes have…
too many?

Stop it, Adam. He shook off the niggling paranoia,
downed half his coffee and returned to his work.

Adam got back to the apartment he shared with Izzy in
Ealing shortly after 6pm. Izzy normally got back half an
hour later because her commute was longer, but today
she'd had to work late, so he wasn't expecting her back
till half-seven. Ish.

He got changed out of the suit that was the only part of
working for Million Eyes he didn't like. He'd always
thought his shoulders weren't broad enough for a suit, and
his head was too small. But Miss Morgan wanted
everyone in the company, male and female, in suits. And
pristinely polished shoes. And the men had to wear plain
ties because she hated patterned ties, apparently. It was
over the top, but it didn't make Adam admire her any less.

He watched a bit of TV, then started cooking a cheese and
tomato pasta bake for dinner. Izzy's request. She said she'd
been feeling sick all day and fancied some comfort food.

Izzy arrived home looking tired and red-faced. Adam

gave her a cuddle as she dropped her bag down and came into the kitchen.

"Still feeling rough?" said Adam.

"Yeah," she murmured.

He pulled away to look at her, placed his hand on her forehead. "You're warm. Maybe you should go to the doctor's tomorrow."

Izzy shook her head. "No need." She walked to the fridge to grab a can of Coke. Popping it open, "I'm just pregnant." She threw back her head and glugged.

Wordless, Adam stared at her, blinked twice, mouth agape. A moment later, "What?"

She shrugged, expression deadpan. "Yeah. It's just a baby."

Adam felt the smile tugging at the corners of his mouth. A rush of excitement made his skin tingle.

Finally Izzy's blank expression surrendered to a smirk.

"Oh my God!" Adam cried. "Are you shitting me? An actual baby?"

Izzy arched her eyebrow. "No, no. A rubber baby."

Adam looked at her with mock scorn. "When? When did you find out?"

"Did the test a few hours ago."

Adam took the Coke can out of Izzy's hand, placed it on the worksurface and pulled his pregnant girlfriend into his arms. "This is amazing. We're gonna be parents." Euphoria coursed through his veins like a Class A. He couldn't believe it. They'd been trying for a while now, but so far, nothing. He'd started worrying that one or the other of them might have a problem.

This was the best thing ever.

Unwrapping from each other's arms, Adam framed Izzy's face in his hands, ran his fingers through her long auburn hair and gazed into her eyes. "You're going to be a great mum."

Straight-faced, Izzy nodded, "I know."

It was funny. On their first date four years ago, Adam remembered thinking that he couldn't really see Izzy as a mum. He wasn't sure why, perhaps just that she'd seemed so ambitious and career-driven, and so sensible. But then he saw her with her nieces and nephews for the first time and this whole other side of her came to light. She was in her element playing with them, chasing them, being silly with them. Honestly, it was the day he knew he wanted to spend the rest of his life with her.

That said, Izzy had every intention of being a mother *and* a career woman. They'd agreed that Adam would take more parental leave than Izzy because Izzy didn't want to be off work for too long. (And because she earned more.) That worked for Adam. He loved his job, sure, but he wasn't as wedded to it as she was, and being a stay-at-home dad for a while had always appealed to him – probably because his own dad had done the bulk of the childcare when he was a kid.

They talked about who they would tell. Izzy wasn't sure whether to tell anyone until they'd had their first scan – her mum and both her aunties had had several miscarriages, but she conceded to them telling their parents.

"We should go out for dinner," Adam said. "To celebrate."

"Sweety, you've got a pasta bake in the oven."

"I know, but we could freeze that. I want to treat you."

"That *is* a treat. I've been looking forward to it all day. Plus, I still feel rough. Been sick a bunch of times. Last thing I feel like doing is getting dolled up to go to a restaurant. Just want to get in my PJs and curl up with you and watch crap TV."

He kissed her. "That's fine, babe. Whatever you want."

Izzy went and got changed. Adam finished loading the dishwasher. He couldn't stop smiling. He couldn't wait to tell his dad; he would be over the moon.

Then a wave of sadness washed over him as he thought of the person he wanted to tell the most – Mum. Two and a half years ago, that cunt called breast cancer snatched her away. She'd always wanted to be a granny.

Adam pushed the sadness back. He was going to be a

dad. Mum wouldn't want anything to spoil this moment.

"Woah – have you seen this?" said Izzy from their lounge-diner, where she was laying the table for dinner.

"What?" said Adam, pulling their pasta bake from the oven, cheese suitably brown and crispy.

"Come see."

Adam popped the dish down on the side, slipped off the oven gloves and went into the lounge.

The news was on and showed a bunch of people excavating what looked like a dinosaur. The headline scrolling across the bottom of the screen read, *BREAKING: DINOSAUR DISCOVERED WITH HUMAN SKELETONS IN ITS STOMACH.* A newsreader speaking over the images, now zoomed in on the apparent human skeletons below the creature's ribcage, was saying that everybody was at a loss as to what the discovery meant.

Adam frowned. "What the hell?"

The newsreader said that the palaeontologist in charge of the dig, Dr Samantha Lester, from the London Institute of Palaeontology and Archaeology, was about to give a live statement. A moment later, the camera was on a woman with brown hair bunched up in a short ponytail, who looked late thirties, early forties, and was wearing jeans and a two-tone white and blue top.

Adam's pulse quickened. Was that the Dr Lester who rang him?

"I can confirm that we are in the process of exhuming what appears to be the fossilised remains of a previously unknown species of dinosaur," said Lester. "It's well preserved and we're estimating it to be about eighty percent complete. We will not know if it is authentic until the bones have been fully excavated in our labs and a detailed analysis has taken place. If, however, the bones *are* authentic, then we believe that this creature may have been closely related to the Spinosaurus, living during the Cretaceous period."

She paused, took a deep breath, blinked and visibly swallowed. "We have also discovered what *appears* to be the skeletons of two humans in the creature's stomach region." This time she strongly emphasised the word 'appears'. Well you would, wouldn't you?

"Visual inspection suggests that they were modern humans – homo sapiens – like the rest of us, and... children," said Lester. "We haven't excavated enough of the bones to offer any further detail as to their condition, their age, their sex et cetera."

"But that's impossible," a reporter interrupted loudly. "Isn't it?"

Lester nodded, "Based on everything science presently tells us, yes. But again, we won't know if these skeletons are authentic until they've undergone a full examination."

"What about the red pills you found?" shouted another reporter.

Adam swallowed. *Red pills?*

Lester frowned. "Where did you hear that?"

"Is it true?"

Lester hesitated and looked at her colleagues.

The same reporter added, "We understand they were found in one of the children's hands. Several small, red items that resemble medicinal pills. Can you confirm that?"

Turning back to the reporters, Lester said uncomfortably, "Yes. I can confirm that."

"Can you tell us what they are?"

"They're being packaged and shipped to our labs for examination as we speak. That's as much as I can tell you."

No, it isn't. Adam's conversation with her came flooding back. Lester said that Jennifer had travelled in time using red pills. He wondered if any of Lester's colleagues knew about Jennifer's letters.

"How could pills have been preserved for that long?" said another reporter.

"That's a good question," said Lester. "We won't know till we examine them."

"Could this be a hoax?" said someone else.

"Again, we won't know for certain till we've fully excavated the bones and run tests."

"Do you think they time-travelled?"

Adam saw Lester's jaw clench. Most of the other reporters laughed.

Lester replied carefully, "All I can say is that if this dinosaur skeleton is authentic, then conventional science tells us that it has to be at least sixty-six million years old. And conventional science also tells us that humans first emerged long, long after that, around three hundred thousand years ago."

"This is mental," murmured Izzy.

As the press continued to fire questions at Lester, which were mostly met with 'I don't knows', Adam darted over to the sofa, where he'd left his MEc. He ran a search and found Dr Lester's staff profile page on the London Institute of Palaeontology and Archaeology website. He read her bio: Lester was a senior project officer who'd worked at various county council archaeological units and did a stint at the Natural History Museum, and had a bunch of qualifications in palaeontology, archaeology and palaeoanthropology, including a PhD from the University of Paris.

There was a phone number. Adam pulled his phone from his pocket.

"Who you calling?" said Izzy.

"The woman who was just on the TV."

"What?"

"I'm pretty sure she's the one who called me months ago about Jennifer, that friend I mentioned."

"You mean the friend we're not allowed to talk about." There was a hint of annoyance in her voice. Izzy didn't like not knowing things. She'd asked about Jennifer a couple more times after the night of Lester's phone call, but Adam had shut her down both times. "So – wait. The woman you said was a conspiracy theorist spouting bollocks about Million Eyes is the LIPA palaeontologist we just saw?"

"Yeah."

"Well she looked pretty sensible to me."

Adam tapped out the phone number from the website.

"What you calling her for?" Izzy pressed.

He wasn't sure himself yet. "I just need to... ask her something."

He pressed 'call' and moved into the hallway of the flat.

After five rings, "Hello, Dr Lester speaking."

"Hi, Dr Lester, it's Adam Bryant. I don't know if you remember me but –"

"Mr Bryant, let me call you back. This isn't a secure line."

"Sure."

Lester hung up. Definitely the same woman then. Adam remembered, the first time they spoke, that she said she'd called him on a secure line – temporarily secure anyway, before it became traceable by the mysterious 'them'.

Was he about to open a can of worms? He'd decided five months ago that she was a crazy.

But that was before he knew that she was a high-up-sounding bod at LIPA.

Lester rang him back. "Hi, it's me."

"How long do we have?"

"Not long. I'm using a scrambler, but it only lasts a few minutes."

Adam swallowed a nervous lump in his throat. "Well, I've... I've just seen you on the news. This dinosaur – with the kids in its stomach – is it for real?"

"Like I told the press, we won't know until all the bones have been fully excavated and we've done tests."

"Yeah, but what do *you* think?"

"I think it's real, yes. And I think those children were time travellers."

"Because of the red pills? I heard one of the reporters mention you'd found red pills..."

"What looks like them, yes."

"You said about red pills when we spoke."

"I know I did. Because I was telling you the truth."

Adam's cheeks tingled. He took a breath. "I'm ready to talk. Can we meet?"

He wasn't sure if it was the right thing, but he'd decided that he wanted to see Jennifer's letters. It was the only way to know for sure that this woman wasn't screwing with him.

"Yes. What are you doing tomorrow evening?"

He popped into the kitchen to check their MEboard, a connected wall display with both their calendars on it. Tomorrow night Izzy was out for dinner with her friend, Stacey. Perfect.

"I'm free tomorrow."

"Okay. We should meet in Central after work. How about Hyde Park? By the Elizabeth II statue. Should be relatively quiet there. Do you know where I mean?"

"I don't. But I'll look it up."

"Fine. Let's meet there at seven o'clock. I'll bring Jennifer's letters."

"Yes, please. I'd like to see them." He wouldn't be going, frankly, if he couldn't.

"See you tomorrow."

Lester hung up. Adam stood in the kitchen for a moment, staring dumbly out of the window at the cars and people below, the pasta bake he'd left on the side going cold, and wondered what he was getting himself into.

8

April 1st 2027

In the driverless LIPA van transporting the latest batch of dinosaur and human bones to the labs at LIPA's Central London headquarters, conservator Keiko Hamasaki sat reading the press and social media explosion that the Tower Hamlets find had triggered, her senses alive with excitement and anticipation. As a member of the excavation team, Keiko was right at the centre of it, and now that it had been on the news, she no longer had to keep quiet; she could already feel the rush of satisfaction that would come from giving her friends and family all the juicy details. Given that this was unquestionably the most important discovery in history, Keiko would soon be famous in a lot of circles.

That said, tons of people were crying 'hoax' over this. Keiko couldn't blame them. Science said firstly that humans evolved sixty-six million years after dinosaurs died out, and secondly that time travel was impossible. For many, hoax was the only possible explanation. And then, at the other end of the spectrum, you had Young Earth Creationists. No surprises that they were going wild. Believing in a literal interpretation of the Book of Genesis, YECs argued that the Earth was thousands of years old, not millions, and that humans and dinosaurs had lived together. Here was, they said, a discovery to prove them right.

What did Keiko believe? Well, as a scientist, she

certainly didn't think the Tower Hamlets find proved human-dinosaur coexistence contrary to all other evidence of dinosaurs and humans that had ever been dug up. She also didn't believe that the humans had travelled back in time, nor that the dinosaur had travelled forwards. That was just dumb. This wasn't *Back to the Future*. This was real life.

To her, what was more likely was that this Spinosaurus-like creature was evidence that some non-avian dinosaurs had survived the Cretaceous-Paleogene extinction event – although that was fraught with difficulties, too. If it had survived to the Middle Palaeolithic, it should have been sixty-six million years more evolved than all other dinosaurs thus far discovered. And yet it looked substantially similar to your average sixty-six-million-year-old.

In any case, she couldn't wait to debate the possibilities with her dad. Dad was super-keen on palaeontology, but to his regret it had always been a hobby, not a job. Keiko's grandma and grandpa had steered him away from 'all that dinosaur nonsense' and made him enter a 'proper profession' – accounting. And yes, Dad was brilliant at maths and a fantastic accountant, but did it bring him joy and fulfilment? No. Palaeontology did. All their trips as a family to museums and dinosaur parks had spurred Keiko to study it and forge a career in it. Now her dad was living his dream through her, and Keiko was only too pleased to let him.

When Keiko was twenty minutes away from LIPA, daylight dwindling fast, the traffic got worse. Even though many of the cars on London's roads were now driverless, dramatically reducing crashes and driver-caused delays, it hadn't made much difference to the congestion, partly because a lot of people who would normally have relied on public transport were now using driverless cars instead. At least Keiko could sit and work, so the time wasn't wasted. If she was in a van that required her to concentrate on wading an inch at a time through a treacle of vehicles, it would've been.

Not that she was working. She probably should've been – she had reports to write. But she was too busy reading the highly entertaining conspiracy theories proliferating on Twitter. The hashtag #DinosAteMan was trending.

Keiko thought about the other big find she currently had in the back of her van, sealed in a polythene bag, in a slim box, next to all the plaster-jacketed bones: the red pills. Or what looked like them. What would the Twittersphere make of those if they found out? They *did* look remarkably like the sort of capsule-shaped compressed tablets you could pick up in a pharmacy, however, Keiko figured that testing would reveal them to be stones. Perhaps gems. That said, even though science was likely to prove them unremarkable, there was no persuading some of the more hardened conspiracy nuts out there.

As the traffic started to ease, Keiko's phone rang. It was Lester. "Keiko, are you on your way to headquarters?" She sounded anxious.

"Yes."

"Did you tell anyone about the red pills?"

Keiko felt a pinch of defensiveness. "You told me not to, so no."

"And you didn't show them to anyone?"

"No."

"Well the press know. Somehow. Somebody must've seen them, or we've got a leak on the team."

Keiko knew that Lester thought Ethan, head of Field Ops, may have tipped off the press about the Tower Hamlets find. Maybe it was him. "Did you tell Ethan about the pills?"

"No. I didn't get a chance."

"Well it definitely wasn't me."

"No. I know. You wouldn't do that. And... and everything's alright?"

Strange question. "What do you mean?"

"No one's... no one's following you?"

Keiko instinctively shot a glance in her wing mirror. At that moment, the nearest car was about two hundred yards behind. "No. Why would anyone be following me?"

"No reason. Just – just be careful. And call me as soon as you get there."

"Sure. Will do."

Keiko hung up. *That was weird.* She decided to search Twitter for references to the red pills. A handful of articles had been posted about them on news sites and were starting to attract retweets and comments, and a new hashtag had appeared: #WhatAreTheRedPills. Imaginations were fired. People were saying they were alien homing beacons, Chinese mind control chips, tiny demon eggs... The list went on.

Keiko wasn't sure why Lester seemed so troubled by the press knowing about the 'pills'. Unless Lester knew something about them that Keiko didn't... And what was all that stuff about people following her?

A few minutes later, the van signalled to go right at the traffic lights up ahead, which turned from green to amber as the van came within a hundred yards.

Suddenly, the van's low hum became a coarse roar. It shot forwards, tyres squealing. Keiko jerked back in her seat, her phone tossed from her hand and landing somewhere behind the seats.

"What the fuck?" Keiko stared ahead as the van swerved round several cars and hurtled through what was now a red light, narrowly missing a car on the intersection.

"Nav, what's happening?" she asked the van's computer.

Nav didn't reply. The speedometer inched past forty-five, in a thirty zone, overtaking a bunch of cars.

How is this happening? Driverless cars can't speed!

"Nav, slow to thirty."

Nav was silent. The van's speed was steady at forty-five.

"Nav, slow to thirty – now!"

Still no reply. Keiko's chest tightened. She felt uncomfortably hot despite the climate control.

The van turned right down a road it wasn't meant to take. This wasn't the way to LIPA headquarters.

Something's really wrong.

"Nav, give me manual control."

Keiko expected pedals to rise out of her foot well and a panel to open in the dash, from which the steering wheel would emerge.

Nothing happened.

Keiko leaned forwards to press the emergency override button.

Still nothing happened. *What?* If the computer wasn't responding, then the emergency override was all she had left. She pressed it again – harder.

No change.

Keiko swallowed. Though her skin was hot, her blood ran cold.

What the hell do I do now?

The van turned right at a roundabout and the speed limit changed to fifty. The van's speed rose to sixty.

Keiko tasted something tangy. She realised she'd been chewing her lip, blood now dribbling onto her tongue.

The van had been hacked. It was the only explanation. Someone wanted these bones.

Keiko craned her neck behind her, looking down into the space behind the seats for her phone. Daylight now fully extinguished, the back of the van and all the artefacts were quilted in a dense darkness intermittently penetrated by dim flashes of streetlamps. The floor behind the seats was where the darkness was at its thickest.

She couldn't see her phone.

"Nav, interior lights on."

She was so used to everything happening automatically she'd forgotten that the computer had stopped responding to her. She reached to flick the switch on the ceiling light

– nothing. She flicked it twice.

Fuck's sake! Nothing works!

Breath quickening, Keiko twisted against her seatbelt and reached behind the seats, hand fumbling about in the dark.

Oh, where are you…

There!

She palmed the phone and tapped the screen with her finger.

It was off. But the battery was at ninety-five percent when she last looked!

She pushed the 'on' button on the rim, waited.

Stared at a black screen.

"Fuck. *Shit!*" A jolt of panic hit her. They'd hacked her phone too? How? She threw the phone into the passenger footwell in frustration.

Now what?

The van was forced to stop behind a line of traffic on a two-lane road, traffic lights ahead and a stream of cars coming the other way. Keiko had no choice. She'd have to get out. Let whoever was controlling the van have it, and the bones.

She pressed the button on her seatbelt buckle.

What?

The expected *click* didn't come. The button did nothing – it wouldn't unclip. She pulled at the strap – hard – but the tongue wouldn't come out.

Shit shit shit.

She pulled the handle on the driver's door. She'd just have to wriggle out of the seatbelt.

"Fuck!" The door was locked – but the switch was in the 'unlock' position. The door should be opening.

No, no, no, no…

Knowing it probably wouldn't work, Keiko tried her electric window. Proven right, her whole body sank.

She stared ahead. The lights would turn green at any moment. She'd lose her chance to escape.

She had to get out of this van. *Now.*

A frisson of desperation threw her elbow at the window. The glass was tough and held out defiantly. All Keiko did was smack her funny bone, pain shuddering up and down her arm.

Pooling all her might into her arm, she slammed her elbow into the window again.

With a smash, the glass shattered, tiny pieces raining into Keiko's lap.

Freedom. She strained to squirm free of the seatbelt – it kept locking.

Finally managing to get her torso free, she thrust her head and shoulders through the broken window and started to climb out.

Then the lights up ahead turned green.

"NO!"

The van accelerated forwards, picking up speed. Keiko quickly pulled herself back in through the window.

Oh God...

Her heart thrummed in her ears. Waves of nausea swept through her. The van turned up a road without streetlights, drenching Keiko in darkness.

Where are you taking me...

It pulled into the empty, minimally lit car park of a huge, shadowy warehouse.

Shit, it wasn't empty. There was a black van of a similar size to hers outside the front of the warehouse.

Keiko shook. Her van parked behind the black one. Her heart stopped as the rear door burst open and four black-clad figures in balaclavas spilled out.

Keiko held her breath as they ran round to the rear of her van and pulled open the doors.

She twisted in her seat, tried her seatbelt again. It wouldn't budge. The men climbed in wielding knives, started cutting the straps that were keeping the plaster-jacketed bones secure. One grabbed the box containing the red pills.

"Please – just take it!" Keiko shrieked, breathless. "Take everything!"

One of the men looked at her with cold, dark eyes and replied in a gravelly voice, "Thank you. We will."

Then he raised his arm, and Keiko stared down the barrel of a pistol.

No! Please don't!

Keiko shut her eyes as the man squeezed the trigger. She didn't hear a bang. She didn't hear anything but her own heart, lurching to an abrupt halt.

9

June 3rd 29

The main thing Jesus still missed about the future was the plumbing. And toilet paper. Shitting in a trench and wiping his arse with stones didn't rank among his favourite experiences. Everything else he'd grown accustomed to. There was something refreshing about people who were truly at one with nature, whose pace of life was so slow and calm. Who wouldn't want that after 2222?

As a member of the Sanhedrin, Joseph of Arimathea couldn't support Jesus publicly, but privately he did what he could. He had helped Jesus become a preacher, taught him how to adapt his message to the thinking of the time. After starting in Nazareth's synagogue, Jesus was now travelling across Ancient Israel, encouraged by Joseph to preach about the Last War and the Apocalypse in every town and city he happened upon.

But Jesus was struggling in his new role. Most of the people he met thought him a madman. He'd been able to win some over by performing 'miracles' with the future medicines and technologies in his medical kit, but it wasn't enough to make the impact he needed.

He knew what the problem was. Him. He was no orator. Public speaking had never come easily or naturally to him. He'd never had to captivate or persuade people like this. He just didn't have the charisma for it. He was a physician. His strength was fixing people.

He met Joseph in a tavern in a city called Hippos, just east of the Sea of Galilee, to once again seek his advice.

"I know someone near here who can help," Joseph said.

Jesus felt a burst of relief. "Who?"

"Somebody who already commands a loyal following. And he believes the world is ending, too. He will be very interested to hear your story. Convince him and you will convince everyone."

Jesus nodded. He knew Joseph would have an answer.

"You should know, however, that he will not accept your story readily," Joseph added. "The man's an egotist. He will not let a stranger steal the limelight unless he is sure that that stranger was sent by God. You must be prepared to ingratiate yourself with him and his followers, join in their rituals."

"I understand."

Joseph took Jesus that evening to a village in a shallow valley through which flowed the River Jordan, where the people, mostly men, lived in limestone caves. Some of the caves were natural, others had been hollowed out by the villagers.

Joseph brought him to a large, dank cave. There, they were greeted by a huge, heavily muscled man with a long beard and piercing brown eyes. He wore a thigh-length goatskin and carried a thick staff. The hour was late and his cave was lit by lamps that were just wicks floating in bowls of oil. Three small dishes of honey and a large bowl of locusts for dipping were laid on a low table, where there were cotton mats on either side for sitting. Jesus winced at the thought of eating locusts but figured it might make a welcome change from goat meat and grain.

Joseph spoke first. "Jesus, I would like to introduce you to John, known among his followers as 'the Baptist'."

10

April 2nd 2027

At ten minutes to seven, Adam got to the Queen Elizabeth II statue in Hyde Park, which stood near the south side of the Serpentine lake. He expected to be first there, but as he walked up the path that skirted the lake, he saw a woman sitting on a bench, staring across the water. Getting closer, he recognised her from the news. She wore dark jeans and a honey-coloured trench coat over a faded violet jumper, and her hair was down in a neat, shoulder-length bob instead of a ponytail. In her lap was a black shoulder bag, the strap still around her neck. She looked in a world of her own but as Adam got nearer, she sensed his approach and turned her head to face him, immediately standing up, holding the shoulder bag close.

"Dr Lester?" Adam said, holding out his hand to shake hers.

"Yes, hello Mr Bryant." She shook his hand. Hers was cold. It was still light but wouldn't be for much longer, and the air had an icy bite.

"Please, call me Adam. I hate people calling me 'Mister'."

Lester gave a restrained, not-very-warm smile. He thought she might've reciprocated the informality, asked him to call her Samantha or even Sam, but she just sat down on the bench, the bag returning to its original position in her lap. Adam guessed that Jennifer's letters were in there. He sat down next to her.

"Thank you for meeting me," said Adam.

"It was me, originally, who wanted to meet with you."

"Yes. Sorry I was rude when you phoned. What you were saying just seemed so... outlandish." That was the polite way of saying batshit.

Lester smiled again. It was a tad warmer this time, but she still didn't seem very relaxed. "It's fine. I might've reacted the same way."

Her admission made him feel a bit less guilty. He launched straight in, wishing he'd worn a thicker sweatshirt when a brisk wind made him shiver. "So I take it you think Million Eyes are something to do with the humans in that dinosaur's stomach?"

"Yes. I think Million Eyes sent those children to the Cretaceous."

"Why?"

"I don't know. But a number of things have happened since we spoke yesterday. One of our vans is missing. The one transporting the red pills and a batch of the bones to LIPA's labs. Went missing last night, along with the staff member driving it."

"Shit!"

"And this afternoon a group of people with Home Office IDs came and took us off the project. Turned up at our labs and confiscated all the bones we'd transported there. Then they took control of the dig site."

"I haven't heard anything about any of that." In fact, Adam had heard nothing about the dig in the news today – surprisingly. You'd think it'd be the talk of the networks.

"No, you wouldn't have," said Lester. "They're blocking the press somehow. An injunction of some kind. None of the news sites are allowed to talk about it anymore."

"Can they do that?"

"I don't know if they *can*, but they *have*."

This was mental, and yet Lester seemed pretty stolid. Her voice was even and her eyes showed little emotion.

Wasn't she furious that they'd taken the find of the century off her?

"You seem awfully calm about it all," he said.

Lester looked down at her hands. "There's not a lot I can do. I tried to keep it out of the press but someone on my team has been tipping them off. I did wonder if Million Eyes might try and shut it all down after it went public. Clearly we got too close to something."

"Do you think your colleague could be…" A pinch of dread swallowed the rest of his sentence.

"Dead?"

"Yeah."

Lester nodded solemnly. "I hope not. But I'm afraid she might be."

"I'm sorry."

Lester sniffed. "Me too." She lifted her gaze to Adam. "They've won this round. I'll make sure I win the next." Her voice was earnest.

"And you think 'they' are Million Eyes?"

"Yes."

"Because of Jennifer's letters?"

Lester nodded.

Adam swallowed. "Can I see them?"

"Yes, of course." Lester glanced around, double checking that there was no one in the immediate vicinity. Adam could see a dog walker a couple of hundred metres down the path by the lake, the occasional cyclist speeding past on the cycleway about ten metres behind them. She opened her shoulder bag and lifted out a large black leather display book. Lifting the magnetic fastener, she opened it to reveal a series of sheets of paper tucked into transparent plastic sleeves.

The paper looked old. Glancing at the first page, Adam saw that it was cracked and mostly yellow, flecked with brown, the colour darkening at the edges and along the two horizontal creases that suggested it had been folded into three. On it was a paragraph of partly faded but still legible handwriting that wasn't English. At the bottom of the sleeve was a strip of white, much newer paper with a paragraph of small, typed-up words that *were* in English.

"In here are four letters, all written on parchment by Jennifer, in Modern English," said Lester. "The first page is a brief cover note of instructions, which was written in Latin by someone else. No name is given but I suspect it may have been a priest Jennifer knew. It was normally only priests who were literate in those days, and Jennifer does mention one in her letters." Lester handed the book to Adam, pointing to the newer strip of paper in the first sleeve. "That's my translation of the Latin note."

"Who are the letters to?"

"Jennifer's younger self."

Adam squirmed on the bench, uneasy.

"They were written at different points in her life, then they were folded and sealed with wax – a practice that was only conducted by the elite at that time. They were placed in a box with the note of instructions, which was folded but not sealed. My team found this box during an excavation of Cawston Manor in the New Forest last year."

"So other people have seen these letters?"

"A couple of the team at the dig saw them – briefly. As soon as I understood what I was looking at, I thought it best to keep a tight lid on this and took personal custody of them. I analysed them and determined their age myself using carbon testing. And I omitted them from the excavation report."

"So you stole them?"

"I borrowed them. Million Eyes could have eyes inside LIPA for all I know. Until I know how far their influence stretches, these letters stay with me." Lester tucked her hand inside her shoulder bag, pulled out a wodge of paperwork. "Do you want to read the carbon dating report? You'll see that the letters really are nine hundred years old."

A carbon dating report was the last thing Adam was interested in right now. "I'll read the letters first."

"By all means."

Chewing on his lip, he read Lester's translation of the brief, anonymous Latin note of instructions.

> It is imperative that these letters be delivered, unbroken, to Jennifer Larson at 35 The Birches, Deepwater, Hampshire, DP25 9JK on 11th September 2019. If for any reason they cannot be delivered to Jennifer Larson, please deliver them instead to Adam Bryant at 82 Whetstone Road, Deepwater, Hampshire, DP25 2QR on the same date.

Swallowing, Adam turned the page to the first of Jennifer's letters.

Oh my God. He felt a flutter of emotion beneath his breastbone. It was Jennifer's writing. He knew that untidy scrawl anywhere.

Don't get ahead of yourself, Adam. This woman could've copied Jennifer's handwriting. There was still a chance he was being played.

He took a breath and started reading.

> Dear Jennifer,
>
> Don't freak out. You haven't lost your memory of writing this letter to a night of tequila slammers. You haven't actually written it yet.
>
> Here goes. Just remember that you're a sci-fi buff. You can handle this. I'm you, Jen. I'm you from the future. Although I'm now in the

past (I'll get to that).

If everything worked out like I planned, you should be reading this letter on 11th September 2019. The day before my life changed. The day before your life is about to. Tomorrow you'll start talking to Gregory Ferro, your favourite blogger. He's in the process of finding evidence that time travellers are fucking about with our history, and you're going to arrange to meet him. You won't believe him at first, but you'll change your mind and agree to help him. About a month from now, he's going to be murdered by the time travellers, who are then going to try and murder you. Twice. You're going to run away to Brighton, live in hiding for a couple of years, before the time travellers catch up with you in 2021. And you're going to travel back in time to escape.

Those are the highlights, but there are some crucial details you need to know. The time travellers are Million Eyes. Ferro found out right before he died. An anonymous whistleblower from inside Million Eyes phoned him, said they have operatives inside the police, the army, the government – you name it. In 2021, before I went back in time, I overheard their operatives talking about assassinating the Queen to advance the 'Mission'. I recorded their conversation in this weird futuristic transcription device I found, which I took, along with one of their bottles of red pills – Ferro thought the pills were basically Million Eyes' time machines. When they came after me, I swallowed one. Sure as hell, I travelled in time. Went from 2021 to 1100. And was stranded, too. Lost the red pills in transit somehow.

Totally insane, I know. I can barely believe it myself. Actually, I can. Because I'm bloody well having to dip a quill in an ink pot every two seconds to write this. It's definitely 1100 here.

Adam felt an ache. Somewhere. He wasn't sure where. He figured it was easy to imitate someone's handwriting but this *sounded* like Jennifer too. This was so surreal.

Oh yes, I should add that a couple of knights took me to the king after I arrived here. That king being William II. He took the transcriber and threw me in the Tower of London. William II's death was one of the events that Ferro was investigating so, in effect, history's coming full circle. I think William II was killed for that transcriber. It has information that could seriously damage Million Eyes' rise to power, so it makes sense that they'd want it back.

Anyway, I stayed at the Tower for a bit, then one night, one of the guards — who'd been trying to get in my pants since I got there — came into my cell, drunk, and jumped me. Fortunately he was so plastered he just collapsed before he could do anything, so I snatched his keys and ran. I got myself out of London and now I'm living and working in a village called Cawston as a villein, trying to keep my head down. It's actually not that bad going. The lord of the manor, Roger de

Grayfort, is decent and I'm friends with the village priest, Father Stephen. Yeah, I know. Jennifer Larson – friends with a priest?! You're probably doubting I'm you again now. But he's been teaching me to speak Old English and he's the one who very kindly gave me ink, paper and a quill so I could write this letter.

But I'm not going to lie. This is NOT how I wanted my life to turn out. And the reason I'm telling you all this is so that none of it happens to you. Don't meet with Gregory Ferro. Don't get involved in whatever the fuck Million Eyes are doing. If you do, you'll lose everything. Like I have. I lost Mum, Jamie, all my friends. Adam...

A lump of emotion lodged in Adam's throat. He swallowed it away.

... And I lost someone I was in a relationship with after I ran away, too. Her name was Toasty and she was awesome, but meeting me got her killed. I need to stop that from happening. YOU need to stop that from happening.

If my plan works, history will change and the events Ferro was investigating might not happen. So you might not even be following Ferro's blog right now. He might not even have one. He might still be happy with his wife and kids. And he might never get murdered. Hopefully I've saved his life as well.

Technically, if all that happens, then I'll

never come back in time to begin with. I'm not sure what that would mean for me exactly. Would I disappear, *Looper* and *Back to the Future*-style? Possibly. Not that the disappearing thing made sense in those films. Maybe I'll just carry on existing, despite the future I came from being erased. Who the fuck knows?

Just please, Jen, don't let it all happen again.

Jennifer.

11

"So her plan didn't work," Adam murmured, his mind spinning with so many questions he was starting to feel dizzy. "These letters weren't delivered in time."

"Unfortunately not," said Lester. "At some point in the last nine centuries, the box with the letters in was forgotten about and became a piece of debris that was eventually built over. If a farmer hadn't happened upon some old coins in the vicinity, we might never have identified Cawston Manor as a potential archaeological site. And those letters might've stayed buried for hundreds more years."

Adam wished Jennifer had told him what was going on. She shouldn't have tried to handle all that on her own.

He turned to her next letter and started to read.

> Dear Jennifer,
>
> The year is 1105. I have no way of knowing if my plan worked and history has changed. I really hope it has. The fact that I'm still stuck here in medieval Cawston and haven't disappeared makes me wonder. But then, I remember some sci-fi author saying that if you go back in time and change stuff, you'll carry on existing because the very act of time travelling takes you 'outside' the timestream, so that the changes to history

can't affect you. Maybe that's what's happened here.

Anyway, I've decided I'm going to write you a letter every five years, just to let you know how I'm getting on.

The last five years have gone by slowly. Life is so simple here. Compared with 21st-century life, that is. If you're reading this on 11th September 2019, then you're in a bit of a rut, career-wise. (Unless, of course, my interferences with history have totally altered your personal timeline and you're now a lawyer or a pilot or something.) I remember, in my 2019, I was working in a call centre not knowing what I wanted to do. Well, here in 1105, I brew beer. I remember learning about this when I did my degree. It was a female-dominated profession for centuries. 'Alewives' we're called. Except I'm nobody's wife. I'm not marrying a bloke just because that's what everybody does. And of course you can't be a gay in Norman times. Not easily, anyway. Not publicly. I've had some dalliances. Have to get my kicks somehow. But I have to be careful. Lesbianism is strictly prohibited by the Church. And the Church dominates everyone and everything here. You can't be an atheist in Norman times either.

Adam fought back a tear. The more he read of Jennifer's words, the more he felt like he could hear her voice in his ear. Oh, how he wished he could. For real.

Anyway, I make a living and I have a few friends. Particularly Rexanne and all her many kids. Her husband Durwyn, the village blacksmith, is an absolute cockwomble though. I'm pretty sure he hits her. I'm thinking I might start hitting him.

Of course, none of my friends know who I really am or what I'm really like, but how could they? I'm an actress who never gets to break character. It's exhausting. But it's life, I guess. There was a time, when I first arrived in 1100, when I thought about jacking it all in, thinking, what's the point. But then I thought, hey, we only get one life. And life is, ultimately, what we make of it. Happiness is not something that happens to us. Happiness is a choice.

So I'm choosing to be happy. It's not always easy, but I try every day to find something to enjoy.

Jennifer.

The plastic sleeve trembled in Adam's fingers. Good on Jennifer for making the best of a bad situation. She'd always been stronger than he was. He was proud of her.

He moved on to her third letter.

Dear Jennifer,

It's 1110. It's hard to believe I've only been here 10 years. Feels like 30, but that's because the pace of life is so slow here.

A few things have changed since my last letter. I still live in my little house in Cawston. 'Jen the Maiden', they call me (because I'm still not married). And although

I still brew beer, I'm also sort of a doctor now. I kept seeing people dying around me of really basic illnesses that could easily have been prevented with better hygiene. And while my knowledge of medicine in the 21st century is nothing next to an actual doctor, here I'm an expert. I don't know why it took me so long to realise I could be helping these people. Perhaps it was just my own selfishness.

I've also realised that what I told you to do in my first letter was short-sighted. I told you to stay away from Million Eyes, to not get involved, in case it messes up your life. That was selfish advice. Million Eyes are poison. Power-hungry killers. And that conversation I overheard, the one about assassinating the Queen, those two operatives said that Million Eyes had been de facto running the country since the 17th century, which means democracy in Britain is a sham and always has been. Something needs to be done. Adam is working for Million Eyes but I suspect he has absolutely no idea what they're really up to, or capable of.

She was right there. He'd been rejecting all the conspiracy theories for years. On what Jennifer was saying, some of those theories weren't that wide of the mark.

Talk to him. He won't believe you at first. He didn't believe me, when I told him at the pub I was starting to come round to Gregory Ferro's theories, minutes before I was run over. And although I told him at the hospital that someone was trying to kill me, I never told him who. I should never have shut him out.

But you don't have to shut him out. He's your best friend. Trust him. Show him these letters. Find help. Do what you can to find out what Million Eyes are doing. And stop them.

We only get one life, Jen. We should use it to make a difference. So make a difference.

Jennifer.

Adam sniffed. The tear that had been teetering on his eyelash escaped down his cheek. He sat back, staring across the Serpentine lake. The sun had sunk behind the trees and the sky was streaked with pink and orange, the soft light on the water dimming with the thickening dusk.

He turned to the final letter, immediately wondering why there were no more after this one, since Jennifer had pledged to write one every five years.

Dear Jennifer,

It's 15 years since I came to this century, and to Cawston. I feel like I've completely forgotten what 21st-century life was like. But that doesn't mean I don't think about Mum, Jamie, Adam and Toasty every day.

I'm still here, still getting by, still playing doctor and brewer, still going to church and pretending to pray. I'm a free woman now, so I pay less rent and don't have to abide by as many rules. I can leave Cawston if I want to, too. Not that I really want to. I quite like it here. I don't even miss TV anymore. It would be nice to read something other than the frickin' Bible, but I've taken up writing stories instead. I was never a writer, but I'm rather enjoying it.

Oh, and a traveller came to the village a

> week ago. A woman, alone, on a horse, with a handful of possessions. She's asked Lord Grayfort if she can become a villein and he's given her a small plot of land where she's currently building a house, just like I did when I came here. She's living with me till it's ready. Her name's Oshilda and, I have to say, there's something about her. She's hot and funny and so mysterious. I've been trying to get her to open up about her past and where she came from. She definitely has a guard up but I think I'm slowly getting through. She reminds me a lot of myself, actually. I'm starting to think she might be drawn to me like I am to her. There's chemistry for sure. Definitely a closet gay. Or at least flexible. We'll see. Planning to work my usual magic.
>   Jennifer

Adam looked at Lester, handing the display book back to her. "And you're sure there aren't any more?"

"There weren't any more at the site. Perhaps Jennifer wrote more but they were lost."

Adam swallowed. It was disconcerting that Jennifer's story had ended so abruptly. Perhaps she simply didn't want to write more. Perhaps, as Lester said, she did write more but they were misplaced or destroyed. But then, why would these four letters have survived?

The other more depressing possibility – something had happened to her. Before she'd had a chance to write any more letters.

A disorienting mix of emotions rose inside him. Relief that Jennifer had escaped Million Eyes and lived. Melancholy that she was still stranded nine hundred years in the past, unable to be herself, living a pretend life. Worry about what had happened to her after 1115.

And guilt. Over not believing her, over not doing more

to try and help, over working for the people who did this to her. That was the prevailing emotion, steadily drowning out everything else. It was so overpowering he started to feel like his collar was closing around his neck.

Lester didn't say anything for several moments. She just let Adam ruminate. Jennifer's mother – Kerry Larson – popped into his head and another pang of guilt hit him, made his collar tighten even more. He hadn't spoken to her in years. He should've kept in touch.

"Did you consider contacting Jennifer's mother? I don't know if she still lives at the same address – the one Jen gave – but she might."

"Kerry Larson? Yes, I did. After I couldn't get you to listen, I did some research, found a phone number for her. Unfortunately she had much the same reaction you did, albeit angrier. Said I was besmirching her daughter's memory, swore a lot, and hung up."

Yeah, that sounded like Kerry Larson. It was where Jennifer got her temper from.

"I see."

"Did you want to see the carbon dating report?"

Adam felt the tug of reality, remembering that this could still all be an absurdly clever and sophisticated fabrication designed to intensify conspiracy theories about Million Eyes.

But he wondered what the point would be, and what possible motive Lester could have for concocting it. This was an experienced, well-regarded woman of science according to everything he'd read on the internet. Why would she risk her job, her reputation, to spread lies about a computer company?

"Do you have a copy I can take home?" said Adam. He didn't really want to read it now.

"Yes." She pulled several sheets from her stack of papers. "There's also photocopies of Jennifer's letters there. I figured you'd want them. But please, do *not* show anyone. Not till we've worked out how we're going to play this."

A question occurred to Adam in that moment. "How do you know you can trust me with all this?"

Lester compressed her lips. "Well, I don't. But Jennifer trusted you. I decided that would have to be enough. And you're the only person I know who works at the Looming Tower. You're right at the centre of it all. Which makes you best-placed to find out what they're up to."

"How so?"

"Well, you're a computer whizz, aren't you. Perhaps you could find a way to hack their systems."

"Hack Million Eyes' systems? Are you kidding?"

"Obviously you'd need to find some way in undetected."

"Yeah, that's not possible. It's Million Eyes. You have *heard* of Million Eyes, right?"

The flippant comment might've seemed like it was triggered by Lester's apparent naivety about how powerful Million Eyes were. It wasn't, really. It was the jumble of feelings about Jennifer and her letters that were coursing through him like a bowl of soup in the microwave getting too hot and starting to spatter everywhere.

Lester said nothing, just raised her eyebrows, a bit like a teacher might look at a misbehaving student. He shook his head, "Sorry."

"It's okay. I know this is probably overwhelming. And I'm not saying it's going to be easy. I'm just saying you have access, and we should use it."

"I have minimal access. Million Eyes are a multi-billion-pound global company with hundreds of thousands of employees, many of them much further up the chain than I am."

"Minimal access is still more access than I have. It's a start."

Adam gave an uneasy sigh. "What would I be looking for?"

"Jennifer mentioned a whistleblower. Someone on the inside told Gregory Ferro that the time travellers he was looking for were Million Eyes. We should see if we can find out who that whistleblower was."

Needles in haystacks sprang to mind. "Like I said, hundreds of thousands of employees."

"Let's start with Gregory Ferro himself. I'll start looking into his death. I have a friend in the police who can help. Someone I can trust. Perhaps there'll be some record of the phone call from the whistleblower, and we'll be able to trace it back. Once I have something – anything – I'll pass it to you so you can join the dots at your end."

"Won't this... be dangerous?"

Lester sat back, looked out over the darkening water. "Yes, it could be. Given what Jennifer says Million Eyes have done. What they're capable of doing."

"Well, I don't know about you, but I've got a family. Found out yesterday that I have a baby on the way."

Her eyebrows flickered as a look of anguish flitted across her face, throat rippling slightly as she swallowed. Almost reluctantly, "Congratulations."

Adam knew that look. Grief. Grief that you don't want to admit in case you actually feel it.

Had she lost someone? *A child?*

Lester's expression hardened again. "You don't have to help me, Adam. I might not get very far without you but I can try. I came to you because I thought you'd want to find out what happened to Jennifer – and why. Jennifer wanted her younger self to find some way of stopping Million Eyes, only her younger self didn't get the letters in time. So now I'm taking up the mantle for her."

Adam looked down at Jennifer's letters. Izzy would kill him if he got involved in something that could put him in jeopardy.

But perhaps he just wouldn't tell her.

He took a long breath in. "I'm not saying I won't help you. I just need some time. If you let me know what you find out about Ferro and the whistleblower, then we can go from there."

Lester nodded. "Okay." She reached into her shoulder bag again. "In that case, take these." She pulled out a sealed plastic bag containing two items – a phone and a tablet computer, both old Uzu models. "Since the scrambler I've been using only works for short calls, we should use burner phones to communicate. The phone in there is encrypted, unregistered and has prepaid minutes and texts – but no internet or GPS. I have one too. I've inputted the number. The computer is for when – *if* – you want to do any digging into Million Eyes, so it does have internet, but the IP address is hidden."

"Jesus," said Adam, taking the bag. "I suddenly feel like a criminal."

"*We're* not the criminals. And if we want to stay hidden, we don't have a choice. There's a reason they're called Million Eyes."

Adam swallowed hard as Lester stood and did up an extra button on her coat. "We'll talk again soon. Thank you for reaching out. It was good to meet you."

Adam nodded. "You too."

She turned and walked in the direction of the Elizabeth II statue and the cycle path some metres behind it, melting into a line of trees. Adam stayed on the bench for a few more minutes. A streetlamp had come on overhead, offering enough light for him to reread the photocopies Lester had given him of Jennifer's letters.

As he did, a new feeling rose inside him. Determination. Jennifer had been to hell and back thanks to Million Eyes. Well, not even *back*. She was still in hell. She was trapped there. Which meant, of course, that even though Million Eyes hadn't killed her, she was still dead from his perspective. Long dead.

He had to know what on earth was going on.

12

April 1st 33

Jesus's mission to forewarn humanity about the Last War and the Apocalypse had led him to Bethany, a town on the south-eastern slope of the Mount of Olives, near Jerusalem. He was staying with a man – Lazarus – whose life he had saved using his regenerator. He travelled daily into Jerusalem to talk to the people, his apostles accompanying him. These were men he had chosen to help him convey his message to the masses (one of Joseph of Arimathea's ideas).

Jesus was on edge. One of his apostles, Peter, had warned him that the Roman prefect of Judaea, Pontius Pilate, was looking for an excuse to increase his powers over the Jews and that any perceived troublemaking by Jesus would make him the perfect scapegoat. Peter also warned that scepticism about Jesus's 'miracles' and Last War prophecies was growing among the Pharisees, a powerful Jewish sect, and that some of his ever-burgeoning following could be spies for the Romans or the Sanhedrin.

That morning, another apostle, Judas Iscariot, visited Jesus at Lazarus's house. Jesus greeted him at the door and immediately clocked the worry in Judas's eyes.

"Teacher," said Judas, "will you walk with me?"

"I will," said Jesus, smiling warmly in an effort to put Judas at ease. It was early, the sky milky blue, the sun peeking over the top of the Mount of Olives, and there was a chill in the air. Jesus put on his cloak and joined Judas.

They walked through Bethany's streets, which were already busy with traders going about their business, the air filled with the clatter of donkey-drawn wagons and mixed smells of livestock, faeces, fresh fish and bread, and freshly cut timber that Jesus was now accustomed to.

They walked by the almshouse for the poor and sick, many of whom were pilgrims nearing the end of their long, arduous journey from Galilee to Jerusalem. Jesus had tried to help some of them, but his regenerator couldn't fix everything. His drugs, now almost depleted, couldn't either.

Judas didn't speak for several minutes as they walked through the town, prompting Jesus to ask, "Is anything the matter, my friend?"

Judas inhaled deeply and breathed out slowly. "It is about Matthew and James."

Jesus frowned. "What about them?"

"You know that they have been, in the past, more cynical about your teachings than the rest of us – such as myself."

"I do."

"But their loyalty has never, thus far, wavered."

"I have never thought that it would." That wasn't true, obviously. But John the Baptist had taught him to at least pretend to be confident if he wanted to convince people that he'd come from two thousand years in the future to avert humanity's destruction.

Judas sighed again. "I fear it could be about to."

Jesus's stomach fluttered. "What makes you say that?"

"In Jerusalem today, while you were visiting the home of Mary the leper, I saw Matthew and James speaking to a man who I believe was an agent of Caiaphas, the high priest who considers you a heretic. I fear a plot may be brewing. I would recommend vigilance."

Jesus sighed and shook his head. Matthew and James wielded a lot of influence, which was the reason he'd recruited them. They took some convincing but he really thought he'd succeeded. Was he wrong?

Jesus and Judas walked to the edge of the village and stood on a grassy slope so that they could look out over Jerusalem, which was now awash with morning sun, its walls shining bright yellow. The mosaic reds, blues and yellows that decorated the city's tall towers were visible even from miles away, as were the white marble columns and glistening gold entablature of the Temple.

As Jesus took in the splendid vista, he made a decision. "Judas, will you do something for me?"

"Of course."

"I have an ally in the city. Joseph of Arimathea. He is a member of the Sanhedrin. I would like you to arrange for me to meet with him."

"The Sanhedrin? Are you sure he can be trusted?"

Judas was right to ask the question. "Joseph has been a very close friend and adviser to me. Yes. He can be trusted."

"As you wish, Teacher. When would you like this meeting to take place?"

"Tonight, after supper."

"It will be done."

"Thank you, my friend."

When Jesus got back to Lazarus's house, he retrieved the chest that had gone with him on his travels through Judaea and Galilee. It contained his medical kit, his Twelfth Remnant uniform and his scrolls. Four lengthy sheets of vellum on which he'd written a description of the Last War and a chronology of the key events leading up to it. He'd also written about the things he had done since mysteriously and inexplicably travelling back in time.

Joseph of Arimathea couldn't be at Jesus's side while he journeyed across Israel. He was a busy man and had duties in Jerusalem, not to mention the fact that his support of Jesus was still a guarded secret. Since Jesus needed his advice regularly, Joseph had taught him to write in his language so that they could communicate by letter. Jesus learned that Joseph's language was an ancient form of his own, Aramaic, which at least gave him a head-start.

When it came to his scrolls, Jesus had decided he would write those in Joseph's language too. If anything were to happen to him, he wanted there to be a written record that people in this time could understand.

And now that there was a real risk that something *would* happen, he was going to have to hide his scrolls, at least for the time being.

He grabbed his reed pen and ink, unfurled the fourth scroll and added a further entry. Then he wrapped the four scrolls individually in linen cloth, fastened them with leather tabs and thongs, and tucked them inside an earthenware jar kindly gifted to him by Lazarus's sister, Martha, so that they would be preserved. He placed the jar inside the chest.

He charged Judas with carrying the chest when he and his apostles returned to Jerusalem that afternoon. Once again business in the city was brought to a near-standstill by the crowds who gathered to see him. Jesus was a celebrity to these people. It meant that they were listening to him, but it was also the very thing that was putting his life in danger by incensing the authorities.

Jesus and the apostles went to the Temple courts where he preached and performed healings. The atmosphere was tense with the presence of some incredulous chief priests; Jesus got into a heated debate with a few of them. By the time his work there was done, the thought of a cup of wine or two was heavenly.

Supper took place in a house that Jesus and his apostles had rented for the evening and consisted of bread, wine, a hunk of lamb, bean stew, olives with hyssop and dried figs with honey.

In spite of the wine, Jesus couldn't relax. He found himself watching Matthew and James like a security bot as they discussed their plans for the next few days.

Were they really planning to betray him?

Jesus and the apostles had intended to go to Gethsemane to pray after supper. Gethsemane was the olive grove in the Kidron Valley, just outside the city walls. Jesus said he would meet them there.

He left with the chest and walked to a deserted building that was once a meeting place for priests of the Essenes, another Jewish sect, where Joseph of Arimathea had agreed to meet him. He wondered how Joseph would react when he saw him. He supposed that depended on whether Joseph was privy to any kind of plot by the Sanhedrin against him.

He found Joseph waiting for him in a room with a long stone table, a few wooden stools and some empty wicker baskets. He greeted Jesus with a grave look. There *was* a plot, and he knew.

Jesus placed the chest on the table and sat down on one of the wooden stools. The daylight was fading so Joseph had lit several oil lamps. Joseph poured them some wine and sat down.

"Tell me what's going to happen," said Jesus.

Joseph sighed. "The high priest, Caiaphas, called a meeting of the Sanhedrin three days ago to decide what to do about you."

"And what did they decide?"

He saw Joseph swallow. "They want you arrested and tried. They want you dead."

Jesus nodded calmly.

"And please understand me when I say 'they'," Joseph continued. "I did not agree with or consent to this."

"I never doubted it. Are my apostles involved?"

"I am not certain. But I am aware that Caiaphas has informants."

Jesus took a long breath. *I bet it's Matthew and James.* "My friend, you have confirmed what I feared and now I must ask something of you."

"Anything."

"If the worst happens and I am crucified, I want you to

take charge of my burial." He looked at the chest. "And I want you to make sure this chest is buried with me."

"Does that contain – ?"

"The items I brought with me from the future, yes."

"So that 'regenerator' of yours is in there?"

"Yes."

"So should I not use it to try and revive you?"

Jesus smiled. "You can try. But if I'm dead, I'm dead. The regenerator won't be able to bring me back."

"I understand." He nodded. "You have my word. I will give you a proper burial and make sure this chest goes with you."

Jesus stood up and leaned over the table to open the chest. "However, I want you to take this." He lifted out the earthenware jar containing his scrolls and handed it to him.

"What's in it?"

"My scrolls. A written record of what will happen during the Last War, and of my experiences since coming here. I know that your position will make it impossible for you to do anything with them. I just need you to keep them safe. And I need your children to do the same. And their children, and their children after that. My hope is that a future generation will use them to prevent the Last War and the destruction of humankind, in the event that my ministry alone has not had the required impact."

"I am certain that it has," said Joseph softly. "You have armed us all with powerful foreknowledge. It will not be forgotten."

"I hope not. Will you do this for me?"

"I will do anything for you."

Jesus smiled. He left the old building shortly after, knowing that his scrolls were in good hands, and walked out of the city to meet his apostles at Gethsemane. It was dark now and stars glinted over the Mount of Olives. The air had grown cold. He shivered.

When he reached the olive grove, men with swords and clubs, sent by the Sanhedrin, were waiting to arrest him.

13

April 4ᵗʰ 33

Jesus's eyes opened. *I'm alive.* He blinked away the dizziness and soaked up his surroundings. He lay on his back on a gravelly floor, rock about a metre above him. Rising stiffly onto his elbows, his body felt heavy, like gravity was against him. Exhaustion permeated him, his every muscle, bone and organ aching, his throat like sand. He looked down. He'd been wrapped in a loose linen cloth – a burial shroud.

What... happened...

He was in a small cave. A boulder had been placed at the entrance. Daylight leaked through gaps between the walls of the cave and its makeshift door, which were wide enough to insert a hand but too narrow for him to crawl through and escape.

The light was sufficient for him to see that something had been placed in the cave with him: his chest.

He crawled over to it. A note had been placed on top, which he lifted into the path of a thin shaft of daylight so his weary eyes could read it.

I am sorry. I tried. Your friend eternally, Joseph.

Now Jesus remembered. Like a spear in his side, the whole horror of his crucifixion came flooding back.

He looked at his hands and heard the clunk of the

soldier's mallets, felt every sharp stab as they drove thick iron pegs into his palms while he lay on the cross, which was, at that point, horizontal on the ground.

But there were no wounds.

Jesus cast his eyes down to his feet. Not a scratch there either. Yet he remembered the soldiers placing one foot over the other and hammering a much longer peg through both of them. He could still feel the freezing metal sliding through his flesh.

He couldn't recall much after they hauled the cross into a vertical position and left him hanging there, only that it had been the most dreadful pain of his life.

He unwrapped himself from the shroud to look at his torso. He could still feel the awful sting of whips cracking relentlessly against his skin, but just like his hands and feet, there was no evidence of the flagellation by Pontius Pilate's soldiers before they nailed him to the cross. He reached to touch his back, where he should also have had wounds. The skin was smooth.

Jesus now knew what Joseph's note meant. He'd said he was going to try and revive him if he was crucified. He'd clearly used Jesus's regenerator to heal all his wounds. He must've decided that because Jesus had failed to regain consciousness, his efforts hadn't worked and Jesus was dead, thus arranging for him to be buried as discussed.

Joseph should've waited longer. Jesus's body had been through a lot. It needed time to recuperate.

This cave, Jesus realised, was his tomb. He'd been buried alive.

He looked again at the boulder that was blocking the entrance. It was large, but perhaps he could push it just a little, make a big-enough gap to squeeze through…

He crawled over and leaned his right side against it, pushing with all of his body weight. But he was still quite weak and it wasn't enough. After a few minutes he gave up and sat with his back against the stone. He'd have to wait for his strength to return.

Then, as he looked at the chest, an idea came to him. He remembered seeing doctors in 2222 rigging regenerators to emit crude disruptor beams. Not that they did much good in the Last War, but if he could do something similar, he might be able to blow the boulder apart.

He opened the chest and lifted out his medical kit. He removed the regenerator and opened the casing to manipulate its circuitry, struggling to summon some recollection of engineering at school.

It took a while and a couple of electric shocks, but it worked and he was able to generate a narrow beam just powerful enough to crack the boulder down the middle. He shoved himself against it, pushing hard, his whole body screaming at him, and eventually half the stone broke away and landed on its side with a thump. Daylight flooded the cave, making Jesus squint painfully.

Once his eyes had adjusted, he changed into his Twelfth Remnant uniform. They were the only clothes he had. Then he slung his medical kit over his shoulder and, leaving the empty chest, inched out of the cave tentatively, just in case Pilate's guards were nearby. If anybody saw him, it wouldn't take long for the authorities to find out. Then they'd come back and finish the job.

He would have to leave Israel. Go somewhere far away, where nobody knew him. Try to alter the course of history some other way.

Exiting the cave, Jesus found himself amid rolling yellow hills patched with rocks, shrubs and fig trees. He didn't know where he was but suspected it was one of the valleys outside Jerusalem. He couldn't hear anything but birds twittering and a light wind whooshing through the trees.

With a quick glance in all directions, confirming that there was nobody about, Jesus fled, leaving an empty tomb.

14

April 5th 2027

"Morning," said Curtis O'Brien to the security guard at the main door of the Looming Tower. As usual, the expressionless automaton with the charisma of a cactus said nothing, but Curtis insisted on greeting him every day anyway.

Curtis passed through the security scanners in the big white lobby and walked over to the reception desk to clock in. The counter was so tall it hid the receptionist sitting behind it. Curtis hoped it was either Matt with the adorable mini beard and biceps the size of a human head, or Lucy with the dimples and utterly glorious legs. Both equally sweet eye candy. Unfortunately, a new guy with pitted skin and receding hair sat behind the desk. No sugar rush for Curtis today.

Curtis put his hand over the vein scanner on the counter. A high-pitched *ding* and small green light on the panel indicated he was cleared and signed in. He walked over to one of the lifts, the doors opening automatically.

"Floor twelve." His breath quickened with anticipation as the lift started going up. It was his first day as principal software engineer in the MEow office and he was due to present to his new team at the morning's snap meeting in an hour. He couldn't wait to get started. There were lots of exciting developments going on in MEow right now. He'd miss Adam, though. Cute little loser.

Momentarily looking up from his phone, Curtis noticed

that the lift was now going down instead of up. *Strange.* The system was bulletproof, he thought. He repeated his command, "Er – floor twelve."

The lift ignored him and kept going down. It seemed to be returning him to the ground floor.

"Fucking thing. Lift, take me to floor twelve!"

Three, two, one, zero, *minus one.*

"Huh? What the hell is floor minus one?"

The lift doors opened. Curtis took a breath and stepped out into a huge room lined with desks and people tapping at MEcs, not unlike the other communal offices in the building. It was brightly lit with the same panel lights in the ceiling as the other floors, but he couldn't see any exterior windows.

Floor minus one. So, what – *underground?* But the Looming Tower didn't have a floor underground. Did it?

Curtis noted the doors leading to various rooms off the one he was in. He read the plaques on some of the doors. *Temporal Health and Medicine. Library. Temporal Shield Reactor. Wardrobe.*

What the fuck was going on down here?

"Ah – Mr O'Brien."

Curtis turned to his left and instantly shuddered. Miss Morgan was walking down a corridor off the main office floor, straight towards him. She held out her hand to shake his, an uncharacteristically warm smile on her face.

"Er – hi… ma'am," he replied, trying to conceal a heavy swallow. He shook her hand but had come over all weak and feeble and it was probably the limpest handshake he'd ever given. He could feel the blush heating up his cheeks.

"Sorry to blindside you like this," said Miss Morgan, "but we couldn't say anything to you before today. We have to play things very cloak and dagger down here."

Curtis frowned. "W-where am I?"

Miss Morgan's smile widened. "The Time Travel Department."

"I'm sorry – the *what?"*

"Walk with me. Would you like a coffee?"

"N-no, thank you."

Curtis walked with Miss Morgan up the corridor she had just come from. "Again, please forgive the deception. You haven't actually been promoted to principal software engineer for MEow. But you have been promoted. Here. To Time Travel."

A laugh slipped out – he couldn't help it. He gathered himself quickly and looked at the CEO, who was straight-faced. "Is this a joke?"

"Do I look like I'm joking?"

Erica Morgan *never* looked like she was joking.

"No, but… time travel's impossible, isn't it?"

"Nothing's impossible, Mr O'Brien. Some things just haven't been invented yet. But time travel has. By us. The general public simply doesn't know about it."

While Curtis's mind gushed with questions, Miss Morgan stopped at a door marked *Chronozine Production*. She waved her hand over the vein scanner on the wall by the door, which cleared her for entry. She gestured for Curtis to do the same.

As Miss Morgan stepped forwards, the door opened automatically into another large room. Curtis's gaze fell over a throng of people in white lab coats and gloves operating lab equipment. There were people staring at slides through microscopes, siphoning fluids through pumps, loading centrifuges with test cylinders and pushing buttons and levers on big, funnel-shaped, rotating machines.

And then there were workers monitoring screens, control panels and temperature gauges attached to an enormous machine at the centre of the room. Curtis gawped at its complex system of columns, pipes, gears, pistons and huge spinning turrets, all working away around a vast, cubic, transparent tank. Inside the tank was a cloud of thick red smoke, swirling and changing shape continuously, moving around the tank like it was alive.

Curtis's mouth had been open so long it was now bone-dry, his tongue starting to stick to the sides. He closed it and swallowed to work up some saliva. As he tried to process what he was seeing, Miss Morgan said, "Excuse me for a moment," and walked over to a white-coated man standing next to a screen, displaying a matrix of numbers. "Status of the Ratheri, Mr Lennox?"

The... *Ratheri?*

"We're tracking a type-two fluctuation in the provium pulse filters," Mr Lennox replied. "It's causing a small phase differential in the Ratheri's chronokinetic alignment. I'm running a diagnostic to isolate the source."

What the bloody hell did he just say?

"Keep me apprised," said Miss Morgan. "Is James Rawling ready to go on the Ancient Egypt assignment?"

Mr Lennox nodded, "Yes, ma'am. Everything's in place. Rawling will travel tonight."

Curtis remembered meeting James Rawling in the cafeteria once. An odd man, he recalled. Tall, lanky, attractive – in a weird sort of way. He was pleasant and well-spoken but had this dark vibe about him. He claimed to work on floor five in the Marketing Department. A lie, it would seem.

This Lennox guy's mention of 'Ancient Egypt' fired Curtis's curiosity. When he said Rawling would 'travel tonight', was it Ancient Egypt he was travelling to? Whatever for? Find out how the pyramids were built? Surveil a pharaoh?

Miss Morgan walked around inspecting the work of some of the other employees before returning to Curtis. She directed him to the left side of the huge machine, where a narrow discharge chute was depositing small white bottles into a collection bin.

She picked up one of the bottles, twisted the lid off and peered inside to examine the contents. She held it out to show Curtis. Nestled in the bottle were dozens of little red pills.

"What are they?" he asked.

"Chronozine," said Miss Morgan. "It's how we travel

in time." She lifted her gaze to the machine. "We make it using the red gas you can see in the tank over there."

"Is that the... the 'Ratheri'?"

"You catch on quick."

Not quick enough. "What *is* it?"

"It's a long story. Not one for today." Miss Morgan walked over to a woman tapping at a control panel on the 'Ratheri' machine, handed her the bottle of pills and said, "Run a metraspectral analysis on these pills. Bring me the chronotonic density rating." Fuck knew what that meant either.

Miss Morgan walked back towards Curtis. "Come."

As he followed her to the door where they had come in, a small bell started to ring in his head. That dinosaur in Tower Hamlets, the one with the humans inside it. The one none of the news networks were talking about anymore, weirdly.

He was sure he'd heard something about red pills being found. And there were people saying the dinosaur, or the humans, had time-travelled...

Walking with Miss Morgan down a different corridor, Curtis said, "Is all this anything to do with – ?"

"The dinosaur in Tower Hamlets?" said Miss Morgan, reading his mind. "Yes. That was us."

"So those children – who were they?"

They turned down another corridor. "We're in the process of determining that."

They stopped at a door marked *Augur* and scanned their hands again. Entering, Curtis's eyes fixed immediately on the big metal dome at the centre of the room. It was surrounded by four glass columns of pale, cloudy liquid along with various conduits, pistons and injectors and a number of integrated screens, some displaying inexplicable sequences of numbers, others images that looked like electrocardiograms. The staff in this room were standing watching the screens, fumbling with control panels and otherwise sitting at desks on MEcs.

"W-what is that?" Curtis said.

"A tool that makes our lives – as time travellers – a lot easier," said Miss Morgan. "We call it the Augur. We use it to monitor the timeline and track temporal incursions."

"Incursions?"

"Changes. Changes that have been made – or will be made – to the timeline. Before the Augur, we could only rely on the sensor grid. But all that did was tell us what was different about the present. It didn't tell us what had caused the present to change – that was always a guessing game. Our analysts would have to use the data on the changes in the present to work out what changes had been made to the past. It wasn't very accurate. And it was a reactive measure."

None of what Miss Morgan was saying was really going in. Curtis thought for a second that he might still be in bed, dreaming, and hadn't actually come into work today at all. He drove his thumb nail hard into the palm of his other hand. Yeah, that hurt. He was awake.

Miss Morgan continued as Curtis nodded idly. "The Augur, however, feeds Million Eyes data constantly on multiple alternate timelines. It enables us to see time travel missions we're yet to undertake, and see the effects of them. We can actually use the data we receive to check whether the missions we're planning will succeed. We think of it as time travel quality control."

A man came up to Miss Morgan, holding a MEpad, and said nervously, "Miss Morgan, sorry to interrupt. Dr Packard's asked if I could get your sign-off on this."

"Do excuse me again," she said to Curtis. That was fine – he could use a break from all this madness she was bombarding him with.

Standing partly with her back to Curtis, Miss Morgan started reading the data on the man's MEpad.

Something occurred to Curtis in that moment. He realised that this was *so* mad he had to tell someone about it. He knew he'd never be able to keep it to himself, but he also knew no one would believe him if he just *told* them. He needed evidence.

Glancing down surreptitiously at his trouser pocket, he lifted his phone halfway out, tapped through to his last message from Adam and started recording a voice message, then let it drop back into his pocket. He wasn't sure how much it would pick up but it was the only thing he could think of in that moment.

Miss Morgan finished reading whatever was on the screen, pressed her thumb against the bottom of it and handed it back to the man.

"Thank you, ma'am." The man walked off.

Miss Morgan turned to face Curtis again. "Where was I? Ah, yes. The Augur. What's really great about it is that if anyone tries to damage the timeline in a way that doesn't benefit Million Eyes, we know about it in advance and can prevent it. For instance, we just received some very interesting data. About you."

Curtis had been staring at the pale fluid roiling in the Augur's four columns, but snapped his gaze back onto Miss Morgan when she said that. "Pardon?"

"Yeah. The Augur revealed that you would be promoted to Time Travel but betray Million Eyes the moment you learned how to travel in time."

"Wait – what?" Curtis felt suddenly dizzy.

Miss Morgan compressed her lips and raised both eyebrows as if to say, *hey, that's just what the data said.* "According to the Augur, you will exploit our secrets in order to take your revenge on the institution that stole your innocence from you."

Curtis's pulse quickened. He stood rigid. The hairs on the back of his neck bristled. "I – I don't know what you're talking abo –"

"Father Michael Magnus."

Curtis swallowed the rest of his sentence. His racing heart froze, blood turning to ice. He suddenly couldn't speak.

"Your parish priest till you were sixteen," Miss Morgan continued. "The man you served as an altar boy, who made you believe each time he raped you that it was a demonstration of God's love. The man who, when the extent of his abuse was revealed, ended up in prison for thirty years for multiple counts of rape and sexual assault against other young boys just like yourself."

Curtis's toes were shaking in his shoes. A film of sweat broke out across his forehead and down his back. Father Magnus's face and voice came crashing back in his mind and made his stomach churn with dread and revulsion and fear.

"And then there's Archbishop Alexander Brooks. He knew Father Magnus was a paedophile and instead of reporting him to police, moved him from parish to parish while paying his victims to keep quiet, thereby covering up his crimes and enabling him to keep committing them. He was the one who reassigned Father Magnus to your parish, wasn't he? He knew the monster he was, but he did nothing. And it wasn't just him. Several other church officials knew what was going on. And you – and several of your friends – paid the price. But when the cover-ups by Brooks were finally brought to light, what did the Church do? Promoted him. The pope himself made him a cardinal, appointed him archpriest of the Basilica di Via Sacra in Rome, one its most important churches. Talk about rubbing salt in the wounds, hey?"

Curtis wrung his hands. Now his blood was boiling, thickening into syrup. He clenched his jaw and tried to stem the flow of vomit threatening to surge up his throat.

"Mr O'Brien, I know you hide an intense pain – and an even more intense fury – under a cover of humour and jest. And I know your fury is directed at the Roman Catholic Church. You hate it. You would do anything to bring the entire church to its knees."

Why was she saying all this? Why was she raking all this back up? He just wanted to scream. Scream and cry and run away.

"You see, Million Eyes holds the key to the Catholic Church's destruction. But we cannot – *will not* – use it. It

would undermine all the work we have done to further
the Mission."

Mission? What fucking 'mission'?

"What the Augur has told us is that you will decide that
your thirst for revenge against the Church is more
important than the Mission and, in order to satisfy it, you
will travel back in time and steal the scrolls of Jesus."

What!

Curtis's heart stopped. What the fuck was this woman
on about? Clearing his throat, he finally mustered some
words, "The scrolls of Jesus?" Summoning the deeply
Catholic education he'd long since pressed into the
furthermost reaches of his mind, "Jesus didn't write any
scrolls."

Miss Morgan's eyes widened. "Didn't he?"

Curtis felt his legs go weak. "I don't understand. I don't
understand any of this. I'm not planning to steal any
scrolls. I don't *know* about any scrolls!"

"Not yet."

"But... but Miss Morgan, I wouldn't! I... I won't!"

"The Augur says you will."

Curtis shook his head, confusion and turmoil tumbling
through it. One question eclipsed the others. "Why did
you promote me then? If you knew what I'd do, why
bring me here? You could've stopped me from ever
finding out about this place."

Miss Morgan gave an impressed nod. "That is true. But
this isn't about keeping history safe. This is about you.
The Augur has exposed you for what you are. Someone I
can't trust. Someone who lacks perspective and strength,
whose heart will inevitably triumph over his head. I don't
need people like that. I need people capable of rising
above petty emotions."

The fact that she'd just called what he'd been through
'petty' made him want to punch the callous piece of shit
in the face. But his anger swiftly collapsed beneath a
burgeoning sense of panic. Sweat poured out of him like
someone wringing a sponge. "But I don't even know

105

what you're talking about!"

Miss Morgan looked at him coldly. "And now you don't need to."

Curtis's heart leapt into his throat as Miss Morgan pulled a gun from somewhere behind her hip. Before his eyes had even registered what was happening, a massive green surge of light burst out of the gun with a powerful hiss, straight into his chest.

Sitting at his desk in the MEps office, Adam felt his phone buzz. He glanced at the screen: a voice message from Curtis. The bosses having just gone into a meeting, he pressed 'play' and lifted the phone to his ear. All he could hear was indistinct, muffled chatter and rustling. The silly idiot had pocket-dialled him.

He listened for nearly a minute just in case Curtis realised and started speaking. Then he stopped the message and thumbed Curtis a quick text. Oi, bellend. Your pocket just called me.

He tapped 'send'. A moment later, he sent a follow-up. I hope your first day in MEow is going well.

15

December 15th 33

"Are you all right, my love?"

Joseph of Arimathea's mind was elsewhere and his wife's question glanced off him. He sat at the stern of the ship, looking out to sea, remembering.

Sapphira came and sat beside him. She placed her warm gloved hands over his, which were cold and bare. It was a grey, wintry day – getting colder and windier as they got further north – so that warmth felt good.

"What is it?" she said softly.

Finally hearing her, Joseph lifted his gaze from the water to her smiling face. "Just… thinking."

"About Jesus?"

"Yes. I keep… seeing him. When I sleep. When I wake. When I look at you, the children. Dying on that cross. Bleeding. Murmuring in desperate pain."

Sapphira removed a glove and stroked his face with her fingers. "I know his crucifixion still haunts you. But time and prayer will heal it. I promise it will."

"What disturbs me most is the injustice. Jesus the Prophet came to save us and look how we repaid him."

"We? *You* did nothing."

"Precisely. I did nothing."

"Joseph, listen to me. We have been over this. There was nothing you could do. You were not to know who was involved in the conspiracy."

"I could have questioned Caiaphas about it. Found out

which apostles he was working with."

"He would never have told you. And he might have suspected your allegiance to Jesus. You could not have risked that."

"Why not? We would have been in the same position that we are now."

"Perhaps not. Perhaps they would have nailed you to a cross before we were able to make our escape."

Joseph looked deep into his wife's gentle grey eyes. Were their roles reversed, would he have shown such loyalty to her as she to him? It was unwavering. And this was in spite of the fact that he had completely uprooted their family.

He looked over at his children. His son and three youngest daughters were at the bow of the ship playing with little wooden jackals, lions, donkeys and people, which they had sculpted themselves. His eldest daughter, Tabitha, was talking to one of his oarsmen and looking up at the sails; it looked like he was explaining to her how they worked.

His eyes back on Sapphira, "So you do not blame me? For forcing our family to leave our home?"

Sapphira shook her head. "You did not force us to leave. *They* did."

"Yes. Because I allied myself with Jesus."

"Are you saying you regret that?"

Joseph sighed and admitted, quietly, "No."

"Good. Nor should you. You are a good man, Joseph. There is no doubt in my mind that you did the right thing by supporting Jesus in his ministry. You said so yourself. He came to save us. He came to prevent the Last War. And we cannot let him down. We must continue his work. You know this. Do not lose your conviction now."

Joseph looked over at the lead chest that housed and protected the earthenware jar containing Jesus's scrolls, entrusted to him by his late friend shortly before his death.

Sapphira was right. They had come all this way. If

Sapphira's faith in him could be unwavering, then so could his in their mission. In fact, he owed it to her to make sure it was. Upending their family's lives and putting them all at risk had to be worth it. *Had* to be.

"Father, look!" cried Tabitha, pointing across the water.

Joseph stood up and followed Tabitha's gaze. Their destination beckoned. The rugged coastline of the Britannic Isles, all towering cliffs, deep caves, steep, grassy slopes, and huge stacks of jagged rocks strewn over yellow beaches. He remembered it well.

Joseph bade his oarsmen to steer the ship around the headland. He smiled and kissed Sapphira, then walked to the bow of the ship where his children were. Tabitha had joined them and all five were staring at the approaching land.

"Do we have to live here, Father?" said his youngest, Abigail.

He looked at her. Even though she was wrapped in a huge fur cloak, her little face disappearing into its folds, she was shivering. The temperature had definitely dropped in the last hour.

Joseph went and sat with her. She huddled close to him for warmth. "We do, my love," he said. "I have been here many times, done much trade with the people who live here. And I have friends here. We will be safe."

"But it's so cold here. Did you have to bring us somewhere so cold?"

"It isn't always this cold, Abigail. It is winter. But the Britons are used to these temperatures and well equipped to withstand them, and the winds and snow."

Her voice shrill with alarm, "Snow?" There had been no snowfall in Jerusalem in quite a number of years and, being only four, Abigail had never seen a flake of it. Joseph had no doubt that this winter, in their new home, she would experience her first snow.

Joseph smiled. "Trust me. You will get used to it in time."

She sighed. He kissed the top of her head and hoped to

God that he was right. That his children would one day be happy here.

Because there was no going back to Judaea.

Joseph and his family, and the small company of friends and servants that had come with them, sailed north, following the west coast of Britannia. The sky was so laden with cloud that it was difficult to tell the time of day, but sunset was surely not far off.

A few hours later, they entered the estuary of the River Brue and sailed inland along the river. Dark had fallen by the time they came ashore at a village called Glesting, in the territory of the Durotriges tribe, which was near to one of the lead mines Joseph owned shares in. Joseph had stayed in Glesting several times before and had come to consider its chieftain, Truinog – a kind, elderly man who always wore a shining gold tunic – a friend. He was confident he would help them.

He was right. Truinog offered Joseph, Sapphira and the children shelter in his roundhouse. The rest of Joseph's companions and servants lodged with other families in the village.

Joseph had seen many of these roundhouses on his travels through Britannia. With their densely thatched conical roofs and windowless walls of wattle and daub, they were a far sight more rustic and rudimentary than his two-storey stone house back in Jerusalem, but sensible given the climate and available materials, and somehow quaint.

Joseph's children, particularly Abigail, were understandably uneasy and unsure in their new, very different surroundings. Still, they welcomed the warmth that came from the crackling central hearth, which was being stoked constantly by Truinog's wife, Donella, as well as the abundance of animal skins and wool blankets she kindly furnished them with.

In the morning, Truinog granted Joseph a tract of land on which he and his company could start building their own roundhouses. Over the next few weeks, in between building his new home, Joseph made a conscious effort to get to know Truinog better. The chieftain had an interesting faith. He and his people worshipped many gods, much like the Romans. Their most important deity was a goddess called Erona, who lived inside the enormous yew tree that sprawled at the centre of the village.

Spending time with Truinog, Joseph realised that while the man was undoubtedly fixed in his beliefs, he was willing, indeed curious, to hear ones that differed. Like Joseph's. Joseph decided that Truinog was open-minded enough to tell him of Jesus the Prophet.

One night, Joseph was with Truinog in Truinog's roundhouse, sitting on logs by the fire and drinking beer brewed from fermented barley grain by Donella. The rest of Truinog's family were asleep on feather mattresses strewn with blankets in the cosy sleeping quarters on the other side of the house.

"Truinog, can I tell you my real motivation for coming here when I did?" said Joseph quietly.

"I thought it was 'cause of your love of these islands and the people on them," said Truinog, gulping his beer.

"Yes, indeed. That is true. But the timing of my arrival was due to something that happened in Judaea."

"Oh?"

"A few years ago, I met a man, Jesus the Prophet, who was sent by my God from the distant future to prevent the destruction of all people, everywhere, over two millennia from now."

Truinog grabbed the flagon of beer to top up his gold-banded drinking horn. He said nothing, his expression blank.

So Joseph continued, "He travelled through Judaea with men he'd appointed as apostles, preaching about what he described as the 'Last War'. But these men betrayed him, plotted to have him killed, and Jesus the Prophet was crucified by the Romans."

"Bloody Romans," said Truinog, hiccupping.

Joseph was starting to wonder if Truinog would remember this conversation in the morning. He carried on regardless.

"Now the apostles are cannibalising Jesus's ministry for their own ends. They have been spreading a twisted and sanitised version of his prophecies and telling people that he was, himself, a god. Jesus was indeed a prophet and a messenger with extraordinary insights and abilities, but he was no god. He was a man, like you and I."

Truinog frowned. "What sort of abilities?"

"He had... tools. Instruments. Instruments that could heal people. Instantly, in some cases. At first I thought he had been endowed by God with the power to perform miracles. But Jesus stressed that they were not miracles and he was not a magus. He explained that his instruments were from the future, where people are able to do unimaginable things by means of their own ingenuity."

"Did you believe him?"

"I did. Nearly everyone else thought him a miracle maker, but I believed I had heard the truth. Now the apostles are changing his status and his message in order to assert their own power. That has made me determined to convey Jesus's true message to as many people as possible."

"So why have you come here? Don't the people of Judah —"

"Judaea," Joseph corrected him.

Truinog grunted. "Don't the people of Judaea need to hear this truth you speak of?"

"They do. But I didn't have any choice about that. The apostles who betrayed Jesus extracted my identity by torturing Judas Iscariot, the one apostle who'd remained true to the last. I was expelled from the Sanhedrin and banished from Jerusalem, but I knew it would not end there. I knew the apostles would send assassins to silence me, to stop me from preaching the truth. Just as they had Judas. I heard he was disembowelled after he was tortured."

Truinog pulled a face. "And you people say we're the savages."

"The Romans were after me, too. I was accused of all kinds of crimes against the Empire. Falsely, I might add. More lies stirred up by the apostles. That was one of the reasons I chose to come all the way to Britannia. Thus far these islands are beyond the Empire's reach."

"Right. That Julius Caesar tried his damnedest. We resisted. No way I'm kneeling before a Roman."

"Nor should you have to."

Truinog took another gulp of beer, dribbling some down his long white beard. "All right. You've got my attention. Tell me more of this 'Last War'."

Joseph opened his leather bag and took out the earthenware jar that contained Jesus's scrolls. He opened the jar, emptying out the scrolls in front of Truinog.

"It is all here, in these scrolls," said Joseph.

"Jesus the Prophet wrote those?"

"Yes. They are an account of the Last War and of what Jesus did after coming to this century. I would have you read them, but they were written in the language of my people. If you will permit me, I will read them to you."

Truinog nodded. Joseph opened and read the scrolls aloud in Brittonic, Truinog's language. Truinog seemed utterly captivated and did not drink once as Joseph read. Joseph couldn't even hear him breathe.

When Joseph had finished reading, Truinog said immediately, "In the morning, come with me to tell the others of this man."

Over the next few years, Joseph of Arimathea continued to live among the Britons. He travelled often, visiting his mines to source tin and lead and selling it in other villages, his family staying in Glesting. Meanwhile, Truinog, inspired by the story of Jesus the Prophet, built a wattle-and-daub temple in Glesting where his people could come and hear the village druid, Veranacus, speak of Jesus's prophecies about the Last War.

Joseph could not have been more pleased that Truinog and the others had embraced the truth of Jesus so readily. As time wore on, it helped ease his guilt over Jesus's death. It would never disappear, but at least when Jesus looked down from Heaven, he could see that his friend was continuing his ministry, preparing humankind for what was coming. The thought persistently warmed him.

And Sapphira and the children had a comfortable life here, too. The weather might not have been as pleasant, but the people were friendly, and the atmosphere was not tense like it was back in Jerusalem, where the uneasy alliance between the Romans and the Jews was always threatening to crack. Life, for all of them, was good.

Until one day.

Joseph returned home from the nearby village of Priddy. Climbing down from his horse, he noted the quietness of his roundhouse. Perhaps everyone inside was reading, though it was unusual for all five of his children to be reading at the same time.

The door was open as it usually was at this time of day, to let in the daylight. As he got closer, he couldn't feel any heat coming from the hearth, nor hear the crackling of the logs.

Chest pounding, he stepped into the doorway. The fire had gone out, not that long ago, judging by the still-glowing embers. The three-legged stand that suspended their bronze cauldron over the fire had been knocked over. The cauldron itself was on its side, a meat and vegetable broth spilled all over the rammed chalk and flint floor. Baskets of food were turned upside down and

Sapphira's loom had been smashed to pieces. The family's sleeping quarters were reduced to a bundle of broken sticks and torn cloth.

There they were. All six of them – Sapphira and the children – lying together in a heap on the other side of the roundhouse, half-buried in shadow.

Though his feet were dead weights, he willed himself forwards. He felt like there was a hand around his neck, squeezing his throat so he couldn't breathe.

When he saw their beautiful bodies torn open, bowels scattered about them in a horrendous and bloody mess, he could do nothing to stop the earth-shattering caterwaul bursting from his throat.

Dropping to his knees, Joseph barely noticed that the jar containing Jesus's scrolls was shattered, the scrolls taken.

He heard footsteps behind him but was frozen. In a moment, someone was standing over him but he couldn't see for tears.

The silver of a blade flashed through the bleariness. It was quick. Perhaps that's why there was no pain. Just a hot, sharp thrust across his stomach, a powerful tingling, and then something warm, soft and sticky fell into his hands. He looked down, saw a blur of red and fell forwards.

His face landed opposite Abigail's. For a moment her little body sharpened into focus. She was smiling at him. But she was in just her tunic. Where was her cloak? The fire was out. She'd get cold.

Someone cover her up. Abigail doesn't like being cold.

The man who had just disembowelled Joseph of Arimathea was Paul, a Pharisee tent-maker also known by his Hebrew name, Saul. He'd been recruited by Jesus's apostles to travel with a company of men to

Britannia, where Joseph was rumoured to be hiding. The rumours, it turned out, were true.

Paul had already burned the infamous scrolls and killed the village chieftain Truinog and druid Veranacus for peddling Joseph's lies. Now that he'd killed Joseph, the next phase of his mission could begin: setting the record straight on Jesus. To that end, Paul and his entourage remained in Glesting and established the first church in Britannia to be dedicated to the real teachings of the Lord Jesus Christ, Son of God, Saviour of the World.

What Paul didn't know was that the scrolls he'd burned were not, in fact, the originals. They were copies, crafted by Joseph of Arimathea some years before. In a bid to keep Jesus's writings safe, Joseph had copied his words onto new vellum scrolls and placed them in a new jar. Then he'd taken the lead chest that contained the original scrolls, in the jar Jesus had given him, and buried it at the foot of the yew tree in which the Celtic goddess Erona was believed to reside.

And there the scrolls remained.

16

April 16th 2027

Clocking off early and ignoring the ever-lengthening list of work emails she still hadn't dealt with, Lester walked to her car in the LIPA car park, texting Brody. I'm going for drinks with Sheryl tonight. Don't wait up. A lie. But she couldn't say she was following up on a lead that might help her with her Million Eyes investigation, as she hadn't told him anything *about* her Million Eyes investigation. How could she? If he knew she was trying to prove that the world's leading technology company were time-travelling assassins, he would think she'd utterly lost it. That her grief over Georgia had made her crazy. No. She would have to keep all this under her hat for the time being.

As she got in the car, her phone buzzed. Brody's reply. I never do.

Lester sighed as she drove out of the car park. This was happening a lot lately – her getting home late. Some of the time she'd been out with friends. She had legitimately gone for drinks with Sheryl a few times over the last two weeks. More than normal, and her counsellor would say she was avoiding going home, avoiding Brody. She couldn't say with certainty that she wasn't.

Other times it was because she'd been staying late at the office. Not working, mind. Getting caught up in her reading about Million Eyes. She'd been delving into their history, researching and cross-referencing, emailing

117

people who might know something, several of whom had turned out to be conspiracy theorists with nothing sensible or tangible to offer. And just generally getting stuck in Google holes for hours at a time.

Today her investigation could well yield something substantive, although it had meant leaving work early and driving all the way to Coventry. Hopefully it would be worth it.

She pushed back her guilt over Brody. She'd be making things up to him tomorrow anyway. She was going to cook a candlelit dinner, serve his favourite wine and dessert and just talk. Maybe even do that thing they used to do: laugh.

Two hours after leaving LIPA, Lester pulled up outside a redbrick, semi-detached house on a shady street lined with sycamore trees, in the outskirts of Coventry city centre.

Getting out of the car, she could feel her heartrate slow right down as her eyes fell upon Georgia. Standing under one of the sycamores on the pavement on the other side of the road, she was twirling her ginger locks around her finger.

Lester leaned against the side of her car, legs suddenly weak. A car went past in front of her, and Georgia was gone.

That was the fifth time she'd seen Georgia in three weeks. First was that time driving home from work. She saw her a few days later standing in her bedroom doorway; about a week after that in the LIPA car park; then last week, when she was onsite supervising a geophysical survey in Northamptonshire. Now here. A few of Georgia's appearances had made Lester wonder if ghosts were real, despite a lifelong rejection of all things spiritual or paranormal. But she knew it wasn't Georgia who was haunting her. It was her own damned mind.

Shaking it off and pulling a deep breath in, she walked up to the front door of the house and pressed the doorbell.

"Hi, is Beth Ferro here?" Lester said to the man who

opened the door. He looked like he was Lester's age, maybe a little older. He was barefoot, in blue jeans and a light green, short-sleeved shirt that accentuated his V-shaped torso and muscular arms, and had chiselled features, a stubbly beard and wavy black hair. She could smell his woody aftershave.

Lester felt a flutter in her groin. *So you are still alive down there.*

"It's Beth Heaton now," said the man. "Are you Dr Lester?"

"I am, yes."

Lester presumed this impressive specimen of a man was Beth's new husband – a much younger and prettier model than Gregory Ferro it looked like, from the pictures Lester had seen of him. "Come in," he said. "Beth's just finishing up a call."

Lester stepped onto a mat in a carpeted hallway. She took off her shoes and followed the man into the first room off the hallway. A woman she presumed was Beth Ferro – *Heaton* – was sitting at a large desk facing the window with a phone to her ear. The pretty man was definitely a toy boy. Beth looked at least ten years his senior – mid-to-late fifties, with a silvery grey pixie cut and glasses. She threw Lester a restrained smile as she entered. The man indicated for Lester to sit in the chair next to Beth's desk.

"Tea? Coffee?" the man whispered so as not to interrupt his wife's phone call.

"Tea, please," Lester replied quietly. "White with one sugar would be lovely." She'd usually ask for a sweetener but didn't want to impose. The man nodded, smiled and departed for the kitchen.

"That's fine. I'll give the client a call in the morning… No, I don't think so… Yep," Beth was saying to whoever was on the phone. Lester had read on LinkedIn that she was a manager for an insurance broker; she obviously worked from home some, if not all, of the time.

There was a photo frame on a shelf opposite Beth's

desk, next to some books. It was a selfie of Beth, her husband and two twenty-somethings – a man and a woman. The newspaper reports about the house fire that killed Ferro mentioned that his wife and two children had already moved out, Beth having recently filed for divorce. Perhaps the pair in the picture were Ferro's kids.

"Great, thanks. Bye." Beth hung up and looked at Lester. "Hi."

"Hi," said Lester. "Thanks for agreeing to meet me."

"That's okay. I don't have long though."

I've just driven two hours to get here. You can give me fifteen minutes. "No problem. I just wanted to ask you a few questions about your husband's death."

"Why exactly?" Beth frowned softly. "I looked you up. You're a palaeontologist, aren't you? Dinosaurs and what-not?"

People always assumed everything palaeontologists did was to do with dinosaurs. "My area of expertise is a lot broader than that. And I'm an archaeologist as well."

"That still doesn't explain why you'd be looking into my husband's death."

"No. That's… My enquiries into your husband's death aren't to do with my work. I have a… a personal interest."

"A personal interest in my husband?"

"A personal interest in what happened to him. I'm… looking into unsolved deaths in the Hampshire area."

"There's nothing 'unsolved' about Greg's death. A fire started at our house, by accident, and he was killed. End of story."

Lester fetched a notebook and pad from her handbag. "And you're certain the fire started by accident?"

"Yes."

"Why?"

Beth huffed. "Because the police said it did. They said his computer probably short-circuited and caught on fire."

"Probably?"

"They don't know for certain. Greg's body was too... too..." Beth swallowed her words and a flash of anguish crossed her face, making her cheeks flush and her eyes momentarily shine with tears. She'd been coming across as quite hard and aloof but clearly the pain of what had happened to Ferro wasn't gone.

Beth blinked several times and cleared her throat. "They couldn't determine the cause of death, but they didn't think it was suspicious."

"And you were satisfied with that?"

"Yes. Well, I had to be, didn't I? I would've liked more clarification on what happened, why Greg didn't realise there was a fire till" – she breathed out a ragged sigh – "till it was too late. But everything was burned to a cinder. There wasn't much left to investigate."

"Did Greg ever talk to you about his research into time travellers?"

Beth's face changed instantly. Her jaw clenched and her eyes hardened. "Yes, he did. And I'm not talking about that." Her voice was laced with indignation.

Lester was taken aback. "Can... can I ask why?"

"Because Greg's obsession with time travellers is probably the reason he wasn't paying attention when our house burned down around him, leaving our kids without a father."

"Did you never think your husband may have been on to something?"

Beth stood up, bristling. "Of course not. My husband was losing his mind and very likely on the verge of a breakdown. Now if you don't mind, I have things to do."

Lester stayed seated. "Ferro believed time travellers were responsible for Princess Diana's death. Didn't you ever wonder if his death was connected to what he was finding out?"

"Oh my God." Beth stared at her, wide-eyed, and Lester thought for a moment she'd got her attention. Then, after a pause, she said, "You're as crazy as Greg was. You need to leave my house."

Beth's husband came in with a tea for Lester and something hot and steaming for Beth.

"Here's your –" the man started.

"No need, Spencer." Finally, the husband had a name. "Dr Lester is just leaving."

Shrugging with resignation, Lester stood up and walked past Spencer into the hallway. There was no point asking any more questions; Beth clearly wasn't receptive to answering them. Nor was she interested in entertaining the possibility that Ferro's death was anything other than an accident. She'd moved on. Luckily, Lester hadn't.

She slid into her shoes and Spencer opened the front door, flashing her an awkward smile.

Lester walked back to her car, tossing a glance across the road just in case Georgia was there under the tree again.

She wasn't.

Sighing with frustration at having wasted her entire evening, Lester got in the car and began the two-and-a-half-hour journey home to Gravesend.

17

September 19th 993

Another diabolical dream had already woken Brother Cuthwulf by the time the bell rang for Prime, the Early Morning Prayer. Another dream that would remain with him all day. He was being taunted by his own mind.

He knew why. For the past two years, since joining the monastic community at Glastonbury Abbey, Cuthwulf had been deliberately suppressing all memory of the horrific things he had done as a knight for King Aethelred. Even though he confessed his sins at the chapter house on a daily basis, there were some sins he just couldn't articulate in front of his brethren. God was punishing him for holding back. He knew it.

Yawning, Cuthwulf threw off his rough coverlet and peeled himself off his thin, lumpy straw pallet, a relentless source of backache. There was movement and murmuring from the brothers as the dormitory returned gradually to the waking world.

"Are you well, Cuthwulf?" whispered Brother Oswyn, who slept next to him, as he rose from his bed.

"Yes. Why do you ask?" said Cuthwulf, straightening his habit and securing his eating knife to his belt.

"You cried out in your sleep."

Merciful God – did I?

"Just a dream," said Cuthwulf.

"Who's Ivar?"

Cuthwulf felt a tightening in his chest. His whole body

went cold. He said quietly, "Ivar?"

"You shouted that name a few times. You sounded quite distressed."

Cuthwulf didn't reply. He hoped his patent discomfort might lead Oswyn to cease the discussion.

"Ivar's a Danish name, isn't it? I heard you were a soldier for King Aethelred before you came here. Someone you met in battle, perhaps?"

Cuthwulf was very private and never liked to talk about his past with his brethren. Abbot Aelfric knew the most about him but Aelfric was like a father to him, and still there were things – plenty of things – he didn't know either. The fact that Cuthwulf had not joined the abbey at a young age like the others, and had this whole other life before the cloisters, caused the brothers to constantly wonder and be curious about him.

Oswyn's questions, however, were becoming intrusive. Cuthwulf changed the subject. "Are you back in the fields today? I hear the harvest has been particularly good this year, that the granary is already full."

But Oswyn was clearly more interested in prying into Cuthwulf's past than talking about harvests. "So you don't remember who this Ivar was then?"

Cuthwulf turned and faced the younger monk. "Oswyn, please stop. My days as a soldier are behind me. I have a new life now. I do not wish to keep discussing the old one."

He caught Oswyn's nervous swallow. He had quietened the younger monk at last.

Cuthwulf went with a company of brothers to relieve himself in the communal latrine. Then it was on to the lavatorium to wash and finally to the abbey church for Prime. Nobody else spoke to him, which he was grateful for.

The sun barely risen, half a dozen candles had been lit to augment the pale light coming through the round-arched clerestory windows of the church. As Abbot Aelfric proceeded up the nave to the sanctuary and, slowly and stiffly, climbed the altar stairs, the candlelight deepened the grooves in his sagging face and darkened the age spots on his scalp.

Cuthwulf was sad to admit it but the man was ageing fast. Joining the abbey in middle age had made Cuthwulf's transition from secular to monastic life more of a challenge and Aelfric had been his guide and support through all of it. He hoped the dear old man had a good number of years left, but feared that that number was getting smaller by the day.

The abbot took his place in front of the altar, placed his palms flat on its surface and sung the opening prayer. For the next half hour, the church was filled with resonant chanting and song, lifting Cuthwulf's spirits and banishing painful images from his mind.

After Prime, Cuthwulf retreated to the library to continue reading Poletricus, a mysterious author about whom little was known, only that he lived during the 2nd century and was a Christian. His writings were among a vast collection of classical texts discovered a year ago in the ruins of a Roman villa in Devonshire and brought to Glastonbury Abbey to be studied by the monks. Poletricus wrote in Aramaic rather than Latin, which meant that most of England would not have been able to read it. That is, apart from the monks at Glastonbury. Dunstan, the abbot who had instituted Benedictine rule at Glastonbury, had insisted that the monks learn Aramaic, the language of Jesus Christ, after the abbey came into possession of an ancient Aramaic New Testament, which Dunstan came to believe was in fact the original New Testament text. Thus he felt it imperative that the monks be able to read the Gospels in their purest form.

Cuthwulf was about a quarter of the way through the mostly intact codex. Poletricus was recounting the travels of Christ's disciples and their mission to spread the gospel beyond the Holy Lands. Cuthwulf got to a section on St Joseph of Arimathea, the man who buried Christ in the tomb, when the bell rang for the Mid-Morning Prayer,

Terce. He marked his page so he could come back to it later.

His day proceeded much like the previous one. Terce was followed by Abbot Aelfric celebrating Mass. Then the monks gathered in the chapter house to confess their sins, hear the abbot read a chapter from *The Rule of St Benedict*, and be given their instructions for the day. For most of them at this time of year, these consisted of going to the fields surrounding the abbey walls and scything wheat and barley. But Cuthwulf was one of the abbey's healers, a very deliberate choice of vocation on his part. He could think of nothing more fitting than healing people after years of hurting them. So, after the chapter meeting, he made his way as he always did to the lay infirmary, where sick people from the town were cared for. Abbot Aelfric had assigned him there rather than the monks' infirmary because of his prior secular experience and good relationship with the townspeople. It meant that Cuthwulf was one of the few monks permitted to travel beyond the confines of the abbey to tend to those too ill to come to its doors, which he always did with great eagerness. Though his commitment to the cloister was unwavering, he couldn't help but miss some of the freedoms he enjoyed before entering it.

The lay infirmary was a large hall with a high timber ceiling, beds lining the two longest walls, and a central fireplace. As Cuthwulf entered, he could feel the heat from the flames, see the smoke billowing towards the rafters and dissipating through the louvres. He saw that several new patients had come to the abbey early that morning. One of them was Ulric the stonecutter, who Cuthwulf knew well. He attended him first.

"Same trouble, Ulric?" said Cuthwulf.

The stonecutter nodded sadly. "Yes. It is getting harder to do my work. Some days I can barely move. It was a struggle to get here this morning. My legs are so sore." Ulric had been having problems with his joints for some time now.

"I would have come to you, Ulric. You should have sent for me."

"I did not want to cause any bother."

Cuthwulf sighed. "It is not bother. It is what I am here for." He glanced at his novice. "Brother Rhys here will rub monkshood oil into your joints and have you drink a willow bark concoction I prepared yesterday. It is a different mixture to the one I gave you last time." He nodded to Brother Rhys, who went to fetch the monkshood oil and willow bark remedy from the infirmary cupboard.

"Thank you, Brother Cuthwulf." Ulric gave a pained smile.

"And next time, send for me. Understood?"

Ulric nodded.

As Cuthwulf moved on to the next patient, the infirmary door opened and a man entered. He was in a long, black habit and Cuthwulf presumed him to be a fellow brother. However, his hood was up and hung low over his brow, so that the light in the room barely touched his eyes, and his habit was somewhat different to everyone else's. What Cuthwulf could see of his face he didn't recognise.

"Brother Cuthwulf?" said the man, looking at him.

Cuthwulf frowned. "Yes. Who are you?"

"You must come with me."

"Come where?"

"Away from –"

The Hooded Man's gaze jerked to one of the beds behind Cuthwulf. Cuthwulf heard movement from the bed and turned around to see that one of the new patients had risen from it and stood facing him. She had a young, well-cared-for face and wore an ankle-length, pale blue tunic, fastened at the waist with a girdle, and a white headscarf that was draped over her shoulders. Her arm was outstretched towards him and a strange silver object was in her hand.

Cuthwulf glanced back at the Hooded Man, who was

clasping a similar-looking object and pointing it at the woman.

"Brother Cuthwulf, leave the infirmary," he said. "Quickly."

"I will not! Who *are* you?" He looked at the woman. "And who are *you?*"

The Hooded Man's eyes were fixed on the woman, as hers were on him. "Cuthwulf, it is for your own safety. This woman wants to kill you."

"What?" His stomach turned with dread. "Why?"

"Cuthwulf, please just do as I – no, *stop!"*

Cuthwulf looked back at the woman and saw Brother Rhys leap at her from behind, the two of them tumbling forwards onto the stone floor. In that moment, a surge of light – as bright and dazzling as a flash of lightning yet with an unusual green hue – erupted from the tip of the silver object in the woman's hand and streaked across the room with a shrill hiss, making the Hooded Man duck. The surge of light struck one of the infirmary's windows, shattering it.

Swallowing hard, Cuthwulf backed away from this incredible display of power.

The woman and Brother Rhys grappled on the floor. Cuthwulf understood Brother Rhys's desire to protect his mentor, but his heroism in the face of such a potent enemy was reckless and going to get him killed.

The Hooded Man straightened and re-pointed what was likely a similar weapon to the woman's, then another green burst of light knifed through the air, just missing him as it blazed into the wall with a crack, scattering dust and stone chips. The Hooded Man dived for cover behind one of the beds, the patient lying in it apparently sleeping soundly through this utter mayhem.

The woman turned on the floor and kicked Brother Rhys square in the jaw, sending him hurtling backwards and crashing into a table topped with cups, pots, jugs and vials. The table was overturned, receptables emptying herbs and medicines all over the floor.

Now the woman was looking at Cuthwulf with a piercing glare. She got to her feet and raised her weapon.

Cuthwulf closed his eyes and held his breath. His heart raced. Sweat collected around his neck.

"Cuthwulf, get down!"

Cuthwulf opened his eyes as the Hooded Man peeked quickly over the top of the bed that was shielding him and fired a beam of green light in the woman's direction. Cuthwulf didn't see if the beam had hit her because he'd plunged to his knees as per the Hooded Man's instruction and crawled behind the bed that belonged to Ulric. Ulric, too, was out of bed and crouched down on the floor.

"What is this madness, Cuthwulf?" Ulric said, pale as a corpse and breathing quickly.

Cuthwulf shook his head. "I wish I knew."

Suddenly the room was doused in dazzling white light and Cuthwulf was blind. He felt a bite of panic that he'd lost his sight forever, then the infirmary started slowly coming back into view. *Thank the Lord.*

"W-what was that?" said Ulric.

Cuthwulf just shook his head.

The Hooded Man came and stood over them. "It's all right. We're safe now. She's gone."

Cuthwulf stood, clutching his chest and trying to steady his breaths. "Gone where?"

"That's difficult to explain."

Cuthwulf looked around the room. Brother Rhys had climbed to his feet and was tending to a cut on his face. The patients all looked frightened out of their wits, apart from the man who was still sound asleep. Cuthwulf feared that the Lord had gathered him up to Heaven, then caught the gentle rise and fall of his large belly with relief.

Cuthwulf looked at the Hooded Man. "Who are you?"

"Someone who's trying to protect the normal course of events."

What kind of riddle is that? "Who was she?"

"Someone who's trying to do the opposite. We call her the Unraveller."

"*We?*"

"The people I represent."

"And who are they?"

"It doesn't matter, you wouldn't understand. What I do need you to understand is that it is vitally important that you proceed with your day as if none of this ever happened."

"How on earth can I do that?"

"Because you're about to make an important discovery. You can't let this incident interfere with that."

"Discovery? What discovery? How could you know that?"

"Let's just say I… I see the future."

Cuthwulf shook his head in disbelief. "Are you saying you are a prophet of the Lord?"

"Not exactly. I can't say anymore. Just know that the future depends on this discovery."

"But I… I can't just forget what's happened here." Cuthwulf looked around at his horror-stricken patients, his injured colleague, the damaged wall, the broken window, the overturned table, smashed vials and spilled medicines. Turning back to the Hooded Man, "How can you possibly expect me to –"

The Hooded Man was gone, the rest of Cuthwulf's sentence along with him. Cuthwulf heard footsteps up the corridor from the infirmary and ran for the door. "Wait! I have so many questions!"

The corridor was empty. It seemed his questions would go unanswered.

A moment later, Brother Mark – another of the abbey's healers – appeared from around a corner. He was holding a sack of mayweed, one of the nine sacred herbs, which he'd gone to the abbey's herb and vegetable gardens to fill.

"Brother Cuthwulf, I thought I heard a commotion," he said. "Has something happened?"

Cuthwulf sighed. *You could say that.*

The next few hours in the lay infirmary were spent calming down and comforting the patients and cleaning up the mess left by the Hooded Man and the 'Unraveller'. This was broken up by dinner in the refectory and further Divine Offices, during which Cuthwulf struggled to put the frightening encounter out of his mind.

Once his duties were complete, Cuthwulf returned to the library to resume reading Poletricus while there was still daylight. After all, the Hooded Man – whoever he was – had told him in no uncertain terms to continue with his day as normal, and returning to the library was exactly what he had intended to do before the infirmary incident.

When he arrived, he wondered if through reading Poletricus he would make the 'important discovery' the Hooded Man had spoken of. He wasn't sure how else he could make any kind of discovery here. Very little happened at Glastonbury. For all the monks, each day proceeded exactly like the last. The ruckus in the infirmary was more action in a few minutes than this abbey had likely seen in a century.

Cuthwulf sat by a window that looked out at the abbey church. The sun had dipped behind the bell tower, the clear sky just starting to darken. There was sufficient light for Cuthwulf to at least finish reading Poletricus's story of St Joseph of Arimathea.

What? Joseph of Arimathea came to Britain? He'd never heard this story before.

Reading on, Cuthwulf found himself gasping aloud and catching disapproving looks from brothers also seizing an hour's study in the last of the light.

This was it. The discovery. And what a discovery it was.

He closed the old book, swept out of the library and took a brisk walk to the chapter house. Heartbeat quickening fast, he entered, strode past the empty pine benches to the rear of the house and rapped his knuckles against the door of Abbot Aelfric's adjoining private chamber.

"Enter," said the abbot in those coarse, ageing tones of his.

Aelfric was at his study table, hunched over his Bible. He looked up as Cuthwulf came in.

"Ah, Brother Cuthwulf," said Aelfric, smiling. "How are you? I understand there was some trouble in the lay infirmary, although the reports I've heard are somewhat confused."

He had no doubt. Cuthwulf wasn't certain himself what had happened.

"Everything is in order." Now wasn't the time to try and explain the incident. Besides, something much more pressing had arisen. "Father, I must speak with you."

"Of course. What is it?"

Cuthwulf swallowed. "I have learned something remarkable about our great abbey."

"Oh?"

Cuthwulf opened the Poletricus codex to the pages on Joseph of Arimathea. "As we both know, King Arthur and the Knights of the Round Table came to Glastonbury in the 6th century in search of the Holy Grail."

The abbot frowned. "Yes. But he never found it. The Grail wasn't here."

Cuthwulf shook his head. "No, Father. He did not find it because he did not know where to look."

Aelfric's eyes widened. "What are you saying?"

Cuthwulf glanced at the book. "I have been studying Poletricus, a Christian author who was unknown to us until his writings were discovered in Devonshire last year. He recounts a story of St Joseph of Arimathea fleeing Palestine and coming to Britain to spread the word of Christ. Poletricus says that Joseph brought the Holy Grail with him."

"Joseph of Arimathea had possession of the Holy Grail?"

"According to Poletricus, yes. Poletricus says that

Joseph came to Glastonbury, settled here, and founded the first church in Britain. He also says that he buried the Grail in the grounds of the church, at the foot of a yew tree worshipped at the time by the Celts. As you know, Father, the yew tree that stands in the cloisters quadrangle is considered to be over a thousand years old. I believe it is the very same tree."

"You are saying you think the Grail is here? Buried beneath that tree? Beneath our abbey?"

"Yes. I believe it has been here the whole time. Like I said, King Arthur didn't have this information when he came here. No one did – until now."

Aelfric sat down, his old face pale with shock at this incredible revelation. Neither man spoke for a minute or so. The abbot was deep in thought.

Finally Aelfric spoke. "We must find out if this is true. If the Grail is indeed buried here, it could change everything."

"Yes, Father."

"I want you to dig beneath the yew tree in the quadrangle. Enlist some of the novices to help you. Under no circumstances are you to tell them you are looking for the Grail. No one is to know until there is something to know."

"What should I tell them instead?"

"Tell them…" Aelfric, frowning, paused for a moment to think. "Tell them you are looking for the relics of a former abbot believed to have been buried there."

Cuthwulf nodded. "Very good, Father."

The bell rang for Vespers, the Evening Prayer. There were but minutes of daylight left.

"When should we start?" said Cuthwulf.

"After Vespers, find trusted and discreet novices to assist you and gather shovels from the storehouse in the vegetable gardens. After Compline, when the rest of your brethren have gone to the dormitory, go with the novices to the quadrangle. Take enough torches so you can see what you are doing."

"Would it not be best to wait till sunrise?"

"When every brother in the abbey is up and about and watching from the cloisters?"

A fair point.

"This must happen tonight. We must know if the Holy Grail is here. I will remain here after Compline until you bring me news."

"Yes, Father."

Cuthwulf gave a reverent bow, turned and left the abbot's chamber. As the congregation reconvened in the abbey church for Vespers, Cuthwulf found himself struggling to keep his mind focused on the prayers and chants, excitement and anticipation of the copious possibilities keeping his faculties thoroughly preoccupied.

Was he really about to succeed where King Arthur had failed?

18

April 17th 2027

Lester was in her kitchen cooking up one of her random concoctions like they did on *Ready Steady Cook*. She wasn't one to follow a recipe; she preferred raiding the cupboards and the fridge for things that might work well thrown together. Didn't always work, but she and Brody had discovered some tasty original dishes through her experimentation.

And cooking was cheap therapy. It soothed her. Something she was often in need of these days.

Brody had left her to it. Their arrangement was that he would cook during the week, because she got home later than him, and she would cook at weekends. They'd never cook together though. Brody was a strict recipe follower and didn't know how to improvise, so Lester's *just chuck it in* approach drove him slightly mad. Also, Brody was a cook who tidied as he went, whereas she would lay waste to the kitchen like a grizzly bear.

She didn't hear her phone buzz because she had Fleetwood Mac classics blaring from the kitchen speakers. After adding chunks of halloumi to a wok of steak, bacon and butternut squash, frying in a mishmash of herbs and spices, she went to check it. She'd missed a call from Ethan ten minutes ago, and had a text from him. I'm back in the BR. Weren't you supposed to have sent me the excavation plan for Torbury Farm?

She knew he'd be on her back for that. She was

supposed to have finished it this week, but her investigations had caused her to fall behind on a number of projects she was managing. She had actually set aside yesterday afternoon for Torbury, but then Beth Ferro agreed to meet her and Lester took off early to head to Coventry. Shame it had been a total waste of time. She still didn't understand why Beth wasn't at least *a bit* suspicious over what happened to her husband. Lester would be, were their roles reversed.

Anyway, Lester would just get the excavation plan to Ethan on Monday. He'd be pissed at her for making him wait, but he was pissed at everyone and everything right now. Had been since the Home Office took the Tower Hamlets dinosaur off LIPA's hands. Every time Lester spoke to him, he was ranting and raving about a government conspiracy.

The funny thing was, Ethan was bang on. There *was* a government conspiracy, and Million Eyes were at the centre of it.

Lester decided she would reply to Ethan later. She placed the phone on the table and circled back towards the hob. Passing the French doors to the garden, she froze, and her heart gave a flutter.

Georgia was standing next to the stacked pots water feature she just loved to stick her hands in, staring through the glass at her mother. The early evening sun made her ginger hair gleam gold and the rainbow sequins on her dungarees glitter.

Lester felt a strangling heat in her throat. Pain squeezed her middle. She shook her head, blinked hard. Georgia was still there. Smiling now, and turning towards the fountain, and putting her hand under the water pouring from the highest pot.

Lester unlocked the door and opened it. The hissing of the wok made her turn her head. When her eyes were back on the garden, Georgia was gone again.

Sighing, Lester pulled the door shut and locked it. That was the sixth time now, the last time only yesterday.

Georgia's visits were becoming more frequent. But they were always so painfully short. It was like Lester was being teased. Offered a lick of the ice cream, never the whole cone.

Lester waited, eyes on the water feature, wishing Georgia would come back. This was probably the reason she hadn't talked to anyone about her visions yet. She didn't want them to stop.

She felt herself welling up. *Please come back. Just so I can look at you for a bit longer.*

The wok hissed and spat. Now the smell of burning was permeating. Lester fought back her emotions and returned to the hob.

Brody came into the kitchen. "You alright in here?" he said loudly over the music, probably having smelled the burning.

"Yeah, yeah, I'm good. Nearly ready." She removed a couple of burnt chunks of halloumi, the odd black sliver of bacon. No real harm done.

Brody lingered in the kitchen as she finished preparing. There was something on his mind.

"Sean, reduce volume by forty percent," Lester said to the MEye, and the music lowered, creating a gentler ambience for dinner. "You okay?" She poured them both a glass of Châteauneuf-du-Pape, Brody's favourite wine, and lit the candles.

"Where were you last night, Sam?"

"I already told you. I went for drinks with Sheryl."

"Yeah. I know you told me that. And it's been bothering me all day. Because I texted Sheryl last night and she said you left work early to go somewhere, and didn't say where."

Damn. She should've thought this through a bit more. Although she wasn't really expecting Brody to text her work colleague to check where she was. He'd never done that before.

"Since when are you checking up on me?"

"Since we stopped behaving like a husband and wife."

Ouch. A part of Lester understood what he meant. That they weren't seeing or talking to each other much. That they weren't going places together. That they weren't having sex.

But another part of her was angry. Lester thought marriage was supposed to be about good times and bad, for better *and* for worse. This was a bad time and this was arguably how a husband and wife *should* behave after they've lost their child. They were grieving, for God's sake. That wasn't to say their marriage didn't mean everything it always did and that she should lose his trust.

Trying to contain her indignation, "We *are* still husband and wife. Things might not have been easy lately but you can't expect them to be, Brody. Surely I've earned your trust after ten years of marriage."

Brody arched his eyebrow. "Sam, I've literally just caught you in a lie. You can't talk to me about trust right now."

He had a point. She *had* lied to him about where she went. And lying and secrets weren't how a husband and wife should behave either. She knew that. And she knew she'd be mad, and probably saying the same things, had Brody lied to her.

That said, she still couldn't tell him about Million Eyes. Not yet. Not till she had something concrete. Part of it was because Brody would think her crazy. Part of it was that she needed to protect him. From them.

She was going to have to substitute one lie for another. "Okay. I'm sorry. It was work. I had to go do a last-minute site visit. It's a sensitive project and I'm not allowed to talk to anyone about it. I shouldn't even be telling you this much."

"I thought the Tower Hamlets dinosaur was taken off your hands?"

"It was. This was something else."

"What?"

"I just said, I can't talk about it."

"Christ, Sam. You're an archaeologist, not a spy."

She felt a bit like a spy at the minute.

"I know. This one's just... sensitive. I'm sorry. I'm certainly not cheating on you, if that's what you think."

Brody sighed and sipped his wine. "I don't know what to think, to be honest." Quieter, "I just feel like I'm losing you."

She took the wok off the heat and switched off the hob. She walked right up to him, holding it out to the side, and looked him in the eyes. "You're not. I'm right here."

He shook his head sadly. "You're not, though. I miss you."

She walked over to the table, pouring half the mixture from the wok onto her plate, half onto Brody's. "Look. Let's just have a nice meal and watch something on MEss together. Yeah?"

Lester felt a brush of unease when she said 'MEss'. MEss was the 'Million Eyes streaming service'. It included everything from TV series and films to music, podcasts and books. Years ago, there were many competing streaming services: Netflix, Disney+, Spotify, Readeze, Streamboat. Then Million Eyes systematically hoovered them all up, like it had done with a lot of things. That's why there was now so much Million Eyes technology in their home: MEcs, METVs, MEphones, a MEye, a MEboard. She still had a non-driverless Ford Freeze, but Brody had a MEcar, and it was looking likely that Lester would feel browbeaten into getting a MEcar soon, too. There was talk of the law changing so that only autonomous vehicles – which had proven many, many times safer than human-driven ones – would be allowed on the roads. And while there were a couple of other driverless brands, Million Eyes monopolised the market.

Lester felt deeply uncomfortable relying on this much Million Eyes technology given what she knew about them. The problem was, there was no getting away from it. Million Eyes were everywhere. Literally. It made her wonder if she and Adam had a hope in hell of putting even the slightest dent in the all-powerful Million Eyes machine.

She placed the wok in the sink and she and Brody sat down to eat.

Brody frowned as he ate a piece of steak. "What is that I can taste?"

"Cocoa. Found some at the back of the cupboard and thought, why not?"

He smiled. "Weirdly enough, that works."

She smiled back. "It does, doesn't it?" It was delicious, actually. Hopefully she could replicate it, although she couldn't remember everything that was in it now.

"So I was thinking we could go out tomorrow," Brody said. "It's going to be sunny. I thought we could go to Shorne Woods."

They used to go there all the time with Georgia. Lester shook her head, "No." Then, keen to avoid an awkward moment, "Let's go to the beach instead. We haven't done that in ages."

Brody flashed a muted smile. "Sure." A moment later, she caught him smirking at her. "You've got sauce on your chin."

Lester went to grab a napkin. Brody's hand was over hers. "Let me." He picked up the napkin, stood and went to her side of the table. He took her chin in his hand and used the other to wipe off the sauce, looking deep into her eyes as he did so.

He's going to kiss me. For a moment she wasn't sure if she wanted him to. But when he leaned in and their lips met, she knew that, actually, she did.

She fell into the kiss, then a sudden passion seemed to surge through both of them. She wrapped her arms around his back and squeezed, while his were around her shoulders, holding her, leaning her back slightly as he lost himself in her mouth. She felt a slow, tingling heat rise inside her, a heat she'd not felt in months.

Brody pulled her out of her chair, cupping and kneading her breasts, moving his lips to her neck, sucking gently on her skin, before returning to her mouth. They moved as one towards the kitchen island, at which point Brody turned her round, kissed the side and back of her neck, and bent her over the counter. She felt him lift up her dress and pull down her knickers.

But then the heat in her went cold. The tingling ebbed away, the excitement with it. Something about this was wrong. She didn't know what – or why – but it didn't feel right. She shouldn't be feeling this good right now. Her daughter was dead. She was in mourning.

Georgia was dead. *Dead.*

"Stop."

Brody was frantically undoing his jeans. "What?"

Lester straightened and turned to face him, shaking her head. "I'm sorry. I'm just… I'm just not ready."

It was like she'd just blown out the flames in Brody's eyes. His face and shoulders sank with disappointment, and he sighed, rebuttoning his jeans. She bent down for her knickers.

Brody looked so sad, so lost. She put her hands on his shoulders and looked into his eyes. "I'm sorry. I really am." She hated being the cause of his pain, but until she'd got a handle on her own, she didn't know what else to do. Or say.

"Are we ever going to have sex again?"

"Of course we will." She just hoped she'd want to again. Although, she *had* wanted to for a moment there; her guilt just overcame it. And yesterday she'd had that flutter when she met Beth Ferro's attractive husband. Her libido wasn't gone. It was just buried under a ton of crap.

Brody gave a shallow smile and pulled away. He sat back at the table to finish eating.

"I'll be back in a moment." Lester left the kitchen to use the downstairs toilet. On her way back, she checked her Uzu burner phone in her handbag, which was in the hallway. She was surprised to find she had a text message from Gavin, the detective friend she had asked to look into Gregory Ferro's death. I've found something. Let's talk. I'm free tonight if you are.

She wasn't. But damn, he'd found something. How could she resist finding out what it was?

She couldn't. Simple as that.

Returning to the kitchen, Lester pretended she'd had a message on her normal Samsung Galaxy. "Babe, I'm… I'm so sorry. I have to go."

Brody's expression was a mix of hurt and anger. "What? Go where?"

"It's to do with that secret work project. I'm sorry. I can't tell you any more than that."

"I thought this was supposed to be our romantic evening together."

"I know. I'll make it up to you."

Brody shook his head and snorted a laugh. "Yeah. Sure you will."

He was mad. She couldn't blame him. But she had no time for that right now. She had to know what Gavin had found.

She grabbed her coat and handbag, dashed out of the house and got in her car. Fortunately she'd barely touched her wine.

"Evening, Detective," said Lester as Gavin opened his front door. She always called him that.

Gavin reciprocated her mock formality with a respectful nod, "Evening, Dr Lester." He motioned for her to come inside.

Lester slipped off her shoes and followed Gavin into the kitchen. "Coffee?" he offered.

She raised an eyebrow. "How long have you known me? Tea, please."

"Sorry, it's my age."

"Git. You're younger than me."

"Yeah, but you wear it better." He faced his feet to

show her his scalp. "Look at all these greys."

"Trust me. I'd be much greyer than that were it not for this miraculous thing called hair dye."

He grinned. "Remind me how you have it."

"White, strong, one sweetener, please." She sat down on one of the bar stools lining Gavin's kitchen island.

He boiled the kettle. "How are you and Brody doing?"

She knew he was asking about losing Georgia. And while she ought to talk to him about it – he was a good friend – she just couldn't. It's why she'd stopped going to her counsellor. She couldn't talk to anyone about it anymore.

"We're fine." Her next words caught in her throat and she had to push to get them out. "How are you and Laurie? Everything go okay with the latest scan?"

Laurie was pregnant. Lester was only asking out of politeness, which was horrible and selfish but she couldn't help it. Talking about children only reminded her that she'd lost one. It also made her think about the fact that she and Brody should try again and have another – while her biological clock still had battery life – but, of course, that was the last thing she wanted to be thinking about. It made her feel guilty and sick. *Try again.* As if Georgia had been a failure. *Have another.* To replace her? There was no replacing that beautiful little girl. None.

Lester could feel herself getting worked up. She drove her feelings back – she was getting quite good at that.

Fortunately, Gavin kept his answer as brief as he could. "Yes. All good, thanks." The guy was emotionally intelligent enough to know that Laurie's pregnancy was not something she would want to dwell on.

"So, what have you found?" she said as Gavin handed her a mug of tea the colour of rust.

Gavin picked up an old Uzu tablet that was by the microwave and sat next to her at the kitchen island. He was the one who'd sourced the burners and tablets that she and Adam had been using.

"Okay. So I've been looking into Gregory Ferro's death like you asked. I've gone through all the evidence in the case file, but I can't find anything to indicate arson or murder. Ferro's body was burned to a crisp, making it impossible for forensics to determine the cause of death. The police theory is that the fire started upstairs in Ferro's study and that his computer, a really old Toshiba model, short-circuited and ignited. Ferro's body was found downstairs in the lounge. It's a mystery as to why he didn't make it out. He may have fallen asleep and by the time he woke up it was too late. There's also the possibility that he collapsed due to some sort of illness."

Lester sipped her tea. "Or because he was assaulted."

"It's possible. There's just no evidence that he was. However, I looked into this phone call you said was made to Ferro shortly before his death. The case file had a call log for that night. Interestingly, one of the calls has been redacted from the record."

Her eyes widened. Now they were getting somewhere. Gavin tapped the Uzu to open the document and placed the device on the counter, pointing to a line of text that had been obscured with a black bar. It was the call just before the one he made to Jennifer Larson that had been deleted.

"Can it be unredacted?"

"'Fraid not. I know it looks like the data's still there, hidden under that black bar, but it isn't. Digital redaction means removing the data completely from the document. The only way of finding out what was deleted is by getting hold of the original, unredacted log, which, naturally, wasn't in the Ferro case file."

Lester's shoulders sank, then she realised Gavin wasn't finished. "After ages searching, I found the original log in a secure folder. I was able to open the folder using my clearance code, but the log itself was encrypted." He brought up the encrypted file on the screen.

Lester nodded. "So now what?"

"Unfortunately that's as far as my technical skills go.

I'm no codebreaker. This is where your guy at Million Eyes comes in."

Lester fished a flash drive from her handbag and handed it to Gavin so that he could download both the redacted and encrypted logs onto it.

Gavin said, giving it back to her, "You know I'm only giving this to you because you said that Million Eyes had compromised the police, and because I trust you. I'm breaking every rule in the book right now."

"I know."

"Just make sure you keep me in the loop."

"I will, I promise."

Lester finished her tea and left Gavin's shortly after. When she got in the car, she called Adam on her Uzu burner.

"Adam, I have something. Can we meet tomorrow morning?"

19

April 18th 2027

Adam had spent much of Sunday trying to decrypt the call log Dr Lester had given him during their very brief meeting in a park in Barking that morning. The log had been encrypted using a remodulating mutation code, which meant someone *really* didn't want people reading it.

He'd fed Izzy a cover story, told her that he went to see his dad. He'd also had to explain why he had an Uzu computer, on which he was running his decryption program. It was the one Lester had given him at their first meeting, whose IP address was hidden behind a multi-layer VPN. He'd told Izzy that the Uzu was Dad's and that he was extricating a bunch of viruses in order to recover some old files for him. Izzy had bought the lie. She actually had a load of work to do herself, so was quite happy to leave him to it.

While he unpicked the various programming sequences that made up the mutation code, Adam's mind kept wandering to Curtis. He hadn't heard from him since he started his new role two weeks ago, despite messaging him a couple of times now to see how it was going. Normally they would go for lunch or an after-work drink at least a couple of times a week when they'd worked together, which Adam wasn't expecting to stop just because Curtis had moved one floor up. Apparently it had.

Could I have done something? Said something? It was unlikely; Curtis wasn't the easily offended type. Maybe he just wasn't interested anymore. Maybe their friendship meant more to Adam than it did to Curtis.

Adam scolded himself for overthinking. It was a new role with bigger responsibilities. He could just have been too busy – or stressed – to message Adam back. But he would, when he got a moment.

Later that afternoon, Adam finally finished decrypting the call log on the Uzu.

There it was. The name and phone number for a 'Stuart Rayburn'. He was the whistleblower who had spilled the beans to Gregory Ferro and probably cost Ferro his life. It seemed that Rayburn himself hadn't wanted anyone knowing who he was either. The number had a blocking code in front of it – although he must've known that such codes weren't capable of hiding a person's caller ID from the police. Perhaps, at the time, that didn't matter.

Adam tried calling the number but got a *number not recognised* message. He googled Rayburn and began trawling through the thousands of search results, eventually landing on an old news article from October 2019 about a Hertfordshire man who'd been reported missing. Could that be him?

He returned to the call log. His decryption program had exposed the file attributes, which meant Adam was able to isolate the ID number of the person who had encrypted the log. If it was someone inside Million Eyes, he could find out who by running a search on the Million Eyes intranet.

Adam's pulse quickened as he fired up his MEc. He was about to find out if Million Eyes really did harbour the sorts of nefarious secrets the conspiracy theorists accused them of.

He ran a search.

Holy fuck.

The ID number belonged to Pete Navarro, head of Information Security.

Adam took a moment to process what he'd found. Then he phoned Lester on his burner. "I have the whistleblower's name. Stuart Rayburn."

"Brilliant," said Lester. "Have you ever heard of him?"

"No. We've certainly never crossed paths while I've been here. I tried calling his number, it's no longer in use. So I googled him. A Stuart Rayburn did go missing in October 2019. Might be the same one."

"Okay. So the next step is to find him, or at least find out what happened to him."

"I've also managed to find out who it was who encrypted the call log. It was the head of Information Security at Million Eyes, Pete Navarro."

"Which proves everything in Jennifer's letters."

'Everything' was a stretch. But it certainly proved that they were involved in Ferro's death somehow, and hiding something about this Stuart Rayburn chap.

"Can you access this Pete Navarro's computer?" Lester asked. "Find out what he knows about Rayburn?"

Adam sighed. "It's not as easy as they make it look on TV. And like I said to you when we met, it's Million Eyes. They have the best cybersecurity in the world."

"But it's not impossible…"

"No. But I really don't think –"

"Just do what you can. I'm sorry. I have to go. Let me know what you find."

Lester hung up.

For fuck's sake. Getting access to Navarro's system was a tall order. Million Eyes used multi-factor biometric authentication for everything. Fooling or hacking it was incredibly difficult and way beyond Adam.

But then, perhaps he didn't need to. He thought about the possibility of a Trojan horse – programs designed to trick users into running them, typically acting as a backdoor into their systems, covertly bypassing normal authentication. They worked because, in effect, the user was inviting the hacker in. Years ago, as a prank, Adam built a Trojan horse disguised as a video game and got his friend, Malcolm, to download it. This gave Adam remote access to Malcolm's computer and enabled him to download porn onto his desktop, open and close his CD tray, play *Baby Shark* on repeat – that sort of thing.

These days, most Trojan horse programs were capable of being detected and blocked by antivirus software. But Adam had heard of ways of producing masked Trojans capable of temporarily fooling antivirus programs. They weren't easy to make, though, and carried a big risk of simply not working. And the key word was 'temporarily'. No Trojan could remain undetectable for long. He'd need to do some serious research if he was going to find a way of getting past the antivirus software that guarded Million Eyes, and into Navarro's system for long enough to find something useful.

The fact that Adam was an employee meant he could circumvent at least some of the layers of security protocols. Even better, now that he'd obtained Navarro's ID number from the file attributes of the call log, he could in theory apply an innocuous update to MEteams, the Million Eyes conferencing app, targeted solely at Navarro's system. If he were to embed a masked Trojan code in the update, when Navarro downloaded it, he'd download the Trojan with it, giving Adam his way in.

Right now he couldn't think of any other way to do it, short of physically going to Information Security, sneaking into Navarro's office and jumping on his already-logged-in MEc when he was in the bog or something. And that would be dangerous as fuck.

No. This was the only way. So Adam spent the rest of the day writing a Trojan horse program that would unlock Pete Navarro's secrets.

The next morning, Adam was in the office waiting for the right moment to deploy his Trojan horse. He'd masked the Trojan with a *tenebris numerus* algorithm that he'd sourced over the dark web from some guy claiming to be a programmer for America's National Security Agency, and embedded the code in an update to Navarro's MEteams. As soon as he applied the update, Navarro would get a notification asking him to download it. Once he had, Adam would have direct access to his system and be able to search for information without interfering with anything Navarro might be doing at the time.

But the Trojan would only be undetectable for sixty seconds before Million Eyes' antivirus software found it and all kinds of security alerts started flashing up on Navarro's screen. Alerts that would lead straight back to Adam. It wasn't long at all, but it was all Adam had been able to do to get past Million Eyes' ultra-resilient security perimeter.

He had to be in and out. Fast.

At just gone 11am, the opportune moment came. It was unlikely he was going to be tasked with anything in the next few minutes; the office was quiet and his line manager and several others were outside having a fag, which usually lasted ten minutes or so. *God, I could do with one of those right now. Damn Izzy for making me quit.*

Of course, once he had applied the update, he'd then have to wait for Navarro to download it. He'd probably do it straight away, but what if he was away from his desk?

Adam clicked 'apply'.

His whole body tightened when, ten seconds later, he got a notification saying the Trojan program was active. Navarro had downloaded the update. Adam was in. A little icon appeared in the corner of his screen, with a timer that was counting down. He had a minute to find out all he could before he was detected.

"Listen up, everyone."

Adam looked up with a start. MEps manager Peter Elba had emerged from his office into the communal workspace. Everyone quietened down to listen to him.

"We need to run a level-three diagnostic of the OV sockets," said Elba, "so I need everyone to log out."

Panic streaked through Adam. His shirt collar felt hot and tight, like his neck was swelling, his top button threatening to pop off.

He couldn't stop working. The Trojan was active. Navarro was going to detect him in less than a minute.

He swallowed hard and carried on. He opened Navarro's internal emails and ran a search for 'Stuart Rayburn'. In the corner of his eye, he saw Peter Elba turn and walk back into his office and hoped to God he had enough time.

His jaw clenched when his search brought up a conversation between Navarro and Miss Morgan in October 2019. He opened the conversation, eyes flitting over the words.

Forty-two seconds left. *Fuck fuck fuck.*

Reading faster than he'd ever read before, his brain took in bits of the conversation.

We need to apprehend him quickly.

Scans indicate Rayburn breached the X9 Server.

Haven't found him yet, ma'am.

The police mustn't know he called Gregory Ferro.

I'll make sure Stuart Rayburn's name and number are redacted from the police call log.

Adam swallowed. His hands shook. Thirty-one seconds left.

Peter Elba came out of his office and looked directly at him. "Mr Bryant, your MEc is blocking the diagnostic. Why haven't you logged out?"

Think fast.

"I'm sorry, sir. I was just recalibr –"

"I don't care, Mr Bryant." Elba's voice rose. "Log out now."

Shit. Fuck. Balls.

He couldn't log out. Not yet.

He opened Navarro's intranet. As a head of department, he had access to the personnel database, so Adam clicked through, typed *Stuart Rayburn* into the search bar and hit 'search'.

Elba addressed someone speaking to him through his earpiece. "Has he logged out?"

Shit.

Now Elba was coming this way. And looked furious. Adam couldn't let him see his screen.

The search was being slow. Too slow.

Fourteen seconds left.

Adam squeezed his fists, his fingernails cutting into his palms, his collar chafing against his neck.

Come on come on come on.

The search completed and Rayburn's personnel file flashed up on screen.

Elba continued marching towards him, face crimson and contorted with anger. He was moments away from seeing everything.

Heart thumping, Adam used a keyboard shortcut to copy the file to his flash drive. Fingers tapping faster than his brain, he closed the intranet browser.

With three seconds to go, he hit a button on the little icon with the timer, killing the Trojan just as Elba was over his shoulder.

"Why the fuck haven't you logged out?"

"I'm sorry, sir. I was recalibrating the NME. I didn't think I should interrupt it."

"What? An NME recalibration won't be affected by a logout. I thought you were fucking smart!"

Adam felt the blood rushing to his cheeks. He shook his head with pretend realisation. "Yes. Yes, of course, sir. I'm so sorry. I'm not with it today. Didn't get much sleep last night." Not a lie. He'd been writing his Trojan till 2am. "It won't happen again."

"No, it fucking won't." Elba had one hell of a temper. This was the first time Adam had been on the receiving end of it. "When I tell you to do something, I expect you to do fucking do it. Clear?" He was so angry a couple of droplets of spit sprayed from his lips and landed on Adam's desk, about an inch from his hand.

"Y-yes, sir."

"Now log the fuck out."

Heart still racing, Adam logged out, Elba's piercing eyes impaling him through the side of the head as he did so.

"Thank you!" Elba turned and stormed back to his office. Adam heard him mutter, "Twat," under his breath.

Adam leaned back in his chair and took a few deep breaths, staring at his screen while his heart slowed. *Fuck my life, that was close.* He could feel the eyes of some colleagues on him and knew he was probably as red as a beetroot right now.

Still, he had what he needed. He just hoped it had worked and he wouldn't get found out. His Trojan code was airtight – he didn't see how he could be. That being said, Million Eyes had capabilities far beyond what he could've imagined, so who knew?

Adam disconnected his flash drive and sneaked off to the toilets. Locking himself in a cubicle and plugging the drive into his burner, he took a moment to evaluate Stuart Rayburn's personnel file.

Rayburn was a systems analyst based at headquarters. His photograph looked like the one in that news article Adam found, about the Hertfordshire man who'd gone missing. His address was 42 Plunkett's Walk, Meath, Hertfordshire. Next of kin: Alison Rayburn, sister, same address. Although it didn't say why, Rayburn's contract of employment with Million Eyes ended in October 2019 – the same month Gregory Ferro was killed and Jennifer was attacked and ran away.

Adam texted Lester the salient points before tucking the phone back in his pocket and going for a desperately needed piss.

He decided now was a good time to pop upstairs to the MEow office and see Curtis. He'd been planning to at some point today and it was probably a good idea to stay out of Peter Elba's way for a little while. Curtis's silence having made him feel a tad paranoid, Adam just wanted to make sure he wasn't mad at him for something. He headed for the lift and went up to floor twelve.

He entered an office with a similar layout and look to his own. Lots of white, with dabs of deep red, same as the red of the diamond-shaped pupil in the Million Eyes eye logo, which was on the back of every MEc screen. There was a large open-plan space lined with clear glass desks and expensive, Italian-made chairs with red upholstered seats shaped like a petal, along with several private offices and corridors leading off to others. The floor, walls and ceiling were all plain white, apart from the one by the lift, which had a vertical garden tightly packed with verdant, leafy plants.

He couldn't see Curtis. He walked to the nearest desk and quietly asked the woman sitting at it, "Sorry to interrupt, could you tell me where Curtis O'Brien is, please?"

The woman blinked twice at him. "Er – bear with me." She stood up from her desk and walked into one of the private offices. A moment later, she and another woman, who Adam recognised as MEow manager Renee Lampard, emerged.

Lampard walked over to him. "Can I help you?"

A nervous flutter swam through Adam's stomach. "I – er – I was just wondering where Curtis O'Brien is."

Lampard gave him a blank look. "Did you need him?"

He couldn't say, 'yes, I need to find out why he's not speaking to me,' so instead said, "I just need to ask him a technical question, if I may." He tried to keep his voice steady but it cracked very slightly with embarrassment.

"I'm afraid Mr O'Brien is working on something at the Guildford office at the moment. Would you like me to pass on a message?"

Adam forged a smile. "No, that's fine. Thank you. Sorry to disturb you."

Lampard gave him a wide smile, a smile that felt as fake as the one he'd just given her.

He walked back to the lift. *Yeah. He's busy. He's just busy.*

20

September 19th 993

After Compline, the monks of Glastonbury Abbey took themselves to the dormitory to bed. Well, apart from Brother Cuthwulf and five novices, who quietly made their way to the cloisters quadrangle, crossing the freshly scythed lawn to the ancient yew tree in the centre, once believed to be the home of a Celtic goddess. One of the novices was carrying a collection of long- and short-handled shovels; the rest carried torches.

Cuthwulf instructed the novices to plant their torches in the ground in a rough circle around the tree. He chose a spot a couple of feet in front of the dark mass of tentacle-like roots and they began to dig.

Cuthwulf was beside himself with excitement. The others thought they were looking for an old coffin or a collection of bones. Only Cuthwulf knew that the real object of their search was the Holy Grail, the chalice Christ used during the Last Supper to consecrate the wine into his blood. It was said to possess divine powers capable of rejuvenating the body, healing serious injuries and bestowing happiness in infinite abundance, so, if it really was beneath this unassuming patch of ground, it could very well hold the key to freeing Cuthwulf from the guilt that saddled his soul. Not only that but he could use it to heal others, perhaps even raise the dead. *What if...* His limbs tingled with anticipation. *What if I could bring them back?* The hope was hot in his heart.

Their shovels dislodged a couple of large stones and struck numerous roots worming their way through the earth, but that was about it. Half an hour and a fairly substantial hole later, Cuthwulf bade them dig in a different spot.

Again they shifted nothing but soft, rich soil. But Cuthwulf wasn't giving up. If he had to, he'd uproot the entire yew tree.

Several roots straying from the rest were curled and arched in a way that resembled a gnarled old hand. The longest of the knobbly 'fingers' seemed to be pointing at a certain spot in the ground and Cuthwulf decided it was as a good a spot as any to try again.

Ten minutes later, their shovels hit something that wasn't stone or root, the distinct clang sounding more like metal. Cuthwulf threw down his long-handled shovel and picked up a short-handled one. He crouched down and told the novices to step back. The deep, earthy, fertile smell of the soil was in his nostrils as he eagerly dug around the object.

A grey, flat-topped chest began to emerge from the ground.

"Is that supposed to be a coffin?" said one of the novices. "It's tiny."

Cuthwulf instructed one of them to help pull the heavy chest from the ground. He scraped it clean with his shovel and examined it. It was definitely metal. It looked like lead that had tarnished to a dark grey and was scabbed with white corrosion. The novices were standing over him, waiting for him to open it.

Cuthwulf looked at them. "Your work here is done. Return to the dormitory and, as we discussed, tell no one of what we have done here."

"But Brother Cuthwulf," said another, "should we not take a look at what's inside?"

"*We* should do nothing, Brother Ealhstan. *I* will look upon the contents of the chest presently. Now do as I say and go back to the dormitory."

The brothers muttered indignations as they strode out of the quadrangle. When they were gone, Cuthwulf took a deep breath. A chest of lead was a chest built to last, and to protect its contents robustly. Was Cuthwulf about to lay his eyes upon the vessel that once held the blood of Christ the Lord?

Breath still held, Cuthwulf unhooked the latch of the chest. Closing his eyes, he lifted the lid.

He opened one eye, looked inside.

But that's not...

Both eyes sprang open, then instantly dipped in a frown. Cuthwulf lowered both hands inside the chest and lifted out a jar that was on its side, lid still in place. It was not a chalice or any other kind of cup.

This couldn't be the Holy Grail. Well, unless all prior descriptions of it had been erroneous.

The jar was tall, wide and made of clay. Cuthwulf tried to remove the lid. It was stuck in place with some kind of adhesive. He pulled harder on the knob of the lid, eventually breaking the seal and dislodging it. He peered inside and saw what looked like scrolls wrapped in cloth. He emptied them into the bottom of the chest for a closer look.

Four scrolls tumbled out. The cloth wrappings round each one were tied with leather tabs and thongs. Cuthwulf picked one up, loosened its ties and removed the cloth. The scroll looked long, old and brittle. He unfurled the parchment carefully to expose the first few pages of writings. It looked like the continuous roll comprised several pieces sewn together with hair or sinew.

The writings were in Aramaic, just like the Poletricus codex. Cuthwulf sat on the ground and began to read. There were references to John the Baptist, the Sea of Galilee, Jesus's apostles, Jerusalem. He opened the other scrolls in an effort to put together a complete story. It took what felt like an hour, sitting there beneath the yew tree, to read all the scrolls in their entirety.

His blood ran cold. *Can any of this be true?*

At the end of the scrolls, after the final entry, there was an addendum written in different handwriting. Cuthwulf read it, hoping it might allay his confusion…

This is the truth of Jesus the Prophet. When the ink was barely dry on his final words, a heinous conspiracy by Jesus's apostles saw him tried and crucified. I attempted to revive him but failed and saw fit to bury him.

Shortly after, my name and allegiance to Jesus was extracted by his betrayers from Judas Iscariot, the only apostle who had stayed true to Jesus to the last. In an instant, the lies about me spread.

With the Romans and the apostles hungering for my death, I fled Judaea with my family and a company of friends, and with these scrolls.

While the apostles continue to distort Jesus's teachings for their own ends, I have come to the Britannic Isles to pass on his true message: the Last War is coming and we can win it if we are ready.

I truly believe that Jesus the Prophet was sent by God to save His people on Earth. Jesus's death means that God has placed this onus on his followers. As Jesus said himself, the future can and must be changed. May we heed Jesus's words and act.

Joseph of Arimathea.

Swallowing hard, Cuthwulf got to his feet. Pacing around the tree, he tried to take it all in. What to make of it all? His mind heaved with mystification, doubt and wonder. Eventually he rolled up the scrolls and tucked them back in the jar. He stood and, leaving shovels, still-lit torches, untidy piles of earth next to large, deep holes, and the lead chest where they were, dashed back inside the cloisters with the jar.

Cuthwulf hastened to Abbot Aelfric's private chamber in the chapter house. The abbot had said he would not be going to bed until Cuthwulf brought him news of the Holy Grail.

He would not be expecting this.

Aelfric's eyes went instantly to the clay jar in Cuthwulf's arms as the monk entered, confusion making the old man's eyebrows twitch slightly.

"Did you find it?" said Aelfric. "The Grail?"

"No, Father," said Cuthwulf. "But I did find something. A lead chest containing this jar."

"Oh." Aelfric's shoulders and face sank with disappointment. "Is there anything in the jar?"

Cuthwulf nodded and stepped forwards. He opened the jar and spilled the scrolls over the abbot's study table, ironically right next to the Bible he'd been reading. He placed the jar near the edge of the table and stepped back.

Aelfric's eyes narrowed. "What are these?"

"They are…" Cuthwulf wasn't certain how to explain this. "They are the writings of a man. A man professing to be called… Jesus."

Aelfric's eyes immediately widened, but he remained silent.

Cuthwulf continued, "The man claims to have travelled from the far future to the fourteenth year of Tiberius Caesar to warn us of a 'Last War'. He says he was baptised by John the Baptist, travelled across Galilee preaching and, according to the addendum at the end of the scrolls, was betrayed and crucified before he could complete his mission."

Aelfric shook his head with a combination of condemnation and shock.

"You should read them, Father." Cuthwulf remembered the order of the scrolls and handed him the first one. He went and sat silently in the chair by the wall.

The abbot huffed and unfurled the opening pages of the scroll. Cuthwulf sat with his hands squeezed together in his lap, knuckles turning white as he watched him read.

Aelfric only read for a few minutes, then threw the first scroll across his study table. "What is this strange nonsense?"

Cuthwulf stood up and went over to hand Aelfric the fourth scroll. "Read the addendum at the end of this scroll. It gives it some…" He paused to think of the word. "Some context."

Aelfric unfurled the last page of the fourth scroll and read the addendum reportedly written by Joseph of Arimathea. Cuthwulf sat back down. When Aelfric finished, he rolled it back up and leaned back in his chair, shaking his head. "This is what I get for hoping that our humble abbey might have been built on top of the Holy Grail. Instead our hallowed grounds were being poisoned by the ghastliest heresy I have ever read."

Cuthwulf said nothing. He stared uneasily at the floor.

Aelfric noted his silence. "Cuthwulf – what is it?"

Cuthwulf wasn't sure how to say this without sounding like a heretic himself. "Father… what if it isn't?"

"Isn't what?"

"Heresy."

Aelfric's expression turned cold. "I beg your pardon?"

"You should probably read all of the writings. They talk about –"

"I do not care what they talk about. I do not *want* to besmirch myself with this filth any more than I have. We must burn them at once."

Cuthwulf stood. "Father, we should not act with undue haste in this matter. Let's look at the facts."

Aelfric frowned. "What facts are those, Brother Cuthwulf?"

"These scrolls are written in Aramaic. We know this to be the language of Jesus. We know that they have been buried in a lead chest in the ground for hundreds of years. If this were just a fanciful tale conjured up by a heretical mind, why not simply destroy them? Why go to the effort of preserving them in this manner were they not of great importance?"

Cuthwulf realised as he was saying it that he was sounding convinced by these scrolls. Was he? And what was he convinced *of* exactly? His mind was spinning.

Aelfric leaned forwards in his chair. "What are you saying?"

"I'm saying we need to think. I would encourage you to read the entirety of the scrolls before you dismiss them. The detail in them is striking. If these scrolls really were written by Jesus, we need to protect them."

"These scrolls were *not* written by Jesus. They are a heinous, blasphemous and dangerous fabrication."

Cuthwulf felt his neck and shoulders tighten with frustration. How could the abbot be so certain without having read them? "What if they are not, Father?"

Aelfric stood. "This discussion is over, Brother Cuthwulf." He bent over his table to gather up the scrolls.

Cuthwulf swallowed. "What are you doing?"

"What I said I would do. I'm going to burn them."

Cuthwulf shook his head. "Father, you cannot. They must be examined."

"No one will see or know about these scrolls. We are going to pretend they never existed, and our conversation tonight never happened."

The scrolls tucked up in his right arm, Aelfric started out of the room. Without even thinking, Cuthwulf was in his path, blocking him.

Aelfric's eyes flared. "Out of my way."

"Father, you mustn't," Cuthwulf pleaded.

"I said, this discussion is over."

Aelfric barged past Cuthwulf and Cuthwulf's hand gripped his shoulder before he knew it was there. "You mustn't!"

Aelfric's face went taut with rage. Though he was frail, he summoned enough strength to yank free of Cuthwulf's grip. "Return to the dormitory, Brother Cuthwulf."

Aelfric continued to the door and Cuthwulf instinctively darted in front of it.

Aelfric raised his voice, "Move."

There was a fierce determination driving Cuthwulf now, but he had no idea where it would lead. All he knew was that he had to protect those scrolls.

"I cannot allow you to destroy those scrolls," said Cuthwulf.

"Out of my way at once!"

"No."

The abbot tried to push past him. Cuthwulf pushed back and Aelfric stumbled. He steadied himself and looked at Cuthwulf with horror, his wrinkled face contorted and red. He went for the door, left hand out to grab the door handle. Cuthwulf blocked him again and Aelfric tried to tussle with him. Cuthwulf thrust his arms out and pushed the old man harder. This time Aelfric lurched backwards, lost his balance, the scrolls tumbling from his arms as he groped for something futilely to keep from falling.

The back of Aelfric's head caught the rim of his study table with a crack so sharp and loud it made Cuthwulf's stomach turn with hot bile. The impact caused the jar that had contained the scrolls to teeter precariously at the edge, then fall. Less than a second after Aelfric had thudded to the floor, the jar smashed loudly next to him.

Cuthwulf stared, everything else in the room falling away, as dark red blood pooled around the abbot's head like a halo. He saw flashes of *them*. The wives and children of peaceful Danes living in England, who Cuthwulf had helped abduct, torture, rape and murder on the orders of King Aethelred in a vain attempt to deter future Viking invasions. He saw Ivar, poor little Ivar, remembered the small helpless boy's desperate tears as Cuthwulf did all those unspeakable things to him. Things that had turned his very soul black and putrid.

And now he had done it again. Killed. After he had promised himself that there would be no more killing. After he'd come so far, done so well. And it wasn't just anybody he'd killed, but an abbot, a friend, a *father*. In a religious sense and what he'd come to feel as a paternal one too.

He wanted to scream, cry, vomit. Slit his own throat with his eating knife. He had fooled himself that he could make it as a monk. He was a soldier. A killer. He could not change who he was any more than he could change what he'd done.

But then the blur of the scrolls in his periphery, strewn over the floor, pulled him back from the precipice he was about to throw himself off.

Perhaps I was never supposed to change.

The Hooded Man had told Cuthwulf that he was about to make an important discovery. This was clearly it. The hand of God *must* have been upon him when he was digging up those scrolls. This was no mere tale of fancy he had stumbled upon; he knew that much.

Cuthwulf looked at Aelfric's body. If God meant for Cuthwulf to find those scrolls, then perhaps God meant for Aelfric to die. So that Cuthwulf could do God's work.

He knew now what he had to do. God didn't want him to stop being a soldier. God wanted him to be *His* soldier.

Cuthwulf crouched down and stroked his former mentor's face with his fingers. "God has a new plan," he whispered. "I will not fail Him. And I will not fail you." Then he gathered the scrolls into his arms, bolted out of the chapter house, past the church to the gatehouse, and fled the abbey.

21

April 19th 2027

Miss Morgan was working from her two-floored apartment in Central London, six minutes' walk from the Looming Tower, when Dr Neether phoned. Dr Neether had been in charge of examining the dinosaur and human bones that had been discovered in Tower Hamlets, and the results were in. And were, Dr Neether said, 'disturbing'. Miss Morgan didn't want to hear about it over the phone and said she was coming in.

She stopped by her favourite Starbucks on Puttenham Lane on the way. Having barely slept last night, she had a cracking headache that no amount of co-codamol was touching. Absolutely not helping was the four- or five-year-old boy in Starbucks screaming at his mother and bashing his knife and fork against their table, while Miss Morgan was in the line for a take-away cappuccino.

What is it with these morons who can't control their kids?

Miss Morgan kept looking at the mother, blithely reading something on her phone and ignoring her child, like her brain had stuck him on mute. Good for her. Unfortunately, everyone else in the small café – where his shrill shrieks were bouncing off every wall – didn't have that luxury.

Ordering her cappuccino, Miss Morgan almost didn't hear the cashier ask for her money. "Are your ears numb yet?" she asked as she swiped her card.

The cashier gave a defeated smile. "Used to it."

Miss Morgan picked up her cappuccino from the end of the counter and, on her way towards the door, stopped by the woman's table. "Excuse me. Animals aren't allowed in here, you know."

The mother looked up from her phone. "I beg your pardon?"

Raising her voice over the boy's incessant racket, "I said, animals aren't allowed in here."

The woman frowned and shot a glance at her little boy. "Are you talking about my child?"

"Child?" Miss Morgan gestured to the boy. "I'm talking about that beast."

The kid at last fell quiet, gawping at Miss Morgan. The woman pulled him from his chair to cuddle him. "Please don't call him that. He's very sensitive."

An old man sitting at the next table chimed in. "So are my damn ears!"

"I'm sorry, okay! I… I didn't realise he was bothering anyone," she said to the man. Looking at her boy, she said softly, "Olly, be quiet, please."

Miss Morgan shook her head and faced the boy, leaning towards him. "What Mummy means to say is, shut the fuck up or she'll clip you round the ear."

The woman's eyes snapped wide and her jaw dropped with a gasp of shock. She protectively covered her son's ears with both hands. The old man laughed. Miss Morgan strode out of Starbucks.

There were moments when Miss Morgan wished she'd become a mother just so she could show everyone how it was done. Her kids would've been angels – she wouldn't have allowed them to be otherwise. Parents today were mollycoddlers, obsessed with being compassionate, understanding, protecting their children's mental wellbeing instead of nurturing them into tough adults ready to take on the harsh realities of the world. She couldn't stand it. Weak. All of them. Weak. Pathetic. Useless.

Growing up she'd always planned to be a mother. Then she became CEO of Million Eyes and there was simply no room for it. She was fine with that. Her life had become something else, something much more important. Because she wasn't just running the world's biggest technology company. She was leading the Mission, the greatest of all honours and heaviest of all burdens. People bore children to leave legacies. Miss Morgan's legacy was secure.

But she would've been a great mother. For sure. She wouldn't have wrapped her kids in cotton wool or wasted time tending to their 'emotional needs'. She would've armoured them with a thick skin and a sharp tongue. Sensitivity, compassion, warmth – those things turned kids into crybabies. Crybabies who grew to become passive, timid, idle adults. Miss Morgan had not got to where she was through being nice. Hard choices couldn't be made if you were always worrying about people's feelings. Stone-cold logic – that was what really mattered.

Miss Morgan crossed the road and was bathed in shade as the sun moved behind the Looming Tower. Approaching the entrance, she walked past the statue of major Million Eyes shareholder Arthur Pell, which stood at the centre of the otherwise pretty gardens. The only good thing about Jennifer Larson wrecking the timeline five and a half years ago was the erasure of this damned statue. Seeing Pell's fat face every time she came into work had been ruining her day a little bit for almost thirty years. Having said that, she'd rather the statue than the real thing. The real thing, to nobody's surprise, had just been placed under investigation for a string of sex offences going back to the 80s, proving that he wasn't just a boil on the arse of humanity, he was careless too. Which was annoying as fuck for Miss Morgan because the moment the press got wind of his unsavoury extra-curriculars, the PR outcry would land right on her desk.

Although at least, if it did come out, she'd be able to

169

negotiate the removal of his statue from Million Eyes' front lawn.

Every cloud.

Her headache was beginning to ease as she entered the lobby, signed in, and went down in the lift to Time Travel, which sat beneath but also extended beyond the Looming Tower, sprawling under London's streets. Her entrance wiped the smiles from the staff who saw her, as normal. She didn't mind that they were intimidated by her. She wasn't there to be anybody's friend. They were doing important work.

She crossed the main office, past the Temporal Shield Reactor room, down the corridor next to the conference room and the offices of deputy manager Rupert Whistler and head of department Carina Boone. Eventually she came to *Temporal Research and Development,* a huge laboratory where artefacts, natural objects and sometimes people – from the past and the future – were studied and experimented on. It was also where chronodes and cognits and the other secret technologies that Million Eyes relied on when time-travelling, were created.

A large section of the lab had been dedicated to work on the Tower Hamlets skeletons. Miss Morgan walked over to where Dr Neether and a group of technicians were at long tables using dental picks and air-powered scribes to fully separate the bones from their rock encasements, applying glues and consolidants as they went to keep the fossils intact. A few of the bones had been extricated and stored in large, padded trays but hundreds of bones still lay inside the white plaster casts that had been used to transport them, stacked on pallets on the floor.

"Ah, Miss Morgan," said Dr Neether in her strained, throaty tones when she noticed her, looking up from the specimen she was working on.

It always turned Miss Morgan's stomach to look at Dr Neether. The woman was a mess. She'd been left with half a face – literally. She had one eye, one ear and a deep cavity in the left side of her face where her cheek and other eye and ear once were. It had been grafted over with skin, but all of the bones in that side had been sheared off and every attempt at reconstruction thus far had failed. She was continuing to have expensive surgical procedures, but none of them were doing much good.

"You have some results for me?" said Miss Morgan.

Dr Neether blinked her only eye. "Yes, ma'am. If you'd like to come this way, I'll show you."

Miss Morgan followed Dr Neether past the pallets of plaster shapes to a lab table on which sat a bulky machine. It had a metal arm with a square lens that arched over the top and an open compartment for samples; Miss Morgan could see a jaw fragment from one of the human skulls positioned inside. Next to the contraption on the table were several trays of bones.

"We've extricated a good number of the human bones now," said Dr Neether. "As you'd expect, both skeletons were severely maimed. There is evidence of blunt-force trauma to many of the bones – breaks, cracks, dents, holes." She gestured to the machine. "Now, you may not have seen this before, ma'am. This is a chronokinetic resonance viewer. It lets us look at objects at earlier points in time. As you know, we're analysing fossils – bones that have turned to stone over millions of years. Which means they no longer contain any organic material capable of containing DNA. The viewer lets us reach back in time to a point when the fossil had enough organic material for us to run a DNA scan."

"Enough technobabble, Dr Neether. Get to the point."

Her hoarse voice quivered slightly. "Y-yes. Sorry, ma'am. We've analysed several bones and obtained DNA profiles for each human. Both males. Approximately twelve and ten years old. I cross-referenced their profiles with those held in our database and produced a match with a confirmed descendant of Elizabeth Woodville, queen of England between 1464 and 1483. She was the mother of the Princes in the Tower. Edward V and Richard, Duke of York. The bodies belong to them."

Miss Morgan took a deep breath, nodding. "I suspected it might be them. During the Jennifer Larson incident, they travelled out of temporal radius. We had no way of going after them." She let out a sharp sigh of relief. "Well, it would seem their impact on history was minimal. That's something. Right?"

A grave look weighed down the good side of Dr Neether's face. "I'm afraid not. There's a reason the dinosaur that ate them did not digest them. It means that it died shortly after eating them."

Miss Morgan swallowed. "Go on."

"When we analysed the princes' bones, we found trace elements of a rhinovirus – the predominant cause of the common cold in humans. We have analysed some of the dinosaur bones using the same method and found that the same virus is present."

Miss Morgan frowned. "So, the princes had a cold. What are you saying?"

The half-faced woman gave several one-eyed blinks. "I'm saying that the dinosaur that ate them contracted this cold. A virus from sixty-six million years in its future. A virus that advanced would have a devastating effect on Cretaceous-era life. So devastating its spread would likely cause... an extinction-level event."

A wave of dread made the hairs on the nape of Miss Morgan's neck stand on end. "Wait. You're not suggesting that the human common cold is responsible for the extinction of the dinosaurs. Are you?"

"I know how it sounds. So we tested another specimen, used the viewer to look at some bones from a Triceratops discovered in North America a few years ago, now exhibited at London's Natural History Museum. The Triceratops – despite being found thousands of miles from the Tower Hamlets specimen – contained traces of the same rhinovirus. I'm now in little doubt that the princes' arrival triggered a global rhinovirus pandemic that wiped out the dinosaurs."

"Dr Neether, that means *we* killed the dinosaurs.

Through the invention of time travel. Million Eyes is responsible."

Dr Neether nodded grimly. "Yes, ma'am."

Jesus. Of all of Million Eyes' changes to the timeline, this was undoubtedly the most cataclysmic. The Cretaceous-Paleogene extinction event saw the demise of seventy-five percent of all species on Earth. Which begged the question: what if they had stopped the Princes in the Tower from travelling back to the Cretaceous? Would dinosaurs have survived to the present day? Would humans have evolved alongside them? Would humans have evolved at all? Miss Morgan's headache had faded – now the incredible and terrifying implications of what she had just learned were giving her another.

She grounded herself in the here and now, put her business head back on. Too late – and too hard on her brain and blood pressure – to worry about all that now. "Nobody but you and your team know about this, I presume?"

Dr Neether shook her head, "No, ma'am."

"Good. Keep it that way. I can't have this getting back to the board. A number of our directors have already expressed reservations about the way in which we have been using time travel. I can't risk anything jeopardising our work here. Particularly now that Operation Blue Pencil is underway."

"Of course."

"And now that we know who the humans were, cease all further extrication and examination of the bones and have them disposed of. Refocus your efforts on Blue Pencil. That's what really matters here."

Dr Neether nodded and went to relay Miss Morgan's instructions to her team.

Miss Morgan turned to leave, but stopped, remembering her other major source of anxiety of late. "Dr Neether, the oraculum. Has it activated yet?"

Dr Neether faced her. "No. But it will. Soon." She gave

a half-smile, which was all she could muster since the left side of her mouth was frozen in an ugly downwards skew.

"There isn't much time left."

"I know. I wouldn't worry. You and I both know it has to activate before April 28th. Whatever's coming, we'll be ready for it."

Not completely sharing Dr Neether's confidence, Miss Morgan sighed and left.

22

April 19th 2027

"Sam, talk to me about Cawston Manor."

A brush of unease made Lester's knees shake. "What about it?"

Ethan wrinkled his nose and sniffed. "Well, I was in the kitchen the other day and overheard a conversation between a couple of the team who were on that dig. They were talking about the artefacts that were found."

Lester's heartrate climbed. "Oh?"

"Yeah. They mentioned finding some letters in a box."

Stay calm. Feign ignorance. "Letters?"

"Yes. And I didn't remember anything about any letters being found at Cawston Manor. So I checked your excavation report." Ethan had those reading glasses with the lenses you can disconnect at the bridge. She watched him slide the wrap-around neck loop onto his ears and click the lenses together to look down at his MEpad. "The artefacts list doesn't mention any letters, only the box, which you've described as being empty."

She swallowed. "That's because it was. There certainly weren't any letters. They must've been talking about a different dig."

"I definitely heard them say Cawston Manor."

"I don't know what to tell you, Ethan."

Ethan disconnected his glasses and lifted his gaze. Creases lined his forehead and his eyes squinted at her with suspicion. "So you're saying that if I called them in here and they repeated that it was Cawston Manor where these letters were found, that they'd be –"

"Mistaken." She said it more firmly than perhaps she intended. "Yes."

Ethan nodded. "Curious."

One of her two phones buzzed twice in her pocket. She hoped it was the Uzu. "Is that everything?"

Ethan shook his head. "No. Why have I still not seen an excavation plan for Torbury Farm?"

Lester squirmed uncomfortably in her seat. "You'll have it."

"When, Sam? The developers have been on my back again this morning. They need to know when the dig's going to start."

Her phone buzzed twice again. Ethan stared at her.

"I'll do it today," she said.

Ethan gave a frowning nod, clearly unsatisfied. "We've also had a response to the complaint we made to the Home Office about Tower Hamlets. I need you to review it. And Keiko Hamasaki's father has been calling and emailing for information about her disappearance; I need you to phone him and explain that we still don't know anything." He murmured quietly, "Even though we do, really." The words 'government conspiracy' were teetering on his tongue again.

"Fine, I'll do that too." said Lester idly. "Can I go?"

Ethan's frown deepened. "Sam, are you alright?"

"Yes, I'm fine."

"You've been shirking your responsibilities lately. Missing deadlines. Your head always seems elsewhere. I know things have been tough for you since..." His sentence trailed off awkwardly.

"Ethan, I'm fine." She didn't want him thinking this was related to Georgia, so she made up something else. "It's my... my mum. She's been ill and I've been helping her."

"I'm sorry to hear that. If you need time off, tell me. You can't keep letting personal matters interfere with your work like this."

Lester took a breath and stood up. "I know, I'm sorry. I'll make sure it doesn't from now on. And I'll get all that stuff to you today, okay?" Ethan started to say something in response but she was already halfway out of his office.

She hurried back to her own office and sat down at her desk to look at her texts, which were, as she'd hoped, from Adam, sent to her Uzu. There was a file attached to the first one. **Managed to access Stuart Rayburn's personnel file. Here's a screenshot of it. He's the same man who disappeared in October 2019.**

Excellent. They were getting somewhere.

The second text read: **Also found messages between Pete Navarro and Erica Morgan from around the same time. They talked about needing to apprehend Rayburn quickly and said he'd breached the 'X9 Server' – I dunno what that is.**

Lester read through the screenshot of Rayburn's personnel record, noted his address in Hertfordshire. His sister and next of kin, Alison Rayburn, had lived at the same address.

Lester already knew that the phone number for Stuart was no longer in use. But his file listed a number for Alison, too. What if that still worked? Perhaps she could arrange to meet with her, find out if she knew anything about Stuart's disappearance.

She looked up from her desk. The door to her office was ajar, so she got up and closed it, catching her secretary Kevin's speculative look as she did so.

She returned to her desk and spent a couple of moments rehearsing what she was going to say. Then she tapped in the number.

It rang about six times before a small voice answered, "Hello?"

"Oh, hello. Is this Alison Rayburn?"

"Who's asking?"

"My name is Dr Samantha Lester. I'm looking into the disappearance of your brother, Stuart Rayburn, and wondered if you –"

The line went dead.

Damn it.

She wondered if Alison still lived at Stuart's address. What if she just went round? No, she couldn't do that. Could she? Alison clearly didn't want to talk.

At the same time, she had a feeling that she and Adam were really onto something here.

"Go, Mummy."

Lester looked up from her phone and felt a deep throbbing in her chest as her eyes met her daughter's.

"Georgia…"

Georgia was sitting in the chair opposite her, swinging her legs, too short to reach the floor. Her long ginger locks were in a ponytail and she had a moustache of chocolate milk.

"Oh – hi Granddad!" Lester pointed at Georgia's chocolate milk moustache. It was a running joke between them. Georgia would get chocolate milk around her mouth and Lester would mistake her for Granddad.

Georgia hunched and wobbled her shoulders in that adorable giggle of hers, before wiping the chocolate milk from her lip. Oh to hear her laugh again.

"What were you saying, my darling?" Lester said softly.

"The lady!" said Georgia excitedly. "You should go see the lady, Mummy. She'll help you."

Lester smiled. She looked down at her burner and Alison's address. Meath, Hertfordshire, was just outside St Albans. It'd probably take an hour or so to get there, with traffic.

"Alright, darling, you've convinced me." She looked up. The chair opposite was empty. Georgia was gone.

Lester leaned back and breathed a long, deep sigh. She was sad, but not surprised.

This was new though. She'd been having visions of Georgia for a while now, but this was the first time Georgia had spoken to her.

It was nice. Hopefully Georgia would come back and speak to her again. It felt so good to hear her voice.

She stood up from her desk and went to fetch her

trench coat from the back of the door. She left her office and said to Kevin as she passed his desk, "Cancel my afternoon, please. I'm going out."

"But – but Dr Lester, what should I tell Ethan?"

She really didn't care. "Tell him... Tell him it's to do with my mum."

An hour and a quarter later, Lester arrived in Meath. It was a sleepy little place. She passed a couple of pubs, takeaways and posh-looking shops, slowing as she turned onto Plunkett's Walk, her sat-nav telling her to go two hundred metres up. She glanced at the houses on both sides. Beautiful, grandiose, detached, with big front gardens and gated cobbled driveways. And a mesh of styles: Tudor, Edwardian and a few that were more modernist. There were some exceptionally deep pockets on this street.

She pulled up outside number 42, one of the more modern houses. From the car she could see its dark timber cladding, exposed steelwork and large expanses of glass. As she got out, her phone rang. Ethan. She ignored it and returned the phone to her handbag.

She glanced around for anyone who might be 'watching'. No sinister-looking cars with blacked-out windows. No one lurking behind hedges with cameras or binoculars – that she could see anyway.

She turned and approached the Rayburn house. There were two waist-high gates with a brick wall between them, one for the driveway, one for the path to the front door. Lester opened the latter and walked up the colourful crazy paving path through a tidy front garden with an evenly trimmed lawn and half a dozen potted plants at the edges. The house had large floor-to-ceiling windows on the ground and first floor and a smaller, circular window on the second, just beneath the gable roof. There was a steel-framed glass balcony that spanned the whole of the first floor and was furnished with a table and chairs. It wasn't to Lester's taste; she preferred houses that were more traditional, more old-fashioned, like the magnificent Tudor house next door with its black timber framing, brick infill and lovely dormer windows.

Number 42's windows used one-way mirror glass, so she couldn't see inside, although the neatness of the lawn and healthy bloom of the plants were evidence that someone still lived here. The question was whether it was still Alison Rayburn.

Lester walked up to the charcoal grey front door and pressed the doorbell. There was no answer or sign of movement for nearly a minute but as she went to press it again, someone started unlocking the door.

A blonde woman opened it, albeit only a few inches. She had tired eyes and a wary look in them. "Yes?"

Lester smiled warmly. "Hi. Are you Alison Rayburn?"

The woman frowned. "Who are you?"

"Dr Samantha Lester. We spoke briefly on the phone a couple of hours ago."

The woman's eyes widened. "Are you serious? I hung up on you."

"Yes. I know."

"So you thought you'd come to my house?"

"I'm sorry. I just… I want to help. Can I come in?"

"No, you can't come in! I haven't got a clue who you are!"

Lester glanced from left to right to double-check no one was around, leaned a little closer to the door and lowered her voice, "I think that Million Eyes were responsible for your brother's disappearance."

Alison swallowed and looked nervous for a second. Then she shook her head. "I'm very busy and I don't want to talk about Stuart. I thought I'd made that clear. Please leave."

"You know something, don't you."

"I don't know anything." There was something in her

eyes that said otherwise. "Just go."

"Million Eyes aren't what they say they are. I'm just trying to find out what they're doing, what their endgame is. You can trust me."

Alison gave a brief, sarcastic laugh. "I don't know you!" Then she slammed the door in her face.

Lester dug a business card from her handbag. She pushed it through the letterbox, keeping the flap open as she stooped to call through it, "If you change your mind, call me."

She returned to her car and checked her normal phone. She had a voicemail from Ethan: *"Sam, I don't know what's happened with your mum, and I hope she's okay, but I can't have you just swanning off like this without telling me exactly what's going on. It's unacceptable. You're already behind on a lot of your work. We need to talk about this. Call me back as soon as you get this message."*

There was plenty of the day left. She could head back to LIPA and get a few hours' work in. But she really wasn't in the mood for another interrogation from Ethan.

She also had a text from Brody. Going for a drink with Phil tonight. Don't wait up. His brevity was passive-aggressive. She knew he was still pissed off over Saturday night. And the fact that they weren't talking. Frankly she didn't know *how* to talk to him at the moment.

She breathed a long sigh and looked back at Alison's house, wondering if she'd hit a dead end.

"I think she's pretending, Mummy. I think she knows things."

Lester looked in her rear-view mirror at Georgia, smiling at her from her booster seat in the back.

The warm feeling from earlier was back, lapping at her heart like gentle waves on a shoreline. "I think so too, darling." But how was she going to get Alison to open up?

She started the engine and drove away. Not back to the office.

Home.

23

October 6th 1003

Shortly before noon in the village of Congelstede, Northumbria, Elswyth the weaver and daughter of Uhtred – still unmarried, to everyone's surprise but her own – left her cottage and walked along the old road that wound through the village to the forest and the river. The road was rutted from the wheels of ox carts and caused her to stumble twice, almost rolling her ankles. It was in desperate need of some attention from Lord Dreogan, the village thegn; alas, he was too busy fighting, drinking and whoring to worry about repairing a road.

The sun was high and bright and there was a chill in the air. It didn't stop Elswyth sweating beneath her thick woollen dress and cloak, the dread in her stomach growing, tightening. There were moments when she thought she might retch, when she had to stop and calm herself.

She was on her way to the home of Renweard the potter to meet with the local priest, Father Beocca, and his 'associates', one of whom was presumably Renweard. The priest had said that they met once a week, every week, in secret. Lord Dreogan knew nothing about it. This morning, after Mass, Father Beocca had asked her to join them. Now Elswyth was terrified that they had learned the truth about her. That said, if they had, why would they want to speak to her? Why would they not simply hand her over to Lord Dreogan?

Everything about this seemed wrong.

Renweard's cottage was where the road stopped and the forest started. When Elswyth arrived, she could hear the river trickling by a dozen yards into the trees. Renweard's slaves, a man and his daughter who lived in the tiny grub-hut next to their master's cottage, were busy doing chores outside, the man in the pen at the side of the house tending to the cows, sheep and chickens, his daughter at the front raking out excess ash and charcoal from Renweard's potter's kiln.

Elswyth walked up to Renweard's door, took a deep breath and knocked.

Renweard answered. "Ah, Elswyth. Thank you for coming."

She smiled. It wasn't sincere. She was only here to find out what they knew. She tried not to let on.

Renweard stepped aside, allowing her to enter. The smell of fish wafted from the cauldron on the hearth, bubbling with a thick-looking pottage, steam and smoke billowing upwards through the smoke hole in the thatch. She walked past a small workspace in the corner, containing Renweard's tools, his potter's wheel, a bucket of wet clay and a stack of already baked pots, jugs, cups and dishes. In the opposite corner, next to the family's sleeping quarters, were a couple of tables and a storage area for food.

The participants of this mysterious meeting had been sitting on benches around the longer of the two tables, but all stood as Elswyth entered. Along with Renweard, there was Renweard's wife, Lyveva, Father Beocca and someone she really wasn't expecting to see.

"Cuthwulf, *you* are a part of this 'group'?"

Cuthwulf was a former soldier and the village healer. He had befriended Elswyth and her father when he came to the village almost ten years ago, and had cared for her father when he died from an affliction of the bowels one week ago tomorrow. How long had he been attending these secret meetings with Father Beocca?

"He isn't just a part of it," said Father Beocca. "He founded it."

He – *what?*

"And what is *it* exactly?" asked Elswyth.

"All in good time," said Cuthwulf. "Come. Sit. Have some ale. Let's talk."

They all sat down at Renweard's table, Elswyth next to Cuthwulf. Lyveva poured her a cup of ale. Elswyth thanked her for it and took a sip. Renweard and Lyveva's children were not here, which meant they were probably working on Lord Dreogan's land.

"How are you, Elswyth?" said Cuthwulf, placing his hand over hers on the table. It was warm, but the skin on his thick fingers was rough and hard.

He was obviously referring to the loss of her father. 'Not well', was the answer. All of Elswyth's siblings had died young, her mother not long after them, so for years Elswyth and Uhtred had had no one but each other. And they had been bound together by a secret that would have seen them killed were it known, consequently leading two lives – one public, one private. Now the secret was in Elswyth's hands. She was on her own and could no longer turn to her beloved father for guidance.

She was lost without him. That was the truth of it. Utterly and completely lost.

She replied stoically nonetheless, "I am well, Cuthwulf. Please tell me why you have invited me here."

Cuthwulf looked briefly at the others. "Because we are interested in those with the strength of mind and character that you possess." He paused, looking slightly uncomfortable. "And because you are secretly a pagan."

Elswyth shuddered, hopefully imperceptibly. Her heart missed a beat. "Pardon?"

"We know that you are a pagan – like your father was," said Father Beocca.

Elswyth shook her head. "I follow the Church of Rome, like you. I am a faithful servant of Christ the Lord. My father was too."

Cuthwulf leaned towards her. "I was with your father during his final hours. There was a time when he became delirious and forgot I was there with him. He started to pray to Woden. He mentioned in those prayers that you are both followers of the All-Father."

Elswyth frowned and shrugged her shoulders. "I do not know who Woden is."

"He also pulled out a necklace from underneath his tunic, a necklace he always kept hidden."

She knew it well. Her knees began to tremble.

Cuthwulf continued, "He was touching the necklace as he prayed. I saw that it bore the symbol of the gammadion cross."

Elswyth stood up sharply. "I have to be getting back."

"Elswyth, wait," said Cuthwulf. "Don't go. You can trust us."

Can I?

"You have nothing to fear from us," Father Beocca added. "We have long suspected that you and your father could be pagans masquerading as Christians. Your father only confirmed it."

Elswyth continued towards the door.

"We mean you no harm," said Cuthwulf. "I promise you this. We have no intention of turning you over to Lord Dreogan. We have a proposal."

Elswyth stopped and turned around. She remained silent, waiting for further explanation.

Cuthwulf looked at the others and said, "We would like you to join us. The fact that you and your father have continued to believe in the old gods, despite many years of being subjected to Christian teachings, means that you are more likely than anyone else to be open to what we have learned about Jesus."

Elswyth frowned. "What you have learned about *Jesus?*"

"Please. Sit down. Let me explain."

It was probably sensible to hear what they had to say. If she refused to cooperate, they might yet expose her secret to Lord Dreogan. And he was not a man to be trifled with. Ever since Elswyth, at ten years old, had watched him gouge out the eyes of Theodore the ox-herder for apparently looking upon his daughter with lust, she'd made it her mission to stay on the right side of him.

She sat back down and Lyveva poured her some more ale.

"There is much you don't know about me, Elswyth," said Cuthwulf.

Everybody had secrets, she was learning.

"For example, you know that I was a soldier –"

Not that you have ever been particularly comfortable talking about it.

"– But you don't know that I was also a monk. I left the king's army and joined the brotherhood at Glastonbury Abbey."

Curious. Cuthwulf had never come across to Elswyth as an especially pious man. She'd long had this sense that he secretly harboured a loathing for Christianity that was similar to her own, although he had never admitted it and went to church with everyone else – like she did.

Having said that, perhaps he used to be pious and whatever he had learned about Jesus had altered his perspective.

Cuthwulf continued, "Ten years ago, I came upon some information. Information that led me to believe that the Holy Grail itself was buried in the abbey grounds. So, I went and dug it up."

Elswyth nearly spat out her ale. "What? You found the Holy Grail?" Though she didn't believe in the object herself, she knew how important it was to the Christians.

"I did not find what I was expecting to. Instead of a chalice, I found a jar of ancient scrolls." He looked at Lyveva, who stood up and went to fetch something by the wall. She returned with a shallow wooden box, placed it on the table in front of Elswyth and lifted the lid.

"These scrolls," said Cuthwulf. "They were buried in a lead box in the 1st century by Joseph of Arimathea."

Elswyth leaned over the box. Inside were four scrolls.

"Go ahead," said Father Beocca. "Take a look."

Little tabs had been affixed to each scroll and marked with a number. Elswyth picked up the scroll marked *1* and unfurled it to the first page. It was covered in strange marks and symbols, a language she could not understand.

Lyveva then brought over a book and placed it on the table. On the cover, written in English, was *The Gospel According To Jesus.*

"We know that your father could read and write," said Cuthwulf. "Did he teach you as well?"

Had her father divulged *every* family secret on his deathbed? "How do you know my father could read and write?"

"He showed me one of his stories. About a warrior called Beowulf who slays a monster, Grendel." Elswyth's favourite, inspired by tales of their ancestors in Scandia. "It was impressive."

"My father was a keen writer," she admitted. "Full of stories. So was his father. But he was private about it. He never wanted to draw attention to himself. I am surprised he showed you *Beowulf.* However, he wasn't himself at the end."

"He should never have kept his talent hidden."

"I used to tell him so."

"Did he teach you?"

Elswyth nodded awkwardly.

"Then please." Cuthwulf gestured to the book on the table. "This is our translation of the Aramaic writings in the scrolls. We would like you to read it."

The bang of Renweard's door made them all swivel round in their seats. Renweard got to his feet at once.

A man thundered into the house. He was wearing a black hooded robe, not dissimilar to a monk's habit. Elswyth had never seen him before.

"What is the meaning of this?" Renweard demanded.

"You all need to leave now," said the Hooded Man.

"Who are you?" said Renweard. "How dare you just barge into –"

"I know you," Cuthwulf interrupted.

Renweard frowned at Cuthwulf. "You do?"

The Hooded Man nodded. "Yes, Cuthwulf. You do."

"Does this mean she has returned?" said Cuthwulf. "The Unraveller?"

Elswyth's heart started to thump. *She? The Unraveller? What in the world are they talking about?*

"Yes," said the Hooded Man. "That's why we have to leave."

"Could someone please explain to me what is going on!" shouted Renweard.

"I'll explain once everyone's out of the house and at a safe distance from it," said the Hooded Man.

"You will explain now!" Renweard insisted.

The Hooded Man stepped right up to him. His hood hung low over his face and Elswyth could hardly see his eyes.

"Any moment now, this house – and everyone inside – is going to get blown to pieces in a huge explosion. Is that enough for you?"

Elswyth sucked in a breath. "What?"

Lyveva looked at Renweard with panic. "Merciful Lord. Could it be true?"

Redweard's face creased with uncertainty.

Father Beocca stepped forwards and looked at the others. "We should go."

"Yes, we should." The Hooded Man pointed at the box of scrolls and the *Gospel According To Jesus* book. "Make sure you bring those."

Father Beocca frowned. "How do you kn– ?"

"Just do it!"

Father Beocca instantly took up the book in his arms. Lyveva replaced the lid on the box of scrolls and handed it to Renweard. With haste they all followed the Hooded Man out of the house. Renweard's slaves were gone – perhaps the Hooded Man had already warned them.

They ran for the trees that skirted the river.

Then a hot and powerful force slammed into Elswyth's

back and tossed her forwards, accompanied by a noise that was so loud it was like something had crushed her head.

Elswyth landed hard on her front, grazing her palms and knees. The force of the impact emptied her lungs of air and rattled her brain in her skull like the clapper of a bell.

The shock had shut off her airways so that nothing could reach her lungs. Panic gripped her momentarily, then her throat reopened and she coughed and gasped and spluttered for air. Her arms and legs were weak and tingling. Everything looked fuzzy, like it was vibrating. She blinked hard.

The ground, trees, river, Cuthwulf and the others sharpened and stilled. They had all been thrown to the ground by the blast and were struggling to their feet like she was.

"Lord in Heaven!" screamed Lyveva, looking back in the direction they had just run from and throwing her hands over her mouth. "Our house!" Renweard wrapped his free arm, the one not holding the box of scrolls, around his wife's shoulders.

Elswyth was on her feet, ears ringing, the pain of the impact throbbing through her, mud all down the front of her dress. She turned stiffly to follow Lyveva's gaze.

Renweard's house had burst like an overripe fruit. Only pieces remained, burning, black smoke spiralling into the sky. Elswyth clutched her chest in shock. What sort of power could do such a thing?

Red-faced, Cuthwulf shouted, "She will pay for this!" and began marching furiously towards the shattered house.

"No, Cuthwulf!" blared the Hooded Man.

Cuthwulf didn't listen. The Hooded Man went after him. Elswyth and the others followed tentatively.

Now closer to the wreck of Renweard's house, Elswyth was able to grasp the fearsome enormity of the power at work here. A singular act had reduced the entire building to scattered rubble. Most of Renweard's animals had been caught in the blast; there were fragments of their bloody carcasses everywhere. It had even been strong enough to rip through iron, as Renweard and Lyveva's cauldron was in about five or six pieces.

"There she is!" screamed Cuthwulf. Elswyth looked up. He was pointing his arm towards the village, where people who'd heard the blast were starting to gather outside their houses, staring at the expanding cloud of smoke that was billowing across the rooftops.

Near the front of those gathered was a woman in a pale blue dress and white headscarf. Her arm was raised and she was pointing a small, silver object in their direction.

Elswyth froze as a bolt of lightning erupted from the object and surged with great force, straight towards her.

The Hooded Man shoved her hard with his free hand. Elswyth fell on her back, jarring her spine, and the lightning streaked past her, about a metre above her head. She heard the deep crack of wood and looked – the bolt had sheared through a tree and a clump of branches was falling to the ground.

Terror shuddered through her. This woman was a goddess, or at least wielded the powers of one. A vengeful one. Elswyth said a silent prayer to the All-Father.

The Hooded Man pulled a similar-looking object from his robe and pointed it at the woman. Elswyth lifted herself painfully onto her elbows to see a bolt of lightning expelled from its tip. It streaked through the air towards the woman.

Are they both gods?

Villagers screamed. The woman leapt out of the way of the lightning, which struck an ox cart and violently blew it apart. As the villagers scarpered or dived for cover, the Hooded Man hurtled after the woman, who disappeared between the houses.

"Elswyth, are you all right?" Father Beocca stood over her, still holding the Jesus book.

"I – I think so…" She took in several deep, wheezy breaths, still trying to fully reinflate her lungs, which felt like they were on fire. Father Beocca stooped to help her to her feet. She leaned on him heavily, couldn't help it. Her whole body felt feeble and shaky.

Her eyes were back on the road. A bright white light flashed in the distance, near the church. "What was that?" said Father Beocca.

Elswyth shook her head. She had no answer – to any of this.

Not long after, the Hooded Man returned to them, breathless and looking anguished.

"She's escaped again, hasn't she," said Cuthwulf.

"Yes," said the Hooded Man.

"Escaped where?" said Elswyth.

"The question isn't *where*" – Cuthwulf looked at the Hooded Man – "is it?"

Elswyth frowned.

The Hooded Man shook his head.

"You both need to start talking," Elswyth said, her voice firm even though she was shaking. "Who was that woman? Cuthwulf, how did you know her?"

"She's called the Unraveller," said Cuthwulf, "and this is the second time she has tried to kill me. She tried ten years ago, when I was still a monk at Glastonbury. This man here saved me."

"This time she was trying to kill all of you," said the Hooded Man.

"Why does she want us dead?" Lyveva cried, distressed tears streaming down her face.

"She's trying to destroy your organisation."

"Does she not realise what we are trying to do?" said Cuthwulf. "Why would she want to stop us?"

The Hooded Man shook his head. "I can't say any more. All you need to know is that she's failed. Now you have to move on. Go about your lives like none of this ever happened."

"You said the same thing ten years ago," said Cuthwulf.

"It still stands. The Unraveller is interfering with things that are *supposed* to happen. We can't let her. You have to pretend that this incident never took place."

"I don't understand," said Elswyth. "It *did* happen."

"Not according to history."

"What in Woden's name does that mean?" This man wasn't making a scrap of sense.

She felt her cheeks redden as she caught Father Beocca's knowing glance. She'd forgotten herself. She shouldn't have said Woden's name aloud. Her father would be enraged.

Still, it didn't much matter in her present company. Cuthwulf and Beocca already knew her secret.

Cuthwulf seemed to know what the Hooded Man was talking about. "It means he knows what is going to happen. Because he has been sent from the future by the Lord."

What? The future? Cuthwulf was talking in riddles.

"I have to go," said the Hooded Man. "Do everything in your power to not let this incident interfere with your work, please."

Cuthwulf nodded. "I understand."

At least someone did.

The Hooded Man pointed at the box in Renweard's arms. "And look after those scrolls." Then he turned and started back down the road towards the village.

"Will she come back?" Renweard called after him. "The... the 'Unraveller'?"

The Hooded Man looked back briefly. "Not if I can help it."

Elswyth faced Cuthwulf and gestured to the book in Father Beocca's arms. "I think I need to read that book."

Cuthwulf nodded, "Yes. You do." He looked at the others. "Come. Let's all go to my house. It's small but I have what we all need right now. Ale."

Praise the gods. Right now she could drink a barrel of it.

193

Elswyth sensed when reading *The Gospel According To Jesus* that she was being drawn into an elaborate deception. It just seemed so unbelievable. Saying that, was it any more unbelievable than the rest of the Christian Bible? Her father had always said that faith in only one god was folly, that the Bible was a collection of silly fables.

For a while Elswyth didn't know what to make of it all, or of the people who had brought it to her. She went to several more meetings with Cuthwulf and the others, asking questions, re-reading *The Gospel According To Jesus*, studying the original scrolls. Cuthwulf helped her to understand some Aramaic so that she could compare certain lines from the scrolls with their English translation.

One day she asked Father Beocca why, being a priest, he was a part of Cuthwulf's group. He was a young man, perhaps younger than Elswyth, although she didn't like to ask. But his sermons at church had always seemed so sincere. Why had he forsaken it all?

"I have only forsaken the lies told by the apostles in the wake of Jesus's death," he replied. "I have not forsaken God. Or Jesus. I still believe with all my heart that Jesus was our saviour. That he was sent by God from the future to prepare us for what lies ahead. For almost a thousand years we have been misunderstanding his lessons."

Elswyth found herself spending more and more time with Cuthwulf, Father Beocca, Renweard and Lyveva. She felt drawn to them. In a way, these people were just like her and her father. They, too, had rejected the doctrines of the Church of Rome and were following their own path. She admired their fortitude – as they admired hers.

And there was something compelling about the Gospel of Jesus, she realised the more she read it. There was something earnest about this man's story. Something real.

Elswyth became a member of Cuthwulf's group. They were doing the work of Jesus – the *real* work of Jesus –

and she wanted to be a part of it. War was coming. A day would come when no one's gods would be able to save them. It was up to them to save themselves.

And saving themselves started now. The first thing Elswyth and the others set out to do was seek a more effective solution to the Danish problem than Lord Dreogan's over-eager and reckless approach, and find a way of secretly influencing those close to him. Elswyth had heard people in the village speak of an attack; everyone was worried. The King of Denmark had reportedly vowed revenge against the English for the mass killing of Danes in England by King Aethelred on St Brice's Day last year, and being near to the coast, Congelstede was vulnerable to a Viking raid. If there was anything Elswyth and the others could do to help protect the village, they were keen to try.

In time, as others started to join their group, Elswyth decided to give the group a name – the Watchers. She felt that they were the watchers of humankind, charged with guarding it and protecting it, and steering it in a direction that would make it strong and resistant when the Last War came.

Centuries later, as the Watchers grew, they changed their name on the basis that in order to 'watch' humanity, they would have to become many, because they would have to have many eyes.

And so the Watchers became known as Million Eyes.

24

April 20th 2027

"How's my kidney bean?" said Adam as he came out of the bathroom. Izzy shuffled towards the bathroom like a zombie, pale-faced with dark shadows swelling beneath her eyes, the bruises of a week's sleeplessness. Adam kissed her cheek and laid a gentle hand on her belly as she passed him.

"*He's* okay," she murmured. "His mother's sick as a dog."

"Oh babe." He decided he would buy her some flowers on his way home. "Why don't you call in sick?"

"Too much to do," she said from the bathroom around a mouthful of toothbrush.

Adam started getting dressed. Then he realised what she'd said. "Wait a minute. *He?*"

She spat and came to the doorway, towelling her face and nodding emphatically. "Only a guy would do this to me. No offence."

He laughed as he walked over to the full-length mirror to straighten his tie and check his hair. Then he stuffed his feet into socks – always the last thing he put on – and went to the kitchen to make Izzy a coffee, throw some cereal down his throat and text his dad a response about going to see him at the weekend.

A few minutes later, Izzy came in clasping a copy of the *Capital Post*, the London newspaper they had delivered each week, her face shadowed with sadness and worry.

"Honey…" she said softly, shaking her head.

He frowned, lowering his phone mid-text. "What is it?"

She laid the paper down, open, on the kitchen worksurface. His whole body went cold and numb at the sight of Curtis's photo next to an article titled *Body of Million Eyes developer found in Battersea Park.*

"What the fuck…"

The article said that Curtis O'Brien, last seen on 5th April – which was the day he was supposed to start his new role on floor twelve – had been discovered dead in some woods in Battersea Park. The police had declared the death a suicide, although there were no details on how or why.

"I'm so sorry, babe," Izzy said, but Adam barely registered her words. "I know you two were good friends." She pulled out one of the bar stools tucked beneath the overhang of the worksurface. "Sit down. Let's talk about it."

Adam didn't sit down. He read the article again, the words starting to blur on the page. Feeling dizzy, he gripped the rim of the worksurface before surrendering and planting his bum on the stool.

Suicide? Curtis wouldn't do that. He'd always been so… so *together*. And Adam knew him well – at least he thought he did.

That said, Adam knew Curtis had some shit in his past. He didn't know what it was, but he suspected it had something to do with the Catholic Church. Adam's mind flitted back to one boozy night at the Seven Kingdoms pub near headquarters, when a slurring and unsteady Curtis launched into an anti-Catholic rant during a conversation they'd been having about the pros and cons of religion. Adam remembered the pain and rage in Curtis's eyes and thinking it wasn't just a stance, it was personal.

He took in a ragged breath and read the article a third time, trying to focus and take it all in.

Wait a minute.

The article said that Curtis was last seen on 5th April. That couldn't be right. Renee Lampard told Adam yesterday that Curtis was working out of the Guildford office.

Unless Million Eyes had something to do with this. *Fuck.* Could they? Could Million Eyes have killed him? *Why?*

A lump of dread started building in his stomach. Izzy was trying to be comforting but her words just bounced right off him.

Then he thought of something. The last contact he'd had from Curtis was that voice message. Adam hadn't listened to the whole message because he'd presumed Curtis had pocket-dialled him.

But this article was saying that Curtis was last seen the day he left that message.

As soon as Izzy had left for work, Adam snatched up his phone and opened his messages with Curtis. He scrolled up to the voice message and tapped 'play'.

He listened past the drone of muffled chatter and occasional rustling he'd heard before. Suddenly, *"Pardon?"*

The voice was a bit louder and clearer, probably closer to the phone. It sounded like Curtis.

More indistinct chatter, then the same voice said, *"Wait – what?"* And a moment later, *"I – I don't know what you're talking abo –"*

Adam homed in on a voice that may have been a woman's, but all her words melted into the background noise.

After almost two minutes, Curtis said, *"The scrolls of Jesus? Jesus didn't write any scrolls."*

Adam shook his foggy head, heart pounding. What the fuck was Curtis on about?

A moment later, more loudly and distinctly and sounding distressed, *"I don't understand. I don't understand any of this. I'm not planning to steal any scrolls. I don't know about any scrolls!"*

And then, voice now wracked with panic, *"But... but Miss Morgan, I wouldn't! I... I won't!"*

A bolt of shock shot up Adam's spine. His hand shook, so much the phone nearly slipped out of it.

Curtis continued, *"Why did you promote me then? If you knew what I'd do, why bring me here? You could've stopped me from ever finding out about this place."*

Another long pause was capped off with a desperate holler, *"But I don't even know what you're talking about!"*

A loud hiss crackled down the phone, made Adam flinch. It was followed by a heavy thud, then the message ended.

Oh my fucking God.

Adam launched into the study, dug his burner phone from the bottom drawer of his desk and phoned Lester. "We need to meet – now." His voice and hands were shaking.

"Okay," said Lester. "I'll tell work I'll be late in this morning. Are you alright?"

"No." He tried to catch his breath, the sound of his own blood rushing in his ears. "No, I'm not."

"Shall we meet in the middle again? That park in Barking?"

"Yeah."

"Okay. I'll leave now. See you soon."

Adam grabbed the newspaper and took the lift to the basement car park where he and Izzy parked their MEcars. On the way, he emailed his boss saying he was sick and wouldn't be in. Reaching his car, he waved his hand over the vein scanner in the driver's door to unlock it and, sliding into the front seat, said, "Activate," and the air-powered engine quietly awoke.

"Good morning, Adam," said the soothing gender-neutral voice of the car's computer. "Your destination, please."

About to say it, he stopped.

What if Million Eyes were tracking him through his MEcar? This was *their* technology, and given what he knew about them, they could've been tracking anyone who owned one.

Fuck this.

He got out, locked the car and walked to Ealing's London Underground station, catching the next tube to Barking.

Just over an hour later, he met Lester in the same place where they met two days ago, when Lester gave Adam the flash drive – a bench close to a large gushing fountain that was useful for drowning out conversations.

"What's going on?" said Lester as Adam sat down. "Has something happened?"

Adam told her about Curtis and showed her the article in the *Capital Post*. She offered her condolences. Then he gave her his MEphone so she could listen to Curtis's voice message.

Lester's brow furrowed with confusion as she listened, rising at the mention of Miss Morgan's name. When the message had finished, she said, "So... Million Eyes are protecting scrolls written by Jesus? Their motives are... *religious?*"

"God knows." He might've smirked at the pun had he not just learned that his friend had been murdered. "But Miss Morgan clearly thought Curtis was going to steal them, whatever they are. That's why she killed him." He stared dumbly at his hands, knowing that Curtis's death hadn't actually sunk in yet and, when it did, it would hit him like a train.

Lifting his gaze, Adam saw that Lester was looking past him at something, the coldness and marble rigidity of her features warming and softening as the corners of her mouth curled slightly into a smile. He instinctively followed her eyes to the path that wound in front of the bench.

No one there.

Lester continued staring at whatever she could see on the path. She inexplicably nodded, like she was listening to someone.

Adam felt a brush of awkwardness. Neither of them had said a word for what felt like a minute, Lester still staring, smiling and nodding.

The uncomfortable silence needed breaking. "Dr Lester?"

Lester's smile evaporated, her attention snapping back to Adam. "Yes?"

"Are *you* okay?"

"Yes, I'm fine, why wouldn't I be?" She said it quickly and with a touch of embarrassment, eyes darting about uncertainly.

Adam thought it best not to pry. He could tell she was an incredibly private person. There was no way she was going to tell him if something was wrong. "Okay. Well, what's next? Because if I was only half-invested before, I'm fully invested now. I wanna nail these fuckers." In normal circumstances he might've regretted swearing in front of the polite and proper Dr Lester, but right now his emotions over Curtis were running high.

Lester didn't seem bothered, nodding, "The best lead we have is still Alison Rayburn. I'm *hoping* she'll change her mind and reach out. I'm going to give her a bit of time. If she still hasn't contacted me, I'll try reaching out to her again. Meantime, I'll do some research, see if I can find out anything about these 'Jesus scrolls'."

"Is there anything else I can do?"

"Why don't you try hacking into Million Eyes' systems again? See if there's anything about what happened to your friend and these scrolls?"

"I'm not sure. I nearly got caught last time, and if I get caught, that's it, it's over."

He looked up. Lester was distracted again, staring at the path by the bench. Something was definitely 'off'.

"Dr Lester, are you sure you're okay?"

Her lips wobbled with a nervous smile. "Yes. I'm fine. I have to go." She stood up. "Do what you think is best, Adam. I'll let you know what I find." She walked speedily out of the park.

Well that was odd. Adam stared at the fountain, glittering in the sun, a faint rainbow arcing through its spray.

His mind whipped back to their first meeting in Hyde Park and the moment Lester offered a pained congratulations on his baby news, which had left him wondering if she'd lost a child.

He realised he knew virtually nothing about her, nor she him, even though they were working together on something that endangered them both.

Maybe it was time he did some digging into his partner in crime.

25

January 9th 1604

King James VI of Scotland, now James I of England too, had a decision to make. He'd had a meeting earlier that day with Sir Robert Chester and some associates, the latest of several in the last few weeks. Sir Robert owned the house in Royston that James was renting so he could go hunting in the heathland. He was a good friend and a good man. And, James had recently learned, part of something that could be of immense consequence to the future of Great Britain.

The hour was late when James returned to the house. There had been a lot to discuss. He entered his bedchamber to find his favourite household squire, Aubrey, lying naked on the bed, reading, his long, copper-brown locks glowing in the candlelight, his muscly arms and legs as chiselled as a stone sculpture. James felt a heat in his groin.

Aubrey looked up from his book. "Your Majesty," he said, smiling so widely that deep shadows formed in his cavernous dimples, flitting those hypnotising blue eyes that he knew made James feel a touch feeble. He swung his perfect legs off the bed, walked over to James and began removing the king's doublet, boots and breeches.

"How was your meeting?" said Aubrey.

"It went well," said James. "Sir Robert Chester and his friends are quite exceptional."

Aubrey was crouched down, peeling off James's

stockings. He stood up, facing him, and the two men stood naked on the large woven rug that depicted James's royal heraldic badge, an amalgamation of the Tudor rose and the Scottish thistle to represent the Union of the Crowns – James's historic ascension to the English throne.

"I am pleased," smiled Aubrey.

Aubrey had become more than James's squire in recent times. He was now something of a confidante as well, and James felt more at ease telling him things than he did his own wife. But then, Queen Anne had grown insolent and disobedient and ever-so-full of opinion since James had assumed England's throne; she now seemed quite capable of arguing over the colour of the sky.

Aubrey poured them both some wine and returned to the bed. James joined him, feeling it time to seek the young man's insight.

"I would speak with you about these meetings I have been having," said James.

"Of course, my king."

James framed Aubrey's pointed chin in his hand, stroking the prickly bristles of his short beard. What a beauty. They exchanged sultry looks, then James pulled his face close and kissed him with passion for nearly a minute. Pulling away to catch his breath, James reached for his cup of wine and took a sip.

Placing the cup down, he said, "Sir Robert and his friends. They are part of, shall we say, a secret group."

"A secret group?" Aubrey grinned and sipped his own wine. "How exciting!"

"They call themselves Million Eyes."

Aubrey's eyes widened and twinkled with recognition.

"You have heard of them?" said James.

Aubrey nodded. "I have heard rumours. I thought they were a myth."

"As did I. It turns out Million Eyes have existed for centuries, operating from the depths of the shadows."

"What is their purpose?"

"It is nothing nefarious. Sir Robert has been inviting me to these meetings so that I can find out more about them. They are simply trying to make things better for our country. They perform charitable works and find ways of solving problems in their local communities. They have people who are formulating new medicines and transportation methods, and building new machines for farming. They even have people who are working on new kinds of weapons, which could prove very helpful if the peace process with Spain were to fail. Many of the things that we take for granted have been invented by members of Million Eyes."

"Mmm." Aubrey looked at him thoughtfully. "But why the secrecy?"

"It is simply their tradition. They are not seeking credit or recognition. They would rather do their good works without attention."

"Are they Protestants?"

James nodded. "Yes. They are very pious. And their loyalty to me is most humbling. Each of them keeps a copy of the *Basilikon Doron*. They believe wholeheartedly in the divine right of kings."

Aubrey's soft expression wrinkled into a frown. "But, Your Majesty, if Million Eyes are committed to doing their good works in secret, why have Sir Robert Chester and his associates revealed themselves to you – their king? Have they not taken an enormous risk?"

"They trust me. They believe that we can help each other."

"Help how?"

"They have decided that they need to be more effectual. Since the 11th century they have been quietly influencing change, but without any real power. Now they are seeking a more direct role in what goes on in this country."

"I thought they wanted to remain a secret."

"They do. No one will know that they are members of Million Eyes, or what Million Eyes even is."

"And what form would this 'direct role' take?"

James took another sip of wine. "They want voices inside Parliament. They want me to grant peerages to a number of their highest-ranking members so that they can sit in the House of Lords. They believe that only with positions in government can they truly make a difference."

"And how will they help you?" Aubrey leaned forwards and ran his fingers through James's hair. "How does Your Majesty benefit from this arrangement?"

"Million Eyes have pledged to support me in matters of law and policy. A secret alliance between them and the monarchy would serve to strengthen my position in Parliament."

"What will you do?"

James had more or less convinced himself while they'd been talking. He downed the rest of his wine and said, "I am inclined to grant their request. I have been looking for a way to cement my hold on England's throne. This could well be it. I would, however, welcome your thoughts."

Aubrey brushed his hand over James's cheek and twirled his long beard around his forefinger. "Your Majesty, you are God's lieutenant upon Earth. You know His will. If this is the course you have chosen, then it is, and can only be, the right one."

James felt a great warmth in his chest. The young man was right. No one understood God's will as he did. And since it was God who had brought Million Eyes to him, His will was clear.

An alliance was to be forged.

"I fear I may love your brain as much as I love your body," said James.

Aubrey grinned and leaned forwards, kissing James softly. The young man tasted of wine mingled with woodsmoke and sweat. James felt his cock tingle, throb and harden. He seized a fistful of Aubrey's hair, roughly, kissing him back with force. Then, as James lay back, Aubrey slid the tip of his tongue down his body and took his king's full length deep into his warm, wet mouth, and the entire bedchamber fell away.

The next day, the king left the house on a boar hunt and Aubrey took a stroll into Royston town. Although there wasn't a cloud in the sky, the air was glacial and Aubrey was glad of his fur-shouldered sheepskin cloak. He noticed as he walked along Ermine Street that clumps of snow from three days ago remained, despite the flood of sunshine.

As he approached the Royse Stone – the footstone that was once the base of Roisia's Cross and had given the town its name – Aubrey saw Sir Robert Chester walking towards him from the opposite direction, as encased in wool and fur as he was.

"Good day, Aubrey," Robert said brightly.

"Good day, Sir Robert," said Aubrey.

They stopped about a foot apart. Sir Robert's eyes darted briefly back and forth, checking that nobody was around. Then he leaned towards Aubrey's face, the chalky steam of his breath hanging in the air between them. He whispered, "Well?"

Aubrey replied quietly, his own breath leaving his lips in a puff of white, "It worked. He is planning to grant your request."

Robert nodded with satisfaction, his smile widening. "Excellent. At last we can start effecting some real change."

"I see that you have not told the king everything…"

"No. His Majesty is fiercely Protestant. We must tread carefully on that front."

"Is there anything further you need from me?"

"Just keep doing what you're doing. We will be touch." Sir Robert produced a small pouch of coins from a pocket inside his cloak and dropped it into Aubrey's gloved hand. "A very good day to you, Aubrey."

"And to you, sir." Aubrey slipped the pouch of coins into his own cloak and they parted ways.

26

April 28th 2027

Miss Morgan had been wide awake staring at the ceiling for the past three hours, thinking about yesterday's bombshell and whether she was going to be able to keep it from, well, *everyone*. She had to, of course. Her legacy – and the legacy of Million Eyes – depended on it.

There was a more urgent consideration now, too. The oraculum. Today was the day and the damn thing still hadn't activated. Only hours remained. Miss Morgan hated things happening at the last minute. She liked to be prepared.

Something frightening occurred to her in that moment. Could there have been something wrong with it? Could it have malfunctioned? Perhaps the oraculum would *never* activate.

It was impossible to tell.

The heavy darkness played tricks on her tired eyes, making it appear that the swirls in the ceiling paint were moving and changing shape. At 3.00am, the tranquil melody of Bach's *Sheep May Safely Graze* weaved its way around the room from her phone. Its bright screen smeared a gentle blueish glow over the ceiling; it was still again.

The call woke the guy she had brought home last night, who'd fallen asleep, snoring like a sluggish starter motor the moment they'd finished fucking, and whose name right now escaped her. He stirred and rolled over, murmuring, "W-what is that?"

"My phone." Miss Morgan let the airy strings caress her ears for a moment, then reached to grab the phone off the bedside table. It was Carina Boone, head of Time Travel. She tapped the screen to answer just as the bouncy intro was about to segue into the graceful main melody line, and placed it to her ear. "I presume you have a good reason for calling me at 3am, Miss Boone?"

"I'm sorry to disturb, Miss Morgan. We need you at headquarters. Something's happened."

"*Something.* Boone, I hate vagueness. Especially at 3am."

"S-sorry, ma'am. It's the Augur. It's been destroyed."

"What! How?" Miss Morgan sat up straight against her headboard and switched on her bedside lamp. The light hit the bloke she now remembered might've been called Brad in the face and made his brow droop and his gently closed eyes squeeze shut like he was on the toilet and couldn't go. He pulled the duvet over his head.

"Sabotage," said Boone.

Fuck. Sabotaging the Augur meant that someone was planning to alter the timeline without Million Eyes knowing about it in advance. And Miss Morgan knew exactly who that 'someone' was.

Miss Morgan lurched out of bed and walked out of the bedroom to the other end of the landing so that Brad wouldn't hear her. She whispered, "Raise the Shield immediately."

"Already done, ma'am. The tower's in lockdown."

"Alright. Run continuous sensor sweeps. Call me if you detect anything that's changed. I'm on my way."

She returned to the bedroom, threw the phone down on the bed and dashed over to her wardrobe.

"Where you going?" Brad's tiny head poked out from the turquoise lump of duvet.

"Work." She selected her pine green skirt suit and started putting it on.

He grinned at her. "That's a shame. I was hoping for a round two."

"No, thank you."

Brad's grin disappeared and he looked awkward. "Oh. Well, could I at least take you for breakfast when you're back?"

She shook her head, "You're not going to be here when I'm back. I'm not sure why you're still here now."

Now he looked affronted. "You mean you were expecting me to leave after we made love?"

She curled her lip. "I'll pretend I didn't hear that. *That* was not what we made."

"Sorry, I didn't realise you were such an unfeeling –" He stopped himself, catching Miss Morgan's wide-eyed stare and hopefully remembering who he was talking to. "Fine. I'll go." He dug himself out of the duvet and pulled on his trousers, socks and shirt. She, meanwhile, was stooped over the dressing table, hurriedly applying some eyeshadow, mascara and bronze lipstick.

Even though his dignity was running on low, he chose to drain the rest of it on his way out. "Can I see you again?"

She simply raised an eyebrow at him.

Finally getting the message, he shook his head, huffed with disgust and stormed downstairs. A moment later, the front door to her apartment slammed.

Miss Morgan grabbed her handbag and followed him out. Leaving the building she saw that his MEcar was already halfway up the road. Good. Meant she didn't have to look at his pathetic face again. Honestly, he wasn't even that attractive. She'd obviously been wearing extra-thick wine goggles last night, but that was because she'd drunk way more than normal in an effort to forget what had happened earlier in the day.

She walked briskly to the Looming Tower, arriving at 3.17am and making her way to the rear of the building. She walked up to a plain concrete wall on the ground floor and stepped close so it could scan her. Then a rectangular line became visible and, with a smooth, quiet scrape, a door-shaped section of the wall slid inwards and to the left. A hidden entrance, for executive use only, specially designed to open through the Shield.

Miss Morgan stepped inside and the secret door closed behind her, lights flickering on. She walked to the nearest lift and went down to Time Travel.

Nearly everyone working in Time Travel that night was gathered in the Augur chamber. She saw why when she entered. The place was a mess. Nine staff members were lying dead on the floor with burn marks on their chests characteristic of disruptor blasts. It looked like at least one had been stabbed in the neck with something, blood pooling around his head.

The metal dome that housed the biological core of the Augur had been cracked open, doubtless by a high-yield disruptor blast – one of the few things powerful enough. Everything inside the dome was fried. The four glass columns of bioneural infusion were smashed, the whiteish spilled fluid emitting an almost unbearable stench, hence why several staff were hurrying to mop it all up. The machine's screens were ripped out, its numerous conduits and pistons reduced to scorched, smoking rubble. All around, frayed, exposed cables sizzled brutishly.

"What the fuck happened here?" said Miss Morgan loudly.

Carina Boone, who'd been talking to one of the surviving Augur analysts, looked up and rushed over to her.

"Someone dressed in a black stealth suit and armed with a disruptor got past all our security and stormed the Augur chamber," said Boone.

"How is that even possible?"

"We're not sure yet, ma'am. I was a few floors up at the time. I'm still trying to get a full picture from the staff who were down here."

"Do you have any leads on who did this?"

"All we know is that it was someone inside Million Eyes with knowledge of this department and its location and access to our weaponry. External CCTV showed them entering the building at 2.39am using biometric authentication. However, they masked their signature as they went so we couldn't tell whose biometrics were being used."

"Surely we can get around that."

"We can. It'll just take a bit of time."

Miss Morgan nodded. "And the Augur?"

Boone looked at the wrecked machine. "I'm afraid there's no repairing it. The biological core is not responding to any stimuli. It's dead. We're going to have to start from scratch." She paused and qualified her statement. "If we can find another suitable candidate."

"That's unlikely. Evans' abilities were more powerful than anyone else we've encountered."

Rachel Evans was a sensile. Sensiles had a broader, deeper cognisance of time and could remember, in varying degrees, events from multiple timelines. For most of them it was just like déjà vu, but Rachel Evans' perceptions were vivid, coherent, detailed – and a precious source of intel for Million Eyes' time travel assignments. So Miss Morgan recruited her.

Then, years later, Evans went rogue. Miss Morgan didn't want to just kill her – her abilities were too valuable. So Million Eyes' most talented minds came together and found a way to extract Evans' medial temporal lobe, fuse it with cybernetic components and house it inside a central processing unit, transforming her perceptions into data. And the Augur was born.

"We were able to enhance Evans' abilities when we adapted her brain into the Augur," said Boone. "Perhaps we can do the same with another sensile. Make whoever's brain we use as sensitive to the fabric of time as Evans' was."

"Perhaps." But Miss Morgan wasn't confident about that. "Has the sensor grid picked up any changes to the timeline?"

"None yet. The Shield's holding at a hundred percent."

"Alright. Keep monitoring. And assign a team to investigate the break-in. I want to know who's betrayed us."

Boone nodded, "Yes, ma'am." She headed for the

Augur chamber door, removing her phone from her pocket as she went.

Miss Morgan breathed a deep, ragged sigh and felt her shoulders sag as she stood watching the clean-up. Small skid loaders were scooping up debris from the Augur whilst dead employees were being zipped into body bags and wheeled out of the chamber on stretchers.

Getting into the lift to go up to the C-Suite, Miss Morgan winced imperceptibly at the sight of Dr Neether, who was about to step out. Her brown hair looked bedraggled and a couple of damp strands clung to the gaping crater down the left side of her flushed face. She recoiled when she saw Miss Morgan, her solitary eye widening. She brushed the hair out of her face in a vain effort to look more presentable.

"Miss Morgan, I – I –" The woman was breathless. Miss Morgan noticed fresh stitches close to the ear that had been sheared off and remembered that Dr Neether had undergone another minor facial surgery yesterday.

"You're here about the oraculum, aren't you?" The hope that it was finally offloading its secrets was hot in Miss Morgan's chest. Surely that was the only explanation for Dr Neether being here at this hour.

"Yes, ma'am."

"Is it active?"

"Yes." Dr Neether stepped out of the lift, her half-face glimmering with small droplets of sweat. Her one-eyed gaze briefly followed the body bag that went past on a stretcher.

Miss Morgan sighed with relief. "Thank God for that."

Dr Neether took a loud breath in. "The Augur – it's been sabotaged?"

"Yes, it has." Miss Morgan frowned accusingly. "Did the oraculum tell you this would happen?" If it did, surely Dr Neether should've stopped it.

Dr Neether gave a mini head shake. "It activated just after. So while I didn't know that the Augur would be destroyed, I know what needs to happen next."

27

October 24th 1605

Darkness fell as young pauper and apprentice baker Tom Digby finished loading the ovens in Mr Mott's bake shop with fresh firewood, in preparation for tomorrow's baking. The comforting smell of the day's bread was in his nostrils. It was the only thing he liked about the place.

"You've been stealing from me again," said Mr Mott, as Tom closed the last oven door.

A swallow caught in Tom's throat.

He heard Mr Mott's footsteps behind him but didn't turn round. His voice now close to his ear, "You have, haven't you, you dirty little beggar!"

Tom's heart raced. He said quietly, "I haven't, sir."

Mr Mott grabbed Tom's jaw in his worn, scabby fingers, yanked it to face him, the bread smell instantly replaced by the fetid stink of Mr Mott's breath.

"You are a liar and a thief," he spat, a tiny bead of the man's saliva springing from his crusty lips and landing on Tom's cheek.

Tom couldn't look away. Mr Mott was still holding his chin. He just had to stand there, breathe in the man's toxic vapours, look upon his repugnant face – skin haggard, blotchy and scarred, eyes bloodshot, grey beard unwashed and flecked with crumbs of dough.

"I will allow you to make it up to me," said Mr Mott, fingers easing off Tom's chin.

Trepidation filled Tom's gut like a meal he couldn't digest.

The old man stooped towards him, his face inches from Tom's. He shoved his hand between Tom's legs and roughly grabbed his cock and balls through his breeches. "You want to make it up to me, don't you?"

Tom nodded.

Mr Mott released him, stood straight and smiled. "Come."

This was now a daily routine. The shop would close, Tom would finish his jobs, Mr Mott would accuse Tom of thievery – each time completely falsely, as though it was part of some warped role play – and then he would invite Tom up to the tiny attic room on the second floor to 'make it up to him'. There, he'd get Tom to remove his clothes and... he would...

No.

Not again.

Never again.

It all happened so fast. Before Tom even knew what he was doing, one of the large baking peels was in his hands.

Mr Mott had turned around, intending to go upstairs, expecting Tom to follow.

With both hands Tom swung the peel hard.

The edge of the wooden blade connected with the back of Mr Mott's head. He lurched forwards, fell against the banister of the staircase. After a moment, he reached round to the back of his head and wet his fingers with the blood that was seeping from it.

Unsteady on his feet, Mr Mott turned half his body towards Tom and murmured, "What the hell are you doing?"

Tom swung the peel again, slamming the blade into the side of his face. The old man went down, landing flat on his back, dazed. He stared at Tom, wide-eyed and open-mouthed, hand clasping his cheek. Then his expression twisted from shock to fury. "You evil worm!"

Tom brought the flat of the blade down onto his face,

smashing in all his teeth. He raised it, brought it down again. And again.

There was movement upstairs. "What's going on down there?" called Mr Mott's wife.

Tom ignored her. His whole body surged with hate. He couldn't control it. Mr Mott still lived, murmuring, moving his head slightly. Tom raised the peel once more, turned the blade so that its edge faced the floor, and plunged it down. Mr Mott's neck crunched and blood gushed from his lips. Tom wanted to strike his foul, stinking head from his shoulders, but his weapon was a wooden bread peel, not a sword. He brought it down two more times.

He barely registered the fast, clunking footsteps coming down the wooden stairs. Mrs Mott appeared at the foot of the stairs as Tom mashed her husband's neck with a fourth blow, head and body now connected by only a couple of inches of bloody pulp. Alas, the bread peel snapped in half on the fourth blow, leaving Tom unable to complete the beheading – but at least the plague sore was dead.

Tom looked at Mrs Mott – an ugly, obese woman who was losing her hair. Her pinched eyes widened at the sight of her husband's corpse, but she didn't scream. Her eldest son, Lawrence, a stocky, florid-faced twenty-year-old, appeared on the stairs next to her. "Mother?"

Mrs Mott pointed at Tom and bawled, "Seize him!"

Tom threw down the broken shaft of the baking peel and launched across the room towards the door. He tripped over a sack of oats that was leaning against the wall and was brought to his knees. He felt Lawrence's huge hand on his shoulder, spinning him round. Then a glancing blow to his chin flung him backwards. His elbows smashed against the wood floor, searing pains shooting up his arms.

He'd landed right next to a bucket of firewood. As Lawrence lunged, Tom grabbed a log and swung it hard. It connected with Lawrence's head, sent him hurtling into the baker's table.

A gunshot rang out as Tom clambered to his feet, made his heart stop.

It had come from outside. Lawrence recovered quickly after colliding with the baker's table. The gunshot made them all freeze and swing their gaze to the windows. Horses shrieked with fear but it was too dark to see what was going on.

Mrs Mott returned her attentions to Tom, who sprang for the door, swung it open so hard its hinges nearly came apart, and bolted into the street. "Get after him!" he heard her scream.

The sky was now black as ink, Ashfield Lane thick with shadow as the weak light from the lanterns hanging over people's doors limped through them. Tom glimpsed a dimly lit commotion going on, saw Mr Tadley, the tobacconist over the road, wielding a musket.

There was no time to find out what was happening as Lawrence charged out of the shop after him. Tearing off his apron and tossing it to the ground, Tom hurtled up Ashfield Lane.

Where would he go? Not home. Tom had told his hateful father what was happening at Mr Mott's and his father had ordered him to put up with it for the money and skills. As soon as he found out that Tom had forsaken both for freedom, he would have no qualms giving Tom up to a constable to protect himself. Actually, he would beat him bloody first, then hand him over.

Tom ran onto Canley Street. He looked back. Lawrence wasn't far behind. His face was bloodied but in the darkness it looked like mud. There was a sizeable gap between them, but it was closing.

Tom flew past the Globe Theatre, up a pitch-dark and foul-smelling side street, came out by St Saviour's Church and the approach to London Bridge.

There was no way he could stay in the Borough. The Motts – and his father – would find him. He would have to flee to the City.

He hurtled towards the southern gatehouse of London

Bridge. Crowning the parapets of the Great Stone Gateway was a display of tall poles topped with dark blobs. Years ago, when Tom first saw them from a distance, he thought they were giant versions of those delicious-looking candy sticks the rich folk ate, hence why the gulls were so hungrily pecking at them. But no. They were heads. Criminals and traitors' heads, dipped in tar and impaled on pikes, their scraggly hair rippling in the breeze while the gulls feasted on their festering eyeballs.

He'd long hoped to one day see Mr Mott's head up there. It was where it belonged. Actually, Tom knew a horde of people whose heads belonged on that gate, his own wretched father included.

Tom glanced back as he ran beneath the open portcullis onto the bridge, Lawrence but metres behind him.

Shit. Perhaps this was a mistake. Tom was forced to slow to a fast walk, his path now laden with obstruction. Terraced shops and houses were perched on both sides of the bridge, their upper storeys overhanging the road below, forming the appearance of a tunnel. The road was not wide. Tom found himself weaving between pedestrians, wardens and bridge watchmen, swerving round coaches, wagons and packhorses. It was much busier than he'd expected, but the famous structure was the only crossing over the Thames, and from the looks of it, all the shops on the bridge stayed open later than everywhere else.

Tom looked back, breathless from all the running, chin and elbows throbbing from the fight in the shop. Lawrence was pushing people out of the way to get to him. Tom saw him shove aside a watchman, who turned and angrily grabbed his arm. "Oi! Watch where you're going!"

Blood pounding hot and viscous through his veins, Tom continued picking his way through the crowds. It was likely that Lawrence would tell the watchman that Tom was a murderer – then both men would be after him.

Tom came out of the first tunnel of shops onto an open section of the bridge where the crowd was thinner. He was greeted by the wonder that was Nonsuch House, a four-storey, elaborately carved and gaudily painted palace, most of it overhanging the river and balancing even more precariously than the other buildings on a system of struts and supports.

No time to admire its opulence, Tom ran through the palace archway, which straddled the bridge. He glanced over his shoulder. No sign of Lawrence. Had he lost him?

He continued apace into the next tunnel of shops. The smell of candy and hot pork pies mingled with the stink of open latrines. *Damn.* He hit the back of a jam of people squeezing past a broken-down cart and ground to a halt. He glanced back. Still no Lawrence. A few feet of movement later, he looked back again and saw him. Their eyes met and Lawrence's snapped wide with rage. The watchman wasn't with him; perhaps he wanted to deal with Tom on his own.

Tom had no choice but to charge through the queue. Screams of "Oi!" resounded and one man grabbed him but Tom was small and nimble enough to break free.

He sped past the Chapel of St Thomas into another passage of shops and houses. Finally reaching the end of the bridge, he flew up the nearest street. He still hadn't lost Lawrence, the stubborn ape. Perhaps he would have to fight him too, even kill him. But perhaps he deserved it. Tom had always had this feeling that Mr Mott's wife and children knew full well what was going on in the attic room above them and let it happen, as though allowing an old man his indulgences. Which made them guilty, too.

Perhaps I should've killed them all.

Tom was exhausted now. He felt like an anvil was pressing down on his lungs. His heart wasn't long from bursting. He couldn't keep going for much longer.

He turned up another narrow side street, came out near a house that caught his eye and stopped. It was dark, the door was open, the windows unshuttered, the lantern on the outside wall broken. Tom peered inside, straining to see in the low light coming from the house next door. There was nothing but some empty barrels in the large downstairs room. Hanging loosely over the door was a partly broken sign with a picture of a musket, which told Tom that this used to be the shop and residence of a gunsmith. Sadly no guns were in sight.

Tom heard approaching footfalls. Lawrence.

He tiptoed inside, went and sat on the floor in a shadow-draped corner behind a couple of barrels.

He hugged his knees close to his chest and was so covered with sweat his shirt was clinging to him like a second skin.

The footfalls got closer, louder. Tom pressed his fingers into his knees till he could feel them bruising. If he had to, he'd fight and kill Lawrence, but the more he thought about it, the more he hoped it wouldn't come to that. Mr Mott was the only person he'd killed. He knew it would change him. He'd seen how it had changed others.

He had enough blood on his hands for one day.

His heart clobbered his ribs as the footfalls got louder still. Any moment now, Lawrence would come charging onto the street.

The footfalls stopped.

Tom hugged his knees tighter, buried his face in them. Froze.

They started again. But this time they got quieter.

Yes! Lawrence hadn't noticed the house. He'd gone in another direction. He'd lost him. *Finally.*

Tom let out a sigh of relief and released his legs, which had started to stiffen. He sat for a moment, eyes honed on the rope hoops that bound the barrel right in front of him, waiting for his breath to return, his thumping heart to settle, his skin to dry of sweat.

He decided he would stay in the gunsmith's house for a little while, just to make sure Lawrence was far enough away. Then he'd wander the streets and find a workhouse. No one would find him there. He'd give a false name and start his life anew. Free of Mr Mott. Free of his father.

About five minutes later, Tom heard the shuffle and crunch of approaching footsteps.

He swallowed hard, peered through the gap in the barrels in front of him.

Lawrence?

A man stepped inside the front door. Not Lawrence. The light was weak but Tom could just about make him out. He had a handsome face, slim build and long, scraggly black hair beneath a tall, conical hat with a flat top. He wore slender breeches, shiny high-cut boots and a dark-coloured jerkin with prominent shoulder wings, buttoned at the waist and open at the chest, over a plain, light-coloured doublet.

The man stood in the downstairs room, watching through the window. Tom saw him consult a clock-watch that was fastened to his doublet and reasoned that he must be waiting for someone.

A few minutes later, another man entered through the door.

Tom held his breath.

This man was uglier but dressed more richly. He had a finely pleated white ruff and a long, thick cape and jerkin over a slashed, patterned doublet with buttons that glinted gold in the low light, and wider breeches that billowed as he walked. His hat was similar to the other man's but adorned with a feather, and he didn't seem to be able to stand straight. His back was curved, his head bent sharply forwards.

"Well?" said the hunchbacked man. "Is everything in place?"

"Yes," said the handsome man.

"Tell me."

"The thirty-six barrels of gunpowder have been hidden in the undercroft beneath the House of Lords. When the parliament meets on the 5th, one of my men will be down there to light the fuse. He will make his escape across the Thames at midnight."

Tom's stomach lurched. *Gunpowder? Parliament?*

"And what of the situation in the Midlands?" said the hunchbacked man.

"As we speak, another of my men is raising a hunting party to seize the princess as soon as it is done."

Tom felt a chill. Whatever this treason was, it was grave.

"It sounds like you have everything in hand," said the hunchbacked man. "I will continue to ensure that nobody in Whitehall suspects anything."

Heavens – Whitehall? This was one of the king's men!

The hunchbacked man turned to leave.

"Wait," said the handsome man, stepping forwards and raising his arm. "There is something I must make you aware of."

The hunchbacked man stopped and turned. "Yes?"

"Several of the men continue to have doubts."

"Doubts? About what?"

"About you. They believe that you will betray us at the last minute. They know that, as a Protestant, you do not believe in our cause nor our holy duty to do what we must to further it. I have tried to explain to them that you have your own reasons for being involved. That you are trying to cure a… a sickness of some kind within the parliament. But your lack of specifics has left them unconvinced."

The hunchbacked man lunged forwards, came within a couple of inches of the handsome man's face. "They must not back out." He sounded anxious.

"Neither of us wants that. Give us more. Convince us that you are as committed to this as we are."

Tom saw the rise and fall of the hunchbacked man's chest as he gave a deep, frustrated sigh.

"Fine. I am doing this because King James has betrayed not just you and your Catholic friends. He has betrayed us all. He is in league with a secret cabal to whom he has been granting an unprecedented number of peerages. As a consequence, this cabal now controls the House of Lords."

"And what is their purpose? Are they Catholic or Protestant?"

"I do not know if they are either. Their purpose is clear only in its fiendishness. I believe they intend to amass more power until they can rightfully call this country... *theirs*. I do not intend to let that happen. Parliament must be cleansed."

Tom shivered. He had no idea what a 'cabal' was or what the hunchbacked man was really talking about, but the handsome man seemed satisfied with the explanation, giving a pronounced nod that triggered the hunchbacked man to turn and leave the house. The handsome man waited a few moments, then he left as well.

Tom knew what he had to do. Find a priest – someone who was literate and trustworthy and could pen a letter to William Parker, the Baron Monteagle. Until two years ago, Tom and his father were servants in the Baron's household in Hoxton, where Tom had made close friends among the Baron's entourage. Then his father went and stole a vast haul of the Baron's valuables, leading the both of them to have to flee the house and never see any of them again. And the theft didn't make Tom and his father rich anyway. His father had squandered it all on drink within a few weeks.

Tom had always wanted to find a way of saying sorry. Perhaps this was it. As a member of the parliament, the Baron was very likely to be present at the State Opening when these heinous plotters intended to ignite thirty-six barrels of gunpowder. If Tom could get a letter to him, warning him not to go, he could very well save his life.

Tom climbed out of the shadows behind the barrels and slunk out of the house, looking around to make sure the coast was clear. Then he turned to go up the narrow side street he had come down to escape from Lawrence, and began looking for the nearest church.

28

April 28th 2027

Lester was on a written warning with Ethan after swanning off to meet Alison Rayburn. She'd managed to apply herself for just long enough to complete the Torbury Farm excavation plan so that Ethan could give the developers a start date – a stop-gap for keeping him off her back. But she had other work that had been piling up for weeks now. He'd soon be at her door again. The problem was, Lester couldn't be arsed with any of it. It was hard for her to care one jot about archaeology and palaeontology after learning that the past she thought she knew, the history she'd dedicated her life to studying, was a lie. A lie that was bleeding into the present. The British Republic was a secret autocracy. Studying bones and rocks and bits of old wall didn't really compare to exposing the conspiracy of the millennium.

"I hear you told Ethan that the box we found at Cawston Manor was empty," said Marni, one of the conservators on the Cawston Manor dig, as Lester was making a cup of tea in the kitchen that morning.

Ah – the other problem. Ethan was still suspicious that Lester had stolen artefacts from the Cawston Manor dig. She'd insisted that anyone who saw any letters in the box that was excavated was mistaken. Now here was Marni, who was there and probably saw them with her own eyes, asking her about them directly. *Great.*

Lester kept her cool. "That's right, Marni. It was."

"Sam, I saw you take something out of that box. Looked like letters to me. I saw you reading them, before you hurried back to the vans. Didn't see them again after that."

Lester swallowed the lump of nervousness in her throat, tried not to let it show. "I don't know what you're talking about. There were no letters. The box was empty."

Marni frowned. "Why are you lying?"

"Excuse me?"

"Well I just… I *saw* you, Sam."

Lester sighed. "Marni, I like you. I do. But please don't forget your place. I'm your superior, okay? You don't speak to me like this."

Marni's cheeks reddened. "I'm sorry. I was just –"

"Mistaken. You were just mistaken."

Marni shook her head, "Fine." She clomped out of the kitchen with obvious umbrage and Lester breathed an imperceptible sigh of relief. Another successful deflection of questions about Jennifer's letters.

Marni's probing was probably Ethan-instigated. He was looking to catch her out.

At least no one had any proof that she was lying. Yet, anyway.

Lester returned to her office with her tea. "This came for you," said Kevin as she passed his desk, handing her a letter in a fuchsia pink envelope with her mum's calligraphic handwriting on it. A card for her birthday, which was two days ago, but she'd ignored the occasion this year, forbidding Brody from buying her anything or even saying happy birthday.

She closed her office door and sat down at her desk to open the card. There was no age on it. No need to remind her she was now a year shy of forty. Just a cute drawing of some hedgehogs by a flowerbed. She skipped over the generic saccharine rhymes that might've touched her once. However, countless condolence cards and sympathy messages since Georgia died had made her desensitised to shop-bought schmaltz.

Reaching the middle of the multipage card, she saw that her mother had written the usual *Dear Samantha... All our love, Mum and Dad* on the right side and an extensive note on the left. It read:

> Samantha, please call me. We've barely spoken in months.

There was a reason for that. All she wanted to talk about was Georgia.

> You don't answer my calls. You hardly ever reply to my text messages. I feel so distant from you at the moment and I don't like it. I know you're in pain. I spoke to Brody.

So he'd been talking to her mum behind her back again, had he?

> I know I'm not around the corner, but I'm always on the end of the phone. Please, just call. I've never seen you close up like this before. It isn't healthy. Brody told me you stopped going to your counsellor. I really think you should rethink that. Your Dad and I love you. Mum.

Lester felt a tiny ache in her chest. She swallowed it away.

She did miss her. She missed them both. But she needed more time.

Her thoughts returned to Million Eyes. She hadn't checked her burner phone since she arrived at the office. *Best do that.* She took it out of her handbag.

A missed call and text message from Adam. Call me when you get this. Something's happening at the Looming Tower.

She dropped the birthday card into the bottom drawer of her desk and called him back. "Hi, it's me." She spoke quietly, although the soundproofing on her door was pretty good.

"Hi," said Adam. "I got an email first-thing telling me not to come into work today. Apparently headquarters has been locked down due to a security breach."

"That's strange. Have they ever done that before?"

"Not that I know of. Not while I've been there. Do you think they're onto us somehow?"

Lester paused and deliberated her answer for a moment. This past week, she had been researching the 'scrolls of Jesus' which had seemingly led Million Eyes to murder Adam's friend, Curtis O'Brien. In an old Jewish text she'd found a single reference to a rumour that Jesus had written a 'gospel' during his ministry. A gospel that told a very different story to the one in the four of the New Testament. But there were no details and she couldn't find any mention of this rumour elsewhere, with most scholars agreeing that Jesus hadn't written anything.

But all of this research had been on the Uzu computer with the hidden IP address that Gavin had sourced for her, and in libraries, trawling through books. Million Eyes couldn't have known anything. Unless they were already watching her...

Lester wasn't going to let paranoia get the better of her. "No. I don't think so. Is there any way you can find out what's going on?"

"I could go in anyway," said Adam. "See if I can see anything."

"Yeah. Do that. Keep me –"

Another call was coming in. She'd saved the number. It was Alison Rayburn.

"Oh, wow, what timing," Lester murmured.

"What?"

"Alison Rayburn's calling me. I better take this."

"Shit – do you think she's decided to talk?"

"We'll find out."

Lester hung up and tapped to answer Alison's call. "Hello?"

"Hi. Er – is that Dr Lester?" Alison's voice was small, afraid.

"Speaking."

"It's Alison Rayburn. I wondered if we could… if we could talk?"

A small shot of adrenaline flitted through Lester. "Yes. We can. I can come by. Are you busy now?"

"No. Not busy."

"Are you at home?"

"Yep."

"Great. I'll be there before midday."

"Okay."

Lester grabbed her coat and swept out of her office. She noticed Ethan walking up the corridor towards her office with a MEpad in his hand, and ignored him.

"Sam, where are you going?" Ethan said.

"Out. Sorry. Family stuff."

"What family stuff?"

Halfway out of the door to Field Operations as he said it, Lester didn't bother replying. She raced downstairs through Forensic Archaeology to the LIPA car park. Her phone buzzed as she got into her car. Ethan. Sam, you're on a written warning. If you don't come back right now and explain to me exactly where you're going and what you're doing, I can't promise you'll have a job to come back to.

Lester tossed her phone onto the passenger seat, instructed her sat-nav to take her to 42 Plunkett's Walk, Meath, and drove off.

Lester pulled up outside number 42 and got out. The road was as sleepy as the last time she was here, but she still scoured it up and down for anyone who might be surveilling the house.

No one. It was just a harmless residential road. Lester walked up the crazy paving path, pressed the doorbell and waited, glancing through the ground floor-spanning windows and remembering it was mirror glass when she could only see a reflection of the front lawn. Slightly quicker than last time, somebody started unlocking the door.

"Hi," said Alison, opening the door just wide enough to poke her head out and check that Lester was alone.

Lester smiled, "Hi."

Satisfied, Alison opened the door wider and stepped behind it, beckoning Lester in. Lester followed Alison through the spacious hallway, past a floating glass staircase, into a large lounge awash with clean lines, plain surfaces and lots of grey and white. It was as sparse and clinical as the outside, with white-stained laminate floors and nothing on the walls but a wall-mounted TV and a single floating shelf with an artificial potted plant. It felt more like an office than a home.

Lester sat down on one of the two large, black, uncomfortable-looking leather sofas in front of a white coffee table. Alison sat on the other. Lester wondered if Alison was going to offer her a drink after she'd just driven almost an hour and a half to see her. It was looking unlikely as Alison sat silently on the edge of the sofa, taut as an elastic band, knees close together and hands gripping them. Clearly Lester was going to be leading this conversation. She eased her in with a white lie, "You have a lovely house. How long have you lived here?"

Alison exhaled deeply. "This was our parents' house. Stuart moved in here after they died. I moved in after I split up with my husband." She glanced around the room. "It's not quite how I'd have it. Too minimalist. But Stuart liked it. So I haven't wanted to change it."

Lester smiled. "What made you change your mind? About talking to me?"

"I… I don't know, really. I guess… I guess I realised it

was time I trusted someone. And I did a little research on you. You seem legit."

Lester nodded, "I am."

The tiniest of smiles flickered on Alison's lips.

Reaching into her handbag hanging over her shoulder, Lester said, "Do you mind if I make some notes?"

"Sure."

She pulled out a notepad and pen. "Great. So, tell me about Stuart's disappearance."

"Okay." Alison took another deep breath and rubbed her knees. "I knew he was looking into Million Eyes. He said he'd found out that Million Eyes had invented... look, this is going to sound barmy."

"I'm listening."

"Time travel. He found out Million Eyes had invented time travel. And also, and I know this seems like conspiratorial claptrap, he found out that they were involved – somehow – in Princess Diana's death."

Lester nodded, straight-faced. "Okay..." She didn't want to give away that she already knew all that, or discourage Alison from continuing by reacting with shock or disbelief.

"I thought he was crazy," Alison continued, "but he said he had proof. He didn't know what to do. Then he did something to override their security and found out that Million Eyes were controlling the government somehow. I told him we should go to the police, but he said Million Eyes have people inside the police."

"Mm-hmm."

Lester, scribbling notes and periodically looking up, noticed Alison's shoulders slacken and her hands fold together in her lap. She seemed to be relaxing a bit.

"I came home one night, found Stuart drunk," she continued. "He said he'd called a man called Gregory Ferro, some blogger who was posting articles about time travellers interfering with historical events, and had posted something about them killing Diana. He said he'd told Ferro everything – that the time travellers he was looking for were Million Eyes. I told him he shouldn't have done that, but Stuart said he needed to do *something* with the information. And since Ferro was trying to expose the time travellers responsible for Diana's death, he was the only person Stuart could be sure wasn't a Million Eyes mole."

A thin shadow fell over Lester's notepad as Alison abruptly stood up. "I've just realised I didn't offer you a drink."

To be honest, Lester was now so absorbed in the story she just wanted Alison to keep going – even though she was parched and could easily have downed a glass of water.

"No, thank you, I'm fine."

"Oh. Okay." Alison sat back down, looking uncomfortable again.

"Please go on."

She nodded. "We, er, we then heard Ferro had died in a housefire. Stuart was beside himself. He was certain he'd been murdered. He blamed himself. And he knew if they'd got to Ferro, they'd get to him. He'd made himself a target. Exactly what I was worried about."

"What did he do?"

"Dumped his phone and his computers – all his electronics – and ran away. I, er... That was the last time I ever saw him." She paused, swallowing, a deep sadness filling up her eyes.

"I'm sorry," said Lester softly.

Emotion weakening her voice slightly, Alison continued, "It wasn't the last time I spoke to him though. A day or so later, a bunch of people in suits who said they were from the police turned up at the house. Showed me a warrant to search it and said they were investigating Stuart for a series of offences they wouldn't disclose. It was bullshit, obviously. I knew it was *them*."

"Did they find anything?"

"They basically ransacked the place. Stuart had got rid of most of his stuff, so they took my computer, my

234

phone, and a bunch of paperwork – I never got any of it back."

Lester looked down at her notes. "And you mentioned you spoke to Stuart again – when was that?"

"A few days after the search. He called me on a secure line from somewhere up north. He said he was okay, said he was hiding. And... he gave me something."

Lester stopped scribbling and looked up. "Gave you something?"

"Yes. A code. He said that by entering the code into the network mandate extension of any Million Eyes computer, I'd get access to all the information I needed to bring them down. He said to use it if I didn't hear from him."

Lester wrote down *network mandate extension.* She had a feeling it was important. "And did you? Hear from him again?"

She shook her head, lips quivering slightly.

"I really am sorry."

The trace of a sad smile flitted around the corners of Alison's mouth. She wiped a tear from her cheek with her index finger. "Thank you."

"Did you use the code?"

"No. I didn't know what the hell a network mandate extension was – I'm not techie at all. Stuart knew that. I asked him what it was and he said I wouldn't be able to open the extension on my own, that I'd need to find a tech person I trusted to help me."

"And did you?"

Alison shook her head. "I didn't know who I could trust. I didn't trust anyone. And... I was scared. Million Eyes knew where I lived. I figured they were watching me."

"And now?"

"I dunno. I guess I've had enough of living in fear like this."

"You could've run away. Like Stuart did."

"I thought about it. But hiding from Million Eyes

would've meant Stuart wouldn't have been able to find me either. And, rightly or wrongly, I always clung on to some small shred of hope he was still out there somewhere and, when it was safe, he'd come home. I wanted to be here if he did."

Lester gave a small, sympathetic smile. This poor woman's brother was surely dead. He sounded like an enormous threat to Million Eyes – more so than Lester first thought, now that she knew about this 'code' of his. They would never have stopped hunting him.

"Do you have the code here?" asked Lester.

"I don't have it written down anywhere. I couldn't risk anyone finding it, so I keep it in my head. I'm a mnemonist. Means I can remember unusually long lists of data."

Lester knew what a mnemonist was, although she'd not met anyone with the ability before. "Will you write it down for me now?"

Alison nodded.

Lester tore a sheet of paper from her notepad and handed it to Alison with a pen.

Alison scribbled a sequence of numbers, letters and symbols onto the paper and held it out to Lester. "I hope you find –"

Alison's sentence was cut short by a slim green vein of light scoring silently through the front window, straight into the back of her head. Her head jerked, fingers going stiff around the note just as Lester was taking it. Paralysed with horror, Lester let the note go with Alison as she dropped to the floor like a marionette with its strings cut.

29

Lester glimpsed a darkly dressed figure outside the front of the house and a jolt of survival instinct broke her paralysis. *If they can see Alison through the mirror glass, they can see me.* She dived to the floor behind one of the sofas, although if another of those laser beams sliced into the room, a sofa wasn't going to do much. Flat on her stomach, she froze again. *Now what?*

The note was still in Alison's hand. She had to move, had to retrieve it. A panic-fuelled sweat broke out across her skin. She took a breath and used her elbows to push against the laminate and drag herself towards Alison's body, staying as low as she could.

Damn – the note was stuck in her fingers. Wincing, Lester used her other hand to prize them open so she could retrieve the note without tearing it. She shoved it into her handbag.

There was a shrill scraping sound at the front door – the whine of metal being sheared and twisted.

Someone was trying to get in.

Lester launched to her feet and bolted through a door into a large dining room. There were French doors that opened into the back garden. She tried them. *Shit!* Locked.

The front door rattled and hissed. Any moment it would swing open and Alison's killer would be inside.

No keycard in sight and no time to search for it, Lester grabbed one of six dining chairs around the large table, lifted it above her head and hurled it at one of the full-length glass panes in the French doors.

No!

The chair bounced off the tempered glass and crashed to the floor.

Panicked, Lester dived to grab the chair again. She moved closer to the doors and, turning her face away, swung the chair's thick metal legs at the glass, hard.

It bounced off again, flinging her backwards, but this time a small spiderweb crack radiated from the impact point.

Lester swung the chair again, throwing all of her one hundred and fifty pounds behind the blow. The crack was now a large spiderweb, but the glass remained intact.

Shaking, veins flooded with adrenaline, Lester started hammering at the crack with a succession of smaller swings, new cracks zigzagging out in all directions.

Just break, goddammit!

The front door banged.

No, no, no.

Alison's killer was in the house.

She swung again – one last almighty blow – and finally the door exploded in a shower of crystal shards that rained down over her head and shoulders. She threw down the chair and propelled herself through the opening.

She ran for the gate at the side of the garden, lifted the simple latch and yanked it open, the corner of her eye catching Alison's killer charging at the shattered French door.

Terror thundering in her chest, Lester barrelled through the gate, pulling it shut behind her, and ran up the driveway to the waist-high wall and gate at the front of the house.

Glancing back she saw the killer – wearing a black tracksuit and balaclava – burst onto the driveway, waving the weapon that had killed Alison in her direction.

Fearing he'd fire at her, Lester instinctively ducked, then used her arms to launch herself over the gate. She sprinted across a slim grass verge to her Ford Freeze, hand digging around in her handbag for her key fob. She found it, pressed 'unlock' and plunged into the driver's seat, pressed the start button and pulled the gearstick into drive mode before her seatbelt was on. She looked back briefly to see the killer get into a silver Lexus sedan parked on the other side of the road further up, which hadn't been there when she got here.

Her gaze flitted to her back seat, and to Georgia.

"What's happening, Mummy?"

Lester dived between the seats to buckle Georgia in.

"Go, Mummy, go!"

The seatbelt clicked. Shooting a glance through the back window, Lester saw the Lexus pull away from the kerb. She jerked back around, gripped the steering wheel, thrust her foot against the accelerator and hurtled up Plunkett's Walk, briefly releasing her right hand from the wheel to plug in her own seatbelt.

Nearing the end of Plunkett's Walk, she looked at Georgia in her rear-view mirror. "Hold on tight."

"Why, Mummy?"

At the end of the road, Lester turned hard left onto another residential road, tyres screeching.

She sped past a woman pushing a pram on the corner. In her mirror she saw the Lexus cut across the pavement and grass verge where they were walking.

"Noooo!"

Lester's heart froze as she watched the woman thump onto the Lexus's bonnet and the pram shoot up into the air as if fired from a cannon, dispensing a white bundle as it went.

She didn't see any of them land because suddenly there was nothing in her mirror but the Lexus. It shunted her hard, the crash of metal ringing out. Lester jolted forwards, but immediately rammed the accelerator, putting a few metres between them.

How could they? How could they just... do that?

Her limbs felt numb and tingly. Her stomach did a series of loop-the-loops. She wanted to puke.

"Mummy, what was that?" Georgia had her hands over her ears – she must've been terrified.

Lester couldn't think of a comforting answer. She got to a junction and turned hard right onto the main road that wound through Meath, pulling straight out in front of cars on both sides, forcing them to brake. Horns blared all around.

She'd never driven like this before, but what choice did she have?

As she tore through the town doing fifty in a thirty, she saw the Lexus come skidding out of the junction after her, matching her speed.

How am I going to lose this maniac?

She overtook three cars. The Lexus copied her, clinging to her like she was towing it. Its dark-tinted windows made it seem like it had no driver, that it was the Lexus itself that was after her.

Hitting a quieter stretch of road, the Lexus swerved to the right, accelerated, and pulled up beside Lester. Another crash of metal drowned out her own scream as the Lexus ploughed into her right side.

With the Lexus shunting her left, Lester veered onto the pavement, mounting the kerb with a jolt and hurtling towards a dog-walker and a lamppost.

"Aaahhh!" screamed Georgia in the back seat.

Lester yanked the steering wheel to the right, narrowly missing both as she shunted the Lexus back, making it onto the road before accelerating to sixty and speeding past her pursuer.

"Who keeps crashing into us?" shouted Georgia, tears streaming down her face.

"Bad people!" Lester shook her head and a flash of that mother and her baby getting tossed into the air like toys made her fingers tighten around the steering wheel. *The worst people.*

Her heart sank when she saw the traffic lights about half a mile ahead. They were green – for now. She glanced in her mirror. The Lexus was gaining on her again.

Stay green stay green stay green.

About two hundred yards from the lights, they turned amber.

"No!"

She couldn't stop.

"Hold on!"

Heart thumping so hard it felt like it might blow a hole through her ribcage, Lester flew over the intersection. Her peripheral vision caught cars on both sides swerving and braking hard, a MEcar mere inches from clipping her rear bumper.

But she was across.

The squeal and crunch of metal behind her pulled her eyes to her mirror. She saw that the Lexus had also decided to chance it across the intersection, bouncing into another car and slewing sideways. The crimson glow of brake lights surrounded the scene as other cars tried to avoid the accident, several smashing into the backs and sides of others.

Right. Time to lose this bastard.

Lester took the next turning on the left in the hope that the Lexus wouldn't see where she went and instructed the sat-nav to take her home. She checked her mirror second by second. No sign – yet. She came to a roundabout and her sat-nav directed her to take the first exit onto the motorway.

She was about to join the motorway when her next mirror glance caught the Lexus, now somewhat bashed up, careening down the sliproad.

For fuck's sake!

She exited the sliproad and kicked the accelerator to the floor, her speedometer flickering past eighty. She swerved round cars and lorries going at sixty or seventy, swinging from lane to lane. In her mirror she saw the Lexus enter the motorway and do the same.

"Are they back, Mummy?"

"Yes, honey. But don't worry. We'll lose them."

Will we?

Now pushing a hundred miles per hour, her poor Ford Freeze engine howled like a gale. The Lexus was close behind, doggedly closing the gap between them. Her jaw clamped tight, eyes staring, knuckles white on the steering wheel, she willed for the Lexus to run out of charge or its tyres to blow out. Something – *anything* – to get it off her tail.

Now it was inches from her rear bumper. There was no way she was going to lose it on the motorway. She'd have to come off.

The next junction was half a mile ahead. She stayed in the fast lane until the last possible second, so it would look like she was passing the junction.

Screaming through gritted teeth, she pulled the steering wheel and spurted across the entire carriageway, tyres giving off a tortured squeal. Several cars glanced off her, horns blasting, one smashing into her so hard it made her jerk in her seat and the seatbelt slice into her neck. It almost knocked her off course but she regained momentum quickly and flew up the sliproad.

She shot a glimpse in her mirror to see the Lexus, relentless as a shark that's smelled blood, surging up the sliproad towards her.

"At the roundabout, take the second exit to get back onto the motorway," said the sat-nav.

Lester swung left at the roundabout at the top of the sliproad and sped up a quiet country road lined with trees.

"In one mile, use the roundabout to make a U-turn –"

"Shut the hell up!" shouted Lester.

"Mummy?"

"Not you!"

The Lexus shot up behind her, smashing into her rear bumper like an angry animal. Lester jerked forwards and it was like her heart had been ripped from one side of her chest to the other.

She rammed the accelerator but the Lexus shunted her again.

"Mummy – I'm scared!" shrieked Georgia.

"I know, darling! Mummy's scared too!"

The Lexus swerved wildly into her right blind spot and hit her from the side, trying to force her down the steep, tree-strewn embankment they were passing.

"*Mummy!*"

She pulled the steering wheel right, pushing back, the cry of clashing metal perforating both of her ears.

The Lexus pulled up next to her, ready to shunt her again, its tinted windows appearing to stare at her with utter disdain.

A horn blasted, tearing her eyes back to the road.

A lorry the size of a house emerged from the blind bend they were skidding around, the Lexus directly in its path.

Lester felt every muscle in her body snap taut as a bowstring. She saw the Lexus brake hard and swerve. Too late. The lorry smashed into its back end, launching it into an almighty roll. It careered off the road and tumbled down the embankment with an earth-shattering crunch that scattered the birds from the trees.

Hands shaking and perspiration dribbling into her eyes, Lester drove on – and didn't look back again.

30

Highway hypnosis took over as Lester drove the rest of the way home. Her brain was in shock, flashes of Alison Rayburn's dead eyes and the Lexus ramming her and that mum and her baby flying into the air cycling painfully through her mind.

What the hell just happened? It was like it wasn't real, like it happened on TV or something. Alison Rayburn – dead, assassinated right in front of her. Moments after giving her a code. A code that might lead to a smoking gun. Did she still have the piece of paper in her handbag? She checked – yes.

The Lexus driver was a Million Eyes operative – no doubt about that. Had they been watching Alison the entire time? All these years?

By lying low and not telling anyone about the code, Alison had kept herself alive. Her decision to say screw it and confide in Lester out of no longer wanting to live in fear had just got her killed. *Lester* had got her killed. If Lester hadn't reached out to her, none of this would've happened.

And now Lester herself was on the run. It wouldn't be long before more operatives would be dispatched to recover this code. She and Brody were going to have to leave town – today.

She pulled her burner phone from her handbag and tapped in Brody's number. He was working from home today, which was useful because it meant that they could pack a bag and leave straight away.

The dial tone buzzed, then the call went to voicemail. *Damn.* He must've been on a call. "Brody, I'm on my way home. Please can you start packing a bag. We need to get out of the house. I'll explain when I get home but we're not safe there."

Before long, remembering nothing of the journey she'd just made, Lester was pulling onto her driveway. Getting out of the car she noticed that the muscles in her neck were painful and stiff, the skin stinging from where her seatbelt had almost broken it. She probably had whiplash.

Brody's car was outside – he was in. She rushed indoors. "Brody? Did you get my voicemail?"

"Mummy, I'm cold."

Lester turned. Georgia was hugging her bare arms and shivering. She looked pale.

"Let's get you a coat." Lester unhooked Georgia's hooded yellow duffle coat from the wall by the door. Georgia walked towards her and dug her arms in. Lester smiled at her and stroked her cheek. It was chilly, but she'd be warm now.

Lester searched for Brody. He wasn't in his office or anywhere else downstairs. She darted up the stairs.

She froze in the doorway to their bedroom. Her stomach lurched and her hand clutched her chest, an intense pain slashing across it, like someone had torn out her already broken heart and stamped on it.

Brody was on his knees on their bed, naked and red-faced, pelvis slapping hard against the arse of some blonde woman who was on all fours and jerking excitedly with each thrust. Lester caught the side of the woman's face. No, not *some* woman. Connie, one of Brody's work colleagues. Both facing the head of the bed, neither had noticed that Lester was even there. Clothes were strewn everywhere, like they couldn't have got them off fast enough.

If only they were making more noise. Brody was panting and grunting, like he always did; she was moaning quietly. If they'd been screaming the place down Lester would never have come upstairs. Too late now. Now this blunt image of her husband pounding another woman had been scratched into her eyes and her memory forever.

"Mummy, what is Daddy doing to that lady?"

Georgia was standing in the bedroom in her duffle coat, a few metres to the left of the bed, staring at the ugly display with a mixture of confusion and disgust.

"Darling, cover your eyes, cover your eyes now!" Lester cried.

The adulterer spun on the bed. "Fuck – Sam!"

Connie spun round too, gasped. She scrambled off the bed, grabbed a leopard print blouse and punched her arms into it.

Lester was speechless. There were so many words churning through her head but none of them made it to her lips. A quiet rage rose inside her.

Connie pulled on a pair of trousers, quickly. *Sensible.* She needed to get the hell out of their house before Lester said or did anything she'd regret. Brody, meanwhile, just sat there uselessly, staring between the two of them, face consumed by shock and shame. He looked like a complete dope.

"Daddy, put some clothes on!" cried Georgia.

"Georgia, don't look!"

"What?" Brody sprang to life. He swung his bare legs off the bed and stood. "*Georgia?*"

Lester started out of the bedroom.

"No – wait!" Brody lunged forwards, grabbing her arm. "You just said Georgia."

Lester faced him. "Yeah – so?"

He eased his hand off her arm. "Do you *see* her?"

Lester shrugged. "Sometimes."

Connie the slut scooped up a clump of underwear and a handbag and, cheeks glowing with embarrassment, scurried out of the bedroom, avoiding eye contact with Lester. *For the best.* A few seconds later, the front door opened and closed.

Brody barely noticed that she'd left. "Why didn't you tell me you were seeing Georgia?"

The gall. The absolute gall of it. "You are joking, aren't you?"

Brody shook his head. "I knew it. I knew there was something wrong with you."

Lester's anger went from simmer to boil. "Something wrong with *me?*"

He sighed. She could smell Connie on him. His chest and shoulders glistened with perspiration. He'd worked up a sweat fucking her. She wanted to vomit.

"How often have you been seeing her?"

She wasn't having this conversation. She turned out of the bedroom onto the landing.

"No, wait! We need to talk about this." Brody grabbed her arm again, harder.

"Let go of me." Her jaw clenched. "Now."

"Not till you agree to talk to me."

Lester looked down, eyes fixed on Brody's hand clasping her arm, and the little black hairs streaking across the back of his hand and up his fingers. If he'd fingered Connie, then she would be all over those fingers. Now that he was touching Lester, *she* was all over *her*.

Red-hot bile bounced off the walls of her stomach. She violently yanked her elbow to jerk out of the bastard's grasp and thudded towards the stairs.

"Sam – stop!"

Brody lunged forwards again, clamping his dirty cheating hand on her other arm.

She swung round, arms shooting up, hands pressing flat against his chest. She thrust out her arms, hard, focusing all of her surging rage into the shove.

Brody flew across the landing towards the balustrade, grazing the waist-high handrail as he went over it, and plunged ten feet to the floor.

Lester felt like she'd blacked out for a moment. But she hadn't. She was standing there on the landing, hands trembling at her sides, stomach rolling with nausea.

It took a second to process what she'd done. She'd never been violent like that before, but the stubborn idiot just wouldn't let go of her. She snapped. That was all. She snapped. *Why wouldn't you let go?*

She was stuck to the floor, feet nailed down. Her face was numb, lips locked an inch apart. Something touched the small of her back and she twisted her neck around and down.

"Mummy, is Daddy okay?"

Lester's brain switched back on, plucked her out of the deepening trance-like state she was falling into. She thundered down the staircase to answer her daughter's question.

I'm sure he is. He didn't fall far.

Brody lay on his back on the laminate floor in their hallway. His eyes were open and staring and thick, dark blood was pooling beneath his head, a near-perfect circle spreading fast across the laminate, seeping into the tiny cracks between the planks.

"Is he okay?"

Yes. He didn't fall far. He didn't fall far.

Lester knelt down next to him and felt for a pulse. She pressed harder on his neck, then grabbed his wrist. *Where's your pulse?* It had to be there. Had to be.

The pool of blood was spreading towards the door and the hall table. *Why is there so much? It was a bump to the head. Just a bump.*

Just a bump.

"Mummy... is Daddy... is Daddy dead?"

No no no.

Lester stood, backed away, hand clutching her chest, skin tingling with a cold, drowning sweat, legs trembling like a flag in a gale. She pinched her eyes shut and shook her head, back and forth, mindlessly repeating *you're not dead you're not dead you're not dead*, everything around

Brody's body going fuzzy and dark. Then she was hit with a sudden urge to go and raid their bathroom cabinet and swallow every pill that was in there.

Instead, she spun away from the body and all the horror, shock and pain that had been fermenting in her stomach finally erupted from her throat, cascading heavily over the laminate.

It took a few minutes for it all to come out. As it trailed off, Lester took several deep breaths, straightened and stared around the hallway, throat raw.

These stains are never going to come out.

Georgia was standing over Brody's body, tears dropping off her nose and chin. "Mummy, can you wake Daddy up?"

Lester felt her heart crack at the sight of her weeping daughter. Her gaze eased to her husband's body and a hard knot of grief lodged in her throat.

Then a flash of Brody screwing Connie ran across her eyes, making her fists ball so tight her nails bit into her palms.

Her burner phone started ringing. It was in her handbag on the hall table. She had to step through her husband's blood to get to it.

Adam. Taking a deep breath, "Hello."

"Hey," said Adam. "I went to headquarters. Couldn't get close. There were guards at every entrance to the building. How did it go with Alison Rayburn?"

For a moment Lester's voice was stuck in her chest like an undigested piece of food. She stared at Brody. The circle of blood around his head had stagnated and was clotting and darkening on the laminate.

"Dr Lester?" said Adam.

"She's... dead."

"What?"

"They killed... They killed her." The words were a struggle. "Shot her. Then they tried to kill me."

Adam's voice went shrill. "Fuck! Shit! Are you okay?"

What a question. *I feel empty. Hollow. Dead.* Okay,

certainly, was something she could never be again.

"I – I'm okay." The lie was so huge she could only whisper it.

"Are you sure? What did they do to you?"

"Chased me." She inhaled. "Chased me in my car. I lost them."

"Shit! So they're not still after you."

A flurry of images coursed through her head. The Lexus shunting her, the woman and the baby rolling in the air, Brody fucking Connie, Brody hurtling over the balustrade. Innumerable sounds – metal crashing, the wailing of tyres and horns, the grunts and moans of Brody's unfaithfulness, the thump and crack of Brody's body as it hit the floor – mingled in an oppressive cacophony.

"Dr Lester?" Adam's voice shivered through the noise. "Are they still after you?"

She tried to breathe, tried to calm down, tried to push the images and sounds away.

"Are you alright?"

She shook her head, but obviously couldn't tell him the real reason why. "They… they probably are. After me, I mean."

"Where are you?"

"My house. I'm… I'm just grabbing some things. I… I need to go somewhere they won't find me."

"You sound shaken up."

Understatement of the year. The decade.

"What can I do?" Adam continued.

"Meet me. Bring a MEc with you."

"A MEc? Why?"

"Alison Rayburn gave me a code. Right before they…" She didn't want to use the word again. So much death today. So, so much. "Do you know how to open a…" She pulled her notebook from her handbag and leafed through to the notes she'd written at Alison's – not easy with her hands shaking so much. "A network mandate extension?"

"Yeah. Yeah, I do."

"Okay. Let's meet… er…" She paused. Where the hell was she going to go?

In a moment of sudden clarity, it came to her. "There's a building in Croydon. An abandoned office block." Croydon in South London was where Lester grew up and the office block, which had been derelict for decades, had been a regular playground for her and her friends. "I'll text you the address. Don't take your MEcar. Get the train like last time. To East Croydon. Then ask someone at the station for directions to Haverstock Lane." She hesitated, paranoia streaking through her. "No. Actually, don't speak to anyone. Just use the maps on the street corners."

"I – er –" Adam paused and Lester thought for a moment he might say no. "Okay. Fine. Text me the exact address. I'll bring a MEc."

"Thanks."

Lester hung up and dropped the burner back in her handbag. She checked that the note with Alison's code was still in there. As she was about to zip it closed, her other phone vibrated and trilled an email alert. She lifted it out and glanced at the screen. It was an email from Ethan that started, **Dear Dr Lester,** I write to inform you that your employment with the London Institute of Palaeontology and Archaeology has been terminated…

Not bothering to read further, Lester hurled the phone – hard – at the nearest wall, chipping the paint. It landed in her vomit.

"Mummy… what are you going to do?" Georgia stood by the front door, staring at her with sad, hollowed eyes.

Lester walked over to Georgia and took her hand. "Come on, darling. We need to leave."

31

December 5th 1945

Something ain't right. Where the heck are we now?

A knot of dread cramped Lieutenant Charles C. Taylor's gut. His squadron of TBM Avenger torpedo bombers, Flight 19, appeared to be flying into oblivion. The five planes were holding course at two hundred and seventy degrees – they should have hit land by now. They should've hit land bloody ages ago.

Taylor had known something bad might happen on this flight. A few hours before takeoff, he'd had a feeling. Couldn't put his finger on it. Just some weird sense of foreboding. He'd gone and asked the aviation duty officer if he could be replaced as instructor and flight leader, but there was no one else. So here he was.

It should've been a routine flight. A simple mock bombing run and navigation training exercise. Nothing was supposed to go wrong.

Lieutenant Robert Cox, another pilot in the vicinity who'd picked up Taylor on the training channel, and some radioman called Baker at the Port Everglades Communications Centre, had been trying to help Taylor and his men get back to base at Fort Lauderdale. But Taylor hadn't heard from Cox in a good half-hour and now Baker's transmissions were growing ever fainter.

"Dagnabbit, Powers, why haven't we hit land yet?" Taylor said into his radio headset.

The Avengers were flying west in close formation. For

some reason neither of Taylor's compasses were working, so he'd ordered Captain Powers to take over lead.

Taylor got a garbled reply from Powers, laden with static. "We... should... are."

"Powers, repeat your last transmission," said Taylor, waiting. "Powers, do you read? We're on the wrong course. We should turn around and head east."

This time, no reply.

Taylor's chest tightened.

"Lieutenant Taylor, sir, do you read me?" Ensign Bossi's voice.

Thank Christ. *Somebody.* "I read you loud and clear, Bossi," said Taylor. "I've been trying to reach... anyone."

"Sir, I think I can see land," said Bossi. "D'you see it?"

Taylor peered towards the horizon. *Shit – yes!* He could see it. A large, dark, mountainous shape.

He tried to inform Baker at Port Everglades, "FT-28 to Port Everglades. We are approaching what looks like a large island. Over."

Baker uttered a muffled reply, "Port Everglades... transmissions are weakening... repeat."

Taylor sighed with exasperation. "Baker, I repeat, we're approaching a –"

Wait – what?

The landmass they were approaching was... moving. Rising. Out of the sea.

"Lieutenant Taylor, are you getting a load of this?" said Bossi.

"Hot damn, what *is* that?"

"Not an island, sir."

Taylor could see it now they were closer. Bossi was right. It wasn't an island at all. It was...

"Is that a storm cloud?" said Taylor.

"Funny sorta cloud."

Damn right. The cloud was a dark, murky red, even though all the others around it were stark white, a few shadowed with grey. Just nature having a funny moment?

Saying that, as they drew nearer to it, Taylor swore he'd never seen a cloud like it. It swirled and roiled like a thick, muddy liquid, and was changing shape fast. Too fast.

"Powers, if you can hear me, we should go around this... this cloud," Taylor said.

Either Powers had heard him or he'd thought the same thing. His Avenger banked left to circle around the cloud. Taylor eased his joystick left to join him, the others following, the cloud – or whatever it was – now behind them.

"Taylor... Somethin'... Somethin' strange is happening..." murmured Bossi.

"Bossi, what is it?"

"My watch. The hands, they're spinning, fast. Backward. Wait. They've stopped. No. Now they're spinning forward."

Taylor looked at his own watch. *Shit.* The same thing was happening to his. Both hands spinning forwards, hours passing in seconds. *What the heck – ?*

"Oh God!" Bossi's voice was suddenly wild with panic. "Taylor, somethin's wrong... Sir, there's... understand..." His previously crisp and clear words were now being eaten by static.

"Bossi? You okay?"

"No, sir! I'm... Shit, I'm bleeding!" screamed Bossi.

"Bleeding? Bleeding from where?"

"My nose, my eyes... ears... Oh God... God..."

Bossi's Avenger started banking left and right erratically. What the fuck was happening? Taylor looked around at the other planes. Powers – up ahead – seemed okay. But Gerber's and Stiver's planes had broken formation and were dipping and swerving all over the place.

Bossi continued to shout, his transmissions totally mangled by interference. "I don't... happening... somethin'... there's... hands." He was fading.

Taylor's heart pounded. His hands slipped off the

joystick. He wiped the sweat on his trousers and refastened his grip.

He didn't know what to do.

Moments later, he felt a sudden buffeting on his wings, and a deep shadow fell over the cockpit. Taylor turned his head right, saw a huge red mass coming up behind them. The cloud. It was *following them*. Rolling through the skies like a great, swollen wave of blood.

"FT-28... Port Everglades... read?" Radioman Baker was attempting to break through the interference.

"I read you!" bawled Taylor immediately. "A dang red cloud's chasin' us!"

"What?" Baker must've thought he'd gone mad. "You're... chased... cloud?"

"Yes! And somethin's happened to Bossi. Said he was bleeding from his dang eyes!"

"FT-28... you say eyes?"

A violent gust of wind – or what he presumed was wind – blasted the tail of Taylor's plane, rocked the wings almost vertical. He dipped out of formation, altimeter unwinding as he lost a few dozen feet. Stomach in his throat, lap belt slicing into his waist, he yanked the joystick to regain control.

Once the plane was level, Taylor – now shaking and feeling like he might piss himself at any moment – raised the nose to ascend to his original altitude.

"Devlin, Parpart – you alright?" Taylor shouted to his crewmen over the intercom. Devlin was his gunner, Parpart his radioman. Both young, good-looking men who were no doubt shitting their underpants right now.

"Devlin here, sir. Yes, I'm okay."

"Parpart?"

No answer.

"Shit – sir! Where did Gerber and Stiver go?" yelled Devlin.

Taylor looked over his shoulder at the planes behind him.

Fuck.

They were two Avengers down. Gerber's and Stiver's planes were gone. How? Where did they go?

The red cloud was gaining on them. It was alive. *Must be.* It was literally chasing them through the skies.

"Port Everglades! Baker!" Taylor screamed into his radio. "Two of the planes have vanished. Gerber and Stivers – they're gone!"

"Vanished?" Baker's voice crackled weakly. "FT-28... suggest... course to..."

It was no damn use.

"Powers, come in," said Taylor, making a further attempt to hail the plane that was leading them.

He saw that Bossi, out to his left, was still in trouble, swerving and banking violently. The red cloud was on both their tails.

"Bossi, are you –"

The shawl-like fringe of the cloud touched Bossi's stabilisers. In a blink, he was gone.

What?

The cloud was touching... nothing. The plane had vanished. Right in front of Taylor's eyes. Plucked out of thin air like a magician's trick.

Three Avengers down.

"Bossi's gone!" Taylor looked ahead. Powers was still lead. Now it was just the two of them. "Powers, are you there?"

Something jarred Taylor's plane, less violently than before. The next moment he could see nothing but red. Thick, dark, turbid red. Through every window. The cloud had enveloped him.

A chill knifed into the pit of Taylor's spine, made him shiver. "Devlin, d'you see what I'm seeing?" he said to his gunner.

"Yes, sir. It has us."

The plane's engine continued to whir. Taylor eased the joystick left and right to see if it changed their position. It didn't. The red cloud swirled around them, somehow holding them there.

He was about to try and radio *anyone* when a distinct beeping cut through the static.

It was unmistakable. *Dot. Dash. Dot.* Morse code.

"Devlin, Parpart – you gettin' that?"

Dash... Dot. Dot. Dot. Dot.

"I'm gettin' it, sir," said Devlin.

Still no answer from Parpart.

Dot. Dot.

The Morse code transmission ceased. Taylor grabbed a pad and pen from the compartment beneath his controls in case it came back.

A moment later it did, again starting with dot, dash, dot.

Taylor started writing out the letters.

R A T H E R I.

Silence again.

"RATHERI?" he shouted. "What the heck does RATHERI mean?"

The beeps returned a moment later. Taylor started writing it out, in case it was a different word. When he saw his hand, he immediately dropped the pen.

What the – ?

Something was happening to his skin. The backs of his hands were wrinkling like crepe paper. Liver spots started to appear. His knuckles protruded, fingers shrinking and shrivelling like they were being instantly desiccated.

He looked at his other hand. Same thing. All his bones were starting to show through, the skin and muscle wrinkling and contracting and drying up. He closed his skeletal fingers into a hollow fist. *Shit.* They were stiff, arthritic. It hurt to bend them. He went to open his fist again. The pain was intense. He winced. His fingers straightened slightly, then the joints gave up. They froze crooked.

Taylor felt a stab of panic. "Devlin, are you...?" He stopped. His voice had changed. It was deeper, lower. Hoarse. *Like an old man's.*

His face began to itch. He scratched his right cheek

with his crooked fingers. They went right through it, the skin as brittle as a dead leaf. A clump of flesh came off in his hand and a jet of blood fell into his lap.

As he looked at the red rag of flesh hanging off his bony hand – and could taste the salty blood that was seeping into his mouth from the wound – only the adrenaline was keeping him from passing out.

Then, as the cockpit blurred and darkened and the Morse code transmission – still beeping away – faded, he started to laugh.

I'm murdered. Murdered by a cloud. Funny.
Half my face is in my hand.
Funny, funny, funny.

December 8th 1945

Lieutenant-Commander Nick Kellerman, Special Adviser to the Commander of the Office of Naval Intelligence, got back to his office after lunch to find that the initial report on the loss of Flight 19 three days ago had arrived on his desk. Such a tragedy. It was still unclear why the routine training flight had gone so wrong. Hopefully this report would bring some answers.

Coffee in hand, Kellerman sat down and began trawling through the papers. They contained the testimonies of witnesses and the logs of Fort Lauderdale Naval Air Station and Port Everglades Communications Centre. Together they created a strange, disturbing picture. Flight leader Taylor said that both of his compasses had broken somehow. Ensign Bossi reported that his watch was spinning and that he was bleeding from his eyes. And then they were chased by some mysterious red cloud, at which point the planes started disappearing in midair.

The report also said that shortly after all verbal transmissions from Flight 19 ceased, radioman Melvin

Baker at Port Everglades picked up a Morse code transmission on the same frequency.

It was a single word being repeated over and over: R A T H E R I.

Kellerman could understand one of the crew of Flight 19 mistyping a Morse code message in distress, but not continuously. It had to mean something – but what?

Then something else occurred to Kellerman. *Why is that word familiar?*

He was convinced he'd seen it before, and had an inkling where. He stood up from his desk and walked over to the filing cabinet in the corner of his office. He opened it and dug out his file on the USS Cyclops, a cargo ship that went missing some time after 4th March 1918 – in the same region of the Atlantic as Flight 19. Three hundred and six passengers and crewmen were lost along with it.

Shit.

On 10th March, three days before the Cyclops was expected to arrive in Baltimore, the US Army base at Fort Bell, Bermuda, received a Morse code transmission from an unknown source. No one understood it at the time and it could not be definitively linked to the ship's disappearance.

The Morse code message was the same word over and over. R A T H E R I.

Kellerman threw the Cyclops file down on his desk. Then he placed a telephone call to Station 1, a secret underground base in London and the headquarters for Million Eyes.

32

April 28th 2027

"What's happened? Who's shaken up? Where have you got to go?" Adam looked up to see Izzy, who'd been working from home in their study, blasting questions at him from the doorway to the lounge. He quickly lowered the burner phone from his ear and slipped it into his pocket, not wanting to explain that he had a second phone solely for communicating with Lester.

"That was... Dr Lester," said Adam. "I've got to go meet her in Croydon."

"What? Why? Is this about Jennifer? *Again?*"

Izzy knew about Adam's meetup with Lester in Hyde Park, but none of what had come out of it. All Adam had said to her was that she had some information about Jennifer's disappearance, and that he wanted to know what it was. He'd told Izzy post-meeting that Lester had showed him evidence that Jennifer was alive, and safe, and left it at that.

"It's not about Jennifer," said Adam. "I think she – Dr Lester – is in trouble."

Izzy nodded. "Yeah, I gathered that. You said she sounded shaken up. So what's happened? And why is she calling *you* about it?" Irritation inflamed her voice, probably because Adam had been so woolly with the specifics when it came to Lester and Jennifer.

He had to give her something. The truth? Frankly, he wasn't going to be able to think of a convincing lie quick enough. "She was chased in her car." He left out the bit about Alison Rayburn having been murdered. He wasn't sure he had processed that himself yet.

"Chased? By who?"

"Million Eyes."

"What? *The* Million Eyes?"

"What other Million Eyes do you know?"

Izzy frowned. "So you're saying Million Eyes, the computer company, *your* employers, have just chased some random palaeontologist in her car?"

"Yeah."

"Why the fuck would they do that?"

"They were trying to kill her. Because she knows stuff about them."

"What? Hang on a minute. You said you didn't believe any of her conspiracy theories about Million Eyes!"

"I didn't, not at first, but I do now."

"Since when?"

Adam needed to put this conversation on pause. He had to go. "Babe, I'll explain everything when I get back. Right now I have to go see if Dr Lester's alright."

"So why do you need to take a MEc for that?"

"I don't know yet." All he knew was that she needed him to open the network mandate extension. "She just asked me to bring one."

"Adam, if you've got yourself involved in something and not told me, I'm gonna fucking kill you."

Precisely why I haven't told you.

Adam walked up to her, placing his hand on her belly, and leaning to kiss her cheek – but she turned away. "I'll explain later, I promise."

She didn't respond. He would have to fix this later. He fetched his keys from the bedroom, grabbed a MEc from the study and shoved it into a laptop bag, and left the apartment.

He kept his hood raised and his chin tucked into his collar. He probably looked suspicious but didn't want his face getting caught on CCTV, although facial recognition was so good these days that even a flash of his nose might lead to a positive ID for all he knew.

At least the trains were quiet. Because of driverless cars, far fewer people used trains than they used to. Adam had a carriage to himself most of the way.

Getting off at East Croydon, Adam felt his pulse quicken and stomach churn. What if Million Eyes had caught up with Lester by now? He kept looking around to check that no one was following him, immediately wondering if he'd become one of those people in films, who goes around trying not to draw attention but looking so guilty they end up drawing plenty.

He checked the first street map he came across after he exited the train station. Haverstock Lane wasn't far away. He took a photo on his burner phone so he could keep referring to it.

About ten minutes later, in a quieter part of town, Adam saw the derelict building up ahead, standing about twenty metres back from the road. It was a square husk of cracked and graffiti-covered concrete, with some windows boarded up, some smashed, and profuse weeds sprawling from ledges and crevices and wherever else they could. The numerous gaps and breaks in the flimsy metal wire fencing that surrounded it, and the worn and old-looking *KEEP OUT* signs, suggested that the fencing hadn't been maintained for a long time.

Adam felt his chest tighten and ache as he walked through one of the larger gaps in the fencing, across cracked paving that had been overtaken by long grass and moss, texting Lester as he neared the main entrance to the building. Broken plywood sheets around the edges of the entrance were evidence that it was, at one stage, boarded up, but no one had come to repair it.

He entered what used to be a reception area, strewn with litter and broken plasterboard, glass and ripped-up carpet tiles. The smell of damp, dust and rot made his nostrils twitch. There were ceiling panels missing and cables hanging down dangerously through the gaps.

Adam walked up to the curved reception desk. A swivel chair behind it was on its side and missing two of its wheels, and a thick layer of dust and grime covered the used-to-be-white melamine desktop. Looking around, Adam saw missing doors on both sides of the room and a large staircase leading to the first floor.

Footsteps crunching over debris, Adam walked up to one of the doorways, which led to a large, mostly empty office space in similar state of disrepair, thick with darkness apart from a thin shaft of light coming through a window whose boarding had been pried off. A couple of old, stained mattresses surrounded by old pizza boxes and Coke cans suggested that squatters had been here. Adam spotted an empty syringe. Druggies had been here too.

No Lester.

Adam looked down at his phone. She hadn't read or replied to his message.

Had Million Eyes found her? Was she dead?

Adam turned to go check the room on the other side. He jumped back. "Fuck!"

Lester was standing in the reception area, near the other missing door. "Hi," she said quietly. "We haven't much time."

She looked totally different to the last time he saw her. Her hair was dishevelled, her face shadowed with trauma and exhaustion, heavy bags swelling beneath her eyes.

"Bring the MEc through here," she said, ushering Adam into another dilapidated office space, full of broken furniture and collapsed partition walls, but better lit due to more of the boarding on the windows having been ripped off.

"Are you okay?" said Adam. "What the hell happened?"

"I told you. They killed Alison Rayburn. Then they tried to kill me."

"Yeah, but how did they kill her? Did it happen while you were with her? What did you do?"

"We don't have time."

Lester dragged a couple of chairs that still had all their wheels over to a desk and sat down on one of them. She pulled a piece of paper from an inside pocket in her trench coat, which must've had this code on she mentioned.

Adam could tell she didn't want to talk about what had happened. Who could blame her? He swerved round an upturned filing cabinet and kicked past the rubble to join her at the desk. Sitting down on the other chair, he opened his laptop bag and placed the MEc on the desk.

"So you want me to open the network mandate extension?" said Adam.

"Yes. I'm guessing you know what that is, because I haven't the faintest."

"Yeah. The NME allows users to reconfigure a computer's data connections, file transfer protocols and server interfaces, and troubleshoot network issues that aren't fixable from the graphical user interface."

Lester looked at him blankly. He realised he'd just reeled off a bunch of jargon only a techie like him would understand. "It lets you... do stuff."

Lester nodded. "Okay. Well here's the code Alison Rayburn gave me. She didn't know what it did, just that it would get her access to all the information she needed to bring down Million Eyes. She never used it because she was scared Million Eyes were watching her." She sighed, a look of guilt passing over her face. "She was right about that."

Adam looked at the code.

ROOT–HOST3721#232–UNR–47_10–8885.tcp.9 48160*2

What the bloody hell was that?

"Does it mean anything to" – Lester stopped and momentarily turned her head to the side – "Ssshh, Georgia! I'm talking."

Adam frowned, did a fast shake of the head. No one else had spoken. There was no one else in the room.

Lester faced Adam and started her sentence over like nothing had happened, "Does it mean anything to you?"

He'd suspected that there was something not right with this woman after their last meeting at the park. He'd done a little background check on her but hadn't turned up anything beyond her professional credentials. Not a glimmer of her personal life was public and unless she was hiding extremely well behind a different name, the only social media profile she had was on LinkedIn. He'd come no closer to finding out if something had happened to her.

He was a bit closer now. "Lester… are you sure you're alright?"

"Yes, I'm fine."

His frown deepened. "Who's Georgia?"

Without hesitating, "My daughter."

Adam wasn't sure what to say. He hadn't expected her to just volunteer the information. Maybe Georgia was the kid she'd lost.

He swallowed. "And, er, where is Georgia?"

Lester frowned and shot a glance to her side. "She's standing right there."

Oh Jesus. I'm trying to bring down the world's most powerful company and my cohort is a nutbag.

Adam took a deep breath in. Doubt flooded his mind. If Lester was crazy, then perhaps this car chase never happened, and was all a lie. And Alison Rayburn wasn't dead. And maybe Lester really did fake Jennifer's letters.

Except Adam *knew* Million Eyes were involved in Ferro's death and Rayburn's disappearance. He'd seen the evidence himself. And he was all but certain they'd murdered Curtis, too.

Still, Lester was a liability. A liability that could put them both in danger.

He decided to focus his attentions on the code. If it was some bullshit conjured up by Lester, he'd know it before long.

"So?" said Lester again, still waiting for his answer.

"Does it mean something to you or not?"

Adam shook his head. "Nope. I'll open the NME and enter it, see what happens."

He clicked through to the control deck and ran the LINIL program. This brought up a list of advanced administrative functions. He scrolled down and selected System Engineer, opening a window where he tapped a short sequence of numbers and symbols and was prompted to restart the computer.

When the computer restarted, he was asked whether he wanted to open the network mandate extension in 'green mode' or 'blue mode'. Green mode was for reconfiguration, blue mode was for troubleshooting. He selected green.

"I'm in," he said, as the NME interface appeared on screen.

Lester wheeled her chair forwards and the two sides of her trench coat fell off her knees.

Adam noticed that the knees and shins of her grey trousers were covered in dried blood. "Shit – you're hurt."

Lester followed Adam's gaze and, eyes flickering with awkwardness, immediately re-covered her knees with the skirt of her coat. "It's nothing."

"But that looks bad. Surely you need to go to A&E."

"It's not mine."

Oh, shit, then it was probably Alison's. From when they shot her. Maybe Lester knelt in her blood or something.

"So it's Alison's?"

"No."

What? *No?*

"But… Then whose… whose blood is it?"

"Doesn't matter."

It really fucking does actually. "Dr Lester, I –"

"Are you going to enter the code?"

He wasn't sure he trusted this code anymore. He wasn't sure what to think. Or do. What if Lester was tricking him somehow?

He stood up and paced around some of the rubble. "I – I don't know."

"What do you mean you don't know?"

He hesitated. "Well… well, we don't even know what this code is. What it might do. What if it's a… a trap?"

"Clearly this code is something Million Eyes want. That's why they chased me and nearly killed me."

"So where's the blood come from if it's not yours and it's not Alison's?"

Lester blew an exasperated sigh. "Fine. I'll do it." She pulled the MEc towards her and stared at the screen. "Where do I enter it?"

He wanted to believe her, but something was really wrong here. If she wasn't going to be straight with him, then he couldn't risk entering a code he knew nothing about into *his* computer.

He shook his head, "I'm sorry. We're not doing this."

She clicked some buttons on the keyboard to try and do it herself.

Adam dived forwards and plucked the MEc off the desk. "I said we're not doing this."

"Adam, we must! This has gone too far to stop now."

"How far, exactly? Whose blood is that?"

Lester swallowed. "It's mine, okay? It's mine."

"You just said it wasn't."

"I misspoke."

Misspoke? "Fine. Let me see the wounds then. Because I think you need to go to the hospital."

Lester stared silently at Adam, blinked and pulled in a long breath. "Alright. Listen. Million Eyes are coming after me. I suspect it's only a matter of time before they find me. And if you don't help me now, I'll make sure that when they do find me, they'll find you too."

Adam's heart thrummed in his ears. "You're threatening me?"

"Yes. Yes, I am."

Her voice was firm and serious. A chill hit Adam in the pit of the back. They stared tensely at one another, then

Lester's expression softened slightly. "Please. Just do it."

Adam could tell she was desperate. Desperate and losing it were a dangerous combination. He could call her bluff – about taking him down with her – and get out of there.

Or he could suck up his doubts and find out what the hell this code was.

Curiosity prevailing, he sat back down at the desk with the MEc and clicked through to the manual entry window.

"Thank you," Lester murmured.

He glanced at her. "I have no idea what's going to happen, you know."

"I know. Neither do I."

Adam looked at the code on the piece of paper and started typing it in. He held his breath as he clicked 'enter'.

The screen went black.

"Shit." Had he fucked it?

After a moment, the screen came back on.

He was back in MEos, the normal user interface, like nothing had happened.

Then a small window titled *Decoding* appeared, with a loading bar beneath. The bar filled quickly and the window disappeared.

Then another popped up – *Copying*.

After a moment spent loading, that, too, disappeared.

Then another window appeared, titled *MILLION EYES X9 SERVER – CLASSIFIED DRIVE (Copy)*.

Lester leaned closer to the MEc screen.

"A worm," Adam whispered.

"A what?"

"It's a kind of malware that disrupts computer systems or, in this case, makes copies of files or entire drives and moves them remotely to another location. Rayburn must've installed the worm in Million Eyes' computer infrastructure, probably in an old support server he knew would never be updated. The code Alison gave you has

just triggered it. It's copied a classified drive onto my
MEc. From the X9 Server. Which is what Miss Morgan
and Pete Navarro said Rayburn had breached."

"What's in it?" said Lester.

There were a bunch of folders. *Offices. Assets.
Employees. Departments. Operations.* Adam clicked on
Operations. A longer list of folders appeared. Adam
scanned some of the names. *Operation Second Wave.
Operation Wawona. Operation Blue Pencil. Operation
Roundhead.*

He opened *Operation Roundhead* and brought up a list
of documents. He double-clicked *Operation Roundhead –
Proposal.*

Written in the header of the document was *X9
Clearance – Special Handling.* Beneath that was the date,
1st October 2021, and the title, *Establishment of the
British Republic.*

Adam and Lester read the document together.

THE PROBLEM

1. Our sources at Buckingham Palace have
   revealed that Her Majesty Queen Elizabeth II,
   hereafter referred to as The Queen, with the
   support of a rebel faction of Privy Councillors, is
   preparing to make radical use of her
   prerogative powers to block progress on
   various Million Eyes endeavours.

CONTEXT FOR THE PROBLEM

2. The Queen has been undermining and
   interfering with Million Eyes' work ever since
   she assumed the throne. She has acted
   contrary to the Agreement of 1604 between
   Million Eyes and the Crown on almost a dozen
   occasions.

---

3. Publicly revealing that The Queen is overstepping her bounds and acting unconstitutionally would risk shattering the illusion of democracy in the United Kingdom of Great Britain and Northern Ireland, based on the fact that The Queen has previously expressed a willingness to expose her own position in order to force Million Eyes to accede to her demands.

4. For additional context, see Enclosure A.

DISCUSSION

5. The suggested courses of action are based on the premise that The Queen has rendered the Agreement of 1604 unworkable and that Million Eyes must now take steps to govern the United Kingdom of Great Britain and Northern Ireland without the Monarchy.

RECOMMENDATIONS

6. It is recommended that:

a. Million Eyes begin making preparations for the assassination of The Queen in accordance with the suggested arrangements laid out in Appendix A.

b. Million Eyes begin taking steps to reorganise the United Kingdom of Great Britain and Northern Ireland into the British Republic through a series of constitutional amendments laid out in Appendix B.

Well, Alison Rayburn was right. This highly classified drive, reserved only for Million Eyes' highest echelons, had just won them the jackpot – documentary evidence that Million Eyes murdered the Queen.

Adam now understood why it was called Operation Roundhead. Million Eyes' actions weren't that different to those of Oliver Cromwell and the Parliamentarians, or Roundheads, during the English Civil War. Although history wasn't Adam's strong point, he remembered that, following the execution of Charles I, the Roundheads abolished the monarchy, the Privy Council and the House of Lords and reorganised Britain into a republic.

He swallowed. Everything had suddenly become real.

"Open one of the other operations," said Lester.

Adam clicked back through to the *Operations* folder and opened the one for *Operation Blue Pencil.* An even longer list of documents appeared. Adam scanned the titles, saw one titled *Operation Blue Pencil – Proposal*, and opened it.

The title of this one was particularly intriguing: *Recommendations for a Final Solution to the Last War.*

What on earth was the Last War?

Rustling outside made Adam and Lester look up simultaneously – and freeze. Instantly Adam's stomach wound itself into a painful knot. Through the broken window ahead of them they saw six or seven police officers approaching the building.

"No, no, no, no," Lester murmured, launching to her feet, raising both hands to the sides of her head in panic.

Adam stood. "Do you think it's them?"

Lester was bristling with alarm. "Of course it's them!"

"What do we do?"

Lester turned her head left and seemed to be looking at the wreckage of an old Uzu computer. "No, Georgia, it's not about Daddy. Daddy's fine."

What the fuck?

If the blood on Lester's legs wasn't hers, or Alison's, could it have been… *Daddy's?*

Footsteps crunched over broken plaster and glass – the police were in the building.

Adam slammed shut his MEc and swiped it off the desk.

Shit, shit, shit.

Lester was already headed for another door near the rear of the building. Even though the woman was off her rocker, their goal was the same. Escape. Since she knew the building, he bolted after her.

Too late.

A beam of green light slammed into Lester's back. The impact made her head and arms jerk backwards, then the beam stopped and she dropped lifelessly to the floor.

Adam spun round. Two police officers were in the room, pointing silver guns.

Realising they were about to fire, Adam screamed, "Wait – don't sho –"

Then another beam of light came surging towards his face.

33

Adam opened his eyes to find himself sprawled on his front, right cheek squished against a smooth, hard floor, blurry whiteness all around him. His left arm lay in front of him, his right tucked uncomfortably beneath him, and he couldn't feel his legs. Rolling slowly onto his back, he realised both legs, although stiff and cold, were still attached, one folded over the other. As soon as he had freed his arm, a flood of pins and needles cascaded down it.

His eyes focused on the low, white, and intact ceiling, telling him immediately that he wasn't in the derelict office anymore. He lifted himself onto his elbows. The pins and needles easing off, a painful bruise on his hip sparked a memory of hitting the floor, jarring it. He glanced around. He was in a small white room, bare apart from two white chairs. The room had a single door with no handle and a small, rectangular window near the top. Some kind of cell?

Adam remembered a police officer shooting him with some futuristic laser gun. Right after they shot Lester in the back. Then, nothing.

His muscles clenched and his stomach did a backflip. Million Eyes had brought him here, wherever here was, but for what? To torture him? *Kill* him?

He wasn't tough enough for shit like this. He should never have got involved with Lester. Raging fear gripped and clawed at his insides, made him want to curl up in the corner and sob. He didn't want to die, or be tortured, or to be parted forever from Izzy and their child, who'd barely even begun to form. He wanted to go home to them both and forget he'd ever got that phone call from Lester six months ago.

He got to his feet and inhaled deeply. A faint smell of chemicals wafted up his nose. He walked over to the door, looked through the tiny window. Nothing but darkness. A sense of claustrophobia started to press down on his chest. He moved away from the door and stared around the room. The walls were plain and featureless, made of thick white panels separated by vertical grooves. The floor was some kind of smooth, white vinyl and the ceiling, again, was plain and white apart from a large, rectangular panel light. He took in every aspect of the room in about five seconds; now there was nothing left to look at.

The claustrophobia pressed harder. *How long am I going to be in here?*

The buzzing of an electronic lock made him turn round. The door opened with a soft clunking sound. His relief was almost immediately watered down by fear that the person opening it was going to be his torturer.

He pulled in an anxious breath as Miss Morgan stepped into the room, clutching not a taser or a pair of pliers but two paper coffee cups, wisps of steam curling out of the sippy holes in the lids.

"Hello, Mr Bryant," she said, holding one of the cups out to Adam as an unseen someone closed the door behind her. "Coffee?"

Adam felt his heart start to race. He shook his head, "No. Thank you."

"Suit yourself." Miss Morgan sat down on one of the white chairs, placing one of the coffees on the floor and taking a sip from the other. She nodded to the other chair. "Have a seat. We have a lot to talk about."

Adam shuddered as he sat down. He placed his hands in his lap so that she couldn't see them trembling. He had no idea where this would lead, but he suspected nowhere good.

"You've been busy." Miss Morgan crossed one leg over the other and rested her coffee cup on her knee. "So have we."

Adam tasted bile and swallowed it back down. "Whe – where am I?"

"The only place you *can* be right now. Headquarters."

He frowned. "What does that mean?"

"All in good time." She smiled eerily and took another sip of her coffee. "You've got us all wrong, you know. You think we're corrupt. A menace. Out to control everything and everyone. Evil."

That's about the size of it, yeah.

She continued, "You don't know the half of it. You don't know what Million Eyes really is. How important we are. How essential our work is for the future of this planet."

Adam knew CEOs had egos – but this was something else.

"I know you've been killing people," said Adam, the words coming out a little more freely and boldly than he'd intended. "The Queen. Gregory Ferro. Curtis O'Brien." He couldn't hold back the venom making his jaw clench as he said Curtis's name.

Miss Morgan cocked her head and smiled like an adult smiles at a child who's said something cute and silly.

Fucking bitch.

"I can't deny that we've killed people," she nodded. "But did you ever stop and think *why?"*

"Power. Isn't that what it always is?"

"Power is a means to an end for us. It's the end I'm talking about."

"I know you're protecting some scrolls supposedly written by Jesus. It's why you killed Curtis."

She went silent for a moment, stared at him through squinted eyes, a slight smirk lingering on her bronze-painted lips. Now he wished he'd accepted the other coffee, just so he could hurl it in her face.

Although, let's face it, he'd never be brave enough to

do that. He was all foam and no beer and he knew it.

"Tell me, Mr Bryant. What do *you* know of Jesus?"

Adam squirmed uncomfortably in his chair. "I dunno. I'm not a Christian."

"And why is that?"

Adam was confused. "Why is what?"

"Why are you not a Christian?"

He frowned. Was everything Million Eyes had done part of a modern-day crusade to convert heathens to Christianity? *Seriously?* They were a bunch of time-travelling Bible-bashers?

"I'm just not," he replied. "I don't follow any religion. I don't buy any of them."

"And what don't you 'buy' about Jesus?"

This conversation was starting to become very strange. "I don't buy that he was the Son of God, or performed miracles, or came back from the dead. He's a myth. Like Santa Claus. Like the Greek demigods. No one believes *they're* real. I never understood why Jesus was any different."

"You're absolutely right."

What?

"Right about what?"

"About Jesus. He *isn't* any different. The story of Jesus, the one the Church tells, is just that. A story. A fable. A myth. Jesus wasn't divine, he didn't perform miracles, he didn't rise from the dead. He was a man called Dr Jesus M. Hirschfield. An ordinary physician who was transported back in time two thousand, two hundred years from the year 2222. A man whose teachings were deliberately distorted by his disciples at the time of the founding of the Christian Church."

Adam frowned dismissively and folded his arms. "That's... crazy."

"It's the truth. Dr Hirschfield was accidentally transported back in time along with medical technology and knowledge from the future, and stranded there. His 'miracles' were no more than applications of modern science in a primitive world."

Shit. So Million Eyes weren't Christians at all. *They* were the 'heathens'. Bible-bashers in the literal sense. "How could you know all that?"

Miss Morgan arched her eyebrows. "Because of the scrolls. Jesus wrote about his experiences in the future, and in the past, in a series of scrolls that we've been protecting. For a long time these were known as the Gospel According to Jesus. Today they are called, simply, the Mission."

Mission... Jennifer had said something about the 'Mission' in her letters...

She went on, "After Jesus was crucified, the person who buried him, Joseph of Arimathea, fled to England with the scrolls. Centuries later, they were discovered buried beneath Glastonbury Abbey by a man called Cuthwulf, who founded an organisation to guard and protect the scrolls, and to carry on Jesus's work. That organisation became Million Eyes."

Adam had been so absorbed in her words that the loud knock at the door made him flinch. Miss Morgan gave another wry smirk.

"Enter," she said.

The door opened and a man in a suit walked over to Miss Morgan carrying a MEpad. "I have the results of the sensor sweep, ma'am."

Miss Morgan took the MEpad and perused it. Her eyes widened and she shook her head. "Big changes this time. Huge." She handed the MEpad back to the man. "Thank you. Tell Miss Boone I won't be long. Then we can get this show on the road."

The man nodded obediently and left the room, pulling the door closed behind him.

Big changes?

Miss Morgan faced Adam, leaning forwards slightly. "You've heard what the Bible says about Jesus coming to save us, I take it?"

He nodded tentatively.

"Well that part is true. He *was* trying to save us. But not from 'sin'. From a devastating apocalypse known as the Last War."

The Last War... Adam remembered seeing that written in the proposal document for 'Operation Blue Pencil', right before the police showed up and shot him.

"The Last War will begin in 2219. Ships will come to Earth from a distant planet. Ships carrying creatures of unimaginable power, who kill indiscriminately in the most abominable of ways. Creatures we will dub the 'Shapeless'."

Adam's throat tightened and a nervous swallow forced its way down.

"Resistance movements will rise against the Shapeless, but by 2222 humanity will face the very real prospect of extinction. Jesus was part of a resistance movement called the Twelfth Remnant when he was transported back in time. The circumstances of how and why he went back are still unclear. But because he was unable to return, he started gathering followers, started telling people about the Last War. He was trying to warn them, so that we could be ready when the invasion comes and have a chance of either defeating the Shapeless or, better yet, stopping the war from happening in the first place. Then some of his closest disciples decided they couldn't trust him, so they betrayed him to the Romans and twisted his message to serve their own interests."

Miss Morgan paused, downed the rest of her coffee, placed the cup on the floor and clasped her hands together over her knee.

"So you see, Mr Bryant, Million Eyes is not what you think it is. We are trying to do what Jesus intended. Stop the Last War from happening. Or else make the human race stronger and more able to fight the Shapeless when they come. From time to time, we may have to get our hands dirty to achieve that. But we all have to make sacrifices for the greater good. And there is no good greater than humanity's survival."

A question occurred to him, a question that made his heart sink and his stomach tighten as soon as he realised what the answer might be. "Why are you telling me all this?" *Is it because you're going to kill me anyway?*

Miss Morgan gave a flat smile. "To prepare you."

"Prepare me? For what?"

Miss Morgan stood up and walked over to the wall behind him, gesturing for him to join her. He got to his feet and went to stand next to her, facing the wall.

Adam frowned, confused. "Is something about to – ?"

"Wall, up."

With a soft whir, the panels on the wall started rising, revealing a floor-to-ceiling window underneath. A wave of vertigo made Adam reach for a railing that wasn't there. They were much higher up than he'd assumed. Hundreds of metres below was a wide river with rolling fields and forests stretching for miles all around it, dotted with the odd building and what looked like a huge elevated walkway, perhaps a monorail, winding its way across the landscape. Dizzy, Adam took a step back.

But he thought Miss Morgan said that they were in headquarters. This obviously wasn't headquarters, although that river *did* look like the Thames.

Where on earth were they?

"Remember when I said that headquarters was the only place you *can* be right now?" said Miss Morgan.

Adam glanced at her. "Yeah – but this clearly isn't headquarters."

"I'm afraid it is. And I'm afraid that down there is London. Or what's left of it. When I say this is the only place you can be, I mean that if you leave this building, you'll be erased from history. Just like everything else."

Adam shook his head. "What? I don't understand. That can't be London. Where actually are we?"

"Approximately an hour after we brought you in, the timeline changed – dramatically – creating a new, alternate 2027. We are protected from the changes by a temporal shield that we erected around the building for this very reason, in case our time travel assignments caused changes we didn't plan or desire. But anyone who steps outside the Shield will be absorbed into this new timeline in which the chance that they even exist at all is slim to none."

Adam stared at the landscape below. He'd assumed what he was looking at was farmland, although the smattering of buildings didn't look anything like farmhouses or barns. All of them were small and cylindrical and made from what looked like metal, with dome-shaped white roofs. And – *what the hell are they?* A couple of the fields had animals, and although they were tiny from this height, they didn't look like any farm animals he'd ever seen. These things were black and white like cows, had long necks like giraffes and huge branching antlers that were... *blue.*

"W-what the hell happened?"

"The Unraveller."

"The what?"

"We call her the Unraveller. We don't know who she is, just that she's determined to destroy Million Eyes by any means necessary. And all of history along with it."

Adam's heart raced. All of this was like some bizarre virtual reality simulation. He felt like one of his friends was going to burst in at any moment and tell him that none of it was real. That it was all just a game.

If only. Head spinning, he murmured, "What are you going to do?"

Miss Morgan looked at him. "This has happened before. Last time, your friend, Jennifer Larson, was the cause of it. Her actions temporarily erased all of Million Eyes' hard work from the timeline and altered millions of lives in the process."

Adam felt a twinge of emotion skirt through him at the mention of Jennifer.

"Fixing the timeline after Jennifer's incursion was messy and complicated. In theory we should've been able to scan the present and get a full report on the changes so that we could at least attempt to trace them back, but the magnitude of the incursion had overloaded the sensor grid, so we couldn't. It took a lot of guesswork and trial and error to put the timeline back together. Afterwards, we decided we needed a way of stopping incursions like that before they happened. So, we built a machine called the Augur, which continually fed us data about any inadvertent or deliberate contamination of the timeline in advance. In other words, it gave us the ability to anticipate future incursions – and stop them."

"So why didn't you? If you knew all this was going to happen, why didn't you stop it?"

"Because the Unraveller sabotaged the Augur last night."

Adam could feel a headache coming on. A twist of pain ratcheted through his skull.

"That's why we locked down headquarters," said Miss Morgan. "We normally conduct time travel assignments during the night, so that we can lock down the building and raise the Shield without drawing attention. But we had to lock it down this morning because we knew that if the Unraveller had destroyed the Augur, that meant she was planning to change the timeline."

"You're saying she destroyed it so you wouldn't know what she was about to do?"

"Yes."

He shook his head. "So… so how are you planning to stop her then?"

"I have a source. A source telling me *exactly* what she's done and what we need to do to stop her."

That was cryptic. "What source?"

"That's not important right now. What is important is that we know where and when we need to send you to prevent all this."

Adam's heart stopped. "I'm sorry – what?"

"You're going to be the one to fix this, Adam."

"Me? Seriously?"

"Yes."

"Why? Why *me?*"

Vaguely and unhelpfully, "Because this is the way it has to be."

Adam looked down at the alternate 2027, watched one of the blue-antlered cow-giraffes saunter across a field and stick its head in a trough of something. "I can't... I can't do anything to fix this. This is way beyond me. I don't even *understand* all this. Everything you've said – it's just words. Batshit words. What are you expecting me to do? Travel in fucking time?"

Miss Morgan reached into the inside pocket of her suit jacket and pulled out a MEphone. She handed it to him and, seeing him and Izzy at the beach on the home screen, he realised it was his.

"Your girlfriend is Isabelle Dunford, correct?"

"Yes."

Smiling briefly and disingenuously, "I understand she's pregnant with your child. Congratulations."

Adam felt a chill. Only his dad and Izzy's parents knew that. How long had Million Eyes been watching him?

"Call her," she said. "Call Izzy."

Adam frowned and tapped through to his recent calls. Izzy's name at the top – he'd called her from work yesterday – he tapped the call button and lifted the phone to his ear.

"This number has too many digits," said a gender-neutral voice with an accent he couldn't place. *"Please redial."*

He tried it again, got the same response.

Huh?

He scrolled through his contacts to find Izzy's work number. He called it and was greeted with the *too many digits* response for a third time.

He returned to his contacts and found the number for Izzy's mum, Julie.

This time the automated voice replied, *"We detect that you are experiencing problems with your telephone. You are now being diverted to the Royal States of Poland Telephone Exchange."*

He looked at Miss Morgan. "What have you done to my phone? Why can't I call Izzy?"

She sucked in her lips and lifted her eyebrows. "I haven't done anything. You can't call Izzy because Izzy doesn't exist anymore. Neither does your unborn child. Neither do *you*. And if you refuse to do what I've asked, none of you ever will again."

Adam looked at the picture of him and Izzy on his home screen. He took it while they were paddling in the sea at West Wittering, moments before a freezing and larger-than-anticipated wave crashed into their legs and drenched them up to their middles, making Izzy double over laughing. A deep, suffocating ache immediately pressed down on his chest. His gaze wandered back to the window and the new world that lay below. Some kind of extraordinary train with huge, spherical carriages zipped along the monorail.

"What do you need me to do?" he murmured, feeling numb.

She smiled, despite there being nothing to fucking smile about, "We need you to save Jesus."

Oh, is that all?

Miss Morgan's meeting with Adam Bryant had gone down better than she expected. He seemed to have taken everything in his stride, although she sensed some shock in his manner. After having Adam escorted from the cells to the Time Travel Department to be fully briefed by Carina Boone, fitted with a chronode and a cognit and given a crash-course in time travel, Miss Morgan remained in the cell for a few minutes. She sat back down on her chair, stretched both arms above her head and rotated her neck. They weren't in as much of a rush as they were after the Jennifer Larson incursion, having reinforced the Shield with a voron pulse. That said, the stresses of what was an even bigger incursion meant they still only had thirteen hours of Shield power left to fix it. This time, however, Miss Morgan had been given assurances that everything would work out.

She leaned over, placed her elbows on her legs and her hands together, and turned her head towards the wall on her right. "Did you get all of that?"

Dr Neether's voice flowed crisply into the cell via the tiny concealed speaker in the ceiling. "Yes, ma'am. I got it all."

Miss Morgan nodded. "And?"

"Everything's proceeding as it's supposed to."

∃Ꮞ

The same man who'd brought the MEpad to Miss
Morgan in the cell escorted Adam to Floor Minus One,
the Time Travel Department, a secret underground
department he'd never known was there. Adam was in a
daze the whole way, chewing his lips till he tasted blood.
Was this actually happening? Was he actually going to
travel in time?

As Adam crossed the main floor of the department, full
of people sitting at desks wearing headsets and working
on MEcs, it didn't seem that different to the departments
everyone knew about – apart from a lack of exterior
windows. He was taken to *Temporal Health and
Medicine,* a large room off the main floor. Walking in, he
felt like he'd entered a hospital ward. The room was
divided into bays with beds and medical equipment, and
there were people in white coats walking around with
MEpads and pushing instrument trolleys. Most of the
beds were empty but one of the bays had its curtain
drawn and Adam could see at least three pairs of feet
beneath it. They were obviously working on someone.

Adam's escort, whose only words to him had been a
gruff "This way," and "Follow me, please," took him past
the bays and a large nurses' station to an office with the
name *Dr Sheila Ruben* emblazoned on the door. Dr
Ruben invited Adam in and enthusiastically shook his
hand. His escort waited outside.

Dr Ruben was unexpectedly pleasant. She reminded
Adam of the GP he'd had as a child. Her weary,

weathered look – grey, curly hair, papery skin and dark, crinkly bags under her eyes – contrasted with a cheery, youthful demeanour. She talked a lot, and fast, in a voice that was high and crisp. Adam noticed a photo of her with a young couple and two boys who looked under ten, posing for a photo with Mickey Mouse at Disney World. And there was a plate with remnants of lettuce and bacon fat and picked-off brown bread crusts, on a desk strewn with paperwork. You'd think that everyone involved in this side of Million Eyes would be as cold and ordered as Miss Morgan, but Dr Ruben seemed pretty normal.

Miss Morgan had already told him that in order to facilitate his time travelling – still, to Adam, a totally bonkers prospect – he would need to undergo two 'very minor' surgical procedures. He'd wanted to tell her to go fuck herself but knew she'd throw Izzy and his unborn child back in his face. He did wonder, were he to refuse, whether Miss Morgan would've been forced to find someone else to go back and save Jesus. She wasn't about to let the timeline remain in the state it was in, not after all her effervescing about Million Eyes' importance.

In any case, he was afraid she might just kill him if he refused, because she'd have no further use for him. She had made it pretty clear that in the grand scheme of things, one individual didn't matter one jot. Adam was still torn on whether she was right about that. These 'Shapeless' sounded nasty, but did stopping them justify the murders of Ferro, Curtis and the Rayburns? The stranding of his best friend in the past? The assassination of the Queen and Princess Diana?

As Adam lay on the surgical bed in Dr Ruben's office, pondering the philosophical implications of what he was about to do, Dr Ruben, fully equipped with small talk about her grandson and his imminent birthday, made an incision behind his ear and inserted a tiny device called a cognit beneath his skin. Then she injected him in the neck with a liquid containing a microscopic chip called a chronode. She briefly explained what both of them did.

The cognit would generate a psychic field enabling him to understand people not speaking Modern English and enabling them to understand him – a universal translator. The chronode, she said, would automatically make its way through his blood to his brain, lodging itself in his parietal lobe, thereby enabling him to 'time-read', although she didn't explain any further what that entailed. She was far more interested in talking about the new cake recipe she was planning to try out for her grandson's birthday and what to replace the pecans with because he was allergic. Adam had assumed, at first, that she was deliberately trying to put him at ease, but since both procedures were completely painless thanks to some exceptionally powerful anaesthesia, it was probably because she just loved to chat.

She followed the two procedures with an inoculation delivered by injection. She said, "It's to stop you from catching anything in the past due to, you know, all the filthy water and terrible hygiene."

Adam gulped.

"Oh, and I almost forgot!" she exclaimed, eyes bulging like a cod fish, as Adam was preparing to leave her office. She pulled open a drawer in her desk, full of thin glass vials the size of a pinky finger, and handed Adam one. It sloshed with clear liquid that had a pale blue tint. "Drink this right before you use your chronode for the first time. It'll optimise the connection between the chronode and your cerebral cortex."

"What is it?" said Adam, frowning.

Dr Ruben laughed, "A little bit of everything! Amphetamine, caffeine, adrenaline, MDMA, cocaine and... a touch of raspberry syrup." She leaned close to his face and whispered surreptitiously, lips bunched up in a puckered smirk, "But that's just to make it taste good!"

"Did you just say MDMA? And cocaine?" It was a long time since Adam had had either of those. He'd grown up a lot since those days.

"Oh yes – the cocaine's the best bit!" She laughed again.

"Er – thanks."

"You're utterly, utterly welcome, Mr Bryant. Now go and put history back together. And good luck. Be excellent. Safe travels."

What an odd lady.

A tad woozy from the anaesthesia, Adam was escorted down a long corridor, past a room marked *Augur*, which must've been home to that incursion-predicting machine Miss Morgan said had been destroyed. He wound up at the office of Carina Boone, head of Time Travel. Miss Boone was much more in line with Adam's expectations: stony-faced, humourless, no warmth whatsoever. She had a tidy brown bob cut and wore a burgundy skirt suit over a white blouse. She looked a decade or so younger than Dr Ruben – late forties, early fifties, he guessed.

As Adam sat down, Boone said, "So I understand I've got to condense down four weeks of time travel training into an hour – this is going to be fun." Clearly she was as annoyed as he was that he'd been chosen for this assignment, instead of someone who was already a trained member of the Time Travel Department.

"Can somebody not go back in time four weeks and recruit me?" Adam suggested. "Give me the training then?"

Boone looked at him like he'd said something completely inane. "The timeline outside of this building has been rewritten. You no longer exist four weeks ago. I thought Miss Morgan had already explained that?"

"Yeah, but if you go back four weeks, that'll be before the timeline changed, won't it?"

Boone frowned, shook her head and gave an exasperated sigh. "History changed the moment the Unraveller assassinated Jesus. We can only send you back to *before* that happened. After that, it's a new timeline. Now are you going to let me do my job or are you going to continue questioning how this works based on an understanding of time travel that I suspect extends as far as *Back to the Future*?"

Hearing the impatience in her voice, Adam gave a meek nod and let Boone proceed with the training.

First, she showed him a video of what happened when a person travelled in time. Normally, she said, there'd be opportunities for virtual trials but in this case, the video would have to do. Basically, you swallowed a red pill – *chronozine* – and passed into the 'Chronosphere', a plane of existence in which all points in time intersected, where you felt like you were floating among billions of ghosts. This triggered the chronode, which brought up a virtual 'timeline', allowing you to select the exact date and time you wished to travel to. Boone paused the video to explain that without the chronode, focusing on a particular object or person whilst in the Chronosphere would pull you into the time frame in which that object exists, but otherwise there was no way of controlling *when* you'd end up. Adam figured that that was how Jennifer ended up in 1100.

The technobabble she used to explain all this went completely over Adam's head, but one thing she said was painfully clear: "Remember, this is time travel only. Not space-and-time-travel. When you swallow a chronozine pill, you'll move in time, but you won't move in space. If all of history hadn't just been erased, I'd be telling you to catch a plane to Israel and travel back in time from there. Unfortunately, you're going to have to travel back from here at headquarters, and make your way to Israel on foot, horse and boat."

Fan-fucking-tastic.

"And where am I going to get a horse from?" he asked.

"You'll need to buy one from some Celts," said Boone.

Cool. I'll just buy one from some Celts. Easy. Adam resisted the urge to say something sarcastic.

"I don't know how to ride, you know."

"Get whoever you buy it off to teach you."

Sure, no problem! I'll just get a dangerous barbarian to give me a horse-riding lesson.

After the video, Boone went through a bunch of time

travel rules that were similarly convoluted. Adam tuned some of it out, although that probably wasn't sensible. He was about to travel in time, for God's sake. He needed to know what he was doing.

He remembered her saying he had one chance to save Jesus, because the timeline had already been changed, so any further changes made by Adam would be permanent. She also said that if he tried to go back and change anything he'd already done, he'd cause a temporal earthquake. Whatever the fuck that meant.

Boone equipped Adam with an ancient-looking leather satchel, which contained a bunch of items she went through in turn. The first was a refillable water bottle. Next, a medical kit with antibiotics, analgesics, anti-rash creams, and a sterile pack for wounds containing sutures and dressings. The idea of having to stitch himself up made his toes curl in his shoes.

"Wh – what if I get an injury that's really serious and I can't fix it?" said Adam, his voice quivering slightly.

"Don't," said Boone flatly.

Great, thanks.

The next thing she showed him was something soft in a zipped-up fabric tube about the size of a kitchen roll.

"It's a pop-up tent," said Boone.

Adam frowned.

Boone explained, "It uses technology and materials that aren't yet publicly available and can shrink down to almost nothing and erect itself automatically at the touch of a button. And the fabric's super-strong. It can resist attacks by bears, wolves… or Celtic warriors with swords."

A lump of dread lodged in Adam's throat.

"Hopefully you won't attract too much attention though. We've made it resemble goat skin so that it sort-of fits in."

An obvious thought occurred to him. "How will I eat?"

"You'll hunt."

"Hunt?" He shivered. "How? With what?"

"With this."

Boone pulled out the next item from the satchel. It was one of the silver guns the police had shot Adam and Lester with, which reminded him, he'd meant to ask Miss Morgan what they'd done to Lester. Was she alive and at headquarters like he was? Had they left her at the derelict office, meaning she was now very likely erased from the timeline? He'd ask Boone when she had finished briefing him.

Boone showed Adam how to use the silver gun, which she called a 'disruptor' and said could be used to hunt, start fires and ward off animal or human threats. She made surviving in the Iron Age sound like a trip to Tesco's.

She produced three more items from the satchel: a pair of spectacles with inbuilt facial recognition, night vision and the ability to scan for time travellers; an e-reader containing an entire library of historical information; and a 'chronophone'. The chronophone looked exactly like a normal MEphone except, Boone explained, it had been configured for 'temporal roaming', which meant Adam could use it to talk to Miss Morgan in the future. He asked how he would charge electronics in an era with no electricity. Boone said all the items had air-powered fuel cells – tiny versions of the batteries found in MEcars – and would never run out of charge. More technology they were withholding from public consumption.

Next, she pulled out a large, heavy pouch containing several smaller pouches that were labelled. Adam realised when he felt them that they were bags of coins. Boone said to use the one labelled 'Celtic Staters' when he arrived in 28 CE, and that instructions for when and where to use the other currencies were in his chronophone.

Then Boone showed him the most important thing of all: a bottle of red pills – and Adam knew he was skirting frighteningly close to the point when he would be travelling back to the Iron Age. His stomach churned with a million anxious butterflies and he found himself listening more intently as Boone furnished him with instructions on how to take the pills properly and safely.

She finished up with a brief history lesson, reeling off the nuts and bolts on the Celts, the Jews and the Romans, before going back over the minute details of his assignment, which she said was all in writing in his chronophone. "Got all that?"

Adam nodded, though in all honesty the answer was *fuck no.*

"Good. Let's get you into some more appropriate attire."

Boone took him to a room off the communal office where he'd started, which had *Wardrobe* on the door. It was basically a huge walk-in closet with neat rows of clothes from different eras hanging like tired ghosts. There were shirts, dresses, trousers, jerkins, pinafores, tunics, togas and... strange, silver catsuits with gills. *When are people wearing those?* Beneath all the clothes rails were low shelves stacked with footwear – everything from cowboy boots to sandals to clogs.

Boone took Adam to the second of the narrow aisles between the rows and selected a thick, black, woollen robe, ankle-length with baggy sleeves and a wide, deep hood. *I don't like the idea of trekking across Europe in that.* Then she pulled a pair of flimsy-looking sandals from one of the shelves beneath.

"You'll want to strip down to your briefs," said Boone. "The lining inside is made from a special material that will moderate your body temperature according to the conditions you're in. If the temperature is low, the robe will keep you warm. If the temperature is high, the robe will cool you down."

Oh, okay. That's something, I guess.

"Changing room's that way."

He took the robe and the sandals and went to change. The robe was easy enough to put on – it basically went straight over his head. The sandals were just a thick sole and leather straps that went over his foot and around his ankle. Not much protection from the elements. Not very comfortable either. He took Dr Ruben's cocaine concoction from his trouser pocket and slipped it inside his leather satchel.

"Now what?" said Adam, returning to Boone dressed like a monk and handing her his clothes. She passed them to a staff member he'd seen sorting clothes and hanging up outfits, who vanished with them through an unmarked door next to the changing room.

"Now you're ready," said Boone.

He fought back a wave of nausea that almost triggered him to puke in front of her.

Why me why me why me?

"Drink your blue juice," said Boone.

Adam took a breath. "Blue juice?" He then realised she was talking about the cocaine concoction. "Oh. Right." Hands trembling, he opened his satchel, pulled out the vial and drank it, tasting raspberry syrup.

"Now remember," said Boone, "you'll be liaising with Miss Morgan directly from this point on. If you have any questions, just give her a call on your chronophone. All the instructions I've given you – and the time travel rules – have been transmitted to your chronophone."

Adam nodded with no certainty of anything.

Without smiling, Boone said, "Good luck. Don't screw this up."

Yeah, thanks. All of history and billions of lives on my shoulders. Fucking super.

He lifted a red pill to his mouth, and stopped. "Wait. I just thought. We're underground. You said this thing is time travel only. Not space. And since there's obviously no headquarters in the 1st century, won't I materialise underground and... be buried alive?"

"No," said Boone, frowning. "When I say it's time travel only, that's not literally true. But your movement in space is merely adjustment. The chronozine knows to orient you so that you don't materialise underground, or, for example, half inside a tree or a wall... or a person."

Adam gulped. He hadn't even thought of that. "What do you mean the chronozine *knows?*"

Boone huffed loudly and stared at him. "That would take all day to explain. It just *does*. Same way it knows to take your clothes and your satchel and anything you might be holding in your hand with you when you travel. The things you need."

You really couldn't make this shit up.

Boone looked at him like she had zero faith that he was going to succeed. Frankly, Adam wasn't sure he had any either.

That said, he *had* to succeed. Izzy and his baby's lives were at stake – along with everyone else he'd ever known.

Pulling a deep breath in and closing his eyes, he swallowed the pill.

Instantly dizzy, a harsh palpitating hum in both ears, he opened his eyes again. Suddenly encircling him were transparent people, furniture and vehicles, all impossibly occupying the same space, blurred together like thousands of merged video clips.

The ghosts. He was in the Chronosphere. He looked down, unable to feel the floor. Shadows played over dark ground. He looked around for Boone in the mad, hazy throng but couldn't see her. Then again, if the chronozine had 'moved' him above ground, she was still under it.

"Shit!" His heart almost perforated his ribcage as a giant quadrupedal creature with scaly skin, front legs like tree trunks, a neck that must've stretched at least six storeys high and a tail that could flatten a house, lumbered towards him.

Holy fuck balls, a dinosaur!

As he craned his neck to look up, the dinosaur was almost on top of him. He screamed, shut his eyes and threw his arms up as one of the tree trunk legs came plunging towards his face.

Nothing happened.

He opened his eyes, saw the swish of the creature's mighty tail above his head, turned to see this absolute titan of nature plodding onwards, stomping on hundreds of ghosts, but not, because all of them occupied different places in time.

He was getting it now. As ridiculous as it seemed, he was seeing the past, the present and the future all happening at once.

The humming quietened slightly and Adam's dizziness began to lift. A moment later, a horizontal white bar of black numbers overlaid his vision, cutting right through the middle of the ghosts. His chronode was engaged. Here was his 'timeline', his menu of dates. From left to right, he could see years, with 2027 – the present – at the centre.

2	2	2	2	2	2	2	2	2	2	2
0	0	0	0	0	0	0	0	0	0	0
2	2	2	2	2	2	2	2	3	3	3
2	3	4	5	6	7	8	9	0	1	2

Remembering the video Boone had showed him, Adam used his finger to carve into empty air and scroll right. The numbers zipped past his eyes, making him squint. Moving his finger left to slow the scrolling, he saw that he'd gone back before the first millennium, the years in three figures. He scrolled further, slowing and eventually stopping as the years reduced to two figures.

1	2	2	2	2	2	2	2	2	2	2
9	0	1	2	3	4	5	6	7	8	9

He lightly prodded the air where the year 28 was displayed.

The banner dissolved and a new one now spanned his field of view.

J	F	M	A	M	J	J	A	S	O	N	D
a	e	a	p	a	u	u	u	e	c	o	e
n	b	r	r	y	n	l	g	p	t	v	c
u	r	c	i		e	y	u	t	o	e	e
a	u	h	l				s	e	b	m	m
r	a						t	m	e	b	b
y	r							b	r	e	e
	y							e		r	r
								r			

He selected August – he'd been told to give himself three months to get to Nazareth. A new banner of numbers appeared: days. He scrolled to the 17th and selected it. Now he was presented with numbers in twenty-four-hour-clock format.

| 00: | 01: | 02: | 03: | 04: | 05: | 06: | 07: | 08: | 09: | 10: |
| 00 | 00 | 00 | 00 | 00 | 00 | 00 | 00 | 00 | 00 | 00 |

The hour, he was told, was as exact as Million Eyes' time travel got. He couldn't specify the minute. Or second. Not that he needed to.

He hovered his finger over 02:00. Boone had said that although there was no evidence of settlements in the London area at that time, and Roman Londinium wasn't established until 43 CE, Adam should materialise during the night 'just in case'. There'd be no one around then.

Knowing this was the last step, he hesitated, his heart thumping, his stomach in ever-tightening knots and constantly threatening to send a tide of vomit surging up his throat. *Am I really going to do this?*

He felt so tempted to tap the left-facing arrow at the bottom of his timeline 'screen' – the back button. He could scroll all the way back to 2027.

Except that, apart from the Looming Tower, there *was* no 2027. Well, not the 2027 he remembered. He saw a flash of those weird cow-giraffes and his blood ran cold.

There was no going back. *Oh, the irony.*

Swallowing hard, he tapped 02:00 with his finger. *1st-century England, here I come.*

As the humming stopped, silence fell and the banner and the ghosts were absorbed inside a thickening mantle of white, a sudden thought popped into Adam's head.

He forgot to ask Boone about Lester.

35

August 17th 28

"Please, magic-maker, show clemency!"

A woman's voice. Clear, but quiet and far away. *What happened?*

Adam opened his eyes to vivid, blank whiteness, like someone was shining a torch in both eyes. Dazzled, he stumbled backwards, feeling ground against his feet again. He felt stiff, extremities tingling, ears ringing. But all of that passed in a moment, leaving him strong, alert and... *hungry*. Inhaling deeply, he took in a pungent and unsavoury smell, a mix of moist earth, piss, shit and oil, and gagged, his appetite sapped. The brightness ebbed like someone was turning down a dimmer switch – then Adam was plunged into darkness.

"Sir, have you come to pass the judgment of the gods?"

The woman's voice again, except now it sounded like she was right next to him. As Adam's eyes began adjusting to the darkness, he realised it wasn't absolute. He was expecting to reach into his satchel and take out his night-vision-equipped spectacles about now, but he didn't need to. His immediate surroundings were flushed with the warm glow of a solitary oil lamp. And the woman who had spoken *was* right next to him. A couple of metres to his left, barefooted and on her knees, holding the lamp. A chilly night wind moaned through nearby trees and made the woman's white tunic billow around her like drifting snow.

The lamplight showed a face florid and agape in horror. She looked pretty, about twenty, had a wide scar across her left cheek and, while on her knees, shiny black hair fell straight and thick all the way to the ground, the lamplight flickering on it.

Adam's gaze wandered to the limply lit surroundings: the ashes of a dead fire and a rudimentary ridge tent of what looked like animal skin – he suspected that might be the source of the awful smell. Beyond the tent, scattered silhouettes of trees and the soft outline of a horse blurred into the darkness.

Adam took a single, gentle step towards the woman. She instantly shrank back, scrunching up her face as if he was about to hit her. "I fear the gods, sir! Let me earn my way back into their good graces!"

"I'm not going to hurt you," said Adam softly. "I promise."

She opened her eyes, her face loosening. He saw her throat bulge as she swallowed. "What do you wish of me?"

I could use your horse, actually. He shook his head, "Nothing."

"Nothing? Then why have you come for me?"

"What makes you think I've come for you?"

The woman frowned. "Because I'm the only person for many miles."

Fucking typical. And he'd just materialised two metres from her bloody tent.

He remembered one of Boone's time travel rules: avoid all non-essential contact with anyone. Because, you know, *timelines.* Thirty seconds he'd been here and he was already chatting with a Celt, potentially drastically altering history for this woman and all the people who came after her.

That said, Boone had given him permission to buy a horse from the Celts – and get them to teach him to ride it – so he could get to Nazareth.

And here was a Celt with a horse.

"What's your name?" Adam asked.

"Rhienne," said the woman, frowning suspiciously.

"Greetings, Rhienne. My name is Adam." *Shit.* He shouldn't be giving his name, not his real one anyway. Dick move.

Rhienne just stared at him, eyes glazed with fear.

Adam took another step forwards, holding out his hands. "Please, get up. There's no need to kneel." She momentarily recoiled as he touched her pale, bare arms, relaxing a little as she allowed him to lift her gently to her feet – although her eyes stayed wide and fixed, lips frozen, like prey watching a hunter.

"Sir, you have great power. To appear from nothing in a blaze of light as bright and shimmering as the sun makes you mightier than any druid I've met." So much for Boone's *travel during the night when no one will see you* plan.

He contemplated her 'druid' reference. That made sense. Druids were the priests, magicians and judges of Celtic society, who sometimes, he'd read, wielded more power than the tribal and village chieftains.

"Why have you come if not to punish me?" said Rhienne.

Adam was starting to wonder what the hell this woman had done. "Why do you feel deserving of punishment?"

Rhienne lowered her head guiltily. "Because… because I killed the tanner who enslaved me and stole his horse."

So that was why she was alone out here. She was a fugitive. "Enslaved you?"

"Yeah. My father was a sheep farmer. When we were young, he took my brother and I wool trading in Regni territory. On our way home, Catuvellauni soldiers attacked our wagon, killed my father and stole my brother and I. They took us north and I was sold to one of the village tanners as a slave. A few days ago, I saw a chance to escape and took it."

"And where are you headed now?"

"Home. My tribe's the Cantii. I lived in a Cantii village

in the south, on the Dour river, not far from the port of Dubrae." She remembered proudly, "Our village was one of those that gathered atop the white cliffs to fend off the Romans when they tried to invade."

The Regni, the Catuvellauni, the Cantii – Celtic tribes Adam remembered Boone mentioning. And 'Dubrae' was what the Celts called Dover, which meant Rhienne must've been talking about the white cliffs of Dover.

"So that's where you're going?" Adam said. "Home to your village near Dubrae?"

"Yes. Do you not know this already? Is this not why the gods have sent you to me?"

He had two options here. Rhienne, he now knew, was a killer and a thief. He could say that in fact he *had* come to punish her, and that the punishment was that she give up her stolen horse to him. Although he'd need her to teach him to ride it and that wouldn't be very druid-y. And leaving a young woman on her own in the wilderness without a means of getting around wouldn't be very Adam-y.

The second option was more palatable. Rhienne was heading the same way he was. He could go with her. He wouldn't be changing history – she was going there anyway. Plus, she knew the land and the people who lived on it far better than he did. And she had a horse, a horse she knew how to ride.

"The gods have sent me to accompany you on your journey," said Adam.

"They have? Why?"

Er – good question. Time to make up some shit. "To keep you safe. They have decreed that you are special."

Rhienne's eyes widened. "They have? I – I am?"

"Yes."

A smile started tugging at her lips and her eyes shone with tears. "I thought you'd come to offer me as a sacrifice."

"Then you accept?"

"Who am I not to? The gods command it." She sniffed,

blinking, and a tear fell down her cheek. "And they say a druid can't be killed, therefore a traveller's safety is assured by being in the company of one. I'd be glad of the safety, and the company, sir."

So would he. "You don't have to call me 'sir'. Adam is fine." Rhienne already had his name – no going back now. It probably didn't matter though. Boone told him most of the Celts were illiterate.

"As you wish... Adam," said Rhienne. "We should go at first light. Do you agree?"

"Yes."

"At first light, then. I should sleep."

It occurred to Adam that she must've been awake before he got here, since she'd watched him materialise. "How come you weren't asleep when I arrived? It's late."

Rhienne looked up at the night sky, so much blacker than Adam was used to. No light pollution. "Bad thoughts. Bad memories. Worries. Doubts. They make sure I sleep as little as possible. When you came, I was trying to find solace in the stars. I like to trace their shapes."

Adam liked that too. "I'm sorry I frightened you."

"Don't be. The gods have given me a gift this night."

Adam smiled.

Rhienne looked at him. "Do druids sleep?"

He wasn't tired. His hunger was returning though. "We do."

"You may lie with me."

Adam felt his cheeks flush. *She's forward!*

She said quickly, "I only mean that you clearly don't have anything with you but that satchel, and my bed is more comfortable than the forest floor. It's up to you."

The wind made Rhienne's shining black hair flutter about her waist. She gave him a beguiling smile, her brown eyes twinkling in the lamplight.

A stirring in Adam's groin made him turn away from her, suddenly uncomfortable. "I – er – I'll go find a place to sleep, and come back at first light."

"If you're certain."

Adam nodded, smiling awkwardly. "Goodnight."

"Goodnight."

As Rhienne disappeared through the door-skin of her tent, Adam walked into thickening darkness. The sky was clear and the moon bright, but it wasn't enough light to see where he was going. He reached inside his satchel for his spectacles. Putting them on and switching to night vision, his surroundings were illuminated in different shades of green. Now able to properly take everything in, he looked around. The area he was in was wooded but not densely, and on one side he could see a clearing about a hundred metres away. Rhienne's tent, a heap of supplies outside it and a horse tied to a tree were the only evidence of human life.

Adam walked till he was about fifty metres from Rhienne's tent. He took out the tube containing his pop-up tent and unzipped it. The cylinder of very tightly packed fabric that emerged from the tube called to mind those magic flannels that expand in water. There was a small, loose flap at the bottom with a round button. As per the instructions on the side of the tube, he pressed the button, set the cylinder down in a 1.5-metre by 2.5-metre space, and waited ten seconds.

The tent began to expand like a bud opening into a flower in one of those sped-up nature videos. He would've been amazed had he not just travelled in time. It was going to take a lot to bowl him over after that.

It was a ridge tent similar to Rhienne's, the canopy looking like sewn-together sheets of animal skin. Of course, he knew from what Boone had said that it was faux skin for camouflage purposes, which meant he was spared the smell that was the byproduct of old-fashioned tanning methods.

He didn't sleep. Instead he spent a few hours reading about this period in history on his e-reader.

When the sky began to lighten and turn milky blue, Adam collapsed his tent, which involved pressing the same button and watching it shrink down into the compacted fabric cylinder it started as.

Seeing Rhienne emerge from her tent and start saddling her horse, he went to rejoin her. Dew lay heavy on the ground and there was a damp mist hovering between the trees. Rhienne smiled from ear to ear when she saw him; she was even prettier by day. No longer barefoot in her sleeping tunic, she now wore one that was thicker and multi-coloured, with a tartan-like design. A deep blue cloak of wool and fur hung off her shoulders and was fastened with a bronze brooch, and she was in sandals similar to Adam's. Attached to the leather belt around her waist was a wood-hilted sword in a scabbard.

She offered him some water from a teardrop-shaped pouch made of animal skin. Even though the bottle of water in his satchel was still three quarters full – he'd been conserving it till he had started on the road to Nazareth – he accepted out of politeness. He drank without smelling, wondering where she'd sourced the water and hoping the inoculation Dr Ruben had given him at headquarters would protect him from all the nasty critters that might be festering in it.

Together they packed up her tent – oh, he wished hers had a button – and secured it to the pack saddle.

They rode double out of the woods on Storm, Rhienne's mare, Adam behind Rhienne with his hands around her waist, so close he could smell her hair – it had a strong, earthy, natural scent that was much more pleasant than he would've expected. The sky had brightened, the sun and a light breeze brushing away the mist, and the dew-soaked ground was beginning to dry. It looked set to be a fine day.

They dropped down into the valley of a wide river – the Thames. Adam's information said that in the 1st century, the Thames was wider and shallower and there were fords where you could cross to the south side. It was just a question of finding them. Rhienne said she remembered the ford she was taken across when the Catuvellauni abducted her, close to a small Regni farming village on the south side, a village the Catuvellauni raided on their way through. When they got to the ford, Rhienne was pleased to see that the village was still there. They'd rebuilt after the Catuvellauni took everything they had.

Hours passed, the weather staying dry and pleasant, but not too warm. They stopped several times to give Storm a rest; to fill up Rhienne's waterskin and Adam's bottle from streams and rivers; to eat – Rhienne still had some bread and chunks of honeycomb that she'd brought with her from her village; and for toilet breaks. Rhienne wasn't shy at all, lifting up her tunic and squatting in the grass while they discussed where they were headed next. He couldn't tell if her lack of inhibition stemmed from her culture or just her. When it came time for Adam to have a piss, a couple of trees on the hillside allowed him to protect his modesty. While pissing, Adam took the opportunity to surreptitiously check the MEmaps app on his chronophone. Fuck knew how but in addition to being able to make phone calls across time, this thing had GPS. And yes, they did appear to be headed for what would one day be Dover.

After the sun went down, Rhienne called a halt for the night and made a fire. Adam was glad to give his thighs and backside some respite from the uncomfortable saddle. He watched her do the old rubbing-sticks-together routine, knowing he could light the logs a lot quicker with his disruptor but not wanting to frighten her out of her wits like his out-of-thin-air arrival had done. Anyway, she was a pro at fire-making, so it didn't take long.

She was a pro at hunting too. A sharp spear and an even sharper eye caught them a beaver for dinner. Tasted pretty good. Could've used some salt, though.

"What happened to your brother?" Adam decided to ask while they ate. Rhienne had said her brother was taken by the Catuvellauni when she was young – why was he not with her now?

Rhienne dipped her head. "Nyle was... he was

impulsive. He was sold to the blacksmith but he rebelled before it was time and the chieftain handed him over to the druids, who... th – they..." Her voice started to break and she cleared her throat. Her hand that wasn't holding a skewer of beaver meat tightened into a fist. "Nyle died three times. They bashed his skull, drowned him, garrotted him, while I watched. The gods were cruel that day."

Fuck. Adam was surprised Rhienne didn't hate these gods of hers, and the druids for doing their dirty work.

"I'm – I'm sorry for your loss," he said softly. What else could he say?

"Thank you. But the gods are wise and Nyle had a weak will. Though his punishment was severe, he... he brought it on himself." She wiped the tears that streamed from both eyes. Adam wondered if she believed what she was saying.

The next morning was much greyer and grimmer, rain coming down like a million swords stabbing the earth. Whatever Adam's robe was made of was waterproof, so the wetness just rolled off him. Rhienne, of course, was not so lucky, although it didn't seem to bother her. If anything, she seemed exhilarated by it, the way she held up her face to the rain so unflinchingly. He imagined the Celts were much more in tune with nature and the elements than 21st-century city folk like him.

They continued through the waterlogged landscape to Rhienne's village, passing several hillforts characterised by distinctive ramparts following the steep contours of the hillside and guarding villages at the top. They were careful to avoid an army of chariots and horsemen raging across the countryside – Catuvellauni raiders, Rhienne said.

The rain lasted hours, eventually thinning to drizzle and stopping late afternoon. The sun burst through, burning away the cloud, just in time to bid them goodnight in a blaze of red and orange.

They set up camp in a cave in a hillside and ate the rest

of the beaver from the previous day. Adam learned more about Rhienne's colourful past and shared what he could of his own life, in a way that would make sense to her.

Next morning, drawing near to Rhienne's village, Adam fell into a bit of a funk. He'd soon be on his own and even though he'd only been with Rhienne a few days he'd enjoyed her company. She made being in this simple, savage century a little easier.

He noticed his rider go quiet, too. Rhienne had said how excited she was to see her sisters again, and her mother most of all, but because over a decade had passed, there was a significant possibility her mother may have died.

As Storm galloped into the valley of the River Dour, where Rhienne said she could see her village in the distance, flickers of dread began igniting in Adam's gut. As they got closer, they could see what used to be houses, workshops, stables and livestock pens, now just piles of ash and charcoal, gradually being enveloped by grass and damp carpets of moss. Mud, patchy grass and weeds covered the field strips on the hillside that once thrived with crops. Everywhere, remnants of possessions and furniture that couldn't be or weren't worth taking scattered the ground. Also scattering the ground – bodies, now skeletons. Dozens of them.

Rhienne was silent as she dismounted Storm and walked amid the debris and the dead. Adam stayed on the horse. She approached one particular heap of ash and wreckage and crouched down to examine one of the skeletons sprawled next to it. He couldn't imagine there was any way of knowing for sure if it was a member of her family. This carnage happened some time ago.

Shaking her head, Rhienne stood up and returned to Adam and Storm.

"I'm so sorry, Rhienne," said Adam.

She looked at him, lips and eyebrows quivering. She was holding back tears. Sighing deeply, she replied, "They were just farmers. No threat to anyone."

"Who do you think – ?"

"The Catuvellauni."

Rhienne pulled herself back onto Storm and he was able to place a comforting hand on her thigh.

"What will you do now?" he asked.

"Good question. I've no idea. I've abandoned one home, lost another. I've run out of homes."

Before even thinking it through, "Come with me."

She turned her head to face him. "Come with you where?"

"Nazareth."

"Nazareth? Where is that?"

"Across the sea. Far, far from here."

"Why are you going there?"

Keep it simple, Adam. "The will of the gods."

Rhienne nodded. That probably would've been enough for her, but Adam, compelled to make it sound more tempting, added, "A fresh start in a new place. Somewhere very different from here. With no Catuvellauni."

She looked him in the eyes and Adam felt a flutter of warmth in his chest. "I'll go with you."

He smiled. In that moment he felt an urge to kiss her. A flash of Izzy's face in his mind made him stare off into the distance. "I take it you know the way to the port of Dubrae?"

She nodded with evident disappointment that he hadn't kissed her, "Yes."

"Then… shall we go?"

"Let's." She tugged on Storm's reins and tapped the horse's ribs with her heels, and Rhienne's slaughtered village was behind them.

36

Adam and Rhienne rode close to the river, which quickly started to widen, the air smelling more of salt and sand than trees, the wind picking up. Before long, the port of Dubrae appeared before them, majestically overlooked by familiar white cliffs and a hillfort where Dover Castle would one day be built. Close to the harbour, traders and horse-drawn wagons weaved around shops, inns and stables, while the sea, shimmering blue and green in the sun, bustled with ships of all sizes and shapes, carrying traders and their wares to and from the continent.

They rode down to the docks for a closer look. Not wanting to part with Storm if she didn't have to, Rhienne looked for a ship capable of transporting horses. There were two: huge wooden galleys with high bows and sterns, three banks of oars and two tall masts with furled sails made of animal hide, currently being loaded with horses, cattle and other livestock. Rhienne found the captain, but didn't have enough to pay him. Adam did though, and discreetly lifted some coins from his pouch of Celtic staters to give to her. Within an hour, Adam, Rhienne and Storm were on their way to Gaul, the ancient Celtic region of Western Europe that would one day be France, Luxembourg, Belgium and bits of other European countries – now firmly in the grip of the Roman Empire.

Once in Gaul, they rode every day through field, forest and mountain, sleeping in different places each night, doing their best to avoid towns and cities and the Roman

311

garrisons that kept them in line. Rhienne now relied on Adam as her guide, and he relied on the GPS on his chronophone, which he had decided to use openly, telling her it was a druid talisman.

Adam knew he couldn't take Rhienne all the way to Nazareth, that they'd have to part ways in a village close by. He couldn't risk her interfering with what he needed to do, or be distracted by her while he was doing it. He hadn't yet told her.

Four weeks later, reaching Hungary and passing near to the city of Aquincum in future Budapest, Adam faced his most frightening moment yet. He and Rhienne were chased and eventually surrounded by a small band of raiders from the Eravasci tribe, heavily armed with swords, spears and daggers. The psychic field created by Adam's cognit allowed him *and* Rhienne to communicate with the raiders, which surprised Rhienne but meant she was able to threaten them with druid spells. Her threats meeting raucous laughter, she tugged her heavy iron sword from its scabbard and was prepared to fight, but it would be seven men versus the two of them, and Adam was no fighter. Left with no choice, Adam pulled his disruptor from his satchel and pointed it at the ringleader.

"You really want to turn around and leave," he said, trying to hide the fact that he was shaking beneath his robe.

The ringleader laughed again and, nodding at Rhienne, said, "What I *really* want is to get my dick into that."

Adam spied a rocky outcrop a few metres behind the ringleader and adjusted his aim. A shaft of blazing green light blew the outcrop apart with a thunderous *crack*. Shards and fragments of rock blasted outwards, one of them hitting a raider in the eye and likely blinding him. As he screamed, his comrades' arrogant grins vanished, their eyes bulged wide in fear and the colour drained from their faces like water down a plughole. Not needing any more convincing that Adam's threat wasn't idle, they fled.

After that, to Rhienne, Adam was not just a powerful magician but a god. A god with whom she was becoming increasingly enamoured.

One night, in the wilderness of 1st-century Turkey, he and Rhienne were lying in his 'magic' tent amid some Judas trees, yellow-leaved and flushed with burgundy seed pods, in a shallow valley between two rocky, yellow-brown hills, close to a tiny stream. The terrain had been turning drier and more rugged these past few days now that they were in the Middle East, and the sun was harsher, its rays pounding them and Storm unforgivingly. Unaccustomed to this sun, Rhienne and Storm were wearing out. Adam, although suffering from a serious case of saddle-soreness, was really starting to experience the benefits of his robe. Boone hadn't been joking about its acclimatising capabilities.

Adam and Rhienne had been sleeping in his tent for a while now; it was so much easier to pitch and collapse than hers, and it didn't smell like shit. Tonight, Adam couldn't sleep – again. His groin was on fire with raw, unsatisfied need. Flashes of Izzy, naked and writhing beneath and on top of him, turned up the burn and made his cock harden and swell uncomfortably against his fur blanket. He was used to having sex three or four times a week; he'd gone from that to nothing. Not since he was a teenager had he felt this pent-up.

He was about to sneak out of the tent, do what had become a nightly routine and go have a wank under the cover of darkness. But as he threw off his blanket, Rhienne's hot hand clapped onto his bare chest and she whispered, "Don't. Stay here, with me."

Rhienne didn't sleep much, Adam knew that. So she was no doubt aware that he left their tent each night for five minutes. She wasn't stupid either. Though he was quiet, she probably suspected what he was doing. What she didn't understand was why he wouldn't let her help.

He looked at her. The lamplight flecked her eyes with gold and made little shadows dance on her face. She

313

looked more beautiful than normal tonight, which didn't help. He'd felt attracted to Rhienne ever since he met her, which had only made his frustration more acute.

Rhienne stared at him, silent now, and her hand slid down his chest to his briefs. He felt a rush of heat all over as she grasped his cock, hard. She wasn't shy or gentle. She wanted him and tonight she was going to have him. The force of her desire sapped Adam's resolve. In a moment he was on top of her, kissing her roughly, clumsily, losing himself in the softness and sweetness of her mouth, thrusting his hands up her sleeping tunic till her breasts were under his fumbling fingers.

He pulled her legs apart and rammed himself in. It was fast, intense, desperate, and over in a couple of minutes. Rolling onto his back, sweating and breathing fast, instant prickles of shame and guilt licked up his neck and he longed for the ground to swallow him whole. *What have I done?* He wasn't a cheater. He'd never cheated in his life, but he had now. He *was* now. Izzy was having his baby, for God's sake.

Except Izzy wasn't. Izzy didn't exist. And neither did his baby. And Adam was halfway across the world right now, two thousand years in the past. So far away, in space and in time.

Did screwing Rhienne even matter?

Yes, Adam. Of course it matters.

Their final few weeks together were spent circling around mountains, weaving through small forests, and traversing sparse rocky plains speckled with tufts of grass and lichen, with Storm leaving a trail of floating dust behind her as she kicked through sandy, stone-strewn soil. Only small amounts of stilted conversation passed between Adam and Rhienne now; their relationship had completely changed since that night. Adam didn't know how to speak to Rhienne anymore and Rhienne knew it.

They followed a well-maintained Roman road to the town of Capernaum in northern Israel, which is where Adam had decided to part ways with Rhienne. They first had to explain themselves to a patrol of Roman legionaries in leather kilts, breastplates and iron helmets who stopped to ask their business. Adam was truthful in saying that he was a traveller going to Nazareth and was stopping by Capernaum on the way, and would not be there long. The centurion in charge of the patrol, distinguished from the others by his long cloak and the red plume of hair on his helmet, allowed them passage.

Capernaum was a fishing town on the northern shore of the Sea of Galilee, sheltered by green hills, with quaint two-storey stone houses separated by gardens and a stunning white limestone synagogue. Down at the quayside, cobalt-blue waters glistened, fishing boats lined white, shining beaches, and muscly, tanned fisherman could be seen casting huge nets into the water and hauling them back in, packed with fish. Adam's guilt that he was about to leave Rhienne in a strange and foreign place was alleviated slightly by the fact that it was so beautiful.

Adam used Tyrian shekels to pay for a house for Rhienne close to the lake and a stall for Storm in the nearest stables. Rhienne had been expecting to go with him to Nazareth and was disappointed that he was leaving her. Adam cited the gods as his reasons – so easy with someone so devout – but he felt like an arsehole. It was clear she had fallen for him. The problem was, he was falling for her as well.

Leaving her with enough money to get by, he hoped she would be able to build a new life for herself, far away from the old one.

Saying goodbye at the door of Rhienne's new home, Adam kissed her cheek, tasting the tear that rolled down it in that moment. He felt an ache in his chest as he turned and started out of Capernaum, intending to make the rest of the journey to Nazareth on foot.

He knew Rhienne was watching him go, hoping he'd look back.

He didn't.

Rhienne stayed in Capernaum for a time, but was a stranger in a strange land. The people there looked, sounded, even smelled different. The ground beneath her feet was dry and rough and she found herself longing for the soft, damp greenness of Britannia. She tried to learn the language. Even though everyone she and Adam had come across on their journey spoke her tongue, no one in Capernaum did.

She might not have stayed for as long as she did if she didn't think – *hope* – that Adam might come back for her. He never told her what he was doing in Nazareth, or where he was going after, and she never presumed to ask.

A few weeks passed and he didn't return. It pained her to admit that Adam was a light in her life that had now burned out.

She was on her own.

In the end, Rhienne decided to take Storm and leave Capernaum and go back the way she came. The journey would not be so easy, not without Adam and his spells and his talismans. But she was damn well going to try.

Enfeebled by the journey to Capernaum, Storm didn't make it. Rhienne resorted to old habits and stole a horse from a local tribe.

It took a season but eventually Rhienne found her way home. She sailed to a marshy peninsula in the east, there joining a tribe known as the Iceni and catching the eye of the tribal chieftain, Subidasto, who took her as his wife.

When their child was born after only four months, Subidasto would proclaim that the child, a girl, was so strong and powerful that she had simply grown faster than any other.

Rhienne and Subidasto named the baby Boudicca. Boudicca would grow up to become queen of the Iceni and lead them into battle against the Romans in 61 CE. She would become a legend and a cultural symbol of Britain and would, many centuries later, earn herself a statue on Victoria Embankment in London. The statue would portray Boudicca, spear in hand, riding on a scythed war chariot drawn by two rearing horses, her daughters crouching beside her.

While in college, Adam took a trip to London with Jennifer and walked by this statue. Jennifer, who loved her history, stopped to read the inscription on the plinth. Adam was more interested in the latest Aston Martin Vanquish that had just gone past.

He probably would've paid more attention had he known the statue was of his daughter.

37

November 17th 28

Today was the day. *At fucking last.* Adam had arrived in Nazareth with a few weeks to spare and boy had they dragged. If only he could've jumped forwards in time to this day – alas, Million Eyes had warned him that time travel was dangerous and should be minimised, not used for 'shortcuts'.

Nazareth was smaller than Capernaum, with less than a thousand inhabitants. Its streets of cosy one- and two-storey clay-brick houses followed the rise and fall of the hillside and were peaceful and surprisingly clean. The noisier town square was fronted by a simple stone synagogue and home to a bustling marketplace where the prevailing sounds were of carpentry, and the smells of camel and donkey shit mingled with that of newly cut timber. Having explored Nazareth's every nook in a day, Adam had rented a room in an inn on the furthest edge of town and, knowing he was supposed to avoid all non-essential contact with anyone, had spent most of his time lying on an uncomfortable reed-stuffed mattress staring at a cracked wall and stewing in his guilt over Izzy, and Rhienne.

Today that guilt was being overtaken by a fist of trepidation balling in the pit of his stomach. He'd been told the exact time that Jesus would come staggering into the town square – that was when he needed to act. But the market was busy and he didn't know what direction he'd be coming from.

Adam stood at the top of the sloping square, in front of the synagogue, so that he could look out over the market. He watched the townsfolk go about their day unsuspectingly. Men and women in tunics, cloaks and headscarves huddled around merchants' stalls and livestock pens; traders passed through on camels and ox-drawn wagons and smaller carts pulled by donkeys; and queues of women and children went to and from the well in the middle of the square to fill their buckets at the watering trough. Fed by an underground spring, the well was Nazareth's main source of water and often heaving. Adam had had to queue up there himself once. Fortunately, his house had a cistern in the courtyard and, since he arrived, there had been several downpours to fill it up.

Adam noticed he was being stared at by the men sitting talking outside the synagogue.

"Who is that, do you think?" one man said. "He doesn't look like he's from around here."

"I've no idea," said another. "Never seen him before."

Adam pretended not to hear them. This was no time to be drawing attention.

"I saw him two weeks back," said a third man.

Adam gulped.

"Perhaps we should… Lord above, who is *that?*"

Adam frowned and looked at the man who'd just spoken, who was pointing towards the square. Shifting his gaze, Adam noticed that a portion of the crowd had stopped dead, staring in stunned silence, mouths agape. He followed their stares, heart springing into his throat. A man in a silvery blue uniform, with a white, box-like shoulder bag slung over his shoulder, was lurching through the square. He looked drunk, or hurt, teetering from side to side like he might fall over at any moment. The people were moving out of his way like he was diseased.

There he was. Dr Jesus M. Hirschfield. *The man I'm here to save.*

Heartbeat quickening fast, Adam scanned the square for the Unraveller. She'd be here soon too.

He couldn't see her.

Shit.

Shit, shit.

He saw Jesus stumble, nearly collide with a donkey cart, double over and clutch his knees. A man in a white robe and dark blue turban walked up to him. Adam assumed that must be Joseph of Arimathea. They started talking.

Adam slunk behind a huge, ancient olive tree close to the synagogue. He dug his spectacles from his satchel, put them on and engaged facial recognition. He needed to check that he was looking at the right people.

Dr Jesus M. Hirschfield. DOB: 14/05/2193
Joseph of Arimathea. DOB: 09/12/0004 BCE

Yep, it was them. Adam looked around for the Unraveller, the spectacles feeding him the identities of other people in the square. Still couldn't see her. Pulse thrumming in his ears, he lowered the spectacles and walked down into the square.

Moments later, Jesus and Joseph started walking up the dirt road that skirted the square. The people staring scurried to the edges of the road to let the strange man pass.

Jesus started walking really slowly, falling behind Joseph as he looked at something to his right. Adam honed his gaze, eyes landing on a young woman in an ankle-length blue tunic and a long white shawl over her head and shoulders.

Is that her? The Unraveller?

He quickly looked through his spectacles.

UNKNOWN FEMALE. DOB: NO DATA.

It was her.

Staring at Jesus with a sad expression, the woman lifted

a small silver object that looked distinctly like a disruptor and aimed it at him.

Fuck!

With a burst of adrenaline, Adam lunged forwards, sliding on some loose stones and nearly going arse over tit. Arms outstretched, he ploughed into Jesus's side, shoving him to the ground. A green streak of light shot past his line of sight, inches from his head.

Townspeople started running and screaming, shrill voices and scraping, crunching footsteps merging into a single drone. Jesus spun onto his back and stared speechlessly at Adam, his face taut with shock. The Unraveller turned and charged away from the square, disappearing around the side of a carpenter's house. Adam bolted after her, pulled out his disruptor, flying up a narrow street and coming out on a path that wound through more ancient olive trees. Sheep and goats trotted along the path further up, herded by their shepherd, unmoved by what was happening. Adam glanced around. *Where the fuck is she?*

A white light flashed over some houses in the other direction, like lightning, but in the middle of the day.

Adam started moving in the direction of the flash, passing onto a different street. A woman came running down it, clutching the thick shawl billowing about her shoulders to stop it flying off her head. "Demons! Demons walk among us!" she was screaming.

Adam stepped into her path. "What's happened? What have you seen?"

Stopping abruptly, "A woman disappeared in front of me, in a flash of light that almost blinded me! I saw it with my own two eyes! Demon!"

He let her continue.

Fuck. Shit.

That meant the Unraveller was gone. And he was supposed to have apprehended her.

Now what?

He returned to the square, saw that Jesus and Joseph

were walking up a small street that led to a wagon. At least Jesus was okay. He'd still write the scrolls that would lead to the founding of Million Eyes. History was back on track.

But what if the Unraveller went back a few hours and tried to kill him again? Hang on – what if *he* went back too? And caught her as planned? But then there'd be four of them... wouldn't there? Adam's forehead started to pound.

Adam made his way back to the inn where he was staying, taking out his chronophone and placing a call to Miss Morgan. The ringing tone was unusual; it didn't stop and start as you'd expect, but was an eerie, constant ring that got deeper and lower as it went on. Listening, he remembered that Million Eyes had configured the phones so that only fifteen minutes should have passed for Miss Morgan despite three months passing for him.

He felt a tightening in his throat as the ringing tone cut to Miss Morgan's silky voice, "Hello, Mr Bryant. It's good to hear from you."

The words stalled on his tongue. He took a breath. "Miss Morgan, I've just... I've just saved Jesus. But... but I wasn't able to apprehend the Unraveller. She's gone. Travelled in time again."

"Yes, I know."

"You do? How?"

"I told you – I have a source."

Oh yes. Your source. Adam really didn't trust this woman at all. "So is Izzy still..."

"Erased? Yes. As is your baby."

His heart sank, suddenly as heavy as a rock. "Do you want me to go back and try again?"

A lighter clicked. "Not *back*, no. You can't go back. Didn't Boone explain that to you?"

"Do you mean the temporal earthquake thing?" It was starting to come back to him.

"Yes. Any changes you make to the timeline while you're trying to undo the Unraveller's changes will be permanent. Time won't let you go back for a do-over. Really defeats the point of what we're doing if you blow up the universe."

Adam swallowed. "So what do you want me to do?"

He heard her draw on a cigarette, her next words partly strangled by the smoke. "You need to go *forwards*. I'm sending new instructions and mission parameters to your phone."

"To save Jesus again? Does the Unraveller try and kill him later in his timeline?"

"No. You need to go forwards in time to the year 993 and save Cuthwulf, the man who digs up Jesus's scrolls from underneath Glastonbury Abbey and founds Million Eyes. The Unraveller is going to kill him. We don't know where at the abbey the scrolls were found, and I'm guessing the Unraveller doesn't either. She'll kill Cuthwulf to ensure that they're never unearthed."

Adam's stomach lurched. "So you want me to go all the way back to England? To... Glastonbury?"

"Yes. As with Jesus, I'm sending details of exactly when and where you'll need to be to save Cuthwulf from the Unraveller. And I would suggest you make your way back to Britain *before* you travel in time. You're better off travelling during the time of the Roman Empire than the Dark Ages – plus you already know the terrain. When you jump to 993, the instructions I'm sending you will tell you which currencies to use to get by."

So that was why he had a bunch of other bags of coins that weren't used in this time period.

"I don't suppose I've got any other choice, have I," said Adam grimly.

"Not if you want to see Izzy again, no." She said it so coldly and matter-of-factly. Did this woman have any feelings at all? Any compassion? He'd been living in the 1st century for three months and she hadn't even asked how he was, how his journey was, whether he'd run into any trouble.

Then she snapped, "You better hurry, Mr Bryant.

Time's ticking away," and hung up.

No, she hadn't. No feelings. No compassion. She was a fucking robot. Adam couldn't wait for this to be over, then he'd never have to see or speak to her ever again.

Adam put the phone back in his satchel and stared out of the window of his rented room. The farmer who lived near him was ploughing his wheat field with his oxen, a bunch of children picking pomegranates from the trees just beyond.

Rhienne popped into his mind. If he was going to have to go all the way back to Britain anyway, should he stop by Capernaum? Check on her? See if she wanted to come back with him?

No. That would just make things more complicated.

This time he was going alone.

38

April 28th 2027

Miss Morgan walked unannounced into Dr Neether's office. The oraculum was active. The small, square slab of blue-tinted, glass-like metal was projecting a holographic textual display over Dr Neether's desk, which the half-faced doctor's only eye was poring over.

Dr Neether looked up with a start and immediately tapped the oraculum, causing the display to dematerialise. "Miss Morgan, I – I wasn't expecting you. How is everything proceeding with Adam?"

Miss Morgan winced at the sound of Dr Neether's voice – thin, crackly and scratchy, permanently choked and sounding like broken glass underfoot. "Fine – as far as I'm aware. That's what I came to speak to you about."

"You require more details about the Cuthwulf mission?"

"No. I want to know what happens after that."

Dr Neether's only eyebrow squeezed low over her eye, her forehead crumpling in a poor attempt at a frown. "Yes, er... ma'am, as we discussed earlier, we do need to be careful how we go about this." She said it as gently as her gravelly voice allowed, but that didn't stop the anger prickling up Miss Morgan's neck. "It would be better for me to reveal the next steps as and when we –"

Miss Morgan pushed through gritted teeth, "I just want the headlines, not the details."

"Ma'am, I really don't think –"

Enough! "Dr Neether, have you forgotten who you're talking to? You don't give the orders around here. *I* do. And not only am I your boss, I'm also the person who gave you everything you have. Not many others would – not after what you did. I *own* you. So when I tell you to do something, you do it. Clear?"

Dr Neether's half-face flushed scarlet and a swallow the size of a golf ball rippled down her throat. "Y-yes. Of course. I – I'm s-sorry, ma'am. I meant no disrespect."

Miss Morgan shook her head. Hopefully Dr Neether would remember her place from now on. If there was anything Miss Morgan couldn't stand, it was backchat from her employees, the people who were supposed to respect her the most. She was reminded of the mutiny that happened on the night of the Larson incident. *Fuckers.* Dr Neether, of course, was a special case. She didn't just owe her job to Miss Morgan, but her life as well.

"Right then," said Miss Morgan, folding her arms across her chest. "Tell me what Adam has to do next."

Dr Neether nodded meekly and rasped, nervousness making her voice crack and scrape even further, "After he's saved Cuthwulf at Glastonbury Abbey, Adam will need to move forwards in time ten years, to 1003, and make his way to Congelstede."

Congelstede. Of course. The Saxon village where Million Eyes was founded. It made sense that the Unraveller would go there next – try and kill Million Eyes in the crib.

Dr Neether continued, "The Unraveller will blow up the house where Cuthwulf, Father Beocca, Renweard and Lyveva had their first meeting with Elswyth, killing them all. Adam will need to save them before the bomb goes off."

Miss Morgan stared down at the potted plant in the corner of Dr Neether's office, letting the new information sink in. "Okay. And after that, is he done?"

"I'm afraid not. He will then need to jump to 1605 and

go to London, where the Unraveller will kill Tom Digby."

"Tom Digby. The boy who penned the Monteagle letter?"

"Yes, and alerted James I to the Gunpowder Plot."

Miss Morgan felt a flush of anger. "So this bitch wants to make sure Parliament is destroyed on November 5th?"

"And all of Million Eyes' highest-ranking members along with it, yes. Adam must save Digby so that the plot can be defeated."

Miss Morgan nodded, then a twinge of apprehension made her stomach tighten. "And you're certain this will work?"

Dr Neether looked confused. "Yes, ma'am. It can't not. It's already happened."

Timelines. Predestination. The future's the past, the past's the future. Miss Morgan could feel her temples start to throb with the warnings of a new headache.

"Ma'am, what is it?" said Dr Neether. She may only have had one eye, but it was damn sharp.

Miss Morgan said quickly, "Nothing. I'm fine."

"If you're worried about anything, you don't have to be. You already know that we succeed. Because of me."

Miss Morgan nodded. *If you say so.*

Dr Neether turned to her computer and started typing. "In the meantime, I've been looking into the identity of the Unraveller…"

All of Miss Morgan's muscles seized. "No! Don't do that."

Dr Neether frowned. "Don't do what?"

"I don't want you looking into her."

"Why?"

Miss Morgan sharpened her voice. "Do I need to give a reason? Who she is simply isn't relevant right now."

"Forgive me, Miss Morgan, but surely the Unraveller's identity is absolutely relevant."

"I said no."

Dr Neether hesitated, her eye back on her MEc screen.

329

Her scarred throat undulated with another nervous swallow.

Leave it alone…

Dr Neether looked at her again, opening and closing her crooked mouth as she searched for the right words. "Ma'am, I don't wish to speak out of turn, but you don't *already know* who the Unraveller is… do you?"

This woman was too clever for her own good. "No. Of course I don't. I just think we have more important things to think about right now."

Dr Neether nodded uncertainly. She didn't look convinced, but what did Miss Morgan care? She didn't answer to her.

"You'll stop looking into her at once – is that clear?" Miss Morgan reiterated. "Stay focused on analysing the oraculum."

"Y-yes, ma'am."

Miss Morgan started out of Dr Neether's office. "I'll let you know when Adam's done at Glastonbury."

39

October 24th 1605

Adam remembered Jennifer saying in her letters that she'd been stuck in the past for so long she'd forgotten what the 21st century was like. Having been time-travelling for almost six months now, he was starting to understand how that felt. Well, sort of. He still had his chronophone and disruptor and all the other advanced bits and bobs in his satchel to remind him.

Certainly, trekking across Celtic Europe to the Middle East with Rhienne and Storm felt like an age ago. But then, it *was*. Hundreds of ages ago. So much had changed since then. *He'd* changed. He was a killer now, and so hardened to these wild and brutal times that he didn't feel uncomfortable admitting it. On his way back to Britain from Nazareth, he'd happened upon a village in Thracia – future Bulgaria – being pillaged by Roman legionaries. Seeing women being raped and murdered out in the open, he'd used his disruptor to frighten the soldiers away. Most of the men had fled quickly, but one threw a javelin that impaled Adam's horse, causing it to throw him off. Adam dropped the disruptor but reached it in time to fire a bolt into the soldier's chest, scoring straight through his breastplate and tossing him against the stone wall of a house, over which he left half of his brain. Just the very idea of having ended someone's life had left Adam shaken for a day or so, but he'd got over it fast – perhaps unhealthily so. It was as though the Adam of the past and

331

the Adam of the future had become two different people, or that he was playing a role, a character, in a historical video game.

In hindsight, though, he probably shouldn't have stepped in to play hero in that village. The people there were meant to die, and the Roman soldier was not. But hey, what's done was done. And, after that, Adam wasn't so worried about avoiding every town or city in his path. If going through or near it was faster, *fuck it*. He had his disruptor, which meant no one was going to lay a finger on him if they didn't want to get blasted.

Since being back in Britain, he'd travelled in time three more times. He'd encountered the Unraveller in 993 and 1003, on both occasions saving the same guy – Cuthwulf – who was instrumental in Million Eyes' formation. He'd also saved a bunch of others the second time – Million Eyes' earliest members.

What a turn of events. After being determined to bring this company to its knees for what it had done to his friends, here he was, helping it come to power.

What the hell would Jennifer think of all this?

Jennifer. He'd been thinking about her more lately. He was getting used to all this time travelling, and he had plenty of chronozine left. And Jennifer was still stranded in the 1100s, pretending to be someone she wasn't.

He was in the business of saving people now. What if he went back and saved her? Someone he actually cared about?

He'd been trying to work out the time travel implications. He knew he couldn't save her till after she'd written her letters. Dr Lester finding those letters and making contact with Adam was what started all this off. Erasing the letters would mean erasing the events that led him to travel back in time in the first place. It might even cause one of those 'temporal earthquakes' he'd been told about. Which meant he'd need to leave her stranded there for fifteen years. That said, fifteen years was better than forever.

Of course, none of that mattered right now. Today was about saving Tom Digby – the Unraveller's next target. Thus far Adam had succeeded in preventing every one of the Unraveller's murders. He was getting to be a pro at this.

What he wasn't so good at was catching the bitch. He'd been told how to bring the Unraveller back with him. It wasn't very technical; he just had to make her swallow a pill when he did and then be holding her arm, or just physically touching her, when he selected a time zone. So far, he hadn't got close to doing that because she'd escaped every time.

He was damn well going to get her this time. He wanted this over. He wanted to know that history was restored, that Izzy and his baby were alive again.

For the past ten minutes, he'd been in Ashfield Lane in Southwark, standing outside a busy tobacconist's, directly opposite Mr Mott's bake shop, waiting for the Unraveller to make her next scheduled appearance. Frosty autumn air iced and stung his cheeks, but his trusty black robe was otherwise keeping him warm. With the dusk deepening, shopkeepers had been using flint and fire-steel to light the lanterns that hung on their outside walls. As it was about a century before public street lighting would be implemented, they were the only things bringing light to these dismal thoroughfares.

Trade was winding down. Adam watched butchers, greengrocers and florists bringing in their crates and buckets and closing their shutters. Some gathered their families and headed up the muddy, rutted road to the church on the corner for Evensong. Others went straight to the tavern opposite, or the brothel just beyond it.

Adam lifted his copy of Thomas Nashe's *The Unfortunate Traveller*, which was helping conceal his chronophone, and glanced at the screen. He inhaled deeply, now accustomed to the stink that wafted up his nose from the street gutters where everyone emptied their chamber pots, and where you might also find animal entrails and the occasional dead dog.

Four minutes. Four minutes till Tom Digby was going to come running out of the bake shop having killed Mott, and the Unraveller was going to shoot him dead in the street.

This time, Adam didn't feel as torn. Not because he was now convinced that Million Eyes were the force for good that Miss Morgan had made them out to be. It was because the Unraveller was trying to devastate half of London. Physicists in the future had shown that if the Gunpowder Plot had succeeded, the explosion would have taken out not just the Houses of Parliament but Westminster Abbey, parts of Whitehall and scores of nearby houses as well, killing hundreds if not thousands of people. Only a small proportion of those people would be Million Eyes. Most would have nothing to do with Million Eyes. Trying to erase Million Eyes was one thing, but how could the Unraveller justify that level of death and destruction?

No, she'd gone too far this time. Regardless of his instructions, this time Adam *wanted* to stop her.

One minute. *Where is she? Shouldn't she be here by now?* He kept glancing around. *Am I in the right place?*

He confirmed his location with his GPS and swallowed the lump of nervousness in his throat. He was in the right place, but was it the right *time?*

The minute passed. Adam saw a cordwainer serve his last customer of the day and start shuttering his shop. Then a wagon carrying barrels, cases and sacks pulled into Ashfield Lane, the horses coming to a stop outside the tobacconist's.

No signs of an altercation at Mr Mott's, no Unraveller. Something wasn't right.

Adam dropped *The Unfortunate Traveller* and backed into the shadows between the tobacconist's and the now-closed cloth merchant's next door. He pulled up his contacts on his chronophone and called Miss Morgan.

He lifted the phone, then a green light speared towards

him from the other side of the road – "Ahhhh!" It flashed at his ear and a white-hot force ripped the phone from his hand, scattering it in about four or five pieces over the ground. The impact sent a jolt of pain shooting up his arm from his hand. Cradling his hand in the other, he saw that the skin was red-raw and smoking and glistening with forming blisters. *"Fuck!"*

The bolt having momentarily doused Ashfield Lane in florescent green light, several passers-by were standing frozen, throwing confused looks in Adam's direction. The tobacconist, transporting his new stock into his shop, dropped the large case he was carrying. With a crack, the lid sprang off and an assortment of tobacco pipes rolled into the road, several falling into the street gutter.

Adam lifted his gaze to see the Unraveller emerge from a shadow-steeped alley between the florist's and the greengrocer's over the road. Her disruptor was poised and she was in the same simple, pale blue tunic and white shawl as when he first encountered her in Nazareth, and again in Glastonbury and Congelstede.

"About time I was one step ahead of you for a change," she said as she walked towards him. It was the first time Adam had heard her speak. Not a voice he recognised.

His burnt hand itching and throbbing, he replied, "You have to stop."

She shook her head and gestured with her fingers. "Your disruptor. Give it to me."

Adam sighed. *Shit, shit, shit.* He thrust his hand into his satchel, pulled out his disruptor. He looked at it, hesitating.

She taunted, "Are you willing to bet your reflexes are faster than mine?"

He handed it over.

She held his disruptor down by her side, keeping the other pointed squarely at his face. "You're Million Eyes, right?"

"Yes."

"How have you been able to follow me through time

like this? We destroyed the Augur. You shouldn't have any foreknowledge of what I'm doing, and yet you've anticipated every move I've made."

Someone was helping her. "We? Who's we?"

The Unraveller snorted with obvious contempt. "So you don't know everything then."

Adam swallowed. The pain from his hand was still snaking up his arm. "Who *are* you?"

"For a long time, I didn't know. Living rough, cleaning the streets for rich folk, I had no idea. A girl out of time. But I know now. I know now *exactly* who I am. I'm the woman who saves the world."

"*Saves* it? From what I've seen, you're destroying it!"

The Unraveller shook her head. "You don't know the half of it."

"What do you mean?"

"I really don't have time to explain. I'm here to stop Tom Digby and I'm not going to let you interfere again. Now are you going to tell me how you've been able to come after me or not?"

Adam didn't have the answer. Somehow he didn't think *Miss Morgan has a 'source'* was going to be good enough.

"If I tell you, you'll kill me anyway," said Adam.

Not entirely sincerely, "I promise I won't."

There was an angry holler from across the road – *"What the hell are you doing?"* Glancing over his shoulder, Adam realised it had come from Mr Mott's.

He looked back at the Unraveller, admitting, "I don't know how they know. Miss Morgan wouldn't tell me."

"There's a lot of things Miss Morgan hasn't told you."

She hardened her aim. He blinked. His thudding heart froze.

She's going to shoot.

Then a jarring shriek punched him in both ears, "There she is! The witch! She's the woman I saw appear out of thin air!"

Adam snapped his gaze to a woman in a dark red

hooded cape, orange pleated skirt and thick white waistcoat embroidered in orange with a pattern of leaves and peapods, pointing a white-gloved finger at the Unraveller. A watchman carrying a pike and lantern followed the woman's pointing finger, raised his lantern, and stormed towards the Unraveller, blaring, "Oi! You there!"

The Unraveller shifted her aim and, without faltering, sent a steaming shaft of light streaking into the watchman's chest, tossing him several metres into the air, his long dark coat flapping about him like a top-sail in a storm. The well-dressed woman screamed.

Adam didn't think. The moment the disruptor wasn't on him, he charged and launched his full weight at the Unraveller, ploughing straight into her. His right shoulder connected hard with her waist, jerking both disruptors from her hands. She went down like a bowling pin, Adam thudding to the ground with her.

Recovering fast, the Unraveller spun onto her front and scrambled to reach one of the disruptors, the nearest a metre away in a mud puddle, the silver casing glinting faintly in the feeble, dark orange glow of the lantern on the wall of the cloth merchant's. He couldn't see where the other had landed.

Adam lunged, clamping his hands on her back. A hot flash of pain sliced up his arm. His burned hand too painful, he focused his energy on the other, squeezing enough of her tough woollen tunic into his fingers to fasten a firm hold. She pulled against his grip, but he had her. Then she swung her torso and, before he could react, slammed her elbow into his face.

Instantly losing his grip, Adam lurched backwards, landed with a thump on his backside, causing a deep tremor to go from his hips to his chest and suck all the air from his lungs.

The blow would've knocked him senseless were it not for the pure adrenaline surging through him. He leapt to his feet as the Unraveller dived to grab the disruptor and spun round to fix her aim.

Adam launched into the road, whirled round to the back of the tobacconist's wagon for cover. As the Unraveller started curving round the wagon, he scrambled down the side nearest the tobacconist's, caught in his periphery the bolt of light blasting the ground behind him and kicking up a spray of mud and stones. He spotted the other disruptor in the middle of the road. *Fuck, fuck, fuck.* He'd never reach it in time.

The tobacconist came out of his shop just as Adam was passing his door.

He had a musket.

Adam turned, held his breath.

The Unraveller was standing at the back of the wagon, about to fire.

Bang!

The ball from the tobacconist's musket slammed into the Unraveller, flinging her backwards. She fell behind the wagon, out of view. The gunshot made the horses rear up and fight their bridles, filling the air with frightened screams. The carter grabbed the reins quickly and pulled, shouting, "Whoa!" and "Steady!" in an effort to calm them.

At that moment, Tom Digby came charging out of Mr Mott's and a woman's scream rang out from inside the bake shop – "Get after him!"

Saved.

The tobacconist was engaged in the arduous process of reloading his musket. Adam made a dash for the other disruptor. Trigger finger ready, sweat dripping off his chin, he carefully approached the rear of the wagon where the Unraveller had fallen.

Was she dead? If it was a direct hit, maybe. Musket balls were known for causing pretty devastating wounds.

A white, dazzling light blazed from behind the wagon, seared into Adam's eyes and made him recoil. The street was momentarily flooded with daytime-strong light, making several onlookers gasp audibly.

No, she wasn't dead.

He stepped behind the wagon, stared at bare gravel. Gone – again.

"See!" shrieked a woman. "I told you – she can appear and disappear at will! And she killed that watchman with lightning! Witch! We must find her and burn her!"

Adam looked up, saw the woman in the pleated skirt and waistcoat from earlier. Another watchman was with her.

Adam reached into his satchel for his spectacles and put them on to run a scan of the ground behind the wagon.

Shit. This bitch literally couldn't quit. She'd gone forwards in time two days. And he knew why.

He glanced over at the singed fragments of chronophone in the road. He was on his own. No way of contacting or getting help from the future – but he knew what to do.

He sprinted into an alleyway between two houses as the watchman called after him, "Sir! Hold on a minute!" Then he took out a red pill and swallowed it.

40

October 26th 1605

Along a tree-lined lane of huge, resplendent houses with lush, neat gardens front and back, the double-fronted brick mansion belonging to William Parker, 4th Baron Monteagle, started to peek through the trees. Adam didn't go all the way up to it, veering off the lane towards a stable with a large carriage parked next to it. He glanced around to check he was alone – he was, apart from the horses. Easing inside one of the half-doors, he watched the mansion from the shadows and waited.

As dusk blended into night, someone lit the lanterns at the front, painting the impressive facade of herringbone brickwork, decorative timber frames and dormer windows with a fluttering orange hue. Other houses lit theirs, but as they were further from the road than the smaller, more tightly packed houses in the City, their light didn't stretch far enough for Adam to see them properly. He put on his spectacles, switched them to night vision, everything now clear and green. A chilly wind jostled the trees and a single carriage rocked by. Otherwise it was eerily quiet.

Half an hour later, a man in a hooded cloak walked up the road towards the Monteagle house. Adam felt his chest tighten. His non-bandaged hand balled into a fist, his lengthening fingernails biting into his palms.

Even though he knew it was coming, he flinched when a sudden shaft of light coursed into the man's chest with an almost imperceptible hiss, the horses behind Adam reacting to the flash. With the night vision, the beam's brightness was strangely inverted and a deeper, darker green.

The man hurtled backwards and slammed into the ground. A bone-like crack rang out. A plume of smoke started to curl from his chest.

Adam saw the folded piece of paper flit from the man's grip as he went down. The Unraveller saw it too – another beam speared into the ground, right where the letter had come to rest, disintegrating it.

Both beams surged from a high place on Adam's side of the road, the top floor window of a house, no doubt. Where he stood, he couldn't see.

He inhaled deeply, heard the quiver in his own breath. He waited ten minutes. Then he quietly slipped out of the stable and slinked down an adjacent road. He veered off the road into a field which, judging by all the archery butts, was used for shooting practice. Eventually he came to the rear garden of the Monteagle house. He scaled a wall to get into the garden, which had an orchard, a fountain and some gilded benches, and circled round to the front.

He removed his spectacles and took the letter from his satchel. Swallowing hard, he knocked at the door. A servant in a simple green doublet, baggy brown breeches and a dirty white ruff answered the door, "Yes?"

Handing the letter to the servant, Adam said, "Put this in your master's hands – quickly."

The servant frowned and gave a reluctant nod, and Adam swept up the path to the road.

The Unraveller probably thought she'd be successful this time, having destroyed Adam's chronophone. It meant he could no longer receive instructions from Miss Morgan.

But of course, he still had his e-reader, which gave him access to a mountain of historical information. And he knew from his reading that Tom Digby's letter would be delivered by an anonymous stranger to the Lord Monteagle's home here in Hoxton on 26th October, when Monteagle was taking supper. The stranger the Unraveller had just killed. Pulling up an image of the letter, stored in the future in the National Archives, Adam had produced as close an imitation as possible and taken the stranger's place.

He still couldn't check with Miss Morgan that his intervention had successfully defeated the Gunpowder Plot, so he jumped forwards in time nine days. A man called Guy Fawkes had been arrested for trying to kill the king. *Yes.* The plan had worked.

All Adam could do now was hope that the Unraveller would give up. Assume that Million Eyes would always be a step ahead and go back to wherever, and whenever, she came from. Because Adam had no cards left to play. He'd done all he could to save Izzy and his baby.

Please be enough. Please be alive.

He'd find out soon, although not quite yet. There was one person he had left to save.

Jennifer.

On the night of the twentieth anniversary of the Gunpowder Plot, a stern-faced man with long brown hair, a slim moustache and a tuft of hair sitting below his lower lip, stood in a field with his wife, his friends and dozens of people he'd never met. He sipped a tankard of beer, watching a huge bonfire blaze and hiss and crackle and spew a mushroom cloud of smoke into the sky, the biting November air surrendering to its heat. Around him, men banged drums, blew trumpets and twanged lutes, and children danced with joy. This year, straw effigies of the pope and the devil were being tossed into the unrelenting flames. Anti-Catholic sentiment was high, what with the new King Charles having married one. The effigies were appropriate.

A man in a capotain hat, with a face full of pitted scars, came up to him and smiled. "Happy Gunpowder Treason Day," he said.

The stern-faced man forged a smile back. "And to you."

A couple of children threw their effigy of the pope on the bonfire, laughing and pointing as the flames devoured it. The stern-faced man wondered if their parents had explained the very real dangers of popery to them, or if they just saw it as a jolly old lark.

"A part of me is sorry it didn't succeed," said the pock-faced man.

The stern-faced man looked at him. "What didn't succeed?"

"The Gunpowder Treason."

Eyes wide, the stern-faced man fell silent.

"I know." The pock-faced man nodded towards the bonfire. "They'd throw me on there if they heard me." He leaned closer and a whiff of stale sweat and tobacco tickled up the stern-faced man's nose. "But between you and me, the clear-out might have done us all a favour."

The stern-faced man frowned. "What do you mean?"

"I've heard that a sickness festers at the heart of the government. That the king and the House of Lords are in league with a mysterious group who called themselves 'Million Eyes', and have been since the beginning of King James's reign." He straightened and looked at the fire, smirking, "My father always said those Scottish kings were a bad omen."

"How do you know all this?"

"I don't. It is just rumour. Rumour and gossip. But if I got elected to the House of Commons, I would make it my mission to find out what's going on and, if the rumours are true and the sickness real, cure it."

The stern-faced man's curiosity was piqued. "Why don't you then?"

"Don't what?"

"Seek election."

He laughed, the flickering glow of the fire making shadows dip in and out of the craters on his face. "Me? A life of politics? No, my friend. I am not clever enough. But you look like a clever man. Why don't you?"

The stern-faced man mused. Become a member of the Parliament? His father would've liked that. Even more if there was corruption to be uncovered and weeded out.

He watched the flames dance. A pope effigy's head fell off, disappearing into the blistering orange swirls, making all the children splinter with laughter.

"John Lilibourne," said the pock-faced man, offering his hand. "Pleased to meet you."

The stern-faced man shook his hand. "Oliver Cromwell. Pleased to meet you, too."

41

January 1st 1116

A snowstorm in the night had left behind an inch-thick coating on the old dirt road into Cawston, sparkling so brightly in the sunshine it stung Adam's eyes. Although his robe was keeping him acclimated and his anticipation about seeing Jennifer again was bringing on a sweat, his toes in his open sandals were turning into blue sticks of chalk. He trod rapidly to keep the blood circulating.

He came into a village of small, whitewashed wattle and daub huts with shuttered windows and thatched roofs, lining a broad, winding street. He was back in a time with no chimneys; these roofs just had holes spewing smoke. Each house had its own little farmyard for grazing livestock and growing crops, although there were few signs of life in them this morning. A couple of goats and pigs stood in yards where the owners had already cleared the snow. Since peasants and their animals shared the same living space, he figured the rest were probably indoors, keeping warm by the hearth.

What was a bustling modern town in the 21st century was a traditional feudal manor in the 12th. These first homes he'd come to were the ones where the villeins and free peasants lived. They paid rent – in goods and services and sometimes money – to the lord of the manor, Roger de Grayfort, 2nd Earl of Stonebury, who Jennifer had mentioned in her letters.

Adam could see several larger buildings beyond the

peasant huts, where the land sloped upwards. Beside a stream brawling down the hillside stood a wooden corn mill, its big wheel lost in a watery mist of its own raising. Clustered around a small village green was a church, a parsonage, and the only stone building here, Lord Grayfort's manor house, a two-storey building crowned with battlements, which towered above everything. The church was Cawston's original Anglo-Saxon tower-nave church, a modest wood structure, as most Saxon churches were. In 1132, the Normans would tear it down and replace it with a stone one, as they had already done in many places across England.

The village was certainly quiet, but Adam invited stares from a few people out and about. He took particular note of the burly man standing outside in his courtyard, wearing a black apron over a pale, sleeveless tunic and hammering away at an anvil. A brick furnace blazed behind him and Adam could feel the heat from it on his frostbitten cheeks.

The village blacksmith. Jennifer talked about the blacksmith in her letters. Was this the 'cockwomble' who beat his wife?

Adam walked towards him, sandals crunching over the snowy ground.

The man looked up when he heard Adam's footsteps, his bushy eyebrows beetling into a scowl. He had a nasty-looking scar across his right cheek.

"Excuse me, sir," said Adam. "Do you know where I can find" – he almost said her proper name, then remembered her nickname from the letters – "Jen the Maiden?"

Growling, "You mean Jen the slut."

Two thoughts flitted through Adam's mind. The first was – *Oh my God, she's really here.* The second – *Yep, you're the cockwomble.*

"Can you tell me where I can find her?"

"Only a fool would come looking for that dangerous wench. If it's ale you're after, you should go see Zelda."

A woman in a kirtle and apron, with a sheepskin cloak hanging off her shoulders, walked through an open door into the courtyard with a baby tightly wrapped in a shawl in her arms. "Oh Durwyn, stop being difficult. This man obviously wants Jen."

Adam remembered the name 'Durwyn'. Which probably made this woman 'Rexanne', Jen's friend.

The woman looked at Adam. "Please excuse my husband, sir." She pointed up the road with her free arm. "Carry on up the road till it splits. Follow it right to the bridge over the stream. Jen's house is just before the bridge."

Adam smiled. "Thank you, ma'am."

"She gave me this," said Durwyn as Adam started to walk off. Adam glanced back to see him pointing at the scar on his cheek. "Don't say you weren't warned."

Definitely sounds like Jennifer.

He walked up the road, sidestepping a man pulling a two-wheeled cart full of bread. Turning off right, he saw the bridge and the white cottage next to it, quite a bit larger than the others he'd seen.

A knot of trepidation balled in his gut. How would Jennifer react when she saw him? How would *he* react when he saw her? Had she changed? How much?

He walked up to the house, legs trembling slightly. The windows were shuttered and there was no smoke billowing through the roof. Maybe she wasn't in…

"Can I help you?"

Adam's heart skipped a beat. He turned.

A woman in a woollen cloak with a fur-trimmed hood was walking towards him. She lowered her hood.

Not Jennifer.

"I – er – I'm looking for Jen the Maiden," said Adam, his voice small, like someone had reached into his throat and cut the power.

"You're new here."

"Yes. My name is Adam."

The woman looked him up and down. "Are you a

monk? You look like a monk."

"Sort of."

The woman nodded. "Jen is at the manor house, taking ale to Lord Grayfort and tending to his wife. She's had a fever for several days. I'm certain she won't be long if you want to wait."

"Yes, thank you."

"I take it you need her to take a look at that hand?"

Adam looked down at his bandaged hand. It still ached, but the pain was easing. "Y-yes. If she could."

The woman smiled. "Of course. I'm Oshilda."

Oshilda – yes. Another name from Jennifer's letters. This was the mysterious traveller who came to the village, who Jennifer said she fancied.

Oshilda walked up to Jennifer's door and opened it.

"Do you live here as well?" Adam asked.

Oshilda stared at him, wide-eyed. "Live with Jen? Two maidens under the same roof? That would be a great way to raise some eyebrows, wouldn't it?"

He did wonder.

Oshilda shook her head, "No, I live a few houses down. I work here, when I'm not working Lord Grayfort's land. I collect supplies for Jen and help her with her animals. She pays me." She smiled. Jen was right – she *was* pretty. "We maidens need to stick together."

Oshilda welcomed Adam into the large main room of Jen's cottage and went to unshutter its windows. Daylight spilling in, Adam could see that a third of the room was taken up by chickens, pigs and a cow, huddled together behind a wooden fence; the rest was lined with tables, stools and a couple of benches, arranged around an unlit central hearth. If Jen was one of the village's alewives, that made sense – her house was basically a tavern. Medieval villages didn't have dedicated drinking establishments. Taverns were just the homes of those who brewed and sold beer, where the villagers would gather at the end of a work day.

From the looks of it, Jen's tavern doubled as a clinic. In

the corner of the room was a table loaded with dressings, tourniquets, medicine bottles, herb jars, a wash basin, bars of what looked like rudimentary soap, a roll of thread she may have been using to suture wounds, and various metal instruments, including a poker, spring scissors, tweezers and several knives.

He also noticed a dish of mouldy bread and citrus peel. It looked like Jennifer was making penicillin, centuries before anyone knew what bacteria was.

"Would you like some ale?" said Oshilda.

Adam inhaled, took in a mix of ale, animal dung and charred wood. "Yes, please."

As Oshilda grabbed a jug and walked over to one of several casks stacked against the wall, popped out the bung and let the dark liquid spill into the jug, Adam continued looking around. Unlike, he suspected, most of the houses here, Jen's had three rooms. Adam approached the doorway of the second, evidently a kitchen from the large stone stove, the table full of pots and utensils and bowls of fruit, and the bags of grain piled in the corner. The third room was just beyond, dark and windowless. What little light reached it marked out part of a low wooden bedstead and mattress.

Oshilda handed Adam his ale and he sat down at one of the tables while she went to light the hearth. Although she hadn't yet asked for payment, he took a few Anglo-Saxon pennies from his satchel and placed them on the table.

"So what's your story?" she asked, placing some touchwood on the hearth and striking flint against fire-steel to ignite it.

I'm a time traveller. So is Jen. I've come to take her home. "Just… just passing through."

He sipped his ale, then the unmistakable clip-clop of approaching horse hooves and the creak and rattle of a wagon made him freeze and hold the ale on his tongue.

"Ah, here she comes," said Oshilda, the hearth lit and starting to fill the house with warmth.

Adam swallowed his ale. He had his back to the door. He heard it open. Every muscle in his body went taut.

"Good morning, Jen," said Oshilda. "How is Lady Grayfort?"

"Doing better. Lord Grayfort was being more flirtatious than usual. He's clearly aching to bed her. Or bed someone. Who have we here?"

Adam could hardly believe it. That was her. Her voice. It hadn't changed. It was like he only heard it yesterday. His hands started to shake.

"A patient," said Oshilda. "Needs his hand looking at. His name is – sorry, remind me what your name was again?"

Finally he looked round and saw Jennifer's face. A deep warmth rippled up from his middle. Apart from wearing a dress, which she never wore, she didn't look that different. Older. Hair streaked with grey, dark semi-circles under her eyes, a couple of wrinkles here and there. His memory flashed back to a night out they had at the Agincourt, a rock club in Camberley, furnished with vodka slush puppies, dancing to Rage Against The Machine's *Killing in the Name*.

Jennifer's eyes flickered with emotion. She answered for him in a voice that was barely there, "Adam."

He smiled. He wanted to jump up and hug her. Dead, stunned silence hung between them.

Confused, Oshilda broke it. "Er – do you – do you two know each other?"

"We did," Adam said quietly. "A long time ago."

Jennifer gave a quiet snort. "Ago? That word's a bit complicated now."

"Yeah," Adam agreed.

Jennifer blinked and shook her head, as if she wasn't trusting her own eyes. "I... I can't believe it's actually you."

"Me neither."

Jennifer jerked her gaze to Oshilda. "Oshilda, please could you come back a bit later? I need some time to talk with Adam."

Oshilda hesitated, frowning softly, then said, "Yes. Yes, of course," and prepared to leave.

The moment they could no longer see Oshilda's shadow beneath the door, Jennifer and Adam threw themselves into each other's arms and hugged for several minutes. It was like neither of them wanted to let the other go. Finally pulling apart, tears streaming down both their faces, Jennifer murmured, "You dickhead. I haven't cried in yonks."

Adam laughed. "Sorry."

She poured herself some ale and they both sat down.

After downing several inches, she said, "I don't even know where to begin."

"Part of me didn't think I'd actually be able to find you."

"How *did* you find me?"

"Your letters."

"Shit. So that actually worked."

"Sort of. They weren't delivered like you wanted them to be, to your younger self, or to me. They were found several years after you disappeared by an archaeologist. She got in touch with me."

She inhaled. "Wow. Just – wow. But... how are you here? *Why* are you here? Did you come back especially for me? How did you even get the means to come back?"

"It's a long story."

"We've got about nine hundred years."

Adam smirked. An instant reluctance to admit what he'd been doing slowed the words from reaching his lips. He wasn't sure how she'd react.

He decided to just come out and say it. "Million Eyes sent me back."

Jennifer's eyes flared. "What?"

"Not to save you," he clarified. "They sent me back to stop this woman, the Unraveller, from messing up a bunch of historical events."

"So you're *helping* them?"

"Yes, but it's... it's complicated. The Unraveller

caused all of history to, well, unravel. The future was suddenly unrecognisable. Everything was gone. Including my girlfriend, Izzy, and our… our unborn baby." He saw a flash of Izzy and swallowed the lump of emotion in his throat.

Jennifer's expression softened. "Shit. That's awful. But also great. I mean, great that you're gonna be a dad! Fuck. Last time I saw you, you were banging that Rachel girl and trying to get into the pants of another one."

Adam remembered with a grin. "Hannah."

"Hannah! Yes. That's it. Did you succeed?"

"Nope. She thought I was too cheesy."

"You *are* too cheesy! I kept telling you to work on those chat-up lines."

"I know. Guess I needed my wing-woman."

Jennifer looked sad. "The last time I saw you was at the hospital, wasn't it."

Adam nodded. "I wish you'd let me help."

"Guess I was trying to protect everyone. Thought I could handle it on my own." She looked around her house. One of her chickens clucked. "What do you think? Handling it well, do you think?"

Adam laughed. "Actually, I think you're doing pretty fucking awesome." He shot a glance at the mouldy bread and citrus. "Is that penicillin you're trying to make over there?"

"A very unrefined version, yeah. Just trying to give these folks a chance, you know?" She took another gulp of beer. "Jesus, I have so many questions. Like why did Million Eyes choose *you* to go back to repair things?"

"I still don't know. But Dr Lester and I –"

"Dr Lester?"

"That's the archaeologist who found your letters. We started looking into Million Eyes, like you said to. We were able to hack into a classified drive and find tons of top-secret information about their operations. We found proof that they were behind the assassination of the Queen and the reorganisation of the country into a republic."

"Fuck – so they really did it? Ousted the monarchy?"

Adam nodded. He went on to explain how he was captured by Million Eyes immediately after and taken to headquarters, where he was briefed about the Unraveller and given a crash-course in time travel. Jennifer asked whether Adam had ever stopped to think that the Unraveller was doing the right thing. Adam told her what Miss Morgan had said about the Shapeless and the Last War.

"You can't trust that cunt," said Jennifer adamantly, clear disdain in her voice.

"But what if she's right?"

Jennifer shook her head. "I can't believe that everything Million Eyes have done has been for the greater good. And even if it was, can that really justify murdering people?"

"Well, I dunno. If we're talking about the extinction of the human race, can't it? You're a *Star Trek* fan – isn't it Spock who said the needs of the many outweigh the needs of the few? Isn't killing one person, innocent or not, better than letting millions die?"

Jennifer frowned and downed the rest of her ale. "I'm definitely not drunk enough for this debate." She got up and poured herself a fresh jug, and topped up Adam's.

"Whether Million Eyes are in the right or not," Adam continued, "I came back because of what the Unraveller did to the timeline. London was completely gone. There was nothing but empty land and tiny little farms all around the Looming Tower. And some super-fucked-up animals. Billions of lives had been erased or changed."

"I might've done the same thing, to be honest. I dunno." She sighed. "What a fucking mess. The problem is time travel itself, you know. It shouldn't exist. No way. It just fucks everything up."

"Unless it's what saves us all."

Jennifer looked unconvinced. She asked if Adam's interventions had worked, if he'd stopped the Unraveller and restored the future. He explained that he didn't know, that the Unraveller had destroyed his phone during their last encounter. His only way of finding out would be to go back to the future and see. He said that without his phone he wasn't going to be able to find the exact location of the Looming Tower – which he explained was protected from the changes by the Shield – so he was worried about going back and getting absorbed into the new timeline. Whatever that new timeline may be.

"I don't think that'll happen," said Jennifer. "I'm starting to think that once you've travelled in time, you're like *immune* to the changes, shall we say. It's like what that author said: if you go back in time, the act of time-travelling itself takes you outside the timestream, so you're removed from the effects of any changes to history."

"Yeah, you said about that, and him, in your letters. But do you know that for sure?"

"Well, no. Course not. But unless you're going to stay here and never go back, what else are you gonna do?"

"Good point." He stared down at his ale for a moment, then lifted his gaze to his friend. "So let's go."

Jennifer stood up. She fumbled with her hands as though trying to focus her thoughts, then went and stared out of one of the windows. "Come back to the future with you, you mean."

"What else would I mean?"

He saw her throat undulate as she swallowed. There was a battle being waged on her face. Why did she look so unsure?

"What is it?" he asked.

Sighing, Jennifer looked at him wistfully. "Adam, I'm – I'm…" She couldn't seem to say it.

"You're what?"

"Happy."

He frowned and looked around at the crude shack that she shared with her farm animals. "Happy? *Here?*"

"You've only been here, what, a few hours? I've been here fifteen years. I'd fully resigned myself to the fact

356

that I'd be here..." She hesitated and shrugged. "...Forever."

"What about your mum? Your sister?"

Jennifer blinked and a tear slipped down her cheek. "Part of me would do anything for a cuddle with Mum again. But I've built a life in this village. The people here – they're my family now. I couldn't just leave them. I... I wouldn't want to."

"What about that Durwyn guy? He calls you Jen the slut."

She laughed. "Yeah, I know. Alright. Apart from him."

"Did you give him that bloody great scar on his face?"

"Yup, guilty."

"Then I'd say these people need protecting – from you!"

"Oh that arsehole had it coming, trust me."

Adam arched his eyebrow. "Aren't you a doctor now? Mmm, what's that promise doctors make... oh, yes – *do no harm.*" He chuckled.

"He was the one doing harm, beating up poor Rexanne. It was a warning really. I placed the poker to his cheek and said that if he touched her again, I'd put it up his arse. He might hate me, but he hasn't raised a finger to her since."

Adam smiled. "You haven't changed."

"Same old Jen, hey?"

He nodded and was silent for a moment. Then he said glumly, "You're serious, aren't you."

She looked down at her hands, pensive. "Yeah. Yeah, I am. As hard as it is to believe, I like it here. Life's just so simple, you know? Compared to the future. The 21st century is so busy and fast and complicated! It's just not like that here."

Adam felt cold. This wasn't what he was expecting at all.

"And then there's Oshilda, who you met," Jennifer added. "Me and her – we're sort of an item now. Sure, we have to keep it on the downlow. But we're making it work. I wouldn't want to leave her." A smile flickered on her lips. "I love her."

Adam sighed and said pointedly, "You don't belong here, Jen."

"Maybe not. But this is where I want to be."

"But what if…" He hesitated, his stomach tightening. "What if something were to happen to you?"

Jennifer's eyes narrowed. "Do you know something?"

Adam shook his head. "I only know that you don't write any more letters. Only four were found. You've already written your last one. Well, unless you do write more and they end up lost somehow."

Jennifer nodded slowly, taking it in. "Okay. Well, who knows what's around the corner? Until all this time travel bollocks, no one did. And you know what, I think I'd rather it that way. I'm not running. Not anymore. Christ, I've done enough running for one life. And unless you can tell me that I'm going to get trampled by a horse or something tomorrow – in which case I'll happily avoid said horse – there's really no point. Why run from the future when you've no idea what it holds?"

Adam sighed heavily. "I'm not going to be able to persuade you, am I?"

Jennifer laughed. "You still know me well. Listen. Why don't you stay the night? Or even a couple of days? I can catch you up on all my medieval adventures, and you can tell me about Izzy. The future's not going anywhere, right?"

Adam downed the rest of his jug. He was anxious to get back to Izzy, but Jennifer was right. He stared out of the window at her yard, where only fringes of snow remained, twinkling in the sun.

"And I'd love for you to spend some time with Oshilda, too," Jennifer added.

He nodded. "I'll stay tonight." He looked at her, feeling a deep ache in his chest. He was going to miss her so much. "Then I can keep working on persuading you to come back with me."

Jennifer smiled. "Oh mate. You won't. But I wouldn't blame you for trying." She looked down. "Now, tell me. What the hell happened to your hand?"

If anyone was completely in their element in this village, it was the one who wasn't supposed to be. Jennifer eagerly introduced Adam to her animals (all of whom had names, even the ones she'd end up slaughtering) and gave him a guided tour of Cawston, complete with funny stories about the residents, such as the baker's wife being butted into the stream by her own goat, and the miller and the carpenter's daughter getting caught having sex in the fallow fields. He shared a meal with Jennifer and Oshilda and could see the palpable chemistry between them, and then they played a game of skittles, reminding the two friends of the many times Jennifer whooped Adam's arse at bowling. Jennifer even taught Adam how to brew ale.

That evening, Adam watched Jennifer serve her product to the villagers and wondered if he'd ever seen her this happy. As nuts as it was, maybe she did belong here. Maybe 12th-century Cawston was exactly where she was meant to be.

The next day, the best friends said a tearful goodbye. Adam hadn't been expecting to say it, but at least he got to, this time. He left the village and made his way to a remote spot in the New Forest to return to the future.

Over the next few years, Jennifer's relationship with Oshilda continued to grow and deepen and, in time, Jennifer was able to use her earnings to buy Oshilda's freedom from Lord Grayfort just like she had her own. They could leave the village together now, and go anywhere. But they were happy where they were, so they stayed.

The five-year mark came but Jennifer had already decided that she wasn't going to write any more letters.

There was no point. The ones she had written were the ones that would lead Adam back to her for a reunion she would treasure forever. If she were to write any more, she might change the course of Adam's journey. And, by extension, her own. She didn't want that. She'd spent much of her youth and her twenties feeling like the pieces of her life never properly fitted. Now the jigsaw of her life was complete.

Another eight years after that, when Jennifer was fifty-three, she started to get headaches and feel tired often. Still the village physician and alewife, she found taking her regular deliveries to the manor house a struggle. Knowing something was wrong, she tried a number of her own remedies. A few of them eased the headaches, for a time.

One warm spring evening, Jennifer's headache returned after several days' relief. She kicked out her patrons early, got drunk with Oshilda and taught her the lyrics to The Killers' *Mr Brightside,* and they sang and danced and laughed together into the small hours.

That night, Jennifer dreamed of her mother for the first time in years. They were at Whipsnade Zoo, watching the sea lions and slurping strawberry splits, and her mum was saying how proud she was of her little girl.

By the morning, Jennifer had slipped away, peacefully, with a smile on her lips and the love of her life in her arms.

42

April 28th 2027

Adam held his breath and clenched everything as he put his hand over the vein scanner on the door of his and Izzy's apartment. The fact that the building was still here had given him hope that the timeline was restored and everything was back to normal. But was it? Even though the apartment was still here, was it still *his?*

The light went green. Adam's body instantly loosened and he threw his head back in a sigh of relief. Turning the handle, he stepped inside.

"Izzy? Izzy, are you home?"

Please be home.

Please exist.

"Adam?"

Izzy came into the hallway and Adam's legs almost collapsed beneath him. Her long auburn hair shining bronze in the lamplight, she stood barefoot in her trackies, no makeup, looking more gorgeous than ever. Overcome with emotion, he ran at her, pulling her into his arms and sobbing on her shoulder.

"Jesus, Adam, what is it?" said Izzy. "What's happened? You've had me worried sick, I haven't been able to reach you for hours."

Hours. Try six months. Try two thousand years.

He looked her in the face, framing her jaw in his non-bandaged hand. "I love you. I love you so much."

Izzy's eyes darted from side to side. "I love you too.

But seriously – what the hell's going – ?"

He cut her off, kissing her hard on the mouth as tears streamed down his face. Then he slid down her body and kissed her stomach through her top. "Is our baby okay?"

"Yes, Adam, he's fine. Course he's fine!" She grabbed both his arms and lifted him to face her, shaking her head with confusion as she looked him up and down. "Where have you been? And why on earth are you dressed like a monk?" Her gaze shifted to his bandaged hand and her eyes flared with worry. "You're hurt!"

Adam wiped his eyes. "It's fine. I'm okay."

Izzy frowned. "You need to start explaining, Adam. Quickly."

After arriving back in the present, hoping to God it was the present he knew, Adam had wandered back into Cawston, now a dense and busy sprawl of concrete, brick and steel. His wallet and phone still at headquarters, but remembering all the numbers on his debit card, he'd purchased a train ticket to Ealing and spent the entire journey rehearsing what he was going to say to Izzy when he got home.

He'd already decided that, whether she believed him or not, he was going to tell her everything. Nearly everything anyway. He obviously couldn't tell her about Rhienne. Izzy had been cheated on before. She would leave him if she knew, no doubt in my mind.

But he couldn't tell her everything now. There was no time.

"We have to leave," he said.

"What?"

"Million Eyes will be coming after me."

"Adam – what the fuck have you done?"

He knew that even though he'd completed his task and stopped the Unraveller, Million Eyes weren't just going to let him go, not with everything he knew. He and Izzy would have to go into hiding. Maybe even leave the country.

"They made me do something for them," he said. "But

they were never going to let me go once it was done. We need to pack a bag and go. Where are our passports?"

Izzy's eyes widened. "Our passports? Christ, Adam. We're not leaving the country!"

"We might have to."

Adam went into the bedroom and wheeled a suitcase out of their wardrobe. He opened it on their bed and started pulling clothes off hangers and slinging them inside.

"Adam, I can't just up sticks and go," said Izzy. "I have a job. A life."

"If Million Eyes are coming after me, it means they're coming after you too."

"Look. Can we just sit down and talk about this? I'll make us some tea. Yeah?"

Adam swallowed. She wasn't listening. "Izzy, you don't underst –"

The sound of Izzy's phone ringing from the living room stopped his sentence short.

She turned out of the bedroom. "That'll be Mum. She said she'd be ringing me tonight."

Adam called after her, "Don't tell her anything!"

He heard her answer, "Hello?" in a manner suggesting that the caller wasn't someone she knew.

He stopped, listened. There was a silence. Then Izzy said, "Who's calling?" A further silence, then, "How did you get this number?"

Adam started out of the bedroom just as Izzy came back in. She had the phone to her ear and was shaking her head, face contorted in confusion. A moment later, she lowered the phone, pressed the mute button and held the phone out to Adam. "It's for you. Some woman. Wouldn't say her name. Why would she be calling *me?*"

Adam felt a surge of dread. It didn't take a genius to work out who it was.

He unmuted the call and lifted Izzy's phone to his ear. "Hello?"

"Mr Bryant, hello," said the voice he'd hoped never to

hear again. "It's Miss Morgan here." Her tone was unnervingly chipper.

"Hi," he said tentatively.

"We haven't been able to get you on your chronophone."

The knot in his stomach tightened. "The Unraveller destroyed it." He looked at Izzy, her bewildered scowl deepening.

"Ah. I see," said Miss Morgan. "Well done for making your way without it." She sounded like a teacher praising a child for giving in good homework.

"Is everything... back to normal?" Adam asked. "It certainly seems like it is."

He heard the click of a lighter. "It is, yes. Congratulations. You have successfully restored the timeline."

"And the Unraveller?"

"She appears to have stopped her attacks. For now." He heard her puff on a cigarette. "You were instructed to come back to headquarters as soon as you returned to the future, you know." Now she sounded like a teacher admonishing a child.

"I know." His hands started trembling. "I'm... sorry. I'll come in now. I just – I just needed to pop home." He swallowed hard and immediately regretted the lie. This woman wasn't dumb – she'd see through it.

"Totally understandable, Adam," she said. "I'm glad you're there. With Izzy."

Okay. That didn't sound anything like Miss Morgan. And that was the first time she'd called him 'Adam'.

He glossed over it. "So this is over, right? I'm done? You don't need me anymore?"

"Yes, Adam. You're done. And no, we don't need you anymore."

"So you won't come after me?"

"No. We won't need to."

He shuddered. "Pardon?"

A wave of dizziness hit him, followed by a painful

tightness in his chest, like a slab of concrete had just been dropped on it.

"I want to say thank you for all your efforts." Miss Morgan's voice instantly sounded far away. "And I genuinely am sorry it has to be this way."

Adam swallowed but the swallow smacked into something. It was like a tennis ball was suddenly lodged in his oesophagus. A spike of panic coursing through him, he coughed, flicking a dot of spit onto the laminate.

"What are you... what are you talking about?" His words became laboured, his hand shooting up to his throat, white-hot blood rushing to his face.

Izzy lunged forwards when she saw his hand go up. "Adam, what it is? What's wrong?" Her voice, too, was muted, like it had to travel through a triple-glazed window before reaching him.

They've done something. Oh my God – they've done something.

"What have... have you... done to me..." His words collapsed into a fit of coughing. He could feel his airways narrowing. Each time he tried to gulp a lungful of air, the gulp was a sip, the lungful a wisp. Something was crushing his chest.

He barely heard Miss Morgan's frostbitten reply, "It'll be over soon. Goodbye, Adam," before the line went dead.

He dropped the phone, deaf to the clunk, both of his hands at his neck, as if clawing at the skin could somehow drag open his airways. He felt like his lungs were being scalded with hot oil, that all of his insides were being burned from the inside out.

"Adam!" Izzy's screams were getting through – just.

"Call 999..." He jammed the words through a rapidly narrowing throat.

Breathe. Need to breathe.

His legs gave way and the room rushed past him in a soft, dark blur. Looking up he saw Izzy crouching over him with her phone to her ear. He couldn't hear her anymore, but her mouth was moving.

Then the wisps of air still struggling through to his lungs stopped dead. Adam went to inhale but his throat had been hermetically sealed. Nothing could get in or out. His lungs had completely shut down.

And then it was as if his entire body had been instantly unplugged from the panic and pain and terror surging through it. A peaceful numbness swept through him. He couldn't breathe, but he didn't need to.

An image of his mum flitted before his eyes. A memory of her shoving him into a freezing cold paddling pool when he was six, his dad almost falling off his chair laughing.

Izzy was mouthing, "Adam! Adam! Adam!" He just stared at her, smiling. Her face and hair were shining gold and all around her were glowing white pinpricks of light. Like diamonds. Like stars.

It was so beautiful. As was she.

Miss Morgan lowered her phone from her ear and stared out of the window at the thick, dark curve of the River Thames through a now-restored London, yellow lights of buildings and boats and pink streaks of sunset billowing on its surface in a dance of colour. She sighed.

A glimmer of movement made her eyes refocus on the window and its reflection of Dr Neether, who stepped up behind her. Dr Neether's warped face in the glass was like looking in one of those funhouse mirrors.

"Miss Morgan," she said in her characteristic growl, "are you alright?"

Miss Morgan contemplated the Unraveller's next move. The oraculum had no more intel to offer, but there was no way the Unraveller was just going to quit. Not with everything she knew. Miss Morgan would have to find her.

"Adam had to die, you know," said Dr Neether. "It was his destiny."

Oh, Miss Morgan didn't give a fuck about that. Adam's death hardly mattered in the grand scheme. But Dr Neether couldn't know what was *really* bothering her. No one could. The truth would go with her to her grave. It had to, for Million Eyes' sake. And for hers.

"I know," Miss Morgan whispered.

Dr Neether inhaled, her breath ragged and crackly, like she had this permanent clump of phlegm in her throat. "And now we have someone else's destiny to arrange."

Miss Morgan turned and faced her, nodding in agreement. "Shall we?"

43

April 28th 2027

"Giddy up! Giddy up, Daddy! Yee ha!"

Lester watched Brody on all fours crawling around the living room with Georgia mounted on a bright pink, padded saddle on his back, clad in her cowgirl gear and waving a toy revolver. She beamed like a flower drinking in the sun. She looked so happy.

"Mummy, look! I'm the sheriff!"

Lester grinned. "Those bandits better run. Sheriff Lester's in town!"

"Neeeeeigh!" Brody wailed, stopping next to the sofa.

"Oh no," cried Lester. "Sheriff, I think your horse is about to rear up again. Naughty horse!"

Georgia laughed, "No, Daddy, no!"

Brody let out another enormous "Neeeeeeigh!" and lifted straight up, flinging a squealing Georgia into the softness of the sofa cushions. Breathless, Brody got to his feet, smiling warmly at his wife.

Suddenly, Georgia's screams and laughs stopped. Half-buried in cushions, her head and shoulders were hidden. Her little legs, in calf-high brown cowgirl boots with plastic gold spurs, went limp.

"Georgia?"

Brody turned towards their daughter. Lester stood up from her chair and walked over to the sofa.

"Georgia? Honey?"

Lester looked down, cupping her hands over her mouth.

Purple, black and green blotches rippled over Georgia's skin and horrific lesions ravaged her face, neck, arms and legs. Georgia gaped at the ceiling, eyes and mouth stuck open in a dead stare.

Brody, do something.

Get help.

Brody – get help!

"Brody, we need to –"

She faced her husband. Thin red worms of blood crawled down both sides of his neck. A steady drip-drip-drip from the back of his head was forming a neat round puddle on the laminate behind his feet.

And yet he looked at her like nothing was wrong, shrugging, "What?"

"Turn around…" she whispered.

He seemed confused, but turned anyway.

Lester shrank back, hands clapped against the sides of her head.

The back of Brody's skull was caved in. The deep hole burrowed halfway into his head, a mess of blood and brain and shattered bone.

Brody turned back around. "What? What is it?"

"Your head…"

Brody jammed his fingers into the wound and stared at the blood, flesh and brain matter that came off on the tips. "Oh, right. Yeah."

Lester stepped forwards, reaching for him. "We need to get you to a…" She swallowed her words. Both of her hands were red and shiny with still-wet blood, pouring in thin streams through the gaps in her fingers.

She looked at Brody, who stared back blankly. Then his mouth stretched into a grin, his lips parted and his whole body shivered with laughter.

Lester screamed and bolted upright, heart racing, cold sweat pouring off her face and down her sides, soaking into her jumper.

What? Wh – where…

She was sitting up on a hard floor, trembling all over

and swamped in darkness. It wasn't her lounge and it wasn't the middle of the day. She glanced down at her hands. A moonlit sky and some nearby streetlights did little to thin the darkness, so all she could make out was that she still had hands. Rubbing them together, she felt their dryness. No blood. Not wet blood anyway. She inhaled sharply several times. The fast throbbing of her body shredded every breath.

Calm down, Sam. Calm.

Cold tears blurred her vision and escaped down her cheeks and into the corners of her mouth. She tasted vinegar. She dried her eyes and face with her palms and sniffed.

She must've drifted off again. *I remember now.* She was still in the abandoned office block in Croydon, locked in a small, empty room on the second floor that used to be someone's office, or may have been a storage room. There was a door she'd tried several times, but the lock remained defiant and she wondered if it had been reinforced on the other side.

The almost-full moon and a sprinkling of stars shone through the half-boarded-up window. The fact that it was night meant she'd been here for at least six hours, although it could've been longer. No way to tell. She'd fallen asleep several times, who knew for how long, and her watch and handbag, which had both her phones in, had been taken.

All the carpet tiles in the room had been ripped up and Lester felt the cold concrete beneath her trousers. Now that it was dark, she couldn't see all the rubbish and discarded stationery that littered the floor, or the holes in the walls and ceiling.

"Mummy, when are they going to let us out of here?"

Lester lifted up her gaze. Georgia was there, somewhere, fully immersed in the darkness.

"Soon, baby," Lester replied.

"Were you just dreaming about me again?"

Lester nodded. "I was."

"Was it a nice dream?"

It was the worst yet. "Yes, darling. It was a nice dream."

"Then why did you scream?"

The door clunked, rattled and scraped open and Lester was dazzled by a powerful LED lantern that illuminated the entire room like it was day again. Someone stepped inside and stooped to place the lantern on the floor. Adjusting, Lester's eyes travelled up from stiletto-clad feet to firm legs packed tightly into a pine green pencil skirt, to a matching jacket over a white blouse, to a face with bronze lips, framed by long, ebony-black hair fanning over padded shoulders.

You.

Her visitor was Erica Morgan, CEO of Million Eyes, who Lester had previously only seen in pictures and on TV. Following her into the room was a shorter, grey-haired old woman Lester had never seen before, wearing a white doctor's coat and pushing an instrument trolley. And standing in the doorway was a burly-looking man in some kind of security uniform, who'd clearly been guarding the door.

Lester's stomach did a free fall. Laid out on the trolley were several surgical instruments. And... a handbag. A blue-grey, leather, crossbody handbag with two compartments and a concealed magnetic fastening. It looked like a Ted Baker. It looked like *hers*.

Miss Morgan's lips stretched into a hollow smile. "Hello, Dr Lester. I'm Miss Morgan. This is Dr Ruben."

Lester got to her feet, her legs stiff and weak. "Why am I here? Where's Adam?"

Miss Morgan compressed her lips in feigned sympathy. "I'm afraid Adam's dead."

Lester's heart sank into her shoes. *No.* Was she lying? Was Adam really dead?

"Did you kill him?"

The tall woman nodded. She looked mournful – Lester didn't buy it.

"Why?"

"We had to."

"That's not an answer."

"This isn't about Adam. This is about you."

Lester shivered. "You mean you've come to kill me next."

Miss Morgan shook her head. "No. I've come to send you on your way." She looked at Dr Ruben, who passed her the Ted Baker handbag. Miss Morgan walked up to Lester and handed it to her. It *was* hers.

Lester frowned as she took it. "Send me where?"

"Not... *where*."

Miss Morgan looked at the security guard in the doorway and nodded. He started towards Lester.

"Wait – what are you doing?"

None of them said anything. The man grabbed both of her arms, roughly, pinning them behind her back.

"Don't hurt my mummy!" cried Georgia. Lester could see her now. She was standing by the opposite wall with her arms at her sides and her little fists clenched in anger. Her beautiful hair cascaded over her shoulders like polished molten copper.

"It's okay, Georgia," said Lester. "Mummy's okay."

Dr Ruben stepped forwards with a syringe containing a clear liquid. Smiling, she placed one hand on the back of Lester's head. "Don't worry, dear. You'll just feel a tiny scratch." Her voice was warm and grandmotherly, which was incongruous given that they were assaulting her.

Lester felt a sting at the back of her neck. Dr Ruben stepped away and returned the now-empty syringe to the instrument trolley. Whatever that clear liquid was, it was now swimming through Lester's veins.

The guard kept a hold of Lester's arms. There was no point trying to squirm free. They had her.

"What was that?" Lester asked.

"It contained a microscopic device called a chronode," said Miss Morgan. "It allows our travellers to 'time-read' and get to the places, or rather *times*, they need to be.

Although the particular chronode we've just injected you with is slightly different. It's pre-programmed to take you to a specific point in time without you having to do anything."

"You're – you're sending me through time?"

"Yes. Specifically, *back*. To Tuesday 2nd November 2021."

Lester's blood ran cold. She felt it drain from her face.

"Do you remember that day, Dr Lester? I do. It was a fresh autumn day. Rain didn't know whether it was coming or going. I was at my house in Upminster, looking after my dog. And what is it you were doing?"

She knew. Lester could tell by her face. She knew. But why would she do that to her?

"Why then? Why at all?"

"Destiny, Dr Lester." Miss Morgan looked at Dr Ruben, who stepped forwards with her hand out. In her palm was a little red pill that looked exactly like the ones recovered from the dig at Tower Hamlets.

"Swallow this, please, dear," said Dr Ruben.

Lester shook her head. "No. I won't. You can't! Please don't do this. I have a family!"

Miss Morgan made that disingenuous face again. "Oh, Dr Lester. No. You don't."

"What?"

"Your daughter's dead. And earlier today, you killed your husband."

"Mummy, what's she saying?" cried Georgia. "What does she mean we're dead?"

Lester shook her head, which felt like a balloon about to burst. *Lies. Lies lies lies.*

"Your life is over, Dr Lester," said Miss Morgan coldly. "It's time for you to start a new one."

Instinct kicking in, Lester struggled, but the guard's arms were thick and hard like steel chains.

Miss Morgan lunged, placed one hand on top of Lester's head, one hand on her jaw, and tipped it back, squeezing her jaw and yanking her mouth open.

No escape.

Dr Ruben pinched Lester's nose in white-gloved fingers and, with her other hand, placed the red pill at the back of her tongue. Miss Morgan forced Lester's mouth closed while Dr Ruben held her nose, and Lester felt the pill tickle down her throat.

Miss Morgan, Dr Ruben and the guard immediately released her and stepped back.

A dizzy wave of fear, guilt and dread coursed through her. "Wh-what's... what's happening..." A strident hum blasted her in both ears, made her double over. Straightening, she met an extraordinary and chaotic scene – her three attackers were gone, the room now heaving with people and furniture that weren't there before, blurred together in a dim, frenzied haze.

"Mummy, I'm scared."

Lester lowered her gaze to her daughter, who was solid, clear and alive, her little green eyes welling up. Lester opened her arms and Georgia sprang into them, nuzzling into her waist.

Then there was nothing but white.

44

November 2nd 2021

Lester carried Georgia out of the abandoned office block to look for her car, but it wasn't parked where she'd left it. Neither of her phones seemed to be working and she still didn't have her watch, so she had no idea what time it was. However, judging by the quietness of the roads, the dew on parked cars and wheelie bins and the milky blue of the sky, it was morning. Georgia commented that she felt dizzy, which Lester echoed. She could murder a cup of tea, too.

Realising they would have to get the train home, Lester and Georgia headed for East Croydon station. A few minutes from the station, Georgia said she felt funny. Lester looked at her face and her heart sank. She had purple, black and green blotches and lesions all over her face and her neck.

Lester made a dash for the nearest taxi. The train wouldn't get them to the hospital in time.

The car had a driver, which was unusual. Most taxis were driverless these days. "Gravesham Community Hospital, please." She climbed in the back with Georgia.

"What is it, Mummy?" said Georgia. "What's wrong?"

"I'm taking you to see Dr Taylor. She'll know what to do."

"Okay, Mummy." The lesions on her face looked sore, but she didn't seem to be in any pain.

An hour later, they arrived at the hospital. Georgia's

condition seemed stable and she'd been jibber-jabbering the entire journey. Lester was sure that Dr Taylor would be able to help. She'd always been so kind and warm, ever since Georgia was tiny. Georgia loved her. She particularly loved that Dr Taylor would stick a temporary *Ninja Turtles* tattoo on Georgia's arm every time she went for a check-up.

Lester tried to pay the driver with her card, but it wasn't working. *Why?* Rifling through her purse she found a wodge of cash she didn't remember putting in there. More than enough to pay.

They got out in the hospital drop-off and Lester held Georgia's hand as they strode towards the building.

Lester stopped cold when the entrance doors slid open and a man and a woman walked out, the woman holding a baby that looked about one.

The woman was... her.

The blood in Lester's veins froze. Her lungs emptied of air but her body wouldn't let any more in.

The woman had her face, her hair, her clothes, her husband. The man walking next to her – Brody.

And her daughter. The baby in her arms.

Georgia.

Other Lester and Brody were despondent and staring into space through red, wet and hollowed eyes. It was the reason they didn't see Lester's double standing across from them in the drop-off, ten metres away. Their minds were somewhere else.

And Lester knew where. Because she remembered. It was like she'd been dreaming; now someone had shaken her awake.

This was the day a rot began eating away at her family and her life. The day Georgia was diagnosed with necrocythemia. This was five and a half years ago. The woman and the man in front of her were her and Brody's younger selves, right after their appointment with Dr Taylor. The appointment where they'd learned that their beautiful baby daughter's future had been erased. A few weeks from now, Georgia's lungs would collapse and she'd require an emergency transplant, and a few weeks after that, her kidneys would pack up. Lester, Brody and Georgia's lives would become a harrowing routine of transfusion, organ failure, transplant, transfusion, organ failure, transplant. A routine that would last until... *oh God.*

Her frozen blood melted, rushing to her head. It was as though a wire in her brain had snapped, wrenching her to her senses. She looked down at the hand that had been holding Georgia's. There was nothing in it but air.

Because she wasn't real. This whole time, she wasn't real. Lester knew that now.

Miss Morgan had sent her back in time to relive all this. To watch her daughter suffer and die – *again.* Time travel could be used to change things, but no one could change this. Miss Morgan must've known it. The woman was pointing and laughing at Lester's helplessness.

Warm, salty tears leaked into the corners of her mouth as she watched her husband and younger self walk silently down the road to their car, lower Georgia, obliviously burbling to her teddy, into the back, and drive away.

She stood in the middle of the drop-off, numb. Her breath grew shallow. A squall of rain pelted her face. She didn't feel it.

Then, listless and running on autopilot, she was walking. Walking into town. Walking into Macey's Rent-A-Car and hiring a car for the day using the abundance of cash in her purse. Driving out of Gravesend.

To Upminster. Where Miss Morgan said she was. Stupidly.

The weather was schizophrenic. One minute it was dark and rainy, people scurrying past on slippery pavements with hoods and umbrellas raised and chins buried into collars. The next they were unzipping their coats and unfurling their scarves as yellow rays shimmered on wet tarmac and flushed the trees fluorescent. Lester kept searching for a rainbow. Georgia loved rainbows.

Lester knew where the house was. She'd seen it online. It was the one Miss Morgan lived in when she wasn't at her swanky apartment in Central London. It had a gym, sauna, hot tub, wine cellar, pool with a swim-up bar, and was bedecked with marble and smoked wood and ostentatious crystal chandeliers, like something out of Beverly Hills. Even that wasn't enough. No, no. She had to have a mansion in New York City and a whole estate of buildings up in Scotland, too.

Lester parked a couple of hundred yards from the extravagantly large house in the elite neighbourhood and waited.

After an hour, maybe more, the front door opened and Miss Morgan emerged with a black and brown German Shepherd on a lead. They walked up the starlight quartz driveway by the landscaped front garden, towards a black iron gate that opened automatically as they got near to it. Clouds rolled fast like clumps of dirty wool overhead, the brightness of the road dipping every few seconds.

Lester pressed the ignition button. The engine gave a gentle cough and began to whir. As Miss Morgan and her dog started up the road, Lester pulled the gearstick into 'drive' and gripped the wheel.

Miss Morgan got to a zebra crossing, looked both ways and entered the crossing.

Lester slammed her foot on the throttle and flew up the road like a flame over kerosene.

Miss Morgan was in the middle of the zebra stripes, the dog about two metres in front of her, and didn't see Lester coming.

But someone else did.

A split-second before impact, a man lurched into the road, arms out, and shoved Miss Morgan from behind.

Thwhack.

The man plunged onto Lester's windscreen, a huge crack spidering through the glass. With a succession of loud clunks, he tumbled over the roof.

Lester looked back. The man was sprawled in the road, limbs twisted in unnatural directions. Miss Morgan was on her hands and knees near the kerb and the German Shepherd was bolting up the pavement, misty wet spray clinging to its ankles, lead whipping behind it.

Lester would have to go back and try again.

She turned and faced the road ahead. Just in time to glimpse the enormous brick wall rushing towards her face.

Dr Samantha Lester. The identity of Miss Morgan's would-be killer, revealed by a police scan at the scene of the crash. Not someone Miss Morgan knew or had heard of.

But then her assistant at headquarters phoned with a shocking development. At that very moment, while Dr Lester lay broken and bleeding on a stretcher, about to be rushed to hospital, there was another, identical Samantha Lester sitting in her office at the London Institute of Palaeontology and Archaeology.

Two of them?

This alarming turn of events could not be left in the usual hands. Miss Morgan had Lester conveyed to the Million Eyes-owned Providence Hospital in Kingston upon Thames, and had her people inside the police take charge of the investigation into the attempt on her life, and the murder of the man who'd saved it.

Scans at the hospital confirmed that Lester the homicidal maniac driver was, no surprises, a time traveller. That meant the other one, at LIPA, was her younger self.

Future Lester had a few possessions with her in a handbag. When Miss Morgan examined them, she saw something she recognised.

It was Million Eyes who had sent Dr Lester back in time. But why?

She began looking into Present Day Lester for clues as to why Future Lester had tried to kill her. She learned that her daughter, Georgia, had just been diagnosed with necrocythemia, a particularly nasty condition that killed most people who had it within a few years. But she couldn't find any connection between Lester and Million Eyes – yet.

As soon as Miss Morgan heard that Dr Lester had awoken from her coma, she made her way to Providence Hospital. It was time to have a talk with the woman who wanted her dead.

"Good evening, Dr Lester."

Lester had been drifting in and out of sleep for hours. She had no concept of how long she'd been here or what day it was, whether she was still in the past, or whether it had all been a painful dream. It looked like she was about to find out.

She opened the only eye that seemed to work, the other still buried under a hunk of tightly wound bandages. Blinking away a white, water-logged blur, her eye followed the familiar voice to the chair at the side of the bed, finding a face that made her insides sputter with rage. Rage and hate. If she wasn't hooked up to a dozen monitors and drip bags, her limbs trapped in heavy casts, she might've leapt off the bed and smashed that face into the wall.

"Have the doctors told you where you are?" said Miss Morgan.

Lester took in a deep, ragged breath, her chest feeling like it had been trampled. She had to push her reply up her throat, the words coming out a strained rasp through barely parted lips, "They... they haven't told me... anything."

Miss Morgan nodded, thin hands with purple-painted

fingernails clasped together over a stockinged knee, crossed over the other. "You're in Providence Hospital in Kingston, a private hospital owned by Million Eyes. I thought it best for keeping this matter contained, and keeping you out of the press."

"What do you want?"

Miss Morgan snorted. "A little gratitude wouldn't go amiss. The physicians here have saved your life. If I'd left you at the mercy of the NHS, you'd be dead right now."

What? That didn't make sense. Lester had tried to kill her. "Why would you... why would you save me?"

Miss Morgan leaned closer to the bed. "Because I know you're a time traveller. And I believe you are here for a reason."

Lester tried to muster a look of hate with one available eye and what felt like half a mouth. "I'm here because... because *you* sent me here."

"Do you know why?"

"'Destiny, Dr Lester'. That's all you said. Before you..." Lester's voice weakened as tears rolled down her cheek, pooling in her right ear. "... Before you sent me to watch her suffer all over again."

"You mean Georgia?"

"Yes!" She attempted to shout the word, but it came out a guttural, phlegm-soaked whisper, several beads of spit arcing onto the bed and the floor. Her whole body twinged with pain, anger and loss.

Miss Morgan sighed thoughtfully. "I've been looking into you. I know about Georgia's diagnosis. I'm sorry."

No you're not. "You sent me back to watch her die. Again."

Miss Morgan shook her head. "I wouldn't do that. Not without cause."

"Cause?"

Miss Morgan started questioning Lester on dates – when she'd come from and when she'd arrived – and the events leading up to her trip through time. Given that she was fully at her mercy, Lester had no choice but to answer. She told her that she arrived just a few hours before she tried to kill her, on 2nd November 2021, and that Miss Morgan's future self had sent her back from 28th April 2027, five years and six months into the past. And she told her about Adam, about them investigating Million Eyes, finding out about the Jesus scrolls, hacking into the X9 Server and reading all about Operation Roundhead before Million Eyes apprehended them.

Miss Morgan stooped to fetch something from her handbag, pulled out a small, square slab of what looked like thick, blue-tinted glass. "Did my future self tell you anything about this?"

Lester blinked several times and shook her head, stiffly. "I don't know what that is."

"We found it in your handbag, in the car you hired to kill me."

If it was in her handbag, Lester hadn't seen it. Had Future Miss Morgan slipped it in there before sending her back?

"I didn't put it there."

"Which means my future self did." She threaded the object through her fingers. "It's called an oraculum. It's a timed data vault, programmed to activate at a particular date and time and containing instructions for dealing with a future event. It is dormant and inert until that time and its information cannot be accessed or extracted by anyone – even us. The fact that my future self gave this to you means there is something very important that you and I will need to do together."

"Together?" Lester coughed, a stab of pain shooting through her. "You're insane. I tried to kill you."

Miss Morgan nodded. "Yes. You did. And we clearly have a lot of work to do to make this relationship work."

"Relationship?"

"You're going to come and work for me."

Lester tried to laugh but it came out a strangled titter. "Never."

Miss Morgan sat back in her chair. "Let me tell you the story of how Million Eyes came to be. Because it really isn't what you think."

Lester listened to an utterly bonkers tale about Jesus travelling back in time to 1st-century Israel from a war-torn 23rd century, when Earth had been invaded by an alien race called the Shapeless and humanity faced extinction. Miss Morgan revealed the nature of the Jesus scrolls – apparently they were his writings about this 'Last War', which Lester remembered seeing a mention of when she and Adam hacked into the X9 Server. Miss Morgan said the scrolls would lead to the founding of Million Eyes almost ten centuries later, and said that Million Eyes was, to this day, carrying on Jesus's work.

Miss Morgan was right about one thing. It wasn't what Lester was expecting at all. An alien invasion? Jesus Christ: Time Traveller? No. Not even close. She didn't know what to think anymore.

"Ever since Million Eyes' inception," said Miss Morgan, "we have been striving for positive change and progress that will make humanity more prepared and better equipped for when the Shapeless come. That's why we sought positions in Parliament. In the 17th century our leaders decided we needed to work our way into the government of this country in order to really drive change. And it worked. The rate of change accelerated. The Scientific Revolution. The Enlightenment. The Industrial Revolution. The Space Programme. Synthetic Biology. All of this might not have happened were it not for us. We have been working to strengthen the world's defences and to give humanity options when the invasion happens."

There was a faint smile on Miss Morgan's lips as she spoke. It was pride. Pride in everything Million Eyes had achieved. *But at what cost did those achievements come?*

"Time travel, though. That was the game changer. We knew time travel was the thing that could truly make a difference. The ability to control time is the ability to change destiny."

A question crept into Lester's head, one she'd wanted answering ever since the discovery of the red pills at Tower Hamlets, pills she was never able to analyse thanks to Million Eyes seizing control of the project. "The red pills. What are they? How do they work?"

"We call them chronozine, because they're infused with chronotons."

Scientific curiosity stirred in Lester like sediment in a pond. Chronotons were hypothetical particles capable of generating chronotonic energy, which existed outside the space-time continuum and could, if stabilised, be used to control movements in time. But most physicists believed them an impossibility. So did Lester.

"You... you created chronotons?" Lester croaked.

"No. We didn't create them. We found them."

"*Found* them?" A hacking cough made Lester's shoulders shake painfully. "Found them where?"

"The Bermuda Triangle."

Oh, this was ludicrous. Did she really expect her to believe all this? She snorted with disbelief, tilting her gaze to the ceiling and blinking sleepily.

Miss Morgan conceded, "I know how this must sound, especially to a scientist."

Softly but with scorn, "Do you?"

"For a long time, ships and planes have been disappearing in the Bermuda Triangle. Scientists have shrugged off these events as coincidences, but we know the truth."

Lester took in a breath that was half-air and half-mucus, chest crackling uncomfortably. The lining of her throat felt like it had been minced with a cheese grater and stuffed back inside. "And what is *the truth?*"

"There's an entity that resides there. A large red cloud with characteristics and behaviour never observed before. We call it the 'Ratheri' because, after every disappearance attributed to the Triangle, a Morse code message has been transmitted from an unknown source, spelling out 'R A T H E R I'. It first came to our attention in 1945, following the disappearance of Flight 19. The pilots had an encounter with a red cloud that appeared to 'chase' them, interfere with their compasses and watches and cause strange things to happen to their bodies. Then all the planes vanished. None of those details are public, of course. Million Eyes redacted the records after we investigated the phenomenon and discovered what it really was – pure chronotonic energy. Believing that the Ratheri had transported Flight 19 forwards or backwards in time, we extracted some of the particles to experiment on them. It took nearly four decades but finally, in 1984, our scientists were able to stabilise the chronotons and create chronozine."

Lester looked at Miss Morgan. It all sounded fascinating, but it just seemed too incredible to be true. And if Million Eyes really were the good guys, why all the secrecy? Why all the plotting and scheming? "Okay. But if you're using technology and time travel to prevent our extinction, why not come out and say so?"

Miss Morgan uncrossed her legs, planting both feet squarely on the floor. Knees together, she leaned forwards intently. "Our secrecy is how we protect ourselves from our enemies. Enemies who are unable or unwilling to understand what we're doing. The Catholic Church and its adherents would've burned us as heretics if they knew what we were saying about Jesus, and if people today knew the truth about Million Eyes and how far our power and influence really goes, we'd have a full-scale rebellion on our hands. People believe they have a voice, a say in what goes on, but they don't. Not really. But they do need to *think* they do. Humans need to feel free. They wouldn't accept it if they didn't. Would you?"

If she thought she was being controlled for the sake of humanity's survival? Maybe. But maybe not. It seemed like Million Eyes saw the populace as cattle that needed looking after.

Lester gave a slight shake of the head. Exhaustion was starting to set in, her eyes heavy and stinging. She wasn't in the right state of mind to have this discussion. "I don't know."

Miss Morgan arched her eyebrows, nodding. "A lot of people value their liberty over their lives, Dr Lester. Those people simply aren't mature enough to control their own destinies."

Lester coughed. "So you control it for them?"

"Yes."

Lester felt a shiver creep down her broken body. Miss Morgan was describing totalitarianism. How could that ever be good?

"But... but aren't you putting yourselves – and all your secrets – in jeopardy?" Lester wheezed. "You're the biggest... the biggest tech company in the world. Seems like a great way to draw unwanted attention." She flinched. The part of her head that was bound in bandages had started to throb.

"It became necessary to come out of the shadows," said Miss Morgan. "For centuries we were the subject of rumour and conspiracy theory. As our numbers and influence grew, it became harder to keep the rumours at bay. Then, with the development of our time travel programme, we knew we needed a smokescreen. We were aware we'd attract more attention but a smokescreen would enable us to control what kind of attention that would be. Since we've been spearheading new technologies in secret anyway, consumer electronics seemed the most obvious choice."

Lester coughed again. She felt like she was swallowing hot cinders. She shook her head, her eye shutting for longer than a blink. "I don't believe you. There's nothing you can say that would make me trust you."

Miss Morgan smiled condescendingly. "You don't have to believe me. I can show you. I can take you to our headquarters, show you everything. And you don't have to trust me right now either. Do you think I trust you? The woman who tried to assassinate me? All I know is that my future self has put us together. That means, in time, we will learn to trust each other. And we will learn to work together."

"And if I refuse?"

Miss Morgan stood up and walked to the foot of the bed, lifted the computerised clipboard off the rail and perused the patient information. "Well, I can see that the maxillofacial surgeons here haven't yet been able to save your face – given that it was mashed to a bloody pulp when your car hit that wall. You're scheduled to have a further operation. Several more, it looks like."

Lester felt as though the bed had been wrenched out from under her, and she was falling.

"But if you don't want my help, I can always cancel those operations and have you transferred to an NHS hospital. The surgeons there won't be able to do what mine can here. But they'll probably be able to keep you alive. Probably."

Lester gulped, tears streaming into her pillow and making it feel damp and cold beneath her head.

"And then there's the man you ran over. I'm the only thing standing between you and a murder charge. I have the power to stop you from being prosecuted, but if you don't cooperate, where's my incentive? I'm giving you a chance here. It's not one you'll get anywhere else."

Something occurred to Lester as she said that. It made her tears stop and a spark of hope flit through her.

'A chance'.

Maybe, just maybe, that's exactly what Lester had here. An opportunity, even. As terrible and repugnant as it seemed, working for Miss Morgan might just lead to a way of... saving her. Of saving Georgia. After all, Million Eyes had time travel and a lot of other highly advanced technologies. They also seemed to have medical resources no one else had. So what if one day they found a cure for necrocythemia? If Lester was on the inside, she could go back in time and give it to Georgia. Literally bring her daughter back to life.

Yes. *Yes.* If she played this right, she could really turn

this to her advantage.

Miss Morgan walked back down the side of the bed and leaned over her, smiling warmly, even maternally. "Listen. How about I give you some time to think. I'll come back tomorrow. You can let me know then what you decide."

Lester let out a broken sigh as Miss Morgan started towards the door. She'd already decided. She was going to use Miss Morgan like Miss Morgan used everybody else. She was going to use her to save the only thing in the world that still mattered. Her darling Georgia.

"Goodnight, Dr Lester."

She winced. A flash of Brody and Connie made her stomach turn. She couldn't go by that name anymore. 'Lester' was Brody's name. She didn't want to be reminded of him or his betrayal. She didn't want to be reminded of how he'd vowed to be there for her, through thick and thin, unless the 'thick' was their daughter dying, in which case, to hell with his vows.

"Neether," she said quietly.

Miss Morgan faced her. "I'm sorry?"

"I don't go by 'Lester' anymore." She decided she would go by her maiden name from now on. She should never have let Brody make her give it up. "My name is Neether. Samantha Neether."

Miss Morgan nodded. "Well then. Goodnight, Dr Neether."

45

April 28th 2027

James Rawling's heart sank when Harriet Turner walked in the door with a bandaged arm and blood on her tunic. Rawling had been hiding out at the facility since he destroyed the Augur last night. There was no going back to Million Eyes now.

He stood and walked over to her. "What happened? Are you hurt?"

Harriet shook her head. Her face looked pale, tired and gaunt, her hair matted with dirt and grease. "I'm fine."

Rawling wasn't sure he believed her. He wondered how long she'd been in the past. "Nothing's changed. I take it it didn't work."

"No." She sighed. "They were a step ahead of me the entire time."

Rawling frowned. "How is that possible?"

"Destroying the Augur wasn't enough. Miss Morgan must have another source."

"So what now?"

"We need to find some other way of stopping her."

Rawling watched Harriet pour them both a Scotch. *Some other way?* Changing history had been their last resort. Surely there *was* no other way.

Harriet handed Rawling his Scotch and downed hers. She looked lost. Lost and alone. His mind wandered back to their first meeting, in 1888, when Harriet was a spirited eleven-year-old street urchin who caught him relieving himself in a church and accused him of being Jack the Ripper, exactly what he'd unwittingly become.

Now, a hundred and thirty-nine years later, Jack the Ripper and that street urchin were saving the world together. Trying, anyway. It didn't appear to be working.

So what came next was anybody's guess.

ACKNOWLEDGEMENTS

First I have to mention the guy this book is dedicated to: my good friend, Dan Lister. At my book launch for *Million Eyes* last year, Dan was there, looking happy and healthy, catching up with our college friends, hiding wooden spoons in our coats. He came because, despite all the crap he had going on, he was a loyal friend and would never miss a celebration if he could help it. Unfortunately that was the last time I saw him as he passed away shortly after. He always wanted me to succeed in my writing and so, Dan, I hope I'm still making you proud.

In the end, 2020 turned into something of a rollercoaster – if the rollercoaster wasn't going and had no one on it. And I know that many writers and publishers have suffered as a result. I'm so grateful that Elsewhen Press are still going strong and are still as dedicated as they always were to their authors. I particularly want to thank Alison for her incredible front cover design, which I fell in love with the moment it landed in my inbox.

I also want to thank my editors and proofreaders, including Elsewhen Press's Sofia and Pete, my ever-committed muse Vicky Ward, my fellow Rushmoor Writer Louise Page, the lovely Milda Rowlinson, and my wonderful friend of nearly nineteen years, Lucy Morris.

And as always, I want to thank my family and friends for their unwavering support, and I'm not just talking about writing. I'm not sure how I would've coped without Mum and Dad's help getting our new house liveable again after our builder broke it.

Which brings me to the person who, over the past two years, has become the most special person in my life: Katherine Dunford. After my last break-up, I thought it could be years before I found love again. Then, one night at a pub in Petersfield, Katherine and I talked the night away about sci-fi and we were hooked. Her cool head and "it's fine, it's totally fine" outlook have made all this house buying nonsense a LOT easier. And when it comes to writing, her encouragement and nerdy excitement is an unremitting source of inspiration. So I want to thank her for being utterly awesome, and making me feel awesome every moment I'm with her.

C.R. Berry, August 2021

Elsewhen Press

delivering outstanding new talents in speculative fiction

Visit the Elsewhen Press website at elsewhen.press for the latest information on all of our titles, authors and events; to read our blog; find out where to buy our books and ebooks; or to place an order.

Sign up for the Elsewhen Press InFlight Newsletter at elsewhen.press/newsletter

MILLION EYES
Time is the ultimate weapon

What if we're living in an alternate timeline? What if the car crash that killed Princess Diana, the disappearance of the Princes in the Tower, and the shooting of King William II weren't supposed to happen?

Ex-history teacher Gregory Ferro finds evidence that a cabal of time travellers is responsible for several key events in our history. These events all seem to hinge on a dry textbook published in 1995, referenced in a history book written in 1977 and mentioned in a letter to King Edward III in 1348.

Ferro teams up with down-on-her-luck graduate Jennifer Larson to get to the truth and discover the relevance of a book that seems to defy the arrow of time. But the time travellers are watching closely. Soon the duo are targeted by assassins willing to rewrite history to bury them.

Million Eyes is a fast-paced conspiracy thriller about power, corruption and destiny.

ISBN: 9781911409588 (epub, kindle) / 9781911409489 (336pp paperback)

Visit bit.ly/Million-Eyes

MILLION EYES: EXTRA TIME
Twelve time-twisting tales.

Million Eyes: Extra Time is a compilation of short stories set in the universe of C.R. Berry's time travel conspiracy thriller trilogy, *Million Eyes*.

The stories act as an introduction to the Million Eyes world, exploring themes that are central to the trilogy and offering a unique insight into its time-travelling villains. They focus on side characters who (mostly) do not appear in the trilogy while revealing clues to key storylines in all three books.

Many of these stories are inspired by conspiracy theories and urban legends you may recognise.

Think of these tales as a bit like the mini-episodes you get with TV series – Star Trek: Short Treks, Lost: Missing Pieces, and Doctor Who's many prequels, mini-adventures and 'Tardisodes'.

While the stories in Million Eyes: Extra Time can stand alone, you'll notice that a number of them are strongly linked and follow a loose chronology. The author's advice is that you read them in the order that they are presented.

Available for free download in pdf, epub and kindle formats
Visit bit.ly/Million-Eyes-Extra-Time

SIMON KEWIN'S WITCHFINDER SERIES

THE EYE COLLECTORS
A STORY OF
HER MAJESTY'S OFFICE OF THE WITCHFINDER GENERAL
PROTECTING THE PUBLIC FROM THE UNNATURAL SINCE 1645

When Danesh Shahzan gets called to a crime scene, it's usually because the police suspect not just foul play but unnatural forces at play.

Danesh is an Acolyte in Her Majesty's Office of the Witchfinder General, a shadowy arm of the British government fighting supernatural threats to the realm. This time, he's been called in by Detective Inspector Nikola Zubrasky to investigate a murder in Cardiff. The victim had been placed inside a runic circle and their eyes carefully removed from their head. Danesh soon confirms that magical forces are at work. Concerned that there may be more victims to come, he and DI Zubrasky establish a wary collaboration as they each pursue the investigation within the constraints of their respective organisations. Soon Danesh learns that there may be much wider implications to what is taking place and that somehow he has an unexpected connection. He also realises something about himself that he can never admit to the people with whom he works...

"Think *Dirk Gently* meets *Good Omens!*"
ISBN: 9781911409748 (epub, kindle) / 9781911409649 (288pp paperback)

Visit bit.ly/TheEyeCollectors

Coming Soon

THE SEVEN SUCCUBI
THE NEXT STORY OF
HER MAJESTY'S OFFICE OF THE WITCHFINDER GENERAL
PROTECTING THE PUBLIC FROM THE UNNATURAL SINCE 1645

ABOUT C.R. BERRY

C.R. Berry started out in police stations and courtrooms – ahem, as a lawyer, not a defendant – before taking up writing full-time. He's currently head of content for a software developer and writes fiction about conspiracies and time travel. (Note: he's not a tin foil hat wearer, doesn't believe 9/11 was an inside job, and thinks that anyone who believes the Earth is flat or the Royal Family are alien lizards needs to have their heads examined.)

Berry was published in *Best of British Science Fiction 2020* from Newcon Press with a *Million Eyes* short story. He's also been published in magazines and anthologies such as *Storgy* and *Dark Tales*, and in 2018 was shortlisted in the Grindstone Literary International Novel Competition.

In 2021, he bought his first house with his girlfriend, Katherine, in Clanfield, Hampshire, discovering whole new levels of stress renovating it (not helped by a rogue builder running off with most of their budget). The couple are now in the fun stage, going full-on nerd and theming all the rooms – their bedroom is a spaceship, their kitchen a 50s diner.

Now that the dust is settling, Berry is refocusing on the final book in the *Million Eyes* trilogy and getting back to writing his first collaborative novel with Katherine: a space-set adventure with aliens, terrorists, a mysterious wall that surrounds the universe and – of course – conspiracies.

Printed in Great Britain
by Amazon